STARS
MA

SWORD OF
MARS

BOOK SEVEN
OF THE STARSHIP'S MAGE SERIES

This edition published in 2019 by:
Faolan's Pen Publishing Inc.
22 King St. S, Suite 300
Waterloo, Ontario
N2J 1N8 Canada

ISBN-13: 978-1-988035-89-5 (print)
A record of this book is available from Library and Archives Canada.
Printed in the United States of America
1 2 3 4 5 6 7 8 9 10

First edition
First printing: June 2019

Illustration © 2019 Jeff Brown Graphics

Faolan's Pen Publishing logo is a trademark of Faolan's Pen Publishing Inc.

Read more books from Glynn Stewart at faolanspen.com

STARSHIP'S
MAGE

SWORD OF
MARS

BOOK SEVEN
OF THE STARSHIP'S MAGE SERIES

GLYNN STEWART

**FAOLAN'S PEN
PUBLISHING**

faolanspen.com

CHAPTER 1

THE SANTIAGO SYSTEM was relatively calm by the standards of stellar real estate, with most of its comets and asteroids limited to an outer belt outside the gas giants. Those three massive planets shielded the rocky worlds in the inner system from those belts, creating the tropical paradise of Novo Lar.

Currently, it was looking much less paradisiacal to Mage-Lieutenant Roslyn Chambers. The petite redheaded tactical officer of the destroyer *Stand in Righteousness* wasn't really looking at the geography.

She was looking at the lack of in-system traffic between Novo Lar and Cova, the uninhabitable fourth planet that served as the industrial heart of the system. She was looking at the debris patterns from several short and ugly engagements between the Interstellar Navy of the Republic of Faith and Reason and the Royal Martian Navy of the Protectorate of the Mage-King of Mars.

Stand was there to scout the system for the Royal Martian Navy, to see if the Republic Interstellar Navy had reinforced the battered survivors of the Battle of Ardennes.

"I have our runaways on the scopes," she announced aloud to Mage-Captain Indrajit Kulkarni.

Stand in Righteousness's tall black commander sat in the middle of the destroyer's bridge, her hands on a silver model of the pyramid-like ship she commanded. That semi-liquid silver simulacrum linked the Mage-Captain into the runes woven through the ship's hull. From the simulacrum chamber-slash-bridge of the Martian destroyer, Kulkarni could teleport her ship a full light-year—or unleash her own impressive magical powers at a much shorter range.

Few enemies survived entering the range of the amplified magic of the commander of a Martian warship.

"Two battleships," Kulkarni agreed slowly. "We were expecting them. What kind of shape are they in?"

"It looks like they're patching up as fast as they can, but they're also the only battleships in system," Roslyn reported. "I'm not sure if they left cruisers behind when they came to Ardennes or if these are newcomers, but they have friends now."

Every wall of *Stand in Righteousness*'s bridge was covered in finely-constructed video screens. Silver runes were cut through those screens, linking the amplifier to the simulacrum, but the screens themselves showed the world outside the starship.

Overlaid on top of the camera feeds, however, was a vast quantity of data. Roslyn controlled much of that data from her tactical console, and she highlighted incoming data as she spoke.

There were six of the Republic's big twenty-megaton cruisers hanging around the pair of forty-megaton battleships. Accompanying them were two ships that would be a bigger problem.

They were the same mass as the battleships, but where the battleships were built from two twenty-megaton hulls attached to each other, these were built from two fifteen-megaton hulls with the other ten million tons coming from the launch and retrieval decks for a hundred and fifty sublight gunships.

The carriers were, thankfully, the *smaller* version of the Republic's new gunship transports, but they were still a lot more firepower than *Stand* could deal with.

"Carriers," Kulkarni concluded aloud. "How many gunships are we looking at?"

"Those two should carry three hundred between them," Roslyn calculated instantly. "I'd be shocked if the Republic didn't drop off some extras when they were bringing in the bombardment platforms and army troops, though."

Six new stations now orbited Novo Lar and Cova. Even from this far away—*Stand* was almost ten light-minutes away from Novo Lar—Roslyn could identify them as fire support platforms. They were designed to drop kinetic weapons to destroy enemy positions as the Republican Army conquered and held resisting planets.

The Protectorate had never designed an equivalent system. The Protectorate didn't even *have* an army. There were more Republican troops on Santiago—one of over half a dozen systems taken in the opening salvos of the war—than there were Royal Martian Marines.

"From the size, I'd estimate each of those platforms can carry enough bombardment munitions to do their job *and* support ten gunships without issue," Roslyn continued.

She was already having her chief petty officers run their own estimates. She'd never even officially graduated the Royal Martian Navy's academy, receiving a battlefield commission as *Stand* had fled from the sneak attacks that had opened the war.

Roslyn was probably the youngest full Lieutenant in the Navy. She was *definitely* the youngest-ever holder of the Mage-King's Medal of Valor. People seemed to expect more of her than she was sure she could deliver!

"Chief Chey thinks it's more," she told Kulkarni a moment later. "She's eyeballing it at fifteen each." Roslyn shook her head. "I see the Chief's point, but I think the platforms are designed as primarily bombardment stations. The gunships are secondary—and the Republic would probably want an even ten-ship squadron."

"If we split the difference, it's another light carrier's worth of gunships," Kulkarni said grimly. "That'll have to be enough of an estimate; we've been here too long already."

Stand in Righteousness was many things, but she was *not* stealthy.

"What about the cloudscoops?" Roslyn asked. "That was where the stealth ship found them before."

"Agreed, but we're already pushing our welcome," the Mage-Captain replied. "*Furious Hope of Justice* is supposed to be scoping out that side of the system, so let's hope Mage-Captain Becskei gets the look we need."

Roslyn wasn't going to argue with her captain—especially not as her sensors informed her a cruiser had started moving in their direction ten minutes before.

"Even if our friend decides to jump, she's a good hour away," the Lieutenant noted as she flagged the cruiser to her Captain. "But they've definitely seen us."

"I think we know what we need to," Kulkarni concluded. "Jumping us."

The Mage-Captain settled her hands on the model and focused on it for several seconds. Roslyn felt the surge of power ripple through the ship, and then *Stand in Righteousness* was elsewhere, a light-year away.

Kulkarni wobbled. The jump spell took a *lot* out of a Mage, and she slowly levered herself to her feet.

"You have the conn, Mage-Lieutenant," she told Roslyn. "Standard jump sequence. Let's get back to the fleet and report in."

The "fleet" was now something worthy of the name. It had been almost three weeks since the Battle of Ardennes, and most of the Militia ships that had answered the call to defend the system had gone home now.

In their place was a solid core of warships of the Royal Martian Navy.

Her Royal Highness Mage-Admiral Jane Michelle Alexander had brought two battleships and twelve cruisers to reinforce the system when she'd arrived. In the aftermath of the desperate fighting to hold it, a lot more ships had followed.

Now five of the Protectorate's immense battleships hung above the planet, accompanied by twenty cruisers and forty destroyers. Over a quarter of the entire Royal Martian Navy was now under the command of the Mage-King's sister.

Roslyn was *almost* convinced it would be enough. Almost. The problem that the Protectorate faced, however, was that the strength of the RMN had been a matter of public record when the Republic had seceded.

Less than two years wasn't enough time to change that.

"The Admiral is requesting a call with the Captain, the XO and the tactical officer," Lieutenant Armbruster reported. The coms officer was busy catching up on the dozens of messages flying around the star system, but anything from a Mage-Admiral had a priority no lesser mortal could match.

With her royal blood, Mage-Admiral Alexander probably matched the priority a Hand could field, and the Mage-King's handpicked troubleshooters ranked above *everybody* as a rule.

"Inform the Captain," Commander Katz, the destroyer's XO, told Armbruster. "Chambers, join me in the conference room, please? Let's give the Admiral the full update."

Alexander stood through the entire briefing, letting Roslyn and the other officers from *Stand in Righteousness* get through everything as she listened calmly.

"I'll have to wait for *Furious Hope of Justice* to report in to be certain," she finally concluded. "But that sounds positive. You're certain there were no new battleships and no heavy carriers?"

"That we saw," Kulkarni said cautiously. "We did miss the refueling stations, but that's why *Furious Hope* went in. That's also a lot of gunships, sir."

"I'm not concerned about the mosquitos," Mage-Admiral Alexander replied. "I'm worried about the ships that can take my battleships one on one."

Roslyn managed to bite down her response. Those "mosquitos" had wiped out entire fleets. The trail of wreckage that led from *Stand in Righteousness*'s posting in Nia Kriti to Ardennes was made up of wrecked Martian ships and dead Martian crews, many of them dead because they'd misestimated the Republic's gunships.

But she was a Mage-Lieutenant and Alexander was the Mage-King's sister and one of the senior-most military commanders in the Protectorate. She had all of the data, too.

"We'll see what turns up at the refueling stations, but I think we know what we're going to do."

She smiled thinly.

"*Stand* will join the screening elements. There'll be no more scouting runs into Santiago, I think. It's time to free our people."

CHAPTER 2

DAMIEN MONTGOMERY was, without question, among the three most powerful people in the Protectorate. He was the First Hand of the Mage-King of Mars, raised above the Hands, the Governors, even the Council that served as the Protectorate's legislature. He answered to the Mage-King of Mars alone.

As a Rune Wright, he could see the flow of power that defined magic and create the Runes of Power that augmented his own magic. Only the family of Desmond Alexander, the Mage-King himself, could do the same—and Desmond Alexander's children were barely more than children.

Unlike Jane and Desmond Alexander, however, injury had robbed Damien of two of his Runes of Power. He was still the third most powerful adult Mage alive, but he fell far short of the power of his King and the Princess.

The short, slim man wore thin, elbow-length black leather gloves to cover the burn scars he'd acquired saving the Council of the Protectorate. He'd melted the silver polymer of his runes while it was still in his skin. He'd be years recovering.

For now, however, the gloves covered the obvious injury and allowed him to travel the streets of Heinlein Station, the primary orbital of the planet Amber, without drawing attention. A few flashes of the platinum hand emblem of his office had got him into the space station without official notice.

Amber might be the Protectorate's perennial problem child, an anarchic-libertarian ideal that *had* no government as most worlds understood it, but they remained part of the Protectorate. Ships from the Amber Defense Cooperative had fought and died at the Battle of Ardennes—as had outright Amberite mercenaries.

Their problem child, Damien reflected, had also proven a loyal child.

The corridors around him swirled with people. All of them were visibly armed, a relatively unusual situation in most of the Protectorate. Amber culture was such that Damien wore an automatic pistol openly on his hip as well.

He couldn't *use* it, but he wore it anyway. The golden medallion at his throat declared him a Mage, in any case. It bore the stars of the Jump Mage qualifications he'd earned as a young man.

If he'd wanted his medallion to be accurate, it would have needed to be much bigger. He was far more qualified than the youth who'd earned those stars now.

Amber might be safe, but he'd learned the reach of the Republic of Faith and Reason's intelligence network the hard way when their agents had attempted to assassinate him aboard his flagship.

For all of Amber's differences from the Protectorate, her shipyards could build modern destroyers. The Protectorate was going to need those yards—and Damien was certain that the Republic was watching them.

The sign for the Six Red Seasons Hotel caught his eye through the crowd and he adjusted his course. His Secret Service detail had already checked out the route. He might *look* alone, but he was far from it.

The hotel ahead of him was his contact point for a man he hadn't seen in years—a man he knew to be an intelligence agent of the Republic.

James Niska had requested this meeting and Damien was extraordinarily curious to find out why.

The message Damien had received had just said to meet Niska in the bar of the Six Red Seasons Hotel. Nothing more specific.

By the time the Hand entered the bar, three of his Secret Service guardians were already in the restaurant. He didn't look for them, but he knew they'd have scattered themselves around the room, appearing to drink with the rest of the solo patrons.

Damien himself claimed an empty booth and ordered a coffee and a sandwich. He didn't expect to have to wait long, but he knew he was going to have to wait at least a little while.

With his hands crippled, eating and drinking were an exercise in frustration. Doing so in public, when he couldn't be obviously using magic to do so, was even more so. He was lifting the coffee and the sandwich with magic but faking using his hands.

The rotational pseudogravity of the rotating station caused extra issues. He was used to magical gravity, and the sideways "fall" of objects on a station like this could still throw him.

He still managed to eat the sandwich without making too much of a fool of himself and was debating ordering a second coffee when someone dropped themselves into the booth across from him without a word of introduction.

Damien looked up at his expected guest and nodded slowly as he recognized the man. Time had not been kind to James Niska, once a Major in the Legatan Augment Corps. He was still eerily skinny, but his hair had faded from gray to pure white. A thick scar ran along his face and through his right eye.

When they'd last met, Niska had had the square-eyed pupils of a combat cyborg. His eyes were far more normal-looking now...which meant that he now had the eyes of an *infiltration* cyborg.

"I see you've had some upgrades," Damien said softly.

"I hear you've done the same," Niska told him. "It's been a long time."

"It has. The entire world has changed beneath us since we were smuggling your gunships."

The cyborg chuckled and shook his head.

"I won't pretend I didn't know this was coming," he conceded. "I'll admit, I perhaps expected better from my new government than to immediately start a war, but I knew the secession was coming."

"A lot of people are dead because of you," Damien pointed out. "Your message said you had information that might be the Protectorate's only hope. That's the only reason I'm here."

Men like James Niska had waged a covert war against the Protectorate long before the Republic's worlds had ever seceded. None of them seemed to understand that the Protectorate would have let them go without a fight.

Niska leaned back in the booth and studied Damien.

"You know, the height can be deceptive, but I think you've aged more than I have," he observed. "Are the rumors about your hands true?"

"That I'm a cripple?" Damien asked flatly. "Basically. Don't think I couldn't destroy you."

"I didn't come alone any more than you did," Niska pointed out. "I'm not your enemy."

"A hundred thousand dead in the Antonius System at the hands of an LMID agent disagree," the Hand replied. "I don't even *know* how many people have died in the war your Republic has started. If you're not my enemy, you've got a lot of talking to do."

"Antonius was a fucking nightmare," Niska said grimly.

Antonius was a sparsely inhabited mining system that Damien's home system of Sherwood shared jurisdiction of with another star system. A Legatus Military Intelligence Directorate operation had tried to start a war over Antonius—and had destroyed two significantly sized outposts along the way.

"Blade was a psychopath and we didn't realize just how bloodthirsty the bastard was," the older LMID agent told Damien. "He's dead, if that makes you feel better. Ricket would have sent you his head in a fucking *gift box* if he'd thought we could get away with it."

"And that's somehow supposed to make up for the dead?"

"No." The older man shook his head. "We were preparing for war, Montgomery. Now we're *at* war. I may not agree with everything my government decided to do, but there was never any question in my mind which side I was on."

"Then why the hell are you here?" Damien asked.

"Because those are my orders," Niska told him. "Case Prodigal Son was...bullshit. The kind of contingency plan you throw into the mix because you feel it needs to be there but you never expect to use.

"Except Ricket activated it...and so far as I can tell, he's dead," the agent said bluntly. "So is just about every *other* LMID agent who didn't get absorbed by the Republic."

"I thought LMID *was* the Republic?"

"LMID works for Legatus, not the Republic," Niska corrected. "A lot of our people went over to the Republic Intelligence Directorate, but LMID remained independent under Director Bryan Ricket.

"And then he sent out the Prodigal Son codes...shortly before someone murdered him." The cyborg shook his head. "There were about sixty LMID senior agents left. We'd gone from being the primary sword of Legatus to being a second-string network mostly responsible for counterintelligence on Legatus itself.

"Except now everyone's dead. Someone wanted to be *very* sure that whatever Ricket discovered didn't survive him."

"I'm not seeing how this is my problem," Damien replied. "I can probably trade amnesty for everything you know about the Republic, but you didn't need to contact me for that."

"No." Niska was silent for several seconds. "Montgomery...we need to talk away from the crowd. In private, where I can access media systems. Which means you need to trust me."

"I don't," Damien told him. "So, you might be out of luck."

"Montgomery...My Lord Hand. My boss—my *friend*—died because of something he found out about the Republic. Something that my leaders decided was worth killing one of their *fanatic* loyalists to keep from getting out.

"I have enough to point us in the right direction. But if Bryan found something that he ordered me to defect over, then my government can't be what I think it is," Niska said quietly. "I know you can't trust me, not really, but I need you to give me this much."

He snorted.

"Besides, I don't think either of us has any illusions about how I'd fare against even a crippled Hand."

It almost sounded like Niska was extracting the title from himself with pliers. Damien certainly hadn't expected the Republic agent to use it.

"Fine," he said. "My men are coming with me, though. Just in case you've had any clever ideas."

"Fair enough," Niska told him, then grimaced. "I'm glad at least one of us *did* bring security. *I* was bluffing."

CHAPTER 3

THE SIX RED SEASONS HOTEL had a dozen conference rooms of any size a guest might want to use. This being Amber, you could pay extra to have the security cameras turned off—and even more for a rental jammer and white-noise generator.

Niska had brought his own and set it up in the middle of the room as Damien's bodyguards swept the room. The Hand shared a nod with Mage-Captain Denis Romanov as the guards completed their sweep.

There were no unexpected bugs in the room, and Niska's device was shutting down every one that was there.

Romanov was both a Royal Martian Marine Corps Mage-Captain and a Special Agent of the Protectorate Secret Service. He was in charge of Damien's personal security and looked much like his boss. He added another forty centimeters to the same slim and dark-haired build, however, which made him much more intimidating than his boss.

"Denis, you stay with us," Damien ordered. "Have your people secure the outside."

The usual wordless conversation of security professionals followed and Romanov propped himself up next to the door as his agents trooped out.

"All right, Major Niska," he addressed the LMID man. "You wanted privacy. Talk."

"I haven't been a Major in a while," Niska told him. "Moved into Director Ricket's personal staff after the Chrysanthemum operation. Coordinating operations in Protectorate space."

He sighed.

"I'll give you a list of the operations and agents I know," he conceded before Damien could even ask. "That's basically what my orders were, anyway."

"This 'Prodigal Son' case?" the Hand asked.

"Yeah. It's an order to defect," Niska said calmly. "Nothing held back. We're supposed to go over to the Protectorate and give you everything. I wrote the damn case, Montgomery. I never expected to see it activated.

"Only Director Ricket *could* activate it," he continued. "It's an emergency alert and a drastic one. It would only be sent if the Director felt that the Republic had betrayed *Legatus*."

"How is that even possible?" Damien demanded. "The Republic is Legatus."

"Legatus is the capital of the Republic. That does not mean that the Republic and Legatus are the same thing with the same interests," Niska countered. "Usually, yes, but Legatus continues to have our own interests.

"The Republic was created to pursue those interests, but it is its own entity." He shook his head. "I can't see any way that the Republic could betray Legatus...but I suppose it could certainly betray Legatus's people.

"In which case the Republic has betrayed its own people."

Niska pulled a portable holo-projector from his coat and tossed it on the table. It activated, showing a screenshot of a classified ads page from the Legatus datanet.

Four of the ads were highlighted, making up some message.

"There are a bunch of layers of cipher and bullshit built into this, but this was the message that was sent out," Niska told Damien. Three words appeared across the screenshot.

ACTIVATE PRODIGAL SON.

"There's authentication and so forth," he continued. "But it's an emergency signal, so only so much. I validated it and got off-planet. Traded access to a ship with a Jump Mage who'd *really* pissed off his prior Captain, got us both out of the Republic.

"I have no evidence that any other LMID agents managed to make it out," Niska said quietly. "And I know at least fifteen died while I was getting my own ass out of dodge. Something *very* wrong went down in Legatus, Montgomery."

"So, what do you know?" Damien asked.

Niska nodded and tapped a command on his wrist-comp. The screenshot disappeared and was replaced by a rotating globe that Damien recognized as Legatus.

Four blue icons marked it. All of them were in isolated areas, well away from the main centers of a heavily populated world.

"Twenty years ago, the Royal Testers and the UnArcana Worlds had one of their recurring fights," Niska explained. "The result was these. Each of the UnArcana Worlds supports at least one isolated boarding school for the purpose of teaching Mages by Right until they're old enough to decide what *they* want to do with their lives.

"About half were being emigrated to other worlds by their parents, but the Testers insisted that we had to have *some* structure for those that wanted to stay."

It was the job of the Royal Testers to meet with every child in the Protectorate at some point between the ages of ten and twelve to test them for the Gift of magic. For the children born to the semi-aristocratic Mage families that ran many of the Protectorate's worlds, it was almost a formality. It was extraordinarily rare for a child of two Mages to *not* be a Mage.

For the rest of the children of the Protectorate, it was only slightly less of a formality. It was even rarer for a Mage to be born to non-Mage parents than vice versa—but across the teeming billions of humanity, it happened a surprising amount. A world of a billion souls would turn up at least two dozen Mages by Right every year—like Damien himself.

Even with the emigration of young Mages from the UnArcana Worlds, they still would have had schools supporting hundreds of teenagers who hadn't decided if they were going to stay and give up the use of their Gifts or leave.

Now, Damien supposed, they had even fewer choices. Without the Testers, though, few Mages by Right would be found at all. The schools would close and the potential Mages would be lost in the populace.

"I didn't realize the Republic was still running those schools," Damien said. "I'm not sure I see the relevance, though."

"Neither did I when Ricket started asking questions," Niska replied. "I'm not even sure *what* he was looking into, but I know it involved the schools on Legatus. There were other aspects to what he was investigating, but I think he *knew* he was in dangerous waters."

"Why?" Damien asked.

"Because I was his right-hand man on Legatus for four years, and I only had the vaguest idea that he had a side investigation running," the LMID agent replied. "None of our people were engaged in it. He was doing it all himself...and he found something that he ordered us all to run over.

"He didn't even get whatever it was into our hands, but he ordered us to run anyway," Niska concluded. "And someone killed over a dozen loyal operatives of the Republic *just in case* they'd received any data from him."

"You think something's happened with those kids?" Damien asked. "Why would you care?"

Niska was better than many Damien had met, but the man was still one of the enforcers of a society that basically jailed those children and made them either give up their powers or go into exile.

"Because they're *kids*," the cyborg snapped. "And because the promise was that their curriculum and opportunity to leave would be honored. But most of all? I care because someone killed Bryan Ricket over it."

"And what do you want me to do about it?" Damien asked.

"I need resources and support to try and find out what Ricket discovered," Niska said calmly. "I need your help to get back in Republic space and finish what my boss—*my friend*—started."

"We can't get into Legatus to complete his investigation," Damien replied. That wasn't *entirely* true, but he wasn't going to admit that he had access to a hyper-advanced stealth ship. He was prepared to help Niska, especially since it seemed like there was a wedge there that they could use against the Republic, but he wasn't giving up his secrets yet.

"I have enough documentation, access, false papers, et cetera, to get us into any Republic system *except* Legatus," Niska told him. "These schools were in every system. One of the larger ones was in the Arsenault System, which should be relatively easily reached from here.

"I don't have a Jump Mage, though. My deal with the woman who got me here was to get her out of the Republic. So, I have a ship, I have a destination, I have *access*...but I don't have a Jump Mage, I don't have personnel and I don't have firepower."

"You want me to provide a crew and a Mage for your ship?" Damien asked. He could do that, but it was risky.

"I have a crew," Niska admitted. "I have two other LMID Augments and a crew that got me out of the Republic without betraying me. I need a Mage. I could use more gun hands and I could use more weapons."

"I'm assuming you can get all of that."

"I am the First Hand of the Mage-King of Mars," Damien said quietly. "If I believe this is worth it, I can get anything."

He met Niska's gaze and the cyborg looked back at him levelly.

"I want to avenge my friend," the cyborg said quietly. "From your perspective? My friend was one of the loyalists at the heart of the Republic. Whatever he found *broke* that loyalty. If it turned Bryan Ricket against the nation he helped build, it could break the Republic.

"And if something that can break the Republic *exists*, then maybe the Republic deserves to be broken."

CHAPTER 4

RHAPSODY IN PURPLE was one of the most technologically advanced ships in the galaxy. Hanging in Amber orbit, the ship was using a number of signature-augmenting panels to appear like a regular courier ship.

She was actually slightly larger than a regular courier ship, but the angles and absorbent materials used to build her hull made her nearly invisible to regular radar. She was also one of the very few ships in human space to use an antimatter power core as well as antimatter engines.

The saved space was used for additional quarters and several immense heat sinks, allowing her to run dark and cold for extended periods.

There were only a handful of stealth ships like her, and Damien had commandeered her to get him to Amber. He normally traveled on a cruiser, but the war meant the Navy couldn't spare the ship anymore.

"Welcome back aboard," *Rhapsody*'s Captain, Kelly LaMonte, greeted him, with a crisp salute.

He gave her a Look. The currently aqua-blue-haired Martian Interstellar Security Service officer was his ex-girlfriend. She knew perfectly well what he thought of any level of formality.

MISS wasn't overly formal in general—both of LaMonte's spouses served aboard *Rhapsody in Purple,* and he was frankly surprised she even knew how to salute.

"You know better than to salute," he told her. "I need your conference room, you, and your top crew in twenty minutes. Denis"—he turned back to his bodyguard—"you as well. We need to make a plan for how we're taking advantage of Niska's situation."

"So, we're in for this, are we?" LaMonte asked. "Just what did the old cyborg want from us?"

"A Mage and backup as he goes back into the Republic to try and find the secret they killed the head of LMID over," Damien told her. "We'll talk in the meeting. I want as many brains pointed at this as possible.

"I think we've got a solid opportunity here, but any of us wandering into the Republic is dangerous."

"And let me guess...you're going with him?" LaMonte asked.

"I don't trust Niska as far as I can throw a planet," he replied. "And he's going to have a hard time trapping *me*."

LaMonte and her spouses Xi Wu, *Rhapsody*'s senior Ship's Mage, and Mike Kelzin, the senior shuttle pilot, took up a good chunk of the conference table on their own. *Rhapsody in Purple* was also represented by the immense Amazonian form of Captain Jalil Charmchi of the Bionic Combat Regiment of the Protectorate Special Operations Command.

Damien was reasonably sure that Legatan Augments were superior to the gear available to Major Charmchi and her platoon of cyborg commandos. He also had *no* intention of mentioning that to a shaven-headed, cybernetically-augmented woman who towered over Denis Romanov, let alone Damien himself.

Romanov stood behind and to Damien's right. At some point, he'd reassemble the type of staff he'd taken into half a dozen crises before. He hadn't had time since his humanitarian mission into Republican space a few months before had turned into the opening act of a war.

Right now, he had his Secret Service detail and a few Marines, plus LaMonte's crew.

"So, Niska is defecting," he said bluntly. "He's promised us a full dump of what he knows about Republic operations in our space and past LMID operations. The latter should at least let us clean up some of the debris left over from their little shadow war."

"What does he want in exchange?" Charmchi demanded. "Spies don't hand that sort of thing over freely."

"I'd be happy to hand him amnesty for that data dump and bury him in a fancy apartment on some world on the far side of the Protectorate," Damien told them. "However, he's here because the Republic had Bryan Ricket, the current head of LMID and Niska's boss, murdered."

Everyone in the little conference room took a moment to process that.

"Niska is convinced Ricket found something the Republic was prepared to kill one of their key loyalists to keep secret," the Hand continued. "He is, in fact, convinced that Ricket found something that *turned* said key loyalist against the Republic.

"He wants to find out what Ricket died for. I want whatever secret Ricket found—because frankly, people, if this secret could turn the head of LMID against the Republic, I want to see who else it can turn."

"So, what do we do? Pick him up and head into Republic space?" LaMonte asked.

"I'm uninclined to reveal the existence of the *Rhapsodies* to even a defected enemy agent," Damien told her. "I think he's aboveboard, but this could easily be a long game to see what we'll expose of our intelligence operations."

"Or to trap the First Hand," Romanov pointed out.

"That's a risk I have to take," Damien replied. "What information Niska has suggests that this is related to the Mages by Right in the Republic. My worst-case scenario right now is that I'm going to be finding mass graves."

That seemed to silence any arguments.

"I'm going to need to borrow one of your Mages, Captain LaMonte. Niska has a ship but no one to jump her and, well"—he lifted his still-injured hands—"I'm not jumping anytime soon."

"You can't possibly be planning on going alone!" Charmchi demanded.

Damien *heard* Romanov swallow his chuckle. The Marine turned Secret Service agent knew him too damn well.

"No, I'm not," he told the cyborg. "I'm taking my Secret Service detail and I'd like to borrow a fire team of your commandos."

"Done," she said instantly, turning her gaze on Romanov. "Think you can take care of them, Mage-Captain?"

"Like they were my own flesh and blood, Captain," the Marine replied brightly.

"Good boy."

"As for the rest of you...I want *Rhapsody* following us as covertly as possible," Damien told them. "I'm prepared to work with Niska to find out what the hell is going on inside the Republic, but I don't trust him. Having a stealthed ship of Mages, Marines and commandos on call will make me feel *much* better."

"Us, too," LaMonte told him. "I don't want to have to go back to Mars and tell His Majesty we *lost* you."

"I'm sure Desmond would understand," Damien said with a chuckle. "At this point, he knows my bad habits."

Leaving his people to scatter and get things organized, Damien retreated to his quarters, where he was greeted by the querulous displeasure of a small ball of black fur. Persephone, his cat and the physical therapist for his hands, had very clear opinions of how long the First Hand should be away from her.

"Sorry, kitten," he said, letting her leap up into his lap as he took a seat. "I don't think I can sneak you onto a ship I'm sharing with a bunch of Legatan cyborgs."

If Persephone understood what he was saying, she didn't show it. She simply curled up on his lap and purred as he started, very carefully, petting her.

Petting the cat was good therapy for his hands, and her presence was good therapy for his soul. He wasn't going to be able to bring her with him, though.

He was thinking about talking to LaMonte when she knocked on his door.

"Come in."

His ex crossed from the door, gave Persephone a few pets and then dropped into a couch facing Damien.

"I suppose telling you that going with Niska yourself is a bad idea would be a waste of time?" she asked.

"Yes," he confirmed. "It's Romanov's *job* to tell me that. He and I went over it. Other than that, I don't think anyone really gets a say."

LaMonte snorted.

"What about Grace?"

Damien sighed.

Admiral Grace McLaughlin was the commanding officer of his home system's Militia, the Sherwood Interstellar Patrol. She was also his girl-friend, which was looking to be one of the worst long-distance relation-ship hells he'd ever heard of.

"I'll send her a message before we leave," he told LaMonte. "She understands duty, at least."

LaMonte shook her head.

"I guess that's all you can do. You do owe her that, at least."

Damien chuckled. When he'd first been recruited into the service of Mars, he'd broken up with LaMonte because he'd had no idea when he'd even be able to leave Mars, let alone have a relationship.

Now he knew exactly how mobile he was—and how tied to duty. He'd try...but he honestly expected Grace to run out of patience before they managed to sort out how to make it work.

"I do," he conceded. "But I also owe the people of the Protectorate my duty. My service."

"Even after wrecking your hands?"

"Always," Damien told her. "If fate gave me this power, then I must use it. I don't have it in me to stand by, and so I do what I can. And 'what I can' is a lot more than most people."

"So, you're going to sail into hostile territory with a potential double agent in pursuit of a mystery that the Republic killed some of their core people over?" LaMonte demanded.

"Yep." He grinned at her. "If it will make you feel better, I'm not bringing Persephone. Can I get you to look after her?"

Rhapsody's Captain shook her head at him.

"Yes," she agreed. "Promise me you won't get yourself killed?"

"I can't guarantee that," he reminded her. "But I can promise I'm not going to do anything intentionally stupid. And if the Republic does bring me down, they'll know they've been in a fight."

She sighed.

"Is it worth it?"

"I don't know. But there are too many questions about what's going on in the Republic and what happened to their Mages. If there's a mass grave somewhere, we need to know...and so do the people of the Republic."

"Fair enough." LaMonte shook her head. "Liara will be going with you. Everyone should be ready to transfer over to Heinlein and whatever ship Niska is using within an hour or two."

CHAPTER 5

THEY MET NISKA on the main docking ring. The white-haired cyborg was accompanied by a redheaded younger woman who looked positively petite and delicate. The way she moved, however, told Damien that she was also an Augment.

Damien had kept his "team" down to twelve people. Himself, Romanov and Liara Foster, plus five Marines turned Secret Service agents and four cyborg commandos.

Liara Foster was a heavyset woman with short-cropped black hair. She was actually older than Damien—or her own Captain—but she fell comfortably in line with the Secret Service detail and the BCR commandos.

"Montgomery," Niska greeted him. "Bit more than you and a Jump Mage, I see."

"I think Agent Romanov here would tase me into unconsciousness and handcuff me to a pillar if I tried to go anywhere alone," Damien told the other man. "Especially into the hands of a former enemy."

"And you wanted numbers and firepower. You got them."

Nothing in terms of weaponry was illegal in Amber, but the contents of the heavy black cases rolling behind Damien's people would have drawn comment even there. Heinlein Station's administrators, if no one else, disapproved of weapons with enough power to breach the station's hull.

There were three sets of exosuit battle armor in the cases, along with the full-size heavy penetrator rifles those suits carried to kill their counterparts. The other two Secret Service Agents would settle for "merely" the stripped-down and ridiculously expensive carbine that fired similar anti-armor rounds.

The BCR commandos' standard long arm was somewhere between the two weapons in scale, but like the penetrator rifles and carbines, it could fire discarding-sabot tungsten penetrator rounds.

There was more than enough firepower in the cases to wreck a significant chunk of Heinlein Station or fight a small war. Damien might only have brought ten people, but they could fight most armies for him.

And the armies *they* couldn't fight, *he* could.

Niska was eyeing the cases and Damien wondered if he could guess their contents. He probably recognized the "coffins" containing the exosuits, if nothing else.

"No half-measures, I take it?" he said slowly.

"No artificial shortages," Damien told the cyborg. "We have ammunition, penetrator rifles, armor. In all honesty, we should probably get this gear *off* of Heinlein Station. Even an Amberite station's security would complain."

Niska snorted and gestured for them to follow him.

"All right. Let's get everyone aboard *Starlight*."

Starlight was a fast packet, a small cargo ship designed to move a hundred thousand tons of cargo. Damien had never spent any time aboard a fast packet, and he studied the design as they boarded her.

The standard merchant ship of the Protectorate looked like an egg-beater, with three to six "ribs" that rotated around the core to provide gravity. Everything along those ribs could realign to account for thrust while the ship was under power.

Starlight's designers had declined to deal with that level of finicky arrangement and set up the entire living and working areas to realign. She looked more like an upside-down flower than anything else, with three pods hanging from the central core. Those pods were currently extended outward, rotating to provide pseudogravity.

Under thrust, they'd fall into line with the main hull, using the thrust for gravity instead of rotating.

It was a clever design and one that kept the living and working areas clear of the cargo spars. The eggbeater design meant that the ribs had to be stopped to load or unload cargo, but *Starlight* could keep her crew aboard while cargo was loaded in front of the pods.

She was also barely ten percent of the size of the only merchant ship Damien had served on. *Blue Jay* had been almost a kilometer long and carried three million tons of cargo.

Starlight's core hull was a hundred and ten meters long. The pods were roughly fifty meters long, and the cargo would be mounted on the first fifty meters of the hull.

"Never seen a fast packet before?" Niska asked as Damien studied the ship through the window.

"Not closely," he admitted. "It's not a common design."

"It's a Legatan speciality," Niska told him. "Should probably have been more widely adopted, but, well..." He shrugged. "Legatus doesn't build many jump ships, so it never caught on."

"We'll see how it goes," Damien said. "I'm looking forward to seeing how she flies."

"And I'm sure Captain Mere Maata is looking forward to showing you," the cyborg replied.

Mere Maata was a dark-skinned woman with a long, thick braid and complex tattoos woven across her face. Damien didn't even pretend to understand the meaning of the tattoos, but he nodded firmly to her as they came aboard. Handshakes would wait until they were out of the zero-gravity loading area.

"She looks like a fine ship, Captain," he told her. "I look forward to seeing how she does. You have our destination?"

"Arsenault. An old stop for *Starlight*; no one is really going to question us." Maata shook her head. "We've picked up a cargo of our usual mix of small and valuable. Our old contacts will be glad to see us, and no one is going to look too hard at our supercargo."

Damien chuckled.

"It's always good to know where we stand," he told her. He glanced over at Niska with a questioning look.

"Maata is retired LMID. She got trapped in Legatus when her Mage jumped ship to a Guild evacuation vessel. I got her out, and now, well, we're going back in."

"I wouldn't go back into the Republic for anyone else, you know," she told Niska, slamming a heavy hand on the cyborg's shoulder, a carefully practiced gesture in zero-g. "You know what I think of this stunt, and they haven't done anything to make me happier since the secession."

"I know," Niska said quietly. "Obviously, we'll be keeping the identities of your team quiet," he continued to Damien. "Maata knows everything, but her crew is mostly out of the loop."

Which explained, Damien realized, why the boarding area was empty of anyone except Maata herself.

"They know we're carrying passengers they're not supposed to talk about," the Captain noted. "And they trust me. I got them out of the Republic." She shook her head. "Nobody *blames* Davey, but it wasn't like we were going anywhere different than he was!"

Davey, presumably, was the Mage who'd jumped ship to get out of the Republic.

"We go in, we find out what we need to, we get out," Damien promised. "Might need to visit another system or two in the Republic, though. Will that be a problem?"

"*Starlight* has run on spec cargos and desperation for a damn long time, Montgomery," she told him. "The crew will go where I tell them to. I'd rather not hang around in the Republic, but I'm guessing you can make it worth my while."

Damien chuckled. The budget of a Hand was basically defined as "explain what you spent to the accountants after they stop crying." As *First* Hand, he got to make someone else do that explaining.

"I think we can manage that, Captain Maata," he told her.

"Then, what are we waiting for?" she said. "Let's get this old boat moving."

CHAPTER 6

THE BATTLESHIP *Righteous Shield of Valor* was the central vessel of the first element to arrive in the Santiago System. *Stand in Righteousness* and seven other destroyers accompanied Mage-Admiral Alexander's flagship into the occupied system.

Roslyn's ship and the other destroyers were there only to augment the battleship's missile defenses if some evil luck had put a Republic force in position to engage them on arrival. Combined, the destroyers had less than a fifth of *Righteous Shield of Valor's* mass, weapons or defenses, but every antimissile turret could count.

They arrived in the quiet of deep space, however, and no sudden surprises emerged from the darkness to jump the Martian fleet.

The second battleship arrived moments later, roughly a million kilometers away. *Pax Marcianus* brought half of Alexander's cruisers. A few seconds later, *Peacemaker* arrived with the other half of the cruisers.

Foremost Shield of Honor and *Liberation of the Oppressed* appeared together, the last two battleships bringing the rest of the destroyers along with them.

Five battleships. A third of the Protectorate's strength of the ships, accompanied by twenty cruisers and forty destroyers.

The only reason it wasn't the largest single fleet Roslyn had ever seen was because she'd seen it in Ardennes, where dozens of Militia ships still stood guard over the world they had bled to hold against the Republic.

"RIN hasn't noticed us yet," Roslyn reported aloud. "It looks like they've picked up some friends since the last time we were here, but not much."

She could still see the two damaged battleships, plus their two carrier and six cruiser guardians. Every ship they'd seen before was still sitting in orbit of Novo Lar.

The newcomers were in orbit around Cova. A single fifty-megaton heavy carrier and four cruiser escorts.

"It's not a full carrier group," she noted. "It looks like a carrier they broke free from another position and attached a few cruisers to. All big ships." She studied it. "I wonder if they're not building any more of the fifteen-megaton hulls."

Every ship they'd seen so far had been built on cores of either fifteen-megaton or twenty-megaton hulls. All of the cruisers they were seeing now were twenty-megaton ships, though, and the heavy carrier was built on two of the cylinders that made up the core hulls of those cruisers.

"It would make sense if they could manage it," Kulkarni agreed. "Their key limitation has to be their FTL drive. If they can build bigger ships, they get more firepower for the same number of hulls. Do the extras change anything?"

"That gets them up to seven hundred or so gunships," Roslyn replied. "But all told? No. Not when we have five battleships." She shook her head. "I'm going to keep an eye on the gunships."

"Good plan," Kulkarni told her. "I'm more concerned about the 'mosquitos' than the Admiral is."

"We have another minute or so before they see us," Roslyn noted. "Five minutes after that before we know what they're doing in response."

"What do you expect?" *Stand*'s Captain asked quietly.

As they spoke, the four clusters of warships were converging. Spreading out the force had reduced the risk of arriving in a cluster of Republic resistance, but they needed to concentrate before they engaged the enemy.

"Two possibilities," Roslyn replied as she watched the fleet converge. "First, they take one look at a quarter-billion tons of RMN battleships and get the hell out of here."

She tapped another icon on her screen as she spoke.

"That's unlikely, though, since they've still got troops on the ground and they only have enough transportation for maybe forty thousand troops, a single corps. Last intel said they had *three* corps on the surface. They won't abandon them, so...option two."

Roslyn ran the numbers on the gunships' acceleration and nodded.

"Option two is that they converge all of their gunships, probably *here*"—she highlighted a spot on the screen—"and throw them right at us. Seven hundred gunships can dodge or eat a lot of missile fire *and* throw over twelve thousand missiles at us. Battleships or not, that'll hurt."

"It would," Kulkarni agreed. "There's a third option, though."

"Sir?" Roslyn asked. She was still new enough for her role and junior enough for her rank to be willing to be educated. She was, so far as she knew, the youngest Lieutenant and youngest tactical officer in the fleet.

"Your option two makes sense, but they know they're outgunned," the Mage-Captain told her. "In their place, I'd hold the gunships back to stiffen the missile defense and firepower of my main fleet. They don't have enough to really hurt us if they send them in alone, but they'll dramatically augment the defenses and the first few salvos of the main fleet."

Roslyn was calculating again as Kulkarni spoke, and highlighted a second point.

"If they bring their forces together, they'll rendezvous here," she noted. "We'll be in missile range by the time they meet up, but they'll be close enough for a level of mutual support already."

"How long until we start seeing clues?"

"Two minutes—and that's assuming they react faster than I'd expect *anybody* to."

It was just over five minutes after they had to have seen the arrival of the Martian fleet before the Republic ships reacted at all—and their reaction wasn't any of the ones Kulkarni or Roslyn had predicted.

The carriers and stations in Novo Lar orbit started spewing out gunships, but none of the ships in orbit of the inhabited planet moved.

The carriers and stations at Cova did the same. After another minute, over three hundred gunships and two cruisers set out on a course that would bring them to Novo Lar well before the Protectorate ships arrived.

Assuming nothing else changed, they'd be in range for missiles for the last hour or so of their journey, but at a distance where they could be reasonably sure they could defend themselves.

"What are they doing?" Kulkarni asked aloud. "The carrier is just staying at Cova on its own?"

"Look at this, sir," Roslyn told her superior as she highlighted several smaller signatures. "They're dropping shuttles to the surface and it looks like they're evacuating the orbital bombardment platforms. With the gunships gone, that carrier probably has capacity to hold most of a corps of troops."

"If they're writing off the gunships in favor of evacuating troops and crew, that would make sense," the Captain said slowly. "That will probably let them evac everyone on Cova. The smaller carriers can't board as many people, though."

"No, but that'll double the number of people they can get off Novo Lar," Roslyn pointed out. "They'll leave a corps on the surface, probably with orders to surrender, but get two corps and the orbital platform crews out. Save over twice as many people."

"So, they'll concentrate their gunships and capital ships and bring them out to meet us," Kulkarni agreed. "They'll have to, or we'll range on the carriers and transports before they get out."

"And we'll have to watch our acceleration as we come near them," Roslyn said. "Or we'll end up cutting through them at far too high a relative speed."

With the firepower balance sitting on the Martian side, a shorter engagement was definitely to the Republic's advantage, especially if they could cut into laser range without slipping into the range of the amplified Mages aboard the Protectorate ships.

"I'd rather let them evac than take the losses pushing through them will entail," Kulkarni agreed. "Get together with Coleborn and make sure we have courses set up for optimal engagement time based on their most likely sortie times."

Before Roslyn could respond, an alert chimed on Kulkarni's console, and she picked up her headset to listen to a message.

The young tactical officer was well aware of how inexperienced she was, but she could *see* the Mage-Captain's face getting stonier and stonier by the second. Kulkarni didn't say anything, but she put her headset down roughly as the call ended and gestured Roslyn over to her.

"Don't worry about those courses," she ordered, her voice gravelly with frustration. "The Mage-Admiral has the same assessment of the Republic approach as we do, but she doesn't think they have enough firepower to threaten the fleet.

"Our orders are to target the transports and carriers. We're to punch through their fleet at whatever velocity is necessary to guarantee a close-enough intercept that they'll be forced to surrender."

Roslyn shivered.

"Surrendering doesn't seem to be in the Republic's lexicon," she pointed out.

"Each of those ships is going to have over twenty thousand people aboard, most of them not spacers," Kulkarni replied. "Even if they're all technically combatants, the ship crews won't regard them that way. If we have to blow them away, a lot of their people are going to die for nothing."

She shook her head.

"They'll surrender, I'm pretty sure...but the Mage-Admiral is wrong if she thinks those gunships can't hurt us. If we punch through a screen of *seven hundred* of the little 'mosquitos,' we are going to bleed for the privilege."

Kulkarni sighed.

"It's a question of priorities," she admitted. "And Alexander wants an intact Republic starship. With one of those, we can answer a lot of damned questions about why this damn war is even being fought.

"It's worth the risk. I'm just not sure the Mage-Admiral realizes how harsh that risk *is*."

Even if she didn't, there wasn't much Roslyn could do about it. The most junior tactical officer in the fleet definitely wasn't going to be calling up the Admiral to tell her she was making a mistake, after all!

CHAPTER 7

SPACE COMBAT was not measured in seconds or minutes. Even brutal short-range engagements like the ambush in Ardennes that had destroyed the Republic fleet there still lasted five minutes or more, and they were rare.

The weapons available to the Royal Martian Navy and the Republic Interstellar Navy had accelerations over a thousand times as fast as their motherships. Weapon ranges were measured in millions of kilometers. Missiles outranged lasers, and lasers *usually* outranged amplified magic, but both sides' missiles had a range of forty light-seconds if their ships weren't moving.

It would take hours for *Stand in Righteousness* and the rest of the ships to get into range of each other, and hours more for them to actually pass through the range envelopes normally.

The course that the RMN task force was taking wasn't going to be quite so normal.

"Their assault landers are going back for a second wave," Roslyn reported. "It looks like the orbitals are emptied and they've moved one of the corps off the planet."

She checked the data.

"I'd guess that the big army transports are full but they're waiting for the carriers to get loaded up," she concluded.

The army transports were built on the same fifteen-megaton hull as the rest of the older ships of the RIN. Each could carry twenty to twenty-five thousand people, two divisions of ground troops.

The two transports in orbit had probably been cycling back and forth between Santiago and a Republic base of some kind for weeks to bring in more troops. With three army corps, over a hundred thousand troops, on the surface of Novo Lar, there was no way the Republic could evacuate everyone.

"What's the ETA on the gunships from Cova?" Kulkarni asked.

"Still just over two hours. If the next wave with the landers is comparable to the last, they'll arrive about thirty minutes after the transports start moving."

"And the Cova evacuation?"

"They don't have landers," Roslyn pointed out. "They're moving forty thousand people with shuttles that aren't designed for mass personnel transport." She checked the numbers. "Assuming the Republic troops on Cova are equivalent to a standard Legatan Army Corps, they're over seventy-five percent complete pulling them up.

"I wouldn't want to be aboard that carrier with an extra forty-odd thousand people crammed in," she continued. "But they should be ready to go in under half an hour."

No one had suggested splitting the fleet to chase down the carrier. They had the edge in firepower, but the RIN had handled the Protectorate roughly in the first weeks of the war. The RMN would let one carrier go to make sure they took fewer losses when they chased down the transports and carriers in orbit.

Or, at least, that was Roslyn's assumption. She couldn't read Alexander's mind.

"Keep one eye on her," Kulkarni instructed. "It may look like she's running, but that carrier still has more missile launchers than almost anything else in the damn star system. If she wants to run, we'll let her... but I don't want any surprises, either."

Roslyn chuckled and locked the ship into a subroutine of her scanners. It would warn her when the ship moved. There were other officers tracking the ships as well, officers whose warnings would get to Mage-Admiral Alexander faster, but it was always possible she'd be the first one to send the alert.

Every officer watching increased the odds that they'd know about any surprises in time to deal with them.

"Bogey at Cova has brought her engines online and is accelerating. Vector is at seventy-five degrees to the ecliptic and heading away from us at five gravities."

Roslyn finished her report and double-checked that acceleration figure. Unlike the Martian fleets that used magical gravity to help compensate for their acceleration, the Republic ships didn't have that option.

Their cylindrical hulls contained internal rotating sections to provide pseudogravity. The RMN hadn't had an opportunity to examine an intact Republic ship yet, but presumably they adjusted position for acceleration.

But they had no ability to counter acceleration. At five gravities, the crew and the newly added passengers aboard that carrier were being crushed.

"Any orders from the Flag?" Kulkarni asked.

"No, sir," Armbruster confirmed. "We're letting them go."

"All right. Time to weapons range, Chambers?"

Roslyn didn't even need to look. She had a timer for that sitting on her primary screen, and she'd kept one eye on it all along.

"Assuming we don't start decelerating and the Republic doesn't come out to meet us, we'll be in range in seventy-eight minutes," she told him.

Unlike the Republic fleet, they were accelerating at ten gravities without crushing their crews. They could push to fifteen, but that had its risks. Right now, their course was angled just past Novo Lar, giving them mobility to try and intercept the transports when they made their run for it.

"Transports will move in forty minutes," she continued. "The Cova force is pushing their systems. They're holding off on their deceleration and it looks like they're going for a slingshot of Novo Lar."

"Really?" Kulkarni asked. "Are you sure?"

Roslyn passed the diagram she'd put together on her screen over to her CO's screens.

"They're still going to be moving damn fast when they hit Novo Lar's orbit," she pointed out. "They've shaved ten minutes off their arrival time, getting there before we can range on them now.

"But if they don't do something, they're just going to fly right past the planet, and I don't think that's what they're planning. Assuming they can push their acceleration to six or seven gravities, they can get their velocity down low enough to let Novo Lar's gravity catch them.

"They'll slingshot and come back out at us at over a hundred KPS," Roslyn estimated. "Real confirmation will be when the ships already in orbit move. If they move out at five gravities toward us around when the transports take off, they'll match up with the gunships and cruisers after the slingshot."

The Captain studied her diagram and smiled.

"I imagine you're not the only one that picked that up, Lieutenant, but I'm forwarding this to the Flag," she told Roslyn. "Knowing what's coming will help."

Roslyn was already programming the assumption into her systems. The slingshot would change when they came into range. Knowing that the Republic ships would be bringing an extra hundred kilometers a second to the fight added another fifty thousand kilometers to her missile range.

Every little bit counted when she wanted to make sure everyone came home.

"Oh, you clever buggers."

Kulkarni's words echoed in *Stand in Righteousness*'s bridge as the transports turned to run.

Even with the acceleration advantage of the Martian fleet, they still couldn't lose velocity that quickly. Alexander's orders to keep a minimum velocity meant they were coming in fast relative to the planet—and the transports weren't running along the same vector.

They were almost running *toward* the Martian fleet.

"Eighty degrees from the ecliptic, angled toward us," Roslyn confirmed. "We'll be in missile range, but I'm not sure we'll be able to bring them to boarding range. Not with a fleet coming down our throats."

Like the carrier from Cova, the transports and carriers were pushing the limits of what could be considered remotely safe for their passengers. The two carriers had enough defenses to keep the transports safe from long-range missile fire, and their new vector meant they weren't going to see much else.

"New course from the Flag," Armbruster reported. "Passing it to Coleborn, but the fleet is adjusting course to intercept."

Roslyn looked at the sensor screens and shivered. They could do it, she supposed. Even through the gravity runes she felt *Stand's* engines go to full power. At fifteen gravities, they could at least get into a range where they could try to disable the ships, force them to a halt before they could escape.

"We'll catch them," she said slowly. "We might have to destroy them, but we'll get close enough that we can definitely do that."

"I know ground troops count as combatants, but that still feels wrong," Armbruster said quietly.

"Hopefully, they're smart enough to surrender," Kulkarni replied—but Roslyn could tell that the Captain's screen was focused on the battleships and their escorts.

They were just starting to move, exactly on schedule to rendezvous with the slingshot maneuver of the cruisers and gunships from Cova.

"But their friends waited to see what we did in response to that maneuver, and now they're coming out to greet us," the Captain concluded. "Looks like the slingshot will bring them together just inside missile range."

Two battleships. Ten cruisers. Seven hundred gunships.

It *probably* wasn't enough to destroy their fleet, but Roslyn would much rather they were focusing on controlling that range, not chasing a completely different target.

"Range in twenty-two minutes," Roslyn reported. "Then we see what happens."

Firing orders came down from the flag shortly afterward, and Roslyn loaded them into her systems. She had a pattern already programmed in and ready to go, but the orders from the Flag told her *who* she was shooting at.

A quarter of the destroyers were going to be using their missiles in a defensive mode, using their antimatter warheads to shoot down the incoming fire from the Republic ships. The rest, including *Stand*, were to join the heavier ships in targeting the cruisers.

The logic, so far as Roslyn could see it, was that the gunships were going to empty their magazines in the first two minutes, and it would take over *seven* minutes for the Protectorate fire to arrive.

It would take almost a minute longer for the first Republic salvos to travel the distance. Their missiles had lower accelerations but longer flight times, which meant they'd launch *before* the Protectorate, but Roslyn's missiles would arrive long before the Republic missiles did.

The gunships would get all of their missiles into space long before the RMN's fire reached them, and *that*, Roslyn concluded, was their big value in an engagement like this. The first three salvos out of the Republic fleet were going to be hell.

The gunships would still serve a role in the battle to come, and Roslyn wasn't sure she'd have ignored them. The seven hundred gunships actually carried *more* antimissile defenses in aggregate than the ten cruisers did, and they were individually easier to kill.

The cruisers were still active threats after the opening salvos, though, with over a hundred missile launchers apiece. They were much bigger than the Protectorate's cruisers and carried more launchers to go with that mass.

The key was the battleships, Roslyn supposed. The Republic had two of them, both damaged forty-megaton ships. The Protectorate had five, three fifty-megaton ships and two sixty-megaton ships.

The Republic wasn't going to win this battle, but it wasn't being fought the way Roslyn Chambers would have chosen to fight it.

Hopefully, Mage-Admiral Alexander's far greater experience meant she saw something Roslyn didn't.

CHAPTER 8

AS RED ICONS began to spill out onto Roslyn's display, all she could really think to herself was that it was better than Ardennes.

At the final Battle of Ardennes, the Republic had thrown five full carrier groups at the system's defenders. There had been tens of thousands of missiles flying each way that day, and a lot of people—Protectorate and Republican alike—had died.

With the gunships in place, the Republic task force launched almost four thousand missiles. The Protectorate task force could launch more, and could *keep* launching them long after the gunships ran out of weapons.

Those first three salvos were going to *hurt*. The fact that all three would be launched before the Protectorate ships were in their own range was going to hurt even more.

"No new orders from the Flag," Armbruster reported.

"Engage as per prior orders then, Lieutenant Chambers," Kulkarni said calmly.

The young Mage-Lieutenant hit the waiting command on her screen. *Stand in Righteousness* shivered as Republic ships entered her range. At fourteen million kilometers, it would take seven and a half minutes for her missiles to reach their targets—minutes in which *Stand* would fire eight more salvos.

The same pattern repeated around her, but Roslyn's attention was fixed on the enemy. How they handled their gunships was going to decide the real cost of this battle. She was confident that they'd *win*—Alexander had brought over five hundred million tons of warships against three hundred—but the more holes they tore in the Republic command-and-control loop, the better they'd do.

Those holes were usually torn by destroying ships. One thing the Protectorate had learned so far was that Republic ships were incredibly hard to kill. They had better antimissile defenses than their Protectorate cousins, and the armor on their outer hulls was better still.

"Enemy first-salvo arrival in two minutes," she noted aloud. "Initial salvo intercept by our defensive missiles in...twenty seconds."

She had no control over those missiles, and the explosions were going to wreak havoc on her own control loops, but she'd take that over having four thousand missiles coming her way unchallenged.

"Intercept."

Roslyn's calm word didn't really do justice to the energy release taking shape on her screen. Two hundred and forty missiles, each carrying a one-gigaton antimatter warhead, had charged into the middle of the Republic missile salvo and detonated.

Antimatter warheads were far from the most stable things in existence. Cascading explosions took out hundreds of missiles.

Unfortunately, thousands more remained and there were only two more salvos in place to intercept the incoming fire. Salvos after that were being targeted on the next wave of missiles.

"We'll take the first two salvos unopposed," Roslyn said quietly. "Our first salvo will hit before their third wave does, which *should* screw with their command relays."

"Assuming we kill any of them," Kulkarni replied. "Otherwise, those antimatter explosions are going to be our best shield."

"Yes, sir," Roslyn confirmed. She was already flagging high priority targets for the crews of her Rapid-Fire Laser Anti-Missile turrets. The RFLAMs were her key defenses after the countermissile salvos were done, but *Stand*'s role in this fight was as a picket ship.

The missiles heading at her were at the top of her priority list—but it was tied with missiles headed at *Righteous Shield of Valor*. The destroyer's job was to protect the battleship.

"Second intercept," she announced as a new series of antimatter explosions tore through space. The radioactive debris from the explosions was doing a number on their communications with their offensive salvos now.

Hopefully, it was doing the same to the Republic crews!

"RFLAM range...now."

Thirty-six turrets on *Stand in Righteousness*'s hull spun to life at her command. The first Republic salvo had been gutted by antimatter explosions, with over seven hundred one-gigaton warheads going off in their midst.

They were designed for that environment, however, and they didn't look *nearly* blinded enough to Roslyn as her lasers opened fire.

More missiles died, but each death was another antimatter explosion. Like black powder cannoneers in the past, a modern space warship had to deal with "gunsmoke" fouling their targeting. As the missiles approached, magic tore into the storm as well, the amplified magic of the Martian ships' Mages destroying dozens more of the weapons.

Despite everything, missiles made it through. Four of *Stand*'s sisters died in balls of antimatter fire, and a chill ran down Roslyn's spine.

"They're focusing fire on the destroyers, sir," she said as calmly as she could. "Our part of the formation, specifically. I would guess they're using the first two big salvos to degrade the escorts around *Righteous Shield* so they can try and scratch a battleship."

"I wonder if they know Her Highness is aboard," Kulkarni asked, but it was a rhetorical question. "Stretch the gap, Lieutenant Coleborn," she ordered. "Let's put ourselves between the flag and the enemy. No one is taking down the flagship while *Stand in Righteousness* is in front of her!"

It looked like Kulkarni was going to get her wish. With the losses in the first wave, only four destroyers and two cruisers managed to get in front of *Righteous Shield of Valor* before the second Republican salvo came screaming down on them.

Missiles from the rest of the fleet tore gaping holes in the missile swarm, and the lasers from every ship were slashing through space ahead of them, but Roslyn was grimly certain the odds weren't in their favor.

Antimatter explosions filled the space around them, blinding her sensors and leaving her turrets firing almost randomly after the first fractions of a second.

Then she *could* see missiles clearly through the cloud. There was no time for her to do anything, not with missiles moving at over fifty thousand kilometers a second within a few thousand kilometers of her ship. Her part in stopping this salvo was already over.

Her RFLAM turrets fired automatically on the programs she'd loaded in. Four missiles were coming directly at *Stand in Righteousness* and had made it through everything, leaving only the final automatic defensive protocol to save her.

Roslyn didn't even have time to inhale before the destroyer rang like a bell and her screens went completely blank.

Everything had gone blank. They'd lost power to the bridge. Thankfully, their gravity runes didn't require power and neither did the amplifier.

The pale emergency lights were enough for Roslyn to see Kulkarni lock her hands on the simulacrum in a death grip. Without power, the only defense the destroyer had was her Captain.

Roslyn felt power *flash* around her as Kulkarni's magic spoke, shielding her ship from a threat they could barely see.

Something flickered, and then her screens rebooted. The only light in the bridge was the pale emergency lights, but many of their combat-critical systems were coming back online.

"Reactor core is rebooting but we can't bring it back up to full," Engineering reported. "We're running at twenty-five percent. That's coms, minimal engines and RFLAMs."

Roslyn might not have sensors, but having communications meant that she was able to link back into the main tactical network—in time to see the third salvo, the last gunship-augmented one, come crashing over the destroyers.

"Fire incoming," she snapped. "They're targeting the Flag...*engaging.*"

Less than two-thirds of her turrets responded to her commands, and Roslyn tried not to think of what that meant. The systems might be slaved to central control, but those turrets still had crews.

Twenty-two lasers stabbed into space as the missiles charged past the crippled destroyer. The rest of the fleet had already gutted the salvo, but hundreds of missiles still swarmed toward the battleship.

Roslyn's turrets tore into them from an unexpected angle, distracting the weapons' electronic brains for a critical fraction of a second. It wasn't enough to stop them all...but it was enough to tip the balance as the battleship's own weapons tore into the enemy fire.

Three missiles made it through, detonating within meters of the battleship's immense armor. Radiation washed over the big ship...but she emerged untouched.

"*Righteous Shield*'s armor is holding," Roslyn reported slowly. "Fleet is maneuvering to cover the cripples."

That included *Stand in Righteousness*. They were one of the lucky ones. Of the eight destroyers and two cruisers that had been covering *Righteous Shield of Valor,* only two destroyers and a cruiser remained... and those were the "cripples" Roslyn was referring to.

Other ships had been battered as well, but the focus had been on the flagship. Roslyn had to wonder if the RIN had known which ship Alexander was aboard.

"Our fire has been minimally effective," she continued, continuing to download from the tactical network. "One enemy cruiser has been damaged, but the gunships are blunting our fire. They're more effective in the missile defense role than we accounted for."

Stand's bridge was silent for several seconds.

"Damage report," Kulkarni finally said, her voice quiet.

"We took two hits, one on each of our starboard faces," Roslyn detailed as the data flowed onto her console. "Fusion plants went into emergency shutdown and at least one missile flagged us as dead and kept going.

"Ten of my RFLAM turrets are gone and four more are disabled. Main battle lasers are...gone," she continued. "Too much damage to the resonance chambers. It may be repairable but they're offline for now. I can't be sure about the launchers without power, but it looks like we're down at least half."

Roslyn was staring blankly at her screen now, until she finally swallowed and forced herself to look up at Kulkarni.

"I've got at least thirty people headed for medbay and twice that just... gone," she told the Captain. That was half of her tactical department wounded or dead. A quarter of the ship's crew, and Roslyn only knew about her *own* people.

"Engineering is telling me not to push past one gravity," Coleborn added from navigation.

"So, we can't maneuver, we can't shoot, and we can barely defend ourselves," Kulkarni summarized. "It seems this battle is over for us."

Half a dozen ships were now unable to decelerate at the same pace as the rest of the fleet. Adjusting formation was stretching out the entire fleet to cover the cripples, but with the gunships' missiles expended, it was probably safe to do so.

Roslyn hoped, anyway. The first Republic cruiser finally died as she watched, escape pods spewing from the ship as the armored outer hull broke in half under the pounding of antimatter missiles.

Fragments of the RIN's new armor were being examined in Ardennes, and she hoped it was a productive examination. That cruiser had taken over a dozen direct hits from one-gigaton antimatter warheads before the armor finally broke.

As she watched, though, another pair of Martian destroyers came under fire from the Republic missiles. *Song of Guardians* simply vanished in a ball of fire, and *Blade of Glorious Freedom* reeled out of formation, her engines turned to vapor as her own antimatter conduits ruptured.

Safety precautions saved *Blade*, but the fleet was losing destroyers *fast*.

The loss of the first cruiser seemed to be the crack they needed to get through the Republic's defenses, however. A second Republic cruiser reeled out of formation and a dozen gunships blew apart around her.

Without launchers, Roslyn hadn't been watching the tactical network. She checked and saw that a quarter of their salvos were being targeted on the gunships now—and it was starting to show.

The earlier focus on the cruisers had left the gunships focused on defending their bigger sisters. The change wasn't throwing enough missiles at them to wipe them out in one salvo, but suddenly, gunships were dying by the dozen.

Every gunship lost was another three defensive turrets out of the fight. The cruisers had taken three *hundred* turrets with them...but in less than three minutes, the ravaging of the gunship squadrons had removed even more of the Republic's defenses.

One of the battleships moved to try and reinforce the gunships' defenses, and Roslyn smiled coldly. Lightspeed delays meant that the command-and-control cycle of the missiles was taking over a minute to respond...enough for the battleship's crew to think their action wasn't impacting the target assignments.

The second salvo after their movement was unchanged, adding to that image and battering cruisers and gunships. The *third* salvo, well after the targeting orders could have been changed, was not.

Almost four thousand missiles targeted one Republic battleship, and *she* was focused on defending the gunships around her.

Forty megatons of hyper-advanced warship vanished in a series of antimatter explosions that wrecked anyone's ability to see into—or out of—the gunship positions.

"Hammer them," Roslyn whispered, watching as the fleet now tracked their missiles across the Republican fleet with boots of fire. She was half-expecting surrenders at this point—they had to be able to tell that they couldn't escape.

None of them could escape, in fact. They were almost clear enough of the Republic warships to launch assault shuttles toward the fleeing transports. Long-range missile fire would neutralize the carriers' defenses before the shuttles arrived.

None of the Republic ships were getting away. Their choices were surrender or—

Her screens lit up with multiple jump flares and she stared at them in shock.

A Protectorate warship, with fully trained Mages and amplified magic, could jump from orbit of a planet. It was unwise and painful for the crew at best, dangerous and near-suicidal at worst, but a Martian warship could do it.

The Republic ships had never demonstrated that ability before. Now, every surviving capital ship in the defending fleet *and* the fleeing transports tried to jump. The rapidly expanding debris clouds told Roslyn the results.

Some of the RIN cruisers from the defense force *might* have made it, but the surviving battleship had torn herself apart. Pieces of the warship were now scattering themselves across the system at a significant chunk of the speed of light.

Worse, though, was the fleeing transports. The carriers had at least jumped. Roslyn wasn't sure if they'd made it, but they'd jumped. The two transports, each carrying at least thirty thousand people, had not been so lucky,

CHAPTER 9

STARLIGHT, unlike *Rhapsody in Purple,* had the space to carry the number of people they'd shoved aboard her. The fast packet only had a crew of seventeen, but one of the many purposes of the ships was to transport people who could pay.

In theory, a fast packet should have had multiple Mages aboard. *Starlight* had been officially home-ported in the UnArcana World of Nueva Bolivia, though, which meant that Captain Maata had probably always had problems recruiting Mages.

Even with the three LMID defectors and Damien's dozen guardians, there were enough staterooms for everyone to have their own.

Damien could probably have even brought Persephone. Much as he found himself missing the cat, he was happier having her in hands he trusted...and *Starlight* was an LMID asset, even if most of the crew didn't seem to have ever been actual agents of the Legatan government and the ones who had been were retired.

"This ship is about as innocent as a middle-aged actor," Romanov told Damien in the Hand's quarters.

They were both drinking coffees. Damien had quietly made it clear that alcohol wouldn't be permitted among his people until they were back aboard *Rhapsody.*

"So, it's tried everything and grown bored of half of it?" Damien asked.

His security chief snorted.

"Basically. They're being pretty clear with us," Romanov admitted. "I don't think they'd have let most passengers into Pod Bravo."

The guest quarters that Damien and his team had been put up were in Pod Charlie. Pod Alpha was where the crew was staying. The simulacrum chamber bridge was in the core, and the cargo was mounted on spars radiating from the front of the core.

"What's in Pod Bravo?" Damien asked, since Romanov was clearly waiting for the question.

"An armory to put a destroyer to shame," the Marine told him. "Plus, well, six Rapier launchers and the magazines for them."

Damien whistled silently.

"Rapier" was one of the main brands of missiles available to civilian ships for self-defense. Since they could be bought, they also often ended up in the hands of the people the freighters needed them for defense *against*. Even the best licensing and control systems only did so much against professional criminals, after all.

Unlike military missiles, they used fusion drives and didn't have any warheads at all, leaving them with a quarter of the range and perhaps a fifth of the effectiveness of a military missile. They were also a tenth of the price and half the size.

Six Rapier launchers would make quite the mess of most ships that would try to jump a freighter as small as *Starlight*. It also meant they'd sacrificed a significant chunk of their passenger capacity and living space to carry the weapons, which supported *Starlight* being a retired covert ops ship instead of a freighter LMID had occasionally used.

"So, these quarters have probably been filled with Augment commandos before," Damien concluded. "Niska isn't the only defector here."

"No. There are Augment-rated combat exosuits in that armory, too," Romanov told him. "Six suits...so either Niska and his buddies figured they'd need spares, or Maata has a few Augments in her crew no one has told us about."

"What about regular exosuits?"

"None," Romanov told him. "There are some man-portable, bipod-mounted, anti-exosuit weapons in there, but it's mostly small arms and concealable body armor. No equivalent to our penetrator carbines."

"So, this ship is their version of *Rhapsody*, but relying on looking normal instead of being invisible?" Damien asked.

"I think we're still a step or two down from 'black ops pocket warship,' but she was a spy ship," the Marine confirmed. "And they don't seem to be too concerned about us working that out, which is probably a good sign."

The Hand snorted.

"We're still not trusting them."

"Not as far as I can throw this ship, no."

"What's our ETA, Captain Maata?" Niska asked at dinner later.

The Captain had been inviting Damien and Niska to join her for dinner most days of the trip.

"We're going from pretty deep in the Protectorate to almost as deep in the Republic," Maata pointed out. "Mage Foster is *very* good, but we don't want to push her."

Foster, Damien knew, was perfectly capable of running an every-six-hours jump until *Starlight* fell apart around her. She was a fully-trained Royal Martian Navy Ship's Mage that the Agency had "borrowed" for their stealth ship.

Normal procedure, however, called for a Mage to jump no more than once every eight hours. Jumping too often could kill the Mage making the jumps.

Damien had once almost killed himself with exhaustion by pushing his limits for an extended period—and he'd seen footage of the aftermath when a Mage jumped after less than an hour's break.

You only needed to see fatal thaumic burnout in person once to never want to push the limit yourself.

"So, how long?" the old cyborg asked with a chuckle.

"Four more days," Maata told him. "Once there, *Starlight* will get us into orbit much faster than most ships; call it fourteen hours. I'll probably be able to spin out finding buyers for my cargo and finding a new cargo for a couple of weeks, but I can only stay so long before it starts getting suspicious."

"So, two weeks to follow up on your leads, Niska," Damien said. "Think that will be enough?"

"I don't have a damn clue," the cyborg admitted. "Worst-case scenario, I suppose we can stay on the ground and have Maata make a circuit and come back for us. That's risky, though."

Niska grimaced.

"Right now, I'm still officially an LMID agent and have a *lot* of independent authority and access. *You*, however, will be public enemy number one as soon as they realize you're inside our borders."

"That will be harder than the Republic might think," Damien replied quietly. He had more tricks than one to conceal his appearance. Concealing his crippled hands was harder, though, and there were only so many people in the galaxy with elbow-length burns from molten metal.

"If I didn't figure that was the case, I'd have suggested you send someone else," Niska told him. "As it stands, having a Hand for backup is surprisingly appealing."

"Do you have any idea what you're looking for?" Maata asked.

"Not really," Niska replied, with a warning glance at Damien. Maata knew a *lot*, but she didn't know everything. "I know *where* to look, and that should tell me more."

He shook his head.

"Whatever it is, the Republic killed *Bryan Ricket* to cover it up," he pointed out. "We're not key loyalists and founding fathers of the nation. They're not even going to blink at putting any or all of us down, hard."

"Let them try," Maata said grimly. "I never expected to see Prodigal Son activated, James, no more than you did. But if the Republic killed Ricket, they're not *my* goddamned Republic anymore.

"So, fuck 'em. I have nuclear missiles if they want to argue the point."

Damien swallowed. Rapiers didn't normally have warheads, but from what Maata had just said...he might want to have his people check the ones *Starlight* carried.

Just in case.

CHAPTER 10

TWO DAYS was barely enough time for anyone to begin to sort out the consequences of the Republic occupation of Santiago or the Protectorate liberation of the system.

Stand in Righteousness and the other cripples had been towed into Cova's orbit while other ships had moved to Novo Lar to force the surrender of the remaining troops. From what Roslyn was hearing, most of the remaining troops felt that they were the lucky ones.

Some had tried to hold out, however, and the Santiago Defense Force didn't have much of an army left. The Protectorate didn't *have* an army, which meant that the holdouts were being dug out by the Marine contingents of Mage-Admiral Alexander's fleet.

Roslyn was getting updates through the tactical network. They were at least more positive than the updates she was getting from *Stand*'s engineering department.

Of the forty destroyers that had arrived in the system, fifteen were just *gone*. The design of the *Lancer* class was almost a century old, and Roslyn was now grimly aware that it had been built as an anti-piracy ship.

Against a real opponent, even updated *Lancer* destroyers were obsolete, and they'd paid the price for the age of their design. The Protectorate had updated their cruiser and battleship designs over the years, but the *Lancer*s had just seen their weapons and systems upgraded around the same core schematic.

Of the twenty-five remaining destroyers, thirteen were damaged to one degree or another and now hung in Cova orbit. Four damaged cruisers orbited with them.

Four more lightly damaged cruisers were still with the battleships, as were the remaining twelve functioning destroyers. Six more of the massive ten-to-twelve-megaton ships had died in the fight.

Mage-Admiral Alexander's fleet was victorious, but the price had been brutal.

The terrifying part was that the Protectorate search-and-rescue efforts had pulled more of their people out of the wreckage than the Republic's. The best estimates Roslyn was seeing was that there had been eighty thousand people on just the ships that they'd seen fail to jump.

S&R had picked up less than two thousand.

Another thirty thousand had died aboard ships and gunships destroyed in the fighting, but Roslyn could understand those. Could live with those, even if she felt guilty about them...but eighty thousand people had died in an instant because they would rather die trying to run than surrender.

"It's about the drives," Coleborn said over her shoulder.

Roslyn looked up at the navigator in surprise and he shrugged.

"The drives?" she asked.

"We haven't recovered an intact Republic jump drive yet," he reminded her. "Their ships self-destruct or, well, suicide-jump"—he gestured at the screen—"to avoid capture."

"I doubt their crews are *that* determined to keep that secret," Roslyn replied. "That's insane."

"You're assuming the crews even know about the security protocols," the navigator replied. "What happened in Ardennes?"

Roslyn shivered, suddenly feeling very, *very* young.

"They blew up after the rest of the fleet jumped out," she said. "Remote-detonated via their FTL com?"

"Or just one fanatic captain," Coleborn agreed. He gripped her shoulder reassuringly. "Sooner or later, that's going to bite the RIN in the ass. Right now, however, the Captain wants to talk to you."

Roslyn looked up at the bigger man.

"You know about what?"

He shrugged.

"Yeah. So do you, I bet."

Kulkarni was waiting as Roslyn entered her office, *Stand in Righteousness*'s Captain looking exhausted. She gestured Roslyn to a seat and slid a coffee across the desk.

"To play the old 'good news, bad news' game, I have bad news, weird news, terrifying news and good news," the Captain told her. "Drink your coffee; you're going to need it."

Roslyn took a seat and a swallow of coffee—far too large a swallow, given that the Captain had added a significant amount of whisky to the hot drink.

She coughed, and Kulkarni managed to smile through her fatigue.

"The bad news, I think everybody has guessed," she told Roslyn. "*Stand* is irreparable. Her amplifier matrix isn't stable enough to jump, and even if Santiago had the yards to fix her, she just isn't worth it.

"She's going to be scrapped in place for parts to repair ships that *do* have matrices we can fix," Kulkarni said sadly. "We are all now out of a job, though you can imagine that isn't going to last long for any of us."

Roslyn gripped the cup of coffee hard. It was warm enough that it was uncomfortable to do so, so she took another swallow of the whisky-laced drink. She'd been battlefield-commissioned aboard *Stand in Righteousness*. She'd literally never served on another warship.

Stand had been her ensign cruise, a glorified internship in the middle of her academy training. Somehow, everything had gone to hell around her, but she wasn't quite sure what would happen to the youngest Lieutenant in the Navy without her ship.

"The weird news might seem unrelated, but you'll understand when I'm done," Kulkarni continued. She was clearly aware of Roslyn's concern as she gave the younger woman a reassuring smile.

"Through sources I don't have nearly the clearance to know about, we came into a mother lode of intelligence on Republic espionage operations inside the Protectorate. I don't know the details, but I can tell you that the Republic is going to have a very bad few days as the news starts trickling home.

"Given what we know of the Republic's communications, we held off on executing on the intel until everything was in place. That was this morning, which brings me to the *terrifying* news."

Kulkarni grimaced and shook her head a Roslyn's confused look.

"I'm sure you wondered why Mage-Admiral Alexander was so dismissive of the gunships," she asked.

Roslyn nodded slowly.

"It was because her operations officer sold her on a detailed analysis that said they weren't a threat," the destroyer Captain told her. "I've seen that analysis now. It's *really* well done. Without knowing the truth, we would have chalked it up to a couple of misestimates and an overeager officer."

"The truth, sir?" Roslyn asked. Surely, what Kulkarni was suggesting couldn't be the case...

"Lieutenant Commander Louna Nikodem was an operative of the Republican Intelligence Directorate," Kulkarni said flatly. "That's how they knew which ship was Alexander's flagship. Nikodem might have had a plan to escape the destruction of *Righteous Shield*...but then again, she might not have.

"Especially since she committed suicide to avoid capture when the MPs came for her."

Roslyn swallowed hard.

"That's...bad, sir."

"It is," Kulkarni agreed. "The good news is that she's no longer a threat—and the good news for me is that Mage-Admiral Alexander's staff suddenly has an unexpected opening. That's also good news for you, Lieutenant. And me, thankfully."

"You're moving over as her ops officer, sir?"

"Exactly," Kulkarni confirmed. "And you'll be on the shuttle with me."

"Sir?" Roslyn said again. She was starting to feel lost.

"The Admiral wants the most experienced people fighting the Republic at her side, and I think she feels that *you*, in particular, need a staff posting as you catch up with your peers."

A staff posting wasn't exactly what Roslyn wanted, but...it was still a posting.

"I can live with that, sir."

Kulkarni laughed.

"'Live with that,' she says," the Captain echoed. "Mage-Admiral Alexander didn't have a full staff when she arrived in Ardennes. She filled most of the holes, but she never had a Flag Lieutenant.

"That's your job now, Roslyn Chambers. It's a staff posting to let you get your feet under you, sure, but serving as a Flag Lieutenant is generally considered as a necessary checkmark to *flag rank*.

"Don't waste Her Highness's trust," Kulkarni concluded. "I'll be there to back you up, and I'm pretty sure Alexander knows where you're at, but this isn't an easy posting she's giving you. Like Montgomery before her, Alexander seems to think you're worth some extra effort."

Roslyn was very quiet as she met her Captain's gaze.

"That should have gone under the terrifying news, Mage-Captain," she admitted.

"That would only have been if I didn't agree with them, Lieutenant Chambers."

CHAPTER 11

THE SHUTTLE FLIGHT away from *Stand in Righteousness* was grim. The destroyer was already being dismantled behind them, exosuited workers swarming over the hull with cutters and transport sleds.

Stand's sacrifice would get two of the other destroyers online, but it was still morbid to watch your home get chopped up behind you.

"She did her job, Chambers," Kulkarni said from behind her. For all that the older woman was trying to be reassuring, Kulkarni was also watching the ship being dismantled.

Stand in Righteousness had been Roslyn's ship, but she'd been Kulkarni's *command*. Roslyn mourned her home, but she couldn't help wondering just how responsible Kulkarni felt for the loss of the destroyer.

"We did our job, too," the Captain continued. "And look over there."

Roslyn noted that Kulkarni *didn't* look away from the wrecked destroyer as Roslyn did.

She was pointing, however, at *Righteous Shield of Valor,* and the sight of the battleship forced Roslyn to pay more attention to what she was getting into.

The *Guardian*-class battleship was fifty times *Stand in Righteousness*'s mass. They were both white pyramids floating in space, but that was where the similarities ended. *Stand* had been exactly one hundred meters high on a square base a hundred meters across.

Righteous Shield was *half a kilometer* high on a four-hundred-meter base. For every weapon system the destroyer possessed, the battleship mustered ten. Her missiles were comparable, but she had three hundred launchers to the destroyer's twenty-four. Her battle lasers were almost ten times as powerful, and she had four times as many of them.

By any standard, the battleship dwarfed their previous ship. *Pax Marcianus* and *Peacemaker*, still in orbit of Novo Lar, outmassed her by twenty percent, but short of those two ships, *nothing* in space challenged a *Guardian*-class battleship.

There were scars on *Righteous Shield*'s hull now. Sensors and turrets had been replaced, but no one had repainted where the fires of matter-antimatter reaction had seared the battleship's hull.

She'd withstood that fire, though, where no lesser ship could have.

"That's our new home," Kulkarni told her. "Unless Alexander moves somewhere. We're part of Her Highness the Mage-Admiral's staff now. We go where she goes, sleep when she sleeps, follow where she leads."

"I feel underqualified still," Roslyn admitted.

Her now-former Captain laughed.

"That's because you are, Chambers," she said. "But that hasn't stopped you yet!"

Their shuttle wasn't the only one in the battleship's landing bay. Two others had appeared in front of them, and streams of people were already making their way off to meet officers and head deeper into the massive ship.

Powered safety shields were moving out of the way, presumably by remote from the control center. They clearly had been protecting those other passengers and the waiting welcoming parties from the energy of the shuttle's arrival.

Roslyn tried not to look as lost as she felt, falling in behind Mage-Captain Kulkarni and hoping that the older woman knew where they were going.

A few seconds after leaving the shuttle, however, she realized where Kulkarni was headed. There were only two red exosuits in the cavernous bay—and only one organization in the Protectorate wore unmarked red exosuits.

The two suits of armor held Royal Guards, veteran Marine Combat Mages with at least ten years' service assigned to the protection of the Mage-King of Mars and his family.

A second circle of four young-looking women in plain black fatigues carrying overpowered penetrator carbines surrounded the Royal Guardsmen. They were Protectorate Secret Service.

All six of those intimidating-looking guards were gathered around a tall woman with gunmetal-gray hair and pale blue eyes. Roslyn Chambers had never met any member of the Royal Family, but she didn't think anyone born and raised in the Protectorate would have failed to recognize Her Royal Highness Mage-Admiral Jane Michelle Alexander.

The guards let Kulkarni and Roslyn through without hesitation, the protective cordon opening to let them in and then closing behind them as the two women came to a halt and crisply saluted.

"Mage-Captain Indrajit Kulkarni and Mage-Lieutenant Roslyn Chambers reporting, sir," Kulkarni introduced them. "We've been assigned to your staff."

"I know, Mage-Captain," Alexander said lightly. "I apologize for the security." Her head gesture took in the Royal Guards and Secret Service agents around her.

"Lieutenant Commander Nikodem had served with me for five years," she continued. "Her betrayal was unexpected, to put it mildly. You were chosen to replace her, Mage-Captain, because you've had plenty of opportunity to screw us just as badly as Louna did."

"I'd hoped my qualifications were also helpful," Kulkarni replied. "It's comforting to be regarded as trustworthy, though."

Alexander chuckled.

"Right now, Captain Kulkarni, 'trustworthy' is the highest qualification someone can have," she noted. "Come, let's get out of the landing bay."

They reached a set of offices close to where Roslyn thought the flag bridge was. Alexander stopped outside one of the doors and gestured to the blank spot where a nameplate should be.

"I believe they've finished cleaning out Louna's crap," she told Kulkarni. "If you want to go in and get set up, Lieutenant Chambers and I need to have a long chat."

Roslyn swallowed as she was suddenly and unexpectedly separated from Kulkarni. Showing her concern was bad form, however, so she simply smiled and nodded.

"With me, Lieutenant," Alexander told her.

Roslyn fell in behind the Admiral and followed her to her office.

Alexander's office showed every sign of having been her main working space for a *long* time. Roslyn wasn't sure when the Admiral had taken over *Righteous Shield* as her flagship, but she'd clearly had time to make the office her space.

There was no sign of the normal standard-issue furniture in the room. The furniture that had replaced it didn't look particularly expensive, but it had definitely been selected to a specific taste. Everything, from the painting of Olympus Mons on the wall to the cabinets to the desk, matched.

"Have a seat, Lieutenant," Alexander ordered. A tray with a carafe of coffee and two cups floated over to the desk without the Admiral doing anything.

"Take anything in your coffee?"

"No, sir," Roslyn replied.

"Okay." Alexander added a cube to hers. "I take one sugar, nothing else. Remember that."

"Yes, sir." Roslyn wondered if getting coffee was going to be the major part of her job.

The Admiral shook her head at the young woman.

"I haven't had a Flag Lieutenant in a while," she admitted. "I have a secretary, Chief Olivia Sinclair, and a steward, Chief Andres. Between them, they keep my life in pretty solid order.

"That said, we've never actually run a fleet at war before, and we're finding the limits of what I can get NCOs to do without getting pushback from other officers," Alexander noted. "Which is bullshit, but I can only do so much."

"So...you found the most junior officer you possibly could?" Roslyn asked.

The Princess of Mars laughed.

"Exactly!" The humor faded. "Now drink your coffee."

Somewhat intimidated, Roslyn obeyed.

"Your job, at least initially, is going to be as my gofer," Alexander told her. "That means that, yes, you need to know my coffee order. My food allergies and preferences. My birthday—and the birthdays of my staff to make sure *I* don't forget as I get old.

"You'll also need to know the entire org structure of my staff, the fleet under my command, and the command structure of *Righteous Shield of Valor*," the Admiral continued. "You'll need to know who to go to for answers when I ask questions and who to go to for supplies when I'm putting on a party or a dinner.

"Olivia and Andres will know a lot of those answers initially, but you can only rely on our NCOs so far," Alexander noted. "A small and aggravating number of those officers have a stick up their asses and won't answer questions from the NCOs. They don't have that excuse when you speak in my name, so you'll have to get used to politely browbeating officers senior to you."

She smiled.

"Given that you are, as you said, the most junior officer in the fleet, that experience will serve you well."

The job didn't sound fun at all, though Roslyn could certainly see the value of it for *Alexander*.

"A lot of this is better experience for you than it might sound," the Admiral pointed out, "and it's going to suck up more time than you can possibly imagine. What will make it worse is that I will expect you to sit in on all of my meetings, double-checking that the dictation software is taking minutes correctly, making sure the stewards know if we need more coffee or food, and generally keeping your mouth shut. A Flag Lieutenant should be neither heard nor noticed."

That...didn't sound like herself at all to Roslyn, but she could probably make it work.

"That's the key parts of your official duties," Alexander continued. "Your unofficial job will be to keep track of everything going on in all of those meetings, everything going on in the fleet, and giving me your honest opinion of everything that I'm being told.

"In private, obviously," she added. "I just had a cold and harsh awakening as to my need for a second opinion on even what my staff tells me. People *died*, Lieutenant Chambers, because I trusted my ops officer and didn't have anyone else to give me their point of view.

"That's going to be your job," she concluded. "Everyone is going to see you as my shadow at best, but I want your eyes and your ears open as we go through everything, and I want your opinion on everything we deal with.

"The worst case will be that I don't have time to explain why you're wrong and delegate that to Captain Kulkarni," Alexander said gently. "The best case is that you see something I've missed and your observations save lives."

Roslyn swallowed hard.

"No pressure, huh?" she asked softly.

"The pressure is on me, Lieutenant," the Mage-Admiral pointed out. "Your job from here on out is to help me survive that pressure. Understand?"

"I think so, sir."

"Can you do it?" Alexander asked.

Roslyn felt a shiver of fear and anxiety run down her spine, but she met Alexander's gaze levelly.

"Honestly, sir? The hardest part is going to be keeping my mouth shut in the meetings," she admitted. "I assume you know about my history?"

"If you mean the bits about being a juvenile delinquent and your jail stint that aren't in your official record?" the Admiral replied. "Yes. Believe me, Lieutenant, I am *very* familiar with the mindset of a daughter of a privileged family raising hell to get someone—*anyone*—to pay actual attention to them."

She grinned.

"I'm just old enough that everyone has forgotten *my* petty thefts by now!"

CHAPTER 12

"WELCOME TO the Arsenault System," Liara Foster said in an exhausted but cheerful voice after completing the jump.

"I'm going to go fall over. Have fun, kids."

Damien snorted at the Jump Mage and gave her a casual wave as she drifted out of the zero-gravity simulacrum chamber. He was using magic to keep himself anchored to one of the railings in the room.

The chamber had the best access to *Starlight*'s sensors of anywhere aboard ship. There was a reason that Navy warships, which needed to know what was going on at all times, put the bridge *in* the simulacrum chamber—and *Starlight* had followed that design.

With Foster on her way to her quarters, Damien was the only Mage in the rune-encrusted chamber. He lacked the runes to interface with the jump matrix, though, so it wasn't like he could jump the ship anywhere.

Damien was a Rune Wright, one of the extraordinarily rare Mages who could see the flow of magic. Floating in the simulacrum chamber, he could watch the flow of energy through the jump matrix. He could also see where the matrix was ever so slightly wrong, the spots in the rune sequences that filtered energy to make sure the jump matrix could only be used to jump starships.

The core of a jump matrix and a military-grade amplifier matrix were identical. The same runes, the same functions, the same sequences. A jump matrix was actually *more* complicated, because there were extra matrices woven through the runes that negated any spell except the one it was designed for.

As a very young Mage who hadn't known any better, Damien had worked out how to turn a jump matrix into an amplifier. The consequences of that had ended up with the largest criminal organization in the Protectorate in pieces and Damien as a Hand of the Mage-King of Mars.

While running from authorities and criminals alike, however, he'd visited Legatus. Niska had then seen him deliver gunships to Chrysanthemum, another UnArcana World.

That made Manchester, Arsenault's habitable planet, the third UnArcana World he'd visited. Like most, it was more industrialized than an equivalent world that used magic. Massive fusion power plants and solar-panel arrays were positioned in geostationary orbits above Arsenault's equator, with forty-thousand-kilometer-long cables running power to the planetary grid.

A Protectorate world would have used antimatter power plants with magical safeguards to provide the same power in a far safer and more efficient manner. Without Mages to produce the antimatter or safeguard the plants, however, UnArcana Worlds went for fusion on a mass scale.

Even as Damien watched, a two-megaton tanker decelerated into Manchester orbit to dock at one of the huge power stations. Tracing the ship's course back, he nodded as he saw several other tankers on a probably permanent cycle between the cloudscoops on the inner gas giant and the power plants in orbit of Manchester.

Gunships of an unfamiliar design escorted those transports. These weren't the mass-produced Republic ships that the RIN's carriers were using to cause terror across the frontlines. They were older ships, probably built by Arsenault before the Secession.

A collection of more-familiar gunships made up a defensive cloud around Manchester. Presumably, some of the stations in orbit were support platforms for the short-range vessels, but Damien could pick out thirty of the ships scattered around the planet.

There were two more rocky worlds inside Manchester's orbit, and it looked like the closer of them was being strip-mined to support

Manchester's industries. Like the tankers coming from the gas giants in the outer systems, there was a scattered but consistent chain of freighters pulling ore toward the orbital refineries.

For all of the orbital industry, however, the planet they were heading for was almost pristine. His files said that the climate was chilly for a habitable planet and most of the population was around the equator, which simplified the power grid and made the orbital plants practical.

Over two hundred million people called the Arsenault System home. On average, that meant that there was probably a dozen or so Mages by Right being born on the planet each year.

Since the Secession, those kids weren't being identified—and that might be for the best.

Damien was, after all, there to find out what had happened to the children who had already been identified as Mages.

"All right," Captain Maata said calmly in a small meeting room several hours later. "I've made contact with my usual buyers and sellers, and have started the delicate dance of selling and replacing a spec cargo."

She shook her head at Damien and Niska, the only other occupants of the room

"From the tone of those conversations, stretching out our visit here is going to be harder than I anticipated," she warned. "I think I'm going to make this an R&R stop. They've done a good job of keeping Manchester's natural habitat preserved, so the planet has some nice resorts.

"If I cycle my crew through a week off each, that should get us the two weeks I promised. Beyond that, though..." She spread her hands. "If I've run my entire crew through a week's vacation apiece *and* my cargo spars are full, people are going to get suspicious if I'm not moving."

"We could fake an engineering casualty," Niska suggested.

"It's a possibility, but we're already close enough in that 'faking' is going to look a lot like 'causing'," Maata told him. "I'm not breaking my ship for you, James, not without a damn good reason."

"If we'd have to trigger an actual problem, our best timing on that would be to do so as *Starlight* is leaving orbit," Damien cut in, trying to cut off any potential argument. "If we hit the end of two weeks and we're sufficiently on the trail that we need more time, well...then we can talk about breaking *Starlight* to buy that time.

"We don't need it before then."

The Captain grumbled but nodded.

"All right. I'll leave you two to the cloak-and-dagger," she told them. "I'm just the driver. I don't think I *want* to know what you're getting up to."

She rose and walked out, leaving Damien alone with Niska.

The Hand leveled his gaze on the cyborg and made an inquiring gesture.

"All I know about Arsenault is the basic encyclopedia entry and a review of our scan data," he pointed out. "Where do we start poking?"

For that matter, Damien didn't even know what moving around on a Republic world looked like. On a Protectorate world, the platinum fist he wore on his chest opened *every* door. It wasn't going to do the same here.

"Getting close to the school won't be particularly difficult," Niska told him. "We'll shuttle down with Maata's crew and rent a vehicle. It's close to a bunch of those resorts she mentioned, so no one is going to question us driving out in that direction.

"The school itself was only ever accessible by air or by foot, so we'll make our way in quietly once we're close enough, but we can get close without drawing attention."

"All right," Damien agreed. "And backup?"

"I figure we bring your Romanov and my O'Malley," Niska said. Harlow O'Malley was the redheaded Augment who'd been with him when they'd boarded *Starlight*.

Damien wasn't sure if O'Malley had been a direct LMID agent or more like Maata, an LMID "asset" positioned in another service. He was certain that her main role now was keeping the old Augment spy alive.

Two Augments, a Combat Mage and a Hand should be enough to deal with any trouble they encountered, regardless of how crippled said Hand was.

"Romanov and I have ways to make sure we aren't recognized," he pointed out. "What about you and O'Malley?"

"O'Malley is a nobody by any grand standard," Niska replied. "She's a retired Augment Corps NCO, not an LMID agent, not a spy or an assassin.

"I have built-in hardware to change my features, but we're also probably going to need some of my access to pull this off. I checked once we were in system—my codes appear to still be good."

"And what happens when they *stop* being good?" Damien asked.

"We fight our way out," the Augment admitted. "There's more than one reason I'm bringing you, my lord Hand."

CHAPTER 13

MANCHESTER'S MAJOR CITY was named Arndale. Like the rest of the planet's major settlements, it was on the equator. In Arndale's case, it was built around—and over—a massive river that flowed toward the sea from one of the planet's largest mountain ranges.

Even in what Damien's wrist-comp told him was a city of fifteen million people, Manchester's determination to maintain a balance with the ecology was clear. Arndale sprawled for dozens of kilometers in every direction, but part of the reason for that was the massive greenbelt spaces laced throughout the city.

The Great Medlock River was nearly six hundred meters wide as it passed through the city, and the designers had been unwilling to give up that space. Carefully buttressed structures swept out over the river, creating grand and graceful thoroughfares that crossed the water.

Later architects had followed the same concept and added entire neighborhoods suspended above the river, with glittering glass-and-concrete structures rising above the water to provide homes for Arndale's wealthy and crazy.

There were six separate shuttle ports scattered throughout the city, and O'Malley brought them in at the one closest to the mountain range. Their destination wasn't in the big mountains, as Damien understood it, but in an off-spur range still within a day's drive of Arndale.

"Everything's checked and paid for," the Augment reported as she stepped back into the main compartment. "Our cargo will be picked up by its recipient, and one of Maata's people will take the shuttle back up once that's done."

"All right, Niska, this is your show," Damien conceded. "What's the plan?"

"First step, we grab a taxi and get to a hotel," Niska replied. "Officially, we're part of Maata's crew on leave, so let's look the part."

"From the hotel, we can get into the datanet," Romanov said. "I don't know about you three, but I want a better lay of the land before we go poking hornets' nests."

"We should pass without much notice so long as no one goes firing off magic where everyone can see it," the Augment replied distractedly, checking something on his wrist-comp.

Both Damien and Romanov had "lost" their usual medallions and the attached collars. Careful makeup work had even covered up the tan line where a portion of their skin had *always* been covered from the light in the past.

Most of their changed appearance, however, was a sustained spell. Damien couldn't do much about his own diminutive height, but his cheekbones were sharper, his nose was more pronounced and his eyes were now green instead of brown.

He didn't recognize *himself* in the mirror, so hopefully it was enough to fool any image-recognition software the Republic was running.

"Let's go grab that taxi, then," he ordered. "I'll admit, I want to see what the Republic looks like from the inside."

The hotel Niska picked was on the outskirts of the city, a solid but cheap facility clearly being used by exactly the type of people they were pretending to be: starship crew and travelers from outside Arndale who'd landed in the city but were heading to the mountains.

After checking in, Damien made his way down to the hotel-lobby bar and restaurant. He was out of date on the news from the war, and given that the Republic had an FTL communicator, he presumed that the local news would be up to date.

To his surprise, however, the talking heads on the screens in the bar were going on, at great length and detail, about the early stages of forming an interstellar sports league inside the Republic.

Similar efforts in the past had failed for assorted reasons, but it seemed the Republic was going to try again. In terms of building a shared identity, Damien could see the value.

"Can I get a coffee?" he asked the waitress. "And a menu?"

"Can do!" she replied cheerfully, returning only a few minutes later with both.

The news had moved on from talking about the sports league to talking about local news that Damien was unfamiliar with. Something about trying to put together an orbital park around the cinder planet they were basically strip-mining to fuel their industry.

Still nothing about the war.

Damien glanced down the menu, ordered a sandwich and met the waitress's questioning gaze.

"We're off the jump ship in orbit," he told her in answer to her unspoken question. "Trying to catch up on news." He gestured at the screen. "This lot does know there's a war on, right?"

"So they say," she said with a snort. "There might be a few snippets about in the talk-show segments later on, but we aren't getting much news about it. I'd have thought you'd know more? News travels by ship, after all, and we don't see many these days."

He nodded his acknowledgement of that and sipped his coffee as she swung away.

The Republic had the Link, a faster-than-light communicator. They had the devices in sufficient quantity that there'd been one concealed aboard Damien's flagship, allowing them to intercept him as his fleet was randomly jumping around.

Apparently, the civilians weren't aware of that. He wondered if that was because the devices simply weren't common knowledge or if it was because they were being intentionally kept secret.

In either case, there were almost certainly people on Manchester who *had* full knowledge of what was going on with the war, but they weren't sharing that with the news media or their citizenry in general.

Damien watched the news switch over to discussion of a local scandal around dog breeding and shook his head. Hopefully, the news was being kept quiet because it was bad for the Republic. These people weren't really to blame for the war—life on the ground seemed pretty normal to him so far—but their government had started it.

And *his* government had no intention of losing it.

"Anyone else creeped the fuck out?" Romanov asked bluntly as they reconvened in the larger of the rooms they'd booked. A tiny jammer was running on the table, loosely covered by the room-service menu as it shut down any cameras and bugs in the room.

"Perhaps you'd care to explain?" Niska replied. "Is it just being on a Republic World where no one gives you instant deference that bothers you, *Mage*?"

"Cut it," Damien snapped. That was...out of character for the Augment. "Something's bothering you, too, Niska. And I hit a few odd spots watching the news downstairs. So, Denis, what *was* bothering you?"

"This is hardly the first time I've wandered around without a medallion, Niska," Romanov replied. "I'm talking about the undercurrents. Everyone here is putting on a brave face, talking about all the possibilities of the Republic...but if you ask what the Republic has actually *done* for them, everyone gets real defensive, real quick.

"Mention the *war* and oh, boy." The Marine shook his head. "Nobody *knows* anything, but everyone seems to know someone who knows someone who says that it's going just great, just *great*, they'll tell you."

"No news of the war," Damien agreed. "No updates via the FTL com. No information on the handful of ships that do come through. All of the news is aggressively local, and the Republic-wide news is fluff.

"Was it the same on Legatus?" he asked Niska.

The Augment sighed.

"A bit," he admitted. "But not like this. Legatus runs the Republic; the news leaks out even if people aren't supposed to talk about it. The Link—that FTL com you mentioned—is classified. None of the news from it should be getting out to the public, but it does."

"And here it isn't," O'Malley agreed. "And Manchester doesn't seem to be thinking they're benefiting from the Republic—or the war."

When the three men looked at her, she shrugged and grinned.

"Boys," she said calmly. "*I* went and got a manicure and a haircut, then went shopping. It's amazing how much information you can get out of bored personal-service and retail workers."

"Okay, so what did you learn?" Niska asked.

"Nobody here really agrees with the war," O'Malley told them. "Most of the people I talked to? They don't understand why it's happening. There doesn't even seem to be a solid propaganda effort to bring them onside, which is damn weird."

"There should be," the LMID agent noted. "Most likely, there was. But everyone is putting on a good face, so it's at least partially lapsed. It's weird."

"Everyone is being very careful what they say until they've got a solid feel on you," Damien said quietly. "Which makes me wonder if we should be looking around corners for secret police."

The hotel room was silent.

"In theory, something like that would be against the Republic's constitution," Niska pointed out. "On the other hand, there are exemptions for times of war."

"There had to be more reason than that for the war," O'Malley said. "I thought it was about the ban on Mages coming to the Republic."

"But if we have a technological jump solution, why would we care?" Niska asked. "It's harder to see on Legatus, I think. People there bought into the us-versus-them narrative long ago. There's no one questioning the war."

"But here...Manchester was always an UnArcana World but never really hostile to the Protectorate," O'Malley said with a sigh. "They just followed Legatus into the Secession and now into the war."

"And make no mistake, the Republic is in charge here," Damien told them. "I'd bet a good chunk of change that everything that hits the news is being approved in advance."

"That's illegal," O'Malley objected.

"Except in times of war," Niska repeated. "Our Republic is breaking more rules than one."

He sighed, rising from the chair and crossing to the window. From there, he could see the mountains, and the cyborg seemed to be searching for answers somewhere in those distant blue rocks.

"I'm realizing how much of a blind eye I was turning to things I should have been paying attention to," he said quietly. "LMID was running counterintelligence, but the new RID was still operating on Legatus, cutting corners and butting heads.

"They were supposed to be an external entity, but their agents seemed to be everywhere." Niska shook his head. "At some point, they turned into secret police as well, and I didn't notice. Because that was illegal."

He was intentionally echoing O'Malley's words.

"It's not the only change I missed. Even before I got the Prodigal Son order, the excuses for not holding elections for the representatives in the Republic Assembly were starting to get thinner and thinner. The Lord Protectorship was supposed to be a temporary role, to be replaced by an elected President within a few years..."

"Let me guess," Damien said softly. "Except in times of war."

"Exactly. There was a setup in the constitution to temporarily convert the Presidency back to a Lord Protectorship to guarantee continuous leadership during war. I wonder, now, if we'll ever see an elected President before Solace dies."

The room was silent. None of this was really counter to Damien's expectations of the Republic, but he *knew* he was looking at anything the secessionary state did with a strong layer of cynicism.

O'Malley and Niska had helped the Republic be born. Damien didn't think either had been involved in any of the really bloody parts of the covert war, but they'd certainly provided logistics for it all, if nothing else.

"Does this impact our mission?" Damien finally asked. "Given what we know happened to Ricket, are we really surprised that the Republic is getting more tainted by the minute?"

Niska snorted.

"Easy enough for you to swallow the Republic's failings," he said. "Harder for us." He was still looking out at the mountains.

"Related, though, is that while the government here on Manchester still seems to be playing by the rules, the RID is here in the shadows... and the government is getting much more secretive, too."

"Stuff they're not talking about, bases nobody admits to, units of the planetary military that aren't in the records anymore? That kind of thing?" Romanov asked.

"All of that and more," Niska confirmed. "Most relevant to us is that the New Blackstone Edge is now a military reservation."

Damien rolled that around in his mind for a moment.

"That's where the school is, isn't it?" he asked.

"Exactly. The school, a planetary park, half a dozen mid- and high-tier resorts...all shut down eighteen months ago to become a reservation for the Arsenault Guard. Handed over to the Republic Army ten months ago."

The Guard continued to survive as the local militia of the system, though Damien understood that all of their spaceborne assets had been handed over to the Republic government. It made sense that the Republic Army also had facilities on the Republic's planets. They needed recruiting and training centers, if nothing else.

"So, the school is now sealed to the public?" he asked.

"The Manchester Planetary Thaumaturgy Academy is now in the middle of a thousand square kilometers of mountains and foothills closed to anyone who isn't part of the Republic Military," Niska agreed.

"When I was trying to book tickets at one of the resorts—something that may have drawn attention, even though it makes sense for crew of a jump ship that hasn't been here since the area was closed off—I talked to a few of the folks at the travel agency.

"They specialize in hikers and skiers, and they were *very* clear in their warnings," he concluded. "They knew a few people who'd gone too close and been escorted out—and while they talked around the possibility, it sounds like they know *of* at least one person the RA shot dead for violating the reservation's boundaries."

"That seems rather...severe," Romanov noted. "I could see using lethal force to protect specific facilities *inside* the reservation, but the entire point of a secured zone is to give you space to find and catch people before they get to the point where you're shooting."

"It depends," Niska said grimly. "If you're also using the reservation as, say, a training ground for a new corps of elite Augment commandos... it might be useful to have them kill people who stray into the reservation.

"As practice."

The hotel was sturdily built, but it was *not* up to resisting the angry fist of a fully functioning cyborg. Niska's fist slammed at least three inches into the concrete, and the room was suddenly very silent again.

"I spent my *life* working toward this," he snarled. "I gave Legatus my body—*literally*. I gave them my soul, my entire adult career. I let them carve out pieces of me and replace them with *machines*.

"It was supposed to be better. *We* were supposed to be *better*. Not in the sense of faster, stronger, but in terms of morals, of equality. We were supposed to be on the right side of history."

"And now?" Damien asked.

"If they killed even one child, then everything I fought for was a lie," James Niska said quietly. "If they are murdering people to train new commandos that will kill without hesitation, without *question*, then everything I built has been thrown away."

"There are a thousand ways to train soldiers without needing that," O'Malley argued. "The people who died could have simply got too deep, into areas they shouldn't have. Areas where they assumed anyone present was a Protectorate spy."

"You don't believe that."

Niska's response wasn't a question. It was a simple statement of fact.

"If enough people died that the travel agency isn't just aware of the rumors but is trying to warn people about the possibility, it isn't that simple," he continued.

"But right now, what matters is that we're not going to be able to just drive up to a few kilometers away from the Academy and hike the rest of the way. We need a new plan."

Damien sighed, thinking as he crossed over to where Niska had broken the wall. Giving the cyborg a long, mostly sympathetic look, he waved an injured hand over the hole.

Power flared in the room as the shattered concrete lifted back into place. Some of it cloned itself to fill the gaps where his magic couldn't find the debris. A few seconds with Damien's gloved hand above where Niska had punched the wall, and there was no sign the cyborg had ever damaged the wall.

"Augments renting hotel rooms in secret aren't any better than Mages, in terms of catching attention," he murmured.

"I can't teleport us in. Not without a lot more information than we have. Can we go in on the ground still? By foot?"

"I checked the map," Niska admitted. "The Academy is right in the center of the new reservation. Forty kilometers from the nearest edge. We could get an off-road vehicle and get to the perimeter, but as soon as we cross the perimeter with any kind of vehicle, we'd trigger an alert."

"I'm not even sure we could get across the perimeter on foot."

"Assuming most of the interior isn't wired, Romanov and I can arrange that," Damien replied. "But that still leaves us forty kilometers to travel on foot. In the mountains, so I can't imagine the path would be perfectly straight."

"With air and ground patrols out looking for us," O'Malley added. "I don't know if we can sneak our way through forty kilometers of secured mountain—and then back out."

"What about by air?" Romanov asked.

"It's a no-fly zone up to about twenty kilometers," Niska replied. "Suborbital flights will go over it, but anything we could land or jump from would draw suspicion."

"Oh, ye of little of faith," the Marine replied with a grin. "So, there will be flights going over the site? How high?"

"I'll have to check. What *are* you thinking?" Niska asked.

"I'm many things, Niska, but I am first and foremost a Martian Marine." Romanov's grin widened. "Do you mean the Augment Corps never trains to drop from orbit?"

CHAPTER 14

TWELVE HOURS LATER, they reconvened in Niska's hotel room. There was a lot less free space in the room now, with assorted boxes filling every corner.

"We brought a bunch of stuff down from orbit, and I bought things that shouldn't have attracted too much attention here," Romanov noted as he gestured around at the boxes. "For all of that, if anyone puts the pieces together, they'll get suspicious fast.

"Assuming the RID's internal group is better than our people, we still have at least twenty-four to forty-eight hours to launch this, but after that, we're probably going to be seeing Augments knocking on our doors," the Marine admitted.

"And what, exactly, do we do if it turns out that I can't get us onto anything flying over the reservation before that?" Niska asked.

"We start moving around," Romanov replied. "I'm paying cash and using different faces, so while I suspect RID *can* find us, every wrench we throw at them slows the process down."

The Augment spy snorted.

"Fortunately for you, I managed to find a suborbital flight to Grand Leeds that doesn't *quite* go over the reservation but can be adjusted easily enough," he noted. "They go over at sixty kilometers. I'm presuming you've got the proper gear for prebreathing for this stunt?"

"What I didn't have on *Starlight* I found down here," Romanov confirmed. "We'll need to prebreathe for forty-five minutes, but the equipment I've got will handle adjusting pressures as we drop."

"How far are we falling here?" Damien asked carefully.

"Sixty kilometers," Niska repeated instantly. "Straight down. It's not going to be a fast process, but they won't see us coming."

"The HALO gear I grabbed is automatic," Romanov told Damien. "You don't have to do anything other than hold on, my lord."

"That's not particularly reassuring," the Hand replied. He could teleport himself to safety if things went wrong, he supposed, so there was only so much to worry about.

"But it sounds like the best plan," he conceded. "How much can we trust the crew of this transport, Niska?"

"Not at all," the spy admitted. "An LMID badge and a pile of money answers a lot of questions, but we'll be going aboard as cargo and need to override the doors to jump."

"That's risky," Romanov said. "Our jump window is less than ten seconds long."

"So, we override the doors in advance," O'Malley argued. "We've got five minutes in the air before we need to jump, and as soon as the plane is off the ground, we can get to work.

"I like it better than playing hide-and-go-murder with RID hunter-killer teams, that's for sure."

"It's not a bad plan," Damien allowed. "It's just a terrifying one." He looked around the other three people in the room. "I'm guessing I'm the only one of us who's never jumped out of a perfectly good spaceship before?"

The Augments chuckled.

"I don't know about spaceship," Niska admitted. "I've HALO-jumped before, but not from sixty kilometers. We train for forty at most."

"Martian Marines train to drop from orbit," Romanov replied. "Of course, we use magic to protect the troops down to about forty kilometers from the ground, which does make life easier."

"They're not going to see this coming," Niska said. "But I suspect they've got some kind of security at the Academy still. We've worked out how we get in...but how are we getting *out*?"

"I've looked at the maps," Damien replied. "I'll have sightline from the Academy to outside the reservation. Your high-tech solution will get us in. My magic will get us out."

Niska looked uncomfortable but nodded.

"I don't like it, but I'll admit I was hoping that was an option. Are we good?"

The suborbital transport plane was a massive affair, with a wingspan of at least a hundred meters. It was a delta shape, with most of its body acting as both lifting surface and fuel tank.

There was no visible difference between the cargo container or passenger compartment and the rest of the transport. The aircraft used the same engines as a surface-to-orbit shuttle and made more use of lifting surfaces to save fuel.

Its power-to-mass ratio was lower than a shuttle's, though. It could still carry the ten thousand–plus tons of cargo a heavy-lift shuttle lifted, though it never truly left the gravity well of a planet.

"This way," Niska told them. The Augment led the four over to a cargo-loading truck that was idling near the big aircraft. There was a cargo container, far smaller than the big ones mounted on *Starlight* in orbit, with one end open.

The driver was studiously ignoring them as he warmed his hands around a paper cup of some hot beverage. Despite that ignoring, however, the drink was put aside moments after they were aboard, and the cargo container closed behind him.

"I hope that was one good cup of coffee," Niska bitched under his breath. "That driver alone cost us a hundred thousand pounds."

Damien still had to mentally pause whenever he heard the name of the Republic's new currency. The entire Protectorate had operated on the Martian dollar for centuries. Local currencies existed, but interplanetary trade was in dollars.

The Republic, of course, couldn't use Martian dollars. They'd refused to even use the same currency name. So, the Pound Reliant of the Republic of Faith and Reason had been born.

A hundred thousand pounds was about seventy thousand Martian dollars...which was probably about a third again that driver's annual salary.

"Cheap at the price," he murmured as the container slid into the plane's cargo bay. "Prebreathing?"

Romanov was already unpacking the pressure suits and air supplies.

"You need to get the nitrogen out of your blood or you're going to have the bends on fucking steroids," the Marine told him. "Get the mask on first, then we'll get the rest of the suit on around it."

Damien obeyed, locking the breath mask over his mouth and nose and slinging the oxygen tank over his shoulder. The pure oxygen hit his system like a shot of caffeine, but he carefully kept his breaths controlled as the various pieces of the pressure suits came out.

They couldn't drop from sixty kilometers without protective gear. Everything they were currently setting up was contained in the combat exosuits Martian Marines would pull this stunt in, but there was no way they could have smuggled military-grade battle armor onto the surface.

Skydiving gear it was, and Damien had no *clue* what he was doing.

The other three assembled their own gear, and then Romanov set to helping a suit get assembled around Damien.

Having someone else dress him felt damn weird, but it wasn't like his hands worked properly. Even if Damien knew what he was doing, he couldn't have handled most of the catches without using magic.

And the last thing he wanted was for a seal to fail when he was thirty or forty kilometers above breathable air!

"Airborne," O'Malley reported. The Augment was linked into the transport's systems, but even Damien had felt the engines flare to life.

"The clock is ticking," she continued. "We jump in five minutes, thirty-five seconds from...mark."

"Go," Niska ordered. "Let's get this container op—"

Damien was sick of feeling helpless. A gesture cut the chains and bolts holding the container closed with a miniscule blade of force.

"Let them figure that out," he told the others. "We don't have time. Five minutes."

O'Malley snorted and shoved the door open. Their container was one of several in the cavernous void of the transport's belly, but they were at least on the bottom level.

They were still low enough that gravity felt the same as normal, but Damien knew that would change as they got higher.

"Are we expecting security in here?" he asked.

They were all carrying stunguns, short-ranged carbines that fired electric SmartDarts, but he hadn't been expecting to use them aboard the plane.

"Once the bay is sealed, it's left alone," Niska replied as they followed O'Malley through the narrow gaps between the containers. "This section isn't even pressurized. By the time the bird reaches full altitude, it's near-vacuum in here."

Their suits would protect them from that, but that didn't sound particularly fun either way.

"We need to get out of here," Damien said.

"Four minutes, thirty seconds," O'Malley replied absently as they reached the loading doors. "These doors may not be actively pressurized, but they are designed to *not* do what we want them to.

"Let's hope that's enough time."

She was removing a panel next to the door as she spoke, pulling wires out and connecting them to her wrist-comp.

"Do a final check on the suits and the parachutes," Damien ordered Romanov quietly. "Everybody's. We can't afford to have a damn accident at terminal velocity."

His math said that it was going to be a fifteen-minute fall before they activated the parachutes. That was a lot of time to know you were going to die if something went wrong.

On the other hand, if they *knew* something was going wrong, Damien could probably still get them safely to the ground. He wasn't sure he could do so subtly, however—and he'd be shocked if the RID didn't have scanners in orbit looking for the distinctive heat bloom of powerful magic.

There wasn't much a Mage could do that would create that bloom, but the Republic was going to want to know if anyone *was* doing magic on that scale.

"Suits are good," Romanov murmured over the radios. "Sixty seconds to the jump window."

The door was still closed and O'Malley was still working.

"What kind of paranoid *fuckwad* puts this level of security on the doors of a plane in flight?" O'Malley demanded. "I'm close. What's the backup plan?"

"We tear the doors open," Damien told her. "That won't go un-noticed."

"Fuck." The Augment was silent again and Damien added a timer to his own heads-up display.

With a ten-second window, they couldn't risk not getting out. He *would* tear the doors open if necessary, but without anything to close them afterward, that would force a detour of the plane.

And *that* would draw attention they couldn't afford. That would give the defenders fifteen minutes to scramble to intercept them. Best case, it meant they had fifteen minutes less to search the Academy.

Worst case, they got shot down before they hit the ground.

"In! I'm in!" O'Malley snapped. "Doors opening in fifteen, closing in twenty from...now."

That wasn't much time at all, but they were ready. Taking a hard breath of the oxygen feeding through his mask, Damien stepped up to the doors.

Then, as the metal swung open, he closed his eyes and stepped out into the void.

Sixty kilometers was a long way down. Intellectually, he'd known that. Hell, Damien had flown shuttles from surface to orbit; he knew what a planet looked like from sixty kilometers up.

There was something *very* different to seeing it with nothing beneath him. Then he started as the limbs of his pressure suit moved, dragging his arms and legs with them.

"Landing zone should be flagged on your HUD," Romanov's voice told him. "I have remote control of your suit and it's mirroring my drop. Just...relax."

"It's a long way down."

"Fifteen minutes still," Romanov replied.

Above them, the suborbital transport was already a shrinking dot. At this height, terminal velocity was noticeably faster.

"So, what do we do if they have antimissile lasers and decide we're a threat?" Damien asked.

"Well, unless you or I realize in time to do something, we die," the Marine replied calmly. "Most likely, though, we'll pass relatively unnoticed. We are very small targets right now."

"Very small, very high, very fragile," the Hand agreed, looking down again and seeing the gold star marking their destination. Still over fifty thousand meters beneath him.

His suit adjusted again, angling his body slightly to bring him toward that star.

"Bingo. The poor fuckers on the ground will never know what hit them."

An alert popped up on Damien's suit visor.

"I'm getting an overheat warning," he told Romanov, realizing that he was starting to sweat as well.

"We're too high to dissipate your body heat and what friction we are getting," the Marine confirmed. "The suits aren't rated for this, so the software will complain."

"What do you mean, *the suits aren't rated for this*?" Damien demanded. He'd assumed Romanov knew what he was doing.

"*Relax*," his bodyguard ordered. "They're Marine Corps gear; they're built with a fifty percent safety margin. We'll be fine."

Romanov paused thoughtfully.

"I mean, the suits won't be reusable," he added after a moment. "We're burning through layers that are supposed to be used again, but *we'll* be fine."

Damien swallowed his response to that and started paying more attention to what was going on. If things starting going badly, it would probably take his magic to fix things. Denis Romanov was a Marine Combat Mage, a powerful and trained magical warrior...but Damien Montgomery was a Hand and a Rune Wright.

Seconds turned to minutes and horror turned to boredom. The warning lights faded, though several of the icons that stayed told Damien that Romanov was correct in his assessment—they'd survived the excess heat by permanently damaging the suits.

He had enough control to check the parachute status, though, and that *looked* fine.

They plummeted past five kilometers and he swallowed as the mountains began to grow beneath him. The ground was starting to look *very* spiky.

"How low do we go before we open the chutes?" he asked.

"Our terminal velocity is fifty-five meters per second," Romanov replied. "We pop the chutes at roughly twelve seconds' altitude, so around seven hundred meters.

"At that point, it should take us about forty-five seconds to land. It's going to be rough."

Damien considered.

"Are we talking stopping a nuke with magic rough or teleporting a space station with magic rough?" he asked. He'd done both of those. One had knocked him unconscious for days. The other had done that *and* wrecked his hands.

Romanov took a second to stop laughing before he replied.

"Not that bad. Crashing a shuttle rough. Pretty sure you've done that."

Damien sighed.

"That's still not a recommendation," he noted. "I've done a lot of things I wouldn't care to repeat."

"In all honesty, my lord? I made *one* orbital drop, with four Mages providing safety protection for the company. This whole stunt was *already* on my list of things I wouldn't care to repeat."

"Why did no one say things like that *before* we jumped out of the plane?" Damien asked.

"Because I'm not sure Niska or O'Malley would have made the jump if I'd told them that, let alone you," Romanov admitted. "Fifteen hundred meters, my lord. Chutes in twenty."

Damien inhaled and braced himself.

He was expecting a full-body horse kick...and he underestimated it badly. He'd been knocked unconscious during the shuttle crash he'd survived, and it still paled in comparison to the first moment of the chute deploying.

It calmed down after that, though, and he managed to regain his breath as the computers in his suit neatly guided him to the center of the snow-covered courtyard of the Manchester Planetary Thaumaturgy Academy.

CHAPTER 15

THE FIRST THING Damien noticed about the Academy was the silence and the snow. It was late enough in the autumn that snow wasn't unexpected, but it hadn't been cleared. There were no footprints. Several inches of untouched snow had drifted over the entire compound.

"How many students are supposed to be here?" he asked Niska as they disconnected their air supplies. The pressure suits would double as body armor and cold-weather gear, but they didn't need oxygen at this point.

"Two hundred or so," the Augment replied, looking around the buildings. "Two dorms, over there. Two classroom buildings, there. One administration building."

Five buildings and a hangar.

"No heat signatures," O'Malley noted. "There's nobody here except us. This place is abandoned."

"It's not supposed to be," Niska said grimly. "I suggest we stay in pairs and check the place out. Admin building?"

"You and O'Malley take the hangar," Damien ordered. "There may be a way out tucked away in there still. Romanov and I will take the admin building."

Something about the frozen school grounds in the middle of the mountains was reminding him that Niska was a Legatan agent. The cyborg had been their enemy for a long time—and part of his job had been dealing with rogue Mages on Legatus.

He'd trusted Niska to get them this far, but he wanted to look at the most likely source of answers without the Legatan operative looking over his shoulder.

Niska seemed to catch some of Damien's concern and simply nodded his agreement. The two Legatan spies headed for the hangar, and Damien turned his gaze on the faceless mask of Romanov's pressure suit.

"This isn't right," he said aloud. "How long has this place been abandoned?"

"No way to tell," the Marine said. "Not without looking at the computers. Shall we, my lord?"

Damien nodded and led the way to what Niska had indicated was the administration building. Signage confirmed the Augment's description almost immediately, and Damien saw that the doors had been chained shut before ice and snow had blockaded them.

The worry scratching at the edge of his consciousness threw caution to the wind and he cut the chains with a gesture. The snow was easily brushed aside. None of this was powerful enough to set off warning signs, he hoped.

To a certain extent, he wasn't sure he cared anymore. There was a vast difference between being told there was a problem at the academies on the UnArcana Worlds and walking through an empty boarding school that should have been home to two hundred young Mages.

The administration building was just as cold as outside. Possibly colder, even. The front hall was a mess, with a bench overturned and frozen in place and several boxes of files scattered around the area.

"I'd call that signs of life, but I don't think it's even that positive," Romanov said grimly. "Shall I check what's in the files?"

"Go for it," Damien ordered. "Keep me informed; I'm going to go deeper."

There was a directory near the entrance, and Damien quickly located the location of the head administrator, the school's principal. She'd been on the third floor of the building, in an office that overlooked the court-yard and the rest of the school.

The stairs were covered in ice, and Damien had to step carefully as he ascended. There was more evidence of chaos as he climbed...but no evidence of violence. There were clear paths to the exits, and most of what appeared to have been discarded was paper records.

Discarding the paper records made sense, he supposed, if they were in a hurry. A lot of forms were likely still filled out by hand by students or their parents, but all of the information on them *should* have been in the school's computers.

The principal's office door yielded to his ministrations after a few moments. It had been locked when the woman left, but a standard dead-bolt was no match for a stressed-out Hand.

Posters hung on the walls, the kind of motivational crap that rarely existed outside of schools. There were bookshelves around the room, but they were mostly empty. What was left was a few books that the owner hadn't cared about and some cheap bric-a-brac.

It took him a few seconds to confirm that the computer embedded in the desk had been removed. He wasn't sure whether it would have sur-vived the cold on its own for long, but it wasn't present at all.

The papers on the desk gave him at least some idea of what had hap-pened...or at least *when* it had happened.

The main contents of the desk were extra copies of a series of form letters, clearly written to be as reassuring as possible, letting parents know that their child had won the "unique opportunity" to study at an "elite institution" at Tau Ceti. Communication would be enabled as much as possible, but visits wouldn't be doable for several years.

It was a "unique opportunity," so far as Damien could tell, that every student here had "won."

The worst part was that the letters were old. They were all dated early 2458—six months before the Secession.

"I've got a bunch of letters here telling parents that their kid had a unique opportunity to study at Tau Ceti," he told the others over the radio. "A lot of them. Looks like a form letter to cover the students being moved somewhere else.

"What the hell happened to these kids?"

He was growing more and more certain that he needed to search the surrounding hills for mass graves...and if that was what he found, all hell was going to break loose.

Damien wasn't entirely sure he could take on an entire planetary government on his own. The *last* time he'd done that, he'd coopted a rebellion.

Anger *probably* wasn't a sufficient substitute, but if this was as bad as it was starting to look, he was going to have to test that theory.

"The hangar is empty," Niska told him a few minutes later. "There should have been a bunch of helicopters and at least one emergency shuttle here, but they're all gone."

"Any idea where?" Damien demanded.

"Nothing useful. They headed to the spaceport at Arndale. No idea where they went from there."

Damien swallowed a series of curses.

"*Find* something," he snarled.

Cutting the radio channel, he stalked into the corridor where Romanov had gone through the paper files.

"Anything useful?"

"No," the Marine said shortly. "This is a stack of the power-of-attorney forms that the parents signed. They just...gave these people their kids. Full authority."

"It was that or leave the UnArcana Worlds," Damien replied. He didn't have a lot of sympathy for *anyone* involved in this school right now, but he at least half-understood that decision.

"We're going to need to sweep the woods around the school if we have time," he continued. "Looking for..." He trailed off, then swallowed hard. "We need to look for graves."

Romanov nodded. Damien couldn't see his bodyguard's face, but he didn't need to.

"I don't know if we'll have time," he pointed out. "We almost certainly triggered *something* when we landed here. It's only a question of how quickly they get here."

Damien nodded, leaving the Marine to it while he skimmed down the list of names and titles. The accountant was probably his best option, he supposed.

He charged down the hallway and kicked the accountant's door open. It didn't appear to have been locked. Damien didn't really care.

His radio crackled to life.

"This place is a bust," Niska said. "There are no computers, no papers, no clues. I should have known going anywhere except where Ricket was investigating himself was a waste of time. We need to get out of here, Montgomery."

"That's all you have to say?" Damien demanded. "*Two hundred kids* are missing and all you have to say is that this is a *bust*? Is what happened here irrelevant?"

"No," the Augment replied. "It's not. But there's nothing here to lead me anywhere. Something terrible might have happened here. Or something entirely mundane and we missed the news release on it. You don't know anything."

It was probably a good thing that Niska wasn't in the room with Damien. It took a *lot* to make the young man lose his temper, but the cyborg might have been learning to fly if he'd been within sight.

"I know the next thing I can reasonably search for is fucking *mass graves*, Niska," he snapped. "And if murdering children isn't a big deal for you, maybe I should be reconsidering who I'm working with."

The radio was silent.

"You know better," Niska finally said. "I just don't see anything here that can help us find out what happened, and we only have so much time."

Damien muted his microphone and snarled, barely resisting the urge to start blasting out walls.

Glaring at the walls, however, he spotted something he hadn't been expecting to see. The accountant had apparently had the relatively common habit of printing out her invoices for review before she paid them. There were a dozen sheets of paper stuck to a board designed for just that purpose.

But they were all slightly misaligned. Most accountants Damien had met would have made very sure that the sheets were all perfectly straight. He crossed to the wall and shifted a page to line it up.

There was a line drawn on the board underneath. He tore the invoice for a bulk order of soup off the board to see what it covered.

It was an arrow. The other invoices came away easily, revealing a circular set of arrows permanently drawn into the board and pointing at a single invoice that had been covered by the other, mundane ones.

Underneath the invoice, someone had written two words: I'M SORRY.

"I've got an invoice for two hundred and seven seats on an intersystem passenger liner," Damien said slowly. "An invoice the accountant here wanted to be sure someone found."

"A passenger liner?" Niska asked. "Going where?"

"Nueva Bolivia," Damien read off the paper, his anger muted now as he saw a possibility that *wasn't* a pit full of dead kids.

"That's not much," the Augment pointed out. "But if you've got the ship details and dates, I can get their final destination out of the traffic control at Bolivia."

He paused.

"You're right, Montgomery," he conceded. "Something is very wrong here and these kids are in trouble. I don't know if we can help, but if there's even one damn clue here, we have to follow it."

The advantage of them not being in the same room, Damien reflected, was that he hadn't broken any of the Augment's bones before the other man had apologized.

"We have a problem," O'Malley announced as Damien pulled the invoice from the wall.

"I dropped some auditory scanners outside as we were heading into the hangar, and they just started going off. Aircraft inbound."

"Any idea what type?" Damien asked.

"High-powered helicopters," the Augment replied. "Fast, maneuverable. Running it against my database, but I'm guessing Phantom VI gunships."

"I've met the V," he noted. The stealth attack helicopters had ended up in the hands of the rebellion on Ardennes. He'd ended up coopting them, along with the rebels, against Ardennes' treasonous prior governor. "The VI lacks the stealth, has bigger missiles?"

"Exactly," Niska replied. "But if we can hear them, they're ninety seconds out at most."

"Sixty-five and counting," O'Malley told them. "I think we need to execute on that exit plan!"

"Meet me in the main yard," Damien ordered.

He was still less than happy with Niska, but he needed his cyborg allies. Getting the hell out of this creepily abandoned school while they were all alive sounded like a brilliant plan.

He and Romanov were outside first. Damien couldn't pick out the sound of the approaching attack helicopters. From the way the Marine was scanning the air, he could at least hear something.

"Thirty seconds and counting," O'Malley told him as she and Niska left the hangar at a run. "That's until they can do a thermal sweep. If they want visual confirmation of us, longer."

"They won't." Niska's voice was grim. "Their orders will be to kill anyone here."

They reached Damien and the two Augments looked uncomfortable.

"What do we do now?" Niska asked.

"Take my arms." Damien stretched out his gloved hands. Being touched on his forearms wasn't a pleasant experience, but it only took a few seconds for all three of his companions to be holding his arms.

Now even he could pick out the gunships, but he ignored them. From the courtyard of the Academy he had an amazing view out over the foothills and plains. He could even pick out Arndale in the distance.

For the moment, however, he selected what looked like a set of farm fields halfway to the city and focused his energy.

"Swallow now," he ordered. "This will suck for you."

He didn't wait to see if they obeyed. As five armed helicopters swept over the mountains, Damien *stepped* into warmer temperatures and calmer airspace.

Warned or not, augmented stomach or not, Niska promptly stumbled away from him to throw up. O'Malley didn't look much better, scanning the air for a few seconds as she processed that they were somewhere else.

Then the redheaded Augment hit a button and smiled.

"Scanners self-destructed," she told the others. "They'll know there was a Mage there, but we should be good."

"This end of the teleport is less detectable, but they'll find it eventually," Damien warned them. "Let's move. We need to get Captain Maata looking for an excuse to go to Nueva Bolivia."

CHAPTER 16

THE FULL WEIGHT of Roslyn's new position didn't really sink in until the first full flag-officer meeting. In a room full of Admirals and Commodores, she was the only person below the rank of Captain.

Her instructions from Admiral Alexander to "keep her mouth shut" made more sense than ever. She sat slightly off to the left of the tall Admiral, her wrist-comp projecting a continuous stream of the transcription of the meeting.

The repeated "Admiral such and such said" on the transcript warned her of something that was going to be a problem. Technically, Mage-Admiral Alexander, the commander of the fleet, and Mage-Admiral Medici, the commander of only half of the cruisers, held the same rank.

Authority went by seniority and, in Mage-Admiral Alexander's case, the fact that she'd been appointed directly by the Mage-King and that said Mage-King was her brother.

There was no question as to who was in command of the fleet. The argument her transcription software was dutifully recording between Mage-Admiral Medici, the man who'd commanded the desperate defense of Ardennes for First Hand Montgomery, and Mage-Admiral Soner Marangoz, the man in command of Alexander's battleships, told her that no one was quite so sure what the pecking order was below that.

"Enough!" Alexander bellowed. "Marangoz, your battleships are going to carry the brunt of the fighting, but that does *not* magically give you more experience than the man who held Ardennes against the Republic! *Listen* to Medici, damn it."

The dark-skinned Admiral turned a shade darker, but he bowed his head in acknowledgement.

"Good. Continue, Medici."

"We need to work on our counter-gunship tactics," the Mage-Admiral told them all. "As we've seen again and again, they provide a mind-boggling augmentation to the first few salvos of missiles from the Republic. Even with overwhelming force, like Admiral Alexander possessed in Santiago, they allowed the Republic to inflict heavy losses and damage."

"And the success of the battle line tells me that the gunships can't deal with battleships," Marangoz replied. "I'm not afraid of mosquitos, Admiral!"

"That exact phrasing, Admiral Marangoz, was used by Lieutenant Commander Nikodem," Alexander pointed out. "And trusting it resulted in us losing far too many cruisers and destroyers in Santiago.

"Our battleships survived because the gunships didn't target them. They knew they could hurt us just as badly and more efficiently by hammering our escorts."

They'd been reinforced up to twenty-six cruisers now, but Roslyn knew their destroyer numbers hadn't recovered. They only had thirty of the lighter ships, meaning the destroyers were actually *outnumbered* by heavier ships.

"My understanding is that there were some covert armament programs that will bear fruit in the near future, but we are otherwise looking at over a year before we have any additional cruisers or battleships," Alexander said grimly. "Destroyers would be sooner, but my brother and the core Admiralty has agreed with the assessment that we cannot deploy the existing *Lancer* design.

"We have no choice but to put *Lancer*s into the fray for now, but new construction on destroyers has been paused until the design process for the *Aegis*-class ships is complete."

Alexander looked around the room and Roslyn felt a chill run down her spine. *She* knew what the Admiral had decided...and nobody else in the room did. That was a strange feeling.

"Right now, the Battle of Ardennes has badly depleted the Republic's available fleet forces," the Mage-Admiral noted. "Our own losses, while horrific, were mostly felt in the Militia volunteers. The Royal Martian Navy remains fundamentally intact, and the sacrifice and triumph of the Militia has evened the odds.

"All evidence, however, suggests that the Republic will out-build us for at least the next year. Worse, if they are prepared to engage in hit-and-run tactics and expend large numbers of sacrificial gunships, they can make us bleed for every system we hold and every system we retake."

"But we have to advance," Marangoz stated. "We cannot leave Protectorate systems in the hands of the Republic."

"The only thing I *cannot* do, Admiral Marangoz, is throw this fleet away for nothing," Mage-Admiral Alexander said coldly. "I can and I *will* leave the occupied systems in the hands of the enemy. We know from the occupation of Santiago that the Republic is not carrying out vast purges or massacres.

"Yes, people are dying," she admitted levelly. "But we do them no service by dying and *failing* them."

"And what about Santiago's Mages?" Medici asked quietly. "They were being rounded up in internment camps, and we *know* several hundred are missing. We can only assume they were transported out of the system."

"We don't know that," Alexander replied. "But the best way to liberate the occupied systems remains the same: we must neutralize the capacity of the Republic to both build new warships and to resupply the ones they have."

"And how do you plan on doing *that*?" Marangoz asked.

"By taking this fleet to the heart of the enemy and separating the Centurion Accelerator Ring, the only major antimatter production facility the Republic has, from the shipyards at Legatus," Mage-Admiral Jane Alexander said firmly.

"We cannot challenge the fixed defenses of either Legatus or Centurion *and* the mobile forces in the system," she said. "But we can engage those mobile forces *or* the fixed defenses. We can create a situation where we can destroy any force that sorties while we prevent them moving ships or supplies out of the system.

"We can't break the defenses of the Republic's core logistics facilities—but we can damn well make sure that the Republic can't get into them either!"

The meeting exploded into chaos, and Roslyn realized why Alexander had insisted everyone attend in person. It was never a good idea to let anyone else watch a bunch of flag officers attempt to argue with their superiors like uncomfortable toddlers.

The Mage-Admiral waited for a minute to see if anyone was saying anything useful, then slapped her hand down on the desk.

The sound was clearly augmented by Alexander's magic, echoing through the room in a way even a *gunshot* wouldn't have.

"Captain Kulkarni," she said sharply. "Explain. Lieutenant Chambers, a map of the Legatus System, if you please."

Roslyn had known that this part of the meeting was coming and had the map already loaded on her wrist-comp. A single command flicked it to the holo-projector built into the table, and a three-dimensional image of the Legatus System appeared.

Kulkarni rose and gestured to the map.

"Lieutenant, can we dim everything except Legatus and Centurion, please?"

Roslyn had that queued up as well. The other planets of the system dimmed to translucence. None of them were completely unoccupied—only Sol was more heavily developed than Legatus, though Tau Ceti came close and had more people.

Tau Ceti's multiple habitable planets helped there.

"The dimensions of the Legatus System are key to the Mage-Admiral's plan," Kulkarni told the assembled flag officers. "Legatus itself orbits the star at an average of eight point two light-minutes every four hundred days. It's an eccentric orbit, with an aphelion of just over nine light-minutes.

"Centurion, on the other hand, orbits relatively evenly at forty-five light-minutes every four thousand five hundred days and change. We are currently roughly one month away from the absolute furthest the two planets will ever be apart, an alignment that occurs approximately once every hundred and forty years."

Roslyn highlighted the gap between the two planets without being asked.

"Fifty-four light-minutes, people. It's far enough that we'd jump it most of the time rather than taking the week or so it might take to fly in normal space.

"The Republic doesn't have that luxury, with most of their defenses being sublight units. Thanks to efforts by one of our scout ships, we also have a solid idea of what kind of mobile forces and defenses are positioned in Legatus."

Kulkarni gestured to the planet and Roslyn zoomed in, highlighting each group of icons as her former Captain laid them out.

"Legatus's permanent fixed defenses have been vastly upgraded since the Secession. What was once shielded by forty gunships and some concealed defenses is now shielded by an estimated two *thousand* gunships and twenty major orbital platforms. Scans from our scout ship suggest those platforms are based around the Republic's default twenty-megaton hull, but we have to assume that the lack of FTL or even significant in-system mobility means they have increased firepower over the RIN's twenty-megaton cruisers.

"Certainly, twenty of them represent a force that our entire fleet would be hard pressed to overcome," Captain Kulkarni noted.

She raised a hand as the flag officers started to object. "We *could* overcome," she agreed. "But it would stretch our fleet to the limit, and there are currently two full carrier groups in orbit around Legatus."

That silenced the officers for a moment as Roslyn added the icons.

"That's two fifty-megaton carriers, four forty-megaton and two thirty-megaton battleships, and eighteen cruisers. The cruisers are about half-and-half fifteen- and twenty-megaton ships.

"Again, we could defeat that mobile force, but they aren't dramatically inferior to our fleet."

"What about the construction yards?" Medici asked.

"Legatus had significant yards," Kulkarni agreed. "None of the ships currently in those yards, however, appear close to completion—though all of them *are* finished hulls. I would hesitate to assume, but my guess would be that what we're looking at are a new collection of their standard hulls delivered to receive systems and armaments—and probably delivered just before our scoutship came through."

"If they're not building those hulls in Legatus's yards, where are they building them?" Marangoz asked. The Admiral was leaning forward intently now. "You're implying they're only doing final fitting-out at Legatus?"

"The fact that we don't see *any* under-construction hulls in Legatan orbit appears to imply that, sir," Kulkarni noted. "We'd known they hadn't done any major military construction at Legatus prior to the Secession, so that makes sense. The yards in Legatan orbit definitely have the capacity to build ships of this scale, but they seem to only be using them for weapons and systems.

"The hulls themselves appear to be being built at Centurion."

Kulkarni gestured to Roslyn, and the Flag Lieutenant moved the zoom.

They weren't as zoomed-in at Centurion as they had been at Legatus, but the planet still looked bigger.

"We knew they'd built the Centurion Accelerator Ring out here, and we'd known they were paranoid about letting Mages near it," the operations officer told the assembled Admirals. "Now we know that there was a lot more going on out there than we thought."

The Ring itself was surprisingly flimsy-looking to Roslyn, which she supposed made sense. The vast majority of it was simply a particle accelerator and maintenance access for the same. Only small portions of the Accelerator Ring were even pressurized.

A single missile could end the Republic's military logistics. Getting close enough to *launch* that missile, though...

"Here and here"—Kulkarni gestured and Roslyn highlighted—"we see construction yards to put anywhere in the Protectorate to shame. However, they appear to lack much of the equipment necessary to fit out warships with weapons and other systems.

"Here"—Roslyn highlighted the third yard for Kulkarni—"we see their original fitting-out yard. It's smaller than the other two, which is why most of that work is now being done at Legatus.

"Centurion is the source of the antimatter for their missiles and gunships and the hulls for their warships. The complex here is a single point of failure, though..." Kulkarni sighed and shook her head.

"Don't let the scale fool you. We are looking at multiple stations and industrial nodes spread around a gas giant with eighty percent of the volume and mass of Sol's Jupiter. *Each* of those nodes is guarded by half as many fortresses as Legatus itself, but the main defense is this."

At Kulkarni's words, Roslyn lit up eight stations orbiting the gas giant in red. They were much farther out than any other platform but carefully positioned so that no missile attack on the Ring would pass by fewer than two of the stations.

"We're not sure what the Republic calls these guys, but they are the key to the defense of Centurion. Each of them appears to be two of their fifty-megaton carriers attached together. Where their fifty-megaton carriers have one flight deck, these fortresses have *four*. Each of them plays home base to at least a thousand gunships."

Eight one-hundred-megaton fortresses mothering eight thousand gunships. Roslyn concealed a shiver at the thought—that was a *lot* of firepower.

"Any attempt to fire directly on the ring would pass through the RFLAM defenses of multiple fortresses, and I suspect we'll find that they have traded a significant portion of their mobile sisters' weapons and engines for more defensive lasers."

"So that, Admirals and Commodores, is our challenge and our opportunity," Mage-Admiral Alexander said calmly. "Their final fitting-out facility and their source of crews is Legatus itself, but their hulls and their fuel come from Centurion.

"We could take either Legatus *or* Centurion in the absence of mobile forces, but the presence of RIN carrier groups means we can't take either.

"What we *can* do is make certain that neither of them can send support to the other," she concluded. "If personnel, hulls, system components and antimatter cannot flow between these two worlds, the Republic's military logistics infrastructure is functionally disabled.

"Once our final tranche of reinforcements arrives, we will take this entire fleet and proceed to the Legatus System. We will attempt to lure the mobile forces into an open space engagement, where we will destroy them.

"Regardless of whether we can lure the mobile forces out, our destroyers will spread out to secure the system while we hold the main force near Centurion. The RIN has demonstrated that their jump drive is much less capable of jumping into and out of gravity wells than we are, and we will take advantage of that to pin them against their planets.

"Nothing will leave or enter Legatus or Centurion. We will choke them out and grind down their defenses. By removing *their* reinforcements from the equation, we can wait for *our* reinforcements to finish construction."

Roslyn wasn't sure what the reinforcements that Alexander was expecting to be built were, but the Mage-Admiral seemed confident that they would turn the tide.

"We will choke out the RIN and force them to withdraw from the occupied systems. They will have no choice but to relieve Legatus...and we will not let them."

CHAPTER 17

GETTING BACK to *Starlight* proved easier than Damien had dared hope. Once they'd made it to a rest stop for tourists, they'd called a taxi and returned to Arndale, where their shuttle had returned them to orbit.

The fast packet was far from home by any stretch of the imagination, but being back among people who knew who he was made for at least something of a relief.

Damien had barely managed to shower off the sweat from their HALO jump before he was interrupted, though.

"Lord Montgomery?"

The intruder was standing just inside the door to his quarters, careful not to invade his bedroom or bathroom.

"In here," he responded, his magic conjuring a defensive shield around himself even as he used it to wrap a bathrobe over his shoulders.

"Sir."

He stepped out to see one of the Martian cyborgs, the Bionic Combat Regiment commandos, that Romanov had brought with them.

"What is it?"

"Sergeant Van's regards, my lord, but there's something going on on the bridge. Captain Maata hasn't updated us yet, but the Sergeant *suggests* that your presence might be advised."

Damien forced the grin he'd have worn before today. Sergeant Chi Van was the senior Martian cyborg on the ship, and *she* trusted their ex-LMID chauffeurs less than Damien did.

So, of course, she was running security on *Starlight*'s bridge. That both helped keep the people shuttling them around safe and made sure that the Martian contingent was fully advised of what was going on.

He glanced at his reflection in the mirror and his grin become somewhat less forced.

"And I'm guessing that, at my height, I'm not particularly intimidating soaking wet in a bathrobe?"

"Neither I nor the Sergeant would *dream* of saying any such thing... my lord," the commando said levelly.

"And by 'my lord,' you're self-censoring from what, again?" Damien asked.

The woman coughed delicately.

"I'm sure I've heard it before, trooper."

"The BCR calls you Darth Montgomery, sir," she admitted.

"Yup," Damien confirmed after swallowing a moment of old frustration. Why, just *why*, had the latest movie version of that ancient folk tale had to come out while he was First Hand?

"I've heard that one before."

"I don't know what you're going on about, Group Commander, but if you're trawling for bribes, I suggest you find another tree to crawl up," Captain Maata was telling someone as Damien stepped quietly onto the bridge.

He traded a nod with Sergeant Van, recognizing the commando's concerned look. From the woman's body language, the concern wasn't directed at Captain Maata.

"No, I already told you, all of my cargo has been offloaded and I had people on the planet looking for new cargo," Maata snapped. "Everything is registered and licensed. I don't know or care what your problem is, but you can get the hell off my back."

She hit a button to kill the call and turned in her seat.

"Ah, Montgomery. I don't suppose you're up to jumping us the hell out of this system before my new RIN friend decides he's sick of me mouthing off?"

Damien held up his hands, once again wrapped in thin elbow-length black leather gloves.

"I don't have jump runes anymore," he reminded her. "And Mage Foster isn't up for jumping out from this close in. Closer in than most, but not *this* close."

Like any Navy Mage, Liara Foster could jump from closer to a gravity well than most regular Jump Mages. A true amplifier, which *Starlight* did not have and Damien wasn't giving her, might have cut most of the difference.

As it was, they needed to get half a light-minute from the planet to jump safely. Standard civilian safety margin was a full light-minute—and at two to five gravities of acceleration, that could take a day.

"What do the RIN want?" Damien asked.

"They accused me of bringing spies back aboard my ship on the last round of shuttle flights," Maata replied. "Which is technically true, but I'll be fucked if I *admit* it."

"So, what do we do?" he said.

"Well, I give it five minutes before Group Commander Ren over there demands I let them board and inspect *Starlight*, so I figure we get moving before that and flip him a big friendly middle finger as we run."

"And if they shoot at us?" Damien replied. He had his own ace in the hole there, but he hesitated to commit LaMonte's ship this close to a Republic world.

His cat was aboard *Rhapsody in Purple*, after all.

"I can shoot down *some* missiles," Maata told him. "It will take them some time to get their thumbs out and decide to shoot us down, too. That gives us some wiggle room."

"Enough?"

"If we're lucky." The covert ops captain looked grim. "More than we're going to get if we stay in orbit. We're booting the reactors; we'll be under way in ninety seconds."

She shook her head.

"I'm not sticking around to get boarded. There are enough question-able folks and gear aboard *Starlight* to see us all hang!"

Damien was quite confident in his people's ability to wipe out the boarding parties that would be sent aboard a small ship like *Starlight*. That would only aggravate the situation, however, and wouldn't get them any closer to jumping out of Arsenault.

"Carry on, Captain," he told her. "I'm going to hang out right here, though. In case you need me."

Even without being able to access an amplifier—or the jump matrix, for that matter—the simulacrum chamber was the best place for Damien to protect the ship from.

And even crippled and weakened as he was, his magic was more than a match for a few gunships.

"All hands, all hands, prepare for pod gravity transition," Captain Maata announced. "We will cease rotation in thirty seconds and com-mence emergency acceleration in sixty seconds. Prepare for pseudograv-ity transition and then get your asses to an acceleration chair."

Damien took a moment to strap himself into a properly equipped chair on the bridge. Since the simulacrum chamber had to be at the heart of the ship, it was in zero gravity except when the ship was accelerating.

And he'd reviewed *Starlight's* specifications. *Emergency acceleration* was seven gravities, a number he'd never seen on a ship without magical gravity before.

Maata gave it an extra ten seconds beyond her warning, watching some report on her screens that Damien couldn't see, before triggering the engines.

Starlight's adjustment to thrust position hadn't gone unnoticed, either.

"Ren is calling again, demanding to know what we're doing," Maata's coms officer reported.

"Ignore him," Maata ordered—and then hit the command to bring *Starlight's* engines online. "Davies, get the RFLAM turrets live. I don't trust Ren not to get pissy!"

That she managed to speak clearly was impressive. Damien was still trying to regain his breath after a large group of angry men decided to stand on his chest. The gel capsules built into the chair absorbed his body readily, helping support his skin against the pressure being exerted.

There was no way he could speak clearly initially. After a moment, he regained enough breath to use magic to protect himself from the crushing force, but Maata had seemed unbothered from the beginning.

Their captain, it seemed, had some secrets of her own.

"Turrets are live," Zach Davies finally responded. *His* voice, at least, was showing the strain of the seven gravities of acceleration. "I have three gunships maneuvering toward us. Do I engage?"

Maata flicked a glance over to Damien.

The Hand could see the lights of the gunship's engines flaring around the spacecraft, but the data codes attached to them told an interesting story.

The three ships could match *Starlight's* acceleration and their missiles could exceed it a thousandfold, but they weren't pushing their drives. Their maneuvers were much more casual and he wasn't seeing targeting radar.

"You know gunships better than I do," he pointed out. "But this doesn't look right to me."

"They're maneuvering to try to disable us, but if they miss with their lasers, we'll evade them unless they use missiles or pile on the accel."

"Can they disable us?" Damien asked. "I can't stop lasers."

"One-gigawatt beams at under two light-seconds?" Maata laughed. From her disregard of the pressure, Damien had to assume that the Captain was one of the mystery Augments they'd known were aboard *Starlight*.

"Nobody can stop them...but I wish them luck disabling *Starlight*." Her grin continued even as the gunships continued their slow pursuit.

"They'll fire in about a minute," she concluded. "I expect one more call to surrender."

"And after that?" Damien asked.

"I don't know," she admitted. "Every second they trail along at two gravities, they lose velocity and distance they'll never make up."

"So, either they don't think we're *actually* a problem or they have a plan," Damien concluded, studying the Republican sublight warships.

"And they know we have a Mage aboard," he added.

"So, we're a problem...and that means they have a plan," Maata agreed. "I don't suppose you Mages can jump us out from here?"

He looked grimly down his gloved hands.

"I could have once, but not anymore," he admitted. "Foster definitely can't, though she can get us out from closer in than they expect."

"Hopefully, that's enough," the Captain replied. "And that my trick with the lasers works."

Damien didn't even have time ask what the "trick with the lasers" was before the gunships opened fire. The tiny sublight warships didn't have the twenty-gigawatt lasers of the Republic Interstellar Navy's capital ships.

Instead, they each carried three of the one-gigawatt Rapid-Fire Laser Anti-Missile turrets the capital ships carried as missile defenses. At a range of less than two light-seconds and firing on a civilian ship, the nine beams should have been more than enough to not only disable *Starlight*'s engines but to separate them from the freighter.

The flash of light around *Starlight*'s engines told Damien something else had happened. Without access to the displays of an actual console, he had no idea *what*, but the ship was still accelerating at seven gravities.

"Layers of reflective armor overtop of a series of tanks of water," Maata told him in answer to his questioning look. "So, now the space around the usual weak points is full of water and, well, glorified glitter."

A second salvo of lasers hit that cloud of droplets and dispersed. Knowing what to look for now, Damien picked out the bursts of vapor.

"Of course, if they keep that up, we're in trouble," she concluded. "I've only got one layer of reflective armor underneath the tanks, and we're leaving the cloud behind."

She sighed.

"And if we shoot at *them*, they'll blow us out of space with missiles," she said aloud. Shaking her head, Maata tapped the internal coms.

"All hands, stand by for evasive maneuvers and increased acceleration. I'm pushing us to eight gees." She paused. "If you're not an Augment or a Mage, get your ass into an accel chair and bring up the full wrap. I may have to push harder, and I like most of you enough to want to keep you!"

She looked back at Damien.

"Your Mages can handle this, right?"

"Yes," he said shortly. "Foster will be on her way up."

He turned his attention back to the gunships. He could neutralize their lasers, but not without it being obvious that a Hand was aboard. A regular Mage couldn't do that, and it wasn't something he could do subtly. Holding a shield like that close to *Starlight* was more likely to wreck the ship than protect it.

Starlight tore through a series of maneuvers just as the gunships fired again. Laser beams punched through where her engines would have been, and Damien shook his head against the dizziness as the ship spun.

Despite that, Liara Foster walked into the simulacrum chamber bridge as if they were under a mere one gravity. She wasn't looking at the screens, though, so she wasn't worrying about vertigo.

Yet.

"You know where the simulacrum station is," Maata told the Mage. "Anything you can do?"

"Against missiles, yes. Lasers? No."

The small freighter twisted through another series of gyrations, but there was no laser fire to dodge.

"We are definitely still in their range," Damien pointed out. "What are they playing at?"

"They're not trying to wreck us." Foster pointed out what Damien and Maata had been struggling with from the beginning.

"They're trying to *capture* us...and this set doesn't need to."

The Jump Mage had seen what the people already on the bridge had missed. They'd been focused on the ships chasing them, but Foster's job meant she was looking ahead to where she'd need to jump.

"Those three have enough of a velocity to keep us from getting away, but if they need to stop us hard, they have missiles—and they don't need to be in our range to launch them.

"*These* three, on the other hand, we have no chance in hell of evading."

Foster had reached her station and highlighted the three icons of the ships she meant. Like several dozen other gunships, they were flying escort to protect Arsenault's internal shipping. Now, however, they'd broken off and were heading directly toward *Starlight*.

"If we follow any of our shortest-time courses to safe space to jump, the three out there will intercept us at a range where they can board us," Maata concluded, pulling the data on the three gunships.

"If we evade dramatically, the three behind us will either catch up to us or write it off as a bad plan and blow us out of space." She shook her head. "I can't blow through three gunships," she pointed out, looking over at Damien and Foster.

"Can you?"

"If necessary," Damien said grimly. "Hopefully, we'll get luckier than that."

"What kind of luck are you counting on?" Maata demanded.

He didn't answer, just looking out at the apparently empty space along their route.

All right, Kelly, he asked silently. *How close did you get? Just close enough to see what's going on?*

Or close enough to pull me out of the fire again?

CHAPTER 18

ONE PLANET.

The First Hand had needed to get in and out of *one planet* without bringing the Republic down on his head.

Kelly LaMonte shook her head and yanked on a currently pitch-black braid.

"How close can we get?" she asked her tactical officer.

"Are you nuts?" Conrad Milhouse asked bluntly. Despite his objection, however, he started throwing projections up on the screen around them. Red spheres surrounded each of the gunship groups, accompanied by dark-orange thrust cones.

Interception cones.

The ships pursuing *Starlight* were in missile range, and their seemingly lackadaisical acceleration was designed to *keep* them in missile range until the freighter could jump. In fact, from the vector cone Milhouse had projected, they were underestimating how close to the planet Liara Foster could jump the ship.

That would have given *Starlight* a potential opportunity to escape, except for the three gunships coming in from the outer system. Those ships weren't in their missile range of *Starlight* yet, but they would get all the way into *boarding* range unless someone found a miracle.

Rhapsody in Purple was already pushing the limits of the heat sinks that allowed her to stay hidden. Kelly had been about to order them to move away from the planet to somewhere they could vent heat safely.

Her theory had been that if they hadn't been caught in the first forty-eight hours, *Starlight's* crew had at least two more days of relative safety. She'd clearly been wrong.

"You're still nuts," Milhouse finally concluded as he stared at the intricate displays on his screen. "But I *think* we can get to about four and a half million kilometers before the gunships detect us..."

He shook his head.

"*If* the data Niska gave us on those birds' sensors is accurate," he added. "If it is, someone cheaped out assuming they'd have motherships and defensive stations to back them. If it isn't..."

He shrugged.

"Five million klicks is the range on our laser. It might well be the range on *theirs*."

"That's the one good piece of news we have out of *Starlight* getting shot up," Kelly replied. "Those were RFLAM turrets, one-gigawatt beams." She smiled. "Maximum effective range around ten light-seconds—against missiles and civilian ships. Against warships or *Rhapsody*? Half that at best.

"Now"—she held up a hand to backtrack on some of her reassurances—"their *missiles* can rip us to pieces quite handily. Can we take them before they launch?"

Milhouse swallowed.

Rhapsody in Purple was a stealth ship, designed for scouting and inserting commando teams. She had two missile launchers and a single laser.

She had a ten-gigawatt laser to the one-gigawatt weapons her enemy possessed, a full military-grade weapon to go with the Phoenix VIIIs in her magazines.

"If they don't know they're under threat, I might get all three with the laser," he admitted. "But anything I shoot missiles at is going to see us coming a long way away."

Kelly nodded, the math running in her head as she considered the situation.

If they got within five million kilometers, the laser could take down one ship at a time...but that beam had to cycle. If they got within *two* million kilometers, her wife could use *Rhapsody's* full military amplifier to shred the gunships.

They couldn't get that close.

"How fast can we cycle that laser, Conrad?" she finally asked.

Rhapsody in Purple lunged through space as her engineers dug into the guts of her singular battle laser. The scout ship had two RFLAM turrets as well, but Kelly had no illusions that those would suffice in the face of multiple salvos from hostile Republic gunships.

Her two assets in the fight she was about to start were speed and surprise. Her intervention would remove any question of whether *Starlight* was a spy ship or not. Hopefully, the Republic didn't know much about the *Rhapsodies*, but a ship appearing from stealth and blowing away a gunship flight wasn't going to leave many doubters behind. If nothing else, stealthing a ship was still supposed to be impossible over the long term, even with magic.

"Those gunships are going to be in range of *Starlight* when we fire," Milhouse warned as the distance ticked down. "If they open fire with their RFLAMs at maximum range, they could destroy Captain Maata's ship."

"If they were going to try and destroy *Starlight*, the squadron from Manchester orbit would have done it," Kelly replied. "Or they'd have launched missiles."

She wasn't sure what defenses the defected Legatan ship had, but she had no more faith in their ability to stand up to full salvos from three gunships than she did in *Rhapsody in Purple's*.

There was no way for her to tell *Starlight* she was there. From what she understood of Damien Montgomery's plan, none of the ex-LMID crew even knew she was following them. She was supposed to be the ace in the hole if they were betrayed.

Or just plain caught.

"We'll fire as soon as we cross the five-million-kilometer mark," she told Milhouse. "Drop stealth, sequence three shots as fast as Engineering can give them to you."

"They're saying a two-second cycle time," Milhouse replied. "Four shots. No more. Quite possibly only three."

It would have to do. For all the hours that had passed since *Starlight* had broken orbit and the hour-plus that would pass between their intercept and the two ships being able to jump, the survival of both ships was going to come down to four seconds and Milhouse's aim.

"The gunships don't think they're under threat," her tactical officer said in response to her unspoken worry. "Straight and true. Easy targets."

Kelly nodded silently.

Thirty minutes to contact.

CHAPTER 19

"I KNOW you want to keep your secrets, Montgomery, but we will be inside the range of those gunships within a few minutes," Niska said quietly.

Damien hadn't missed the Augment entering the bridge, but his focus had been on the incoming enemy ships.

While *Starlight* was accelerating hard toward deep space and the safety of a magical teleport and had built up quite a velocity, the gunships had already been heading in that direction. They'd adjusted their course, moved slightly in *Starlight*'s direction, and were now accelerating in the same direction as the freighter.

The math was clear: even if *Starlight* were to somehow find even more acceleration, there was no way the jump-ship could avoid interception. The gunships would not merely get her in range of their lasers. They would get close enough to lock on to her hull.

Even without Damien aboard, that would end poorly for them. *Starlight*'s weapons were easily capable of destroying the gunships at close range.

Her weapons were only missiles, however, which meant the gunships would be able to return fire with precision before they were disabled. They'd take one or two of the gunships with them, but then the survivor would destroy Pod Bravo and board the ship.

Between the Augments and Marines, *that* wouldn't end well either... but there were still three more gunships following behind them, well within their missile range.

Another hour or so and Liara Foster could risk the jump. *Starlight* wasn't a Protectorate ship, though, and her jump matrix was ever so slightly odd in a dozen ways. Enough that the Navy Jump Mage wasn't sure she could push it.

Their only hope was to get through the gunships in front of them and deal with the long-range missile fire from their pursuers. That hope depended on a ship that Damien hadn't told his ally was with them.

Damien himself wasn't sure Kelly was with them. There was an encrypted transmitter hidden in his quarters that was letting the stealth ship know where they were jumping to, but there was no return transmission.

"Would you be reassured, Niska, if I had somehow concealed an entire fleet with magic?" he asked. "If all I had to do was whisk away my cloak of spells and the Protectorate would save us?"

The Augment snorted.

"I believe you can hide *a* starship, Montgomery," he said. "Perhaps even several...if you were in the middle of them. Is there another ship out there? A ghost, perhaps, that's been following us since Amber?"

Damien shook his head.

"Somehow, I'm not surprised you noticed."

"I noticed the transmissions first, I have to admit," the old spy said. "So far as I can tell, Maata didn't and her people haven't seen the ship at all. I'm impressed."

"You should be," the Hand replied. "Our ghost's a good ship and the Captain is a good friend. I just hope they are close enough."

"Enemy laser range in thirty seconds," Maata announced. "Two hours after that before they can board us."

Which was probably two hours before an ordinary Mage could jump them. Foster could get them out if the Republic was confident of that, but they couldn't take the risk.

Damien exhaled.

"It's down to either our ghost or the Republic's overconfidence," he admitted. "Bets, Major Niska?"

The Augment looked at the screen.

"These are the crews the Republic assigned to security duty, so over-confidence is possible," he admitted. "I'd still rather bet on your—"

The first of the gunships in their way disappeared in a brilliant flash of light, the laser invisible before it struck.

Two seconds later, the second gunship—still continuing on its fixed course—shared the first ship's fate.

Whoever was piloting the third gunship, though, earned a mental salute from Damien. They had *four seconds'* warning, lightspeed beams entirely invisible until they arrived, and the gunship *still* managed to avoid *Rhapsody of Purple*'s beam.

"Captain Maata?" Damien said loudly.

"Launching."

Six new icons appeared on the screen as the Rapier launchers in Pod Bravo spoke for the first time. Damien didn't expect them to be effective—the Rapier IVs had a little less than a third of the acceleration of Phoenix VIIIs—but they'd make the gunship commander think.

Especially as *Rhapsody in Purple* appeared on their screens and opened fire with her own launchers. Two Phoenix VIIIs screamed toward the gunship at over twelve thousand gravities.

They could probably deal with either salvo, but they couldn't deal with both—and they had to focus on the Phoenixes. For all that *Rhapsody in Purple* was further away, she was moving much faster relative to the gunship.

"I don't suppose *Starlight* has lasers?" Damien asked quietly.

"RFLAMs only," Niska told him. "Missiles are it."

It wasn't like the gunships blocking their way had anything heavier, but *they* had real armor. *Starlight* didn't. If she got into range of the gunships, she'd be destroyed.

More Rapiers flashed out of the launchers and the First Hand held his breath. The gunship had launched her own weapons, six Excalibur V antimatter-drive missiles, at *Rhapsody*. The stealth ship had her own RFLAMs, but that would push her defenses.

Then two of the missiles disappeared and he heard a whoop from Maata's gunner.

"Returning the favor as best we can, sir," the man declared. "Bugger was already in range of us after all."

Damien smiled. *Starlight* couldn't take down six missiles heading away from her, but she could take down some—and while *Rhapsody in Purple* would be pushed to stop six missiles with her two RFLAM turrets and her amplifier, she could almost certainly handle four.

The gunship shot down the first pair of missiles from *Rhapsody*. And the second. The stealth ship wasn't firing her laser, Damien noted grimly, but the missiles were still coming.

They weren't necessary. The gunship had split her fire too badly, and two Rapiers made it through. Most of the civilian missiles didn't have warheads, relying on kinetic energy to finish their opponents.

Captain Maata's turned out to carry two-hundred-megaton fusion bombs.

The intercept squadron was gone, but that was only half of *Starlight's* problems, and Damien's gaze turned to the icons of the three ships that had been pursuing them since Manchester orbit.

"What are they doing?" Maata asked slowly, her attention clearly focused in the same spot. "I assumed they would launch as soon as they saw us, but they haven't even increased their acceleration. Wait...have they cut it?"

Damien's borrowed seat didn't have a console or a repeater screen, but he had linked his wrist-comp in earlier, and now he dug into it to get a proper update on what was going on.

"They cut their acceleration just after we shot down the intercept squadron's missiles," he confirmed for her.

"But they want to catch us. Why cut their acceleration?"

"Because they'll resume it again in about forty seconds," Damien said grimly as he brought up the numbers on the launchers built into the Republic's new *Accelerator*-class gunships.

"And then they'll activate the drives of the missiles they've been launching into space and send them all after us at once," he continued.

"We're not even near their extreme range, so that will be over fifty missiles arriving in a few minutes."

"Can your stealth ship cover us from that?" Maata asked.

"No," Liara Foster interrupted. The Mage was clearly already doing the calculations. "We won't be in range of their amplifier or their RFLAMs at that point. By delaying, they took away our mutual support."

"We can't stop fifty missiles," Captain Maata told them. "This is a freighter with some concealed guns, not a warship."

"Not even a warship this size could stop fifty modern missiles," Damien replied. Magic wrapped around him as he unbelted himself from his seat and crossed the bridge to the simulacrum.

The acceleration would have crushed the mundane members of the crew. Even the Augments could only *survive* eight gees of thrust, not easily walk around in it.

Magic, however, allowed many things. He knew he was getting uncomfortable looks from the crew. Foster had received a couple herself when she'd entered the bridge, but everyone had been too glad to see her to care.

"Liara, we need to go," he said quietly as he reached her. "You're the only person aboard who can save us now."

"We're still too close in," the stocky woman replied, her hands fixed to the simulacrum. "If I jump now, I'll kill us all. Maybe if I was in a warship..."

"Liara, I have studied this for years," he reminded her. "It's not about the amplifier or the jump matrix or the *ship* at all. Whether or not we can jump from here is entirely about the Mage and their training. If you could jump from here in a warship, you can jump from here in a Legatan q-ship."

She swallowed.

"I don't know if I can," she admitted. "I don't know if I'm strong enough."

"You are a fully trained goddamned Mage of the Royal Martian Navy," Damien snapped. "You trained to jump from bloody *orbit* in an emergency. I won't pretend it won't hurt...but—"

He gestured at the screen as the Republic missiles lit up.

"I can't jump us," he reminded her, holding up his gloved hands. "Romanov can't jump us—he doesn't have the runes and never learned how. It's you or we all die."

"Make it happen, Mage Foster."

She took a deep breath and focused on the liquid silver icon at her fingertips. Liara closed her eyes, and Damien felt the power flicker through the ship.

And then they were somewhere else, a thankfully long way away from any Republican missiles.

CHAPTER 20

ROSLYN'S HEAD HURT.

The young Mage-Lieutenant rubbed her temples and blinked several times, hoping that the array of data she had on her screen would come back into focus.

It didn't cooperate and she linked her wrist-comp to the wallscreen in her office. Transferring the data blew it up to roughly forty times the size, and even her tired eyes could read that.

Mage-Commodore Jane Adamant had arrived yesterday with the battleship *Righteous Guardian of Liberty* and another half-dozen cruisers and destroyers. The Commodore had received an incredibly cold shoulder from the locals in Ardennes, but her presence finally brought Mage-Admiral Alexander's fleet up to her target numbers for Operation Bluebell.

Roslyn shook her head as she moved Adamant's task force over to one side of the screen. She'd looked up the officer's history and she could see why the Ardennes Self-Defense Force didn't like her—Mage-Commodore Adamant had earned her star by smashing the *previous* ASDF to pieces at Damien Montgomery's order.

The ASDF ships had obeyed a treacherous governor and been under the guns of a mutinous RMN cruiser squadron. They'd had no choice but to fight—and Mage-Commodore Adamant had had no choice but to wreck their ships.

The older woman hadn't seemed bothered by the cold shoulder, either. She'd clearly known what to expect.

Her ships brought them up to six battleships, thirty-two cruisers and thirty-six destroyers. Unless Roslyn missed her mark, their newly designated Second Fleet was the single largest formation the Royal Martian Navy had *ever* assembled. They had over half of the RMN's surviving cruisers, if nothing else.

The Protectorate had been functionally stripped of ships, she knew. Anywhere with a strong-enough Militia to protect themselves had been left to their own devices. Tasks and missions that would once have seen cruisers or multiple destroyers now saw single destroyers—*nothing* the RMN had heavier than a destroyer was anywhere except the front and Sol.

Coordinating the logistics and meetings for those seventy-four ship captains and the twelve flag officers among them was falling on Roslyn Chamber's young shoulders. Icons glittered next to the ships on her wall screen—a glorified checklist.

She was *almost* certain she'd invited every captain and flag officer to the final briefing aboard *Righteous Shield of Valor,* but missing one would have been unacceptable.

Lost in the review, she missed the admittance chime on her door the first two times it went off. She had barely registered the third when Mage-Captain Kulkarni gave up and entered her office.

"You have a doorbell for a reason, Lieutenant," the fleet operations officer told her. "You also, I should note, have assigned working hours for a reason."

"The Flag Lieutenant sleeps when the Admiral does," Roslyn replied. "Have *you* seen Alexander sleep?"

"Yes," Kulkarni said calmly. She studied the screen. "Sit down, Roslyn. Can you even read this?"

"Not really," the young woman admitted as she obeyed. "I just need to make sure I didn't screw anything up."

"And did you ask me to double-check it?" the ops officer asked. "Did you ask one of the Chiefs to check? Or any of the other officers in the Admiral's staff?"

"No, sir," Roslyn admitted.

"And in what galaxy, exactly, do you think that we expect the most junior officer on the staff to handle an entire fleet briefing on her own?" Kulkarni asked. "Or, hell, *anything*? You literally can't see straight, Roslyn."

She tapped a command on her own wrist-comp and the screen shut down.

"You are two hours past the end of your shift, and Chief Sinclair told me you *started* four hours early," Kulkarni told Roslyn. "I've just transferred your working files to my wrist-comp. I will double-check everything and make sure everyone knows where they need to be and when.

"*You*, Mage-Lieutenant, are going to bed—*your* bed, in case that's currently a question—and you are going to sleep for the next twelve hours so that you are conscious and useful *during* this briefing.

"Am I clear?"

"I haven't enough time to breathe, let alone find someone else to sleep with," Roslyn responded, only half-aware of how stupid she sounded.

"Because you're not supposed to be doing this alone without *any* experience to fall back on," her senior officer told her. "Your quarters, Mage-Lieutenant. *Now*."

Chief Olivia Sinclair was waiting for Roslyn when she finally woke up. She'd already realized she'd overslept the start of her next shift by an hour and was in a panicked rush toward her office when she almost physically collided with the taller woman.

"Slow down, Lieutenant," Sinclair told her. "There are no time bombs or live snakes waiting in your office. I checked."

"I need to get back up to speed on the briefing," Roslyn replied. "We have a lot of work to do."

"We do," Sinclair confirmed. "Which is why I'm going to brief you while we walk to the mess and you are going to *eat* while I finish."

Roslyn opened her mouth to argue, and the Chief shook her head with a smile.

"Kulkarni got the Admiral up to speed. You eat breakfast while I talk, then we catch up with the rest of the staff. Her Highness's orders."

That was an override that the Mage-Lieutenant couldn't argue with.

"Lead the way, Chief," she allowed.

"Kulkarni and I went through your checklist," Sinclair told her as she proceeded toward the mess. "Everyone has confirmed their arrival times, and I got that information to the boat bay. Scheduling of the arrivals has been delegated to the deck officer, so that's entirely under control."

"What about space?" Roslyn asked. Fitting in enough shuttles to get sixty-six Captains and eleven flag officers aboard *Righteous Shield* had been one of her biggest concerns.

"Delegated," Sinclair said cheerfully. "Neither you or I is really qualified to sort out that problem, but Master Chief Intaglio most definitely *is*. Trying to handle that yourself was..."

The Chief trailed off, clearly trying to work out how to phrase that Roslyn had been an idiot politely.

"A mistake," the young woman finished for her older-but-subordinate NCO. "I'll add it to the list."

"Nah, your only actual mistake was not calling me the moment you had a concern," Sinclair replied. "First rule of being a fledgling, sir: always talk to the Chiefs."

"I learned that in Tactical," Roslyn admitted as they reached the officers' mess. "Keep forgetting that it applies to being a staff officer, too."

Technically, Chief Sinclair wasn't supposed to be in the mess except as specifically invited. The stewards had clearly been informed that she was coming—and informed of just what Mage-Admiral Alexander figured needed to happen to her Flag Lieutenant.

The two of them were quickly seated in a corner of the mess, and a tray of food was brought out for Roslyn.

"Eat," Sinclair instructed. "Everything for the briefing is handled except for a tiny handful of final details that Kulkarni *can* take care of if you're late. We need you to backstop the Admiral as she speaks and make sure you're catching everyone's questions for her."

Sinclair grinned at her.

"We also need to make sure you remember to ask for help next time!"

"Officers. We are ready."

The three simple words hung in the massive briefing room like the Sword of Damocles.

Roslyn, feeling refreshed and far more on top of things now that her superiors and juniors alike had forced her to take a breath and rest, knew that those words were all that really needed to be said.

They'd go over the battle plan and the targeting and deployment sequences and the rest in detail again, but Mage-Admiral Alexander's statement was the important part of this briefing.

Even if those details were why they'd hauled over seventy officers aboard *Righteous Shield*.

"I am officially activating Operation Bluebell as of this moment," Alexander continued. "A cruiser squadron of the Tau Ceti Security Fleet will arrive in forty-eight hours to provide additional security to the Ardennes System, but Second Fleet will move out at oh eight hundred hours Olympus Mons Time tomorrow.

"We now represent the single largest force the Protectorate has ever deployed, with half of the battleships and over half of the cruisers currently in commission. Until new construction comes online, we are the *only* offensive force the Protectorate can afford to deploy."

That caused a stir amongst the officers, though Roslyn doubted it was a surprise to any of them. To pull together Second Fleet, they'd stripped the Protectorate's defenses bare. If the Republic resumed their offensive, there might well not be enough ships left to stop them.

"Operation Bluebell, however, represents a strategic strike that the enemy must counter. We are twelve days' flight from Legatus. There, this fleet will challenge one of humanity's oldest worlds and the heart of our enemy.

"We cannot afford to fail."

Alexander smiled broadly at her people.

"Captain Kulkarni had prepared a presentation to update everyone on our planned operations and how we will take advantage of the weakness of the Legatus System. Before that, however, I'm sure some of you have higher-level concerns. Let's get them out of the way."

There was a long moment of silence.

"What about the Militia ships?" Mage-Admiral Medici asked slowly. "They basically carried the Battle of Ardennes. Why aren't we reinforcing Second Fleet with them?"

"Because the Militia that fought and died for Ardennes *died*," Alexander replied. "It is not—it has *never* been—the purpose of the System Militias to fight Mars's battles for us. They stood with us at Ardennes because no one had a choice, and they paid heavily for that stand.

"The Militia ships that fought here were mostly sent home for badly needed repairs. They aren't here for us to call upon again, and I would rather not call on wounded ships to volunteer a second time.

"Most importantly, however, the Militia ships have too few Mages aboard," the Mage-Admiral concluded. "There are certainly systems that are secure enough with powerful-enough Militias that they could assist us, but they have two or three Mages per ship at most. They can't keep up with the Fleet.

"If we are to strike as deeply and quickly as we must, we are left with only Navy ships—and we now have enough Navy ships to carry the day."

Alexander surveyed the room.

"Does that answer your question, Admiral Medici?"

"It does," Medici confirmed instantly...leaving Roslyn to wonder if the question had been prearranged.

That was something to think about for the next time she organized one of these. It would always be useful to have someone softball a question to the Admiral, she figured. Especially if it was a question that needed to be asked.

"Anyone else?"

CHAPTER 21

CAPTAIN MAATA regarded *Rhapsody in Purple* with undisguised envy.

"Heat sinks, radar-absorbing hulls, *antimatter power?*" she asked as she looked over her scan results and glanced back at Damien. "I knew you could use magic for stealth, but everyone in the Republic assumed your technological solutions were behind us."

"The Protectorate is, in the grand scheme of things, technologically stagnant," Damien admitted. "Incremental improvements on existing technologies. On the other hand, the Protectorate contains a hundred star systems and over a hundred billion human beings."

He shrugged.

"Even with magic available to solve many problems, someone is always going to come up with a clever idea. It's hard to stagnate entirely with that many clever humans running around."

Niska snorted.

"I think you might be the first person I've ever seen admit that the Protectorate was stagnant," he pointed out.

"Magic stagnated our technological development," Damien said. "The Protectorate government has been aware of that for at least, oh, fifty years. And has been working on it for most of that time."

And if the Republic had assumed that the Protectorate *hadn't* been aware of that weakness and working to counteract it, they were going to have some ugly surprises coming.

"How long have you had those?" Maata asked. "I might have switched sides sooner if I'd known that was on the table!"

"Long enough that the answer is classified," Damien told her with a chuckle. The people sharing *Starlight*'s bridge with him would have been the last people the Protectorate wanted to discover that the *Rhapsodies* existed.

Time had changed that, it seemed, but he was still glad *Rhapsody in Purple* had been a surprise. Now the two starships floated in deep space, two light-years from the Arsenault System.

"Now that no one is being kept secret, let's pull Captain LaMonte into the planning for our next stop," he continued. "We'll probably want to follow much the same pattern regardless, but if everyone knows we have backup, that does give us options."

"Kelly LaMonte?" Niska asked, arching an eyebrow at him. "Wasn't she aboard *Blue Jay*?"

"She was," Damien confirmed. "And yes, we were an item then. Now she's married to her Ship's Mage and her First Pilot. Does that satisfy your gossip urge?"

The cyborg laughed.

"I don't have much of one of those," he told Damien. "I do like to know where I stand with people, though. How far are we from Nueva Bolivia?"

"Twelve days with one Jump Mage aboard," Maata replied. "If we can borrow an extra Mage from Captain LaMonte...?"

"We'll talk about it," Damien said. He didn't want to commit any of the other Mages from *Rhapsody in Purple* to coming aboard a Legatan ship, however defected and friendly.

On the other hand, the itch at the back of his neck suggested that the sooner they found the answer they were chasing, the fewer people were likely to die.

For the first time since the mission had begun, Damien had all of his people in one conference. Most of them were aboard *Starlight*, with Kelly

LaMonte, her spouses, and Captain Charmchi linked in via a video channel from *Rhapsody in Purple.*

"Captain LaMonte," Niska greeted her. "Time has treated you well, I see."

Damien's ex-girlfriend looked good, he had to admit. Her thirties and command suited her, and neither had prevented her from continuing to change her hair on a whim. Currently, *Rhapsody's* Captain had neon-yellow hair, unusual even for her.

"Major Niska," she responded. "I see time has treated you like shit."

He winced as Damien swallowed a chuckle.

"I probably deserve that," he admitted. "It's been an odd few years for us all."

"Kelly, you and your people were briefed on *Starlight's* officers?" Damien asked.

"Aye. They're trouble," she pointed out. "But we're pretty deep in their home territory, so I guess we should keep them."

Maata snorted.

"So, half of this call knows the other half. Introductions?" she asked.

"Captain Maata, be known to Captain Kelly LaMonte, commander of one of the Protectorate's stealth ships," Damien replied. "With her are her spouses, Ship's Mage Xi Wu and First Pilot Mike Kelzin, and Captain Jalil Charmchi of the Protectorate Special Operations Command."

He wasn't going to specify things like *Rhapsody in Purple's* name or *which* branch of PSOC Charmchi reported to. He needed Niska and Maata, but they didn't need to know everything about his little branch of the Protectorate's intelligence apparatus.

Names were already more than dangerous enough, he supposed.

"It's a pleasure," Niska told them all. "Six months ago, we were all enemies," he continued. "Now it seems there may well be a cancer at the heart of the Republic I helped birth that is our mutual enemy.

"I don't know what my Director discovered, but I do know that he was a founding father of the Republic and they killed him for it." Niska shook his head. "What we found in Arsenault suggests that it has something to do with the young Mages by Right who were still in the Republic at the time of the Secession."

"We know Arsenault's Mages were shipped to Nueva Bolivia," Damien concluded. "We've identified the ship—*Sounds in the Shining Morning*—the flight registry, everything. Once we're in Nueva Bolivia, we should be able to ID where *Shining Morning* dropped them off."

"There's still one question, though, that's going to impact a lot," Romanov said grimly, the Marine sitting to Damien's right. "There shouldn't have been any way that the Directorate could have traced the encounter at the Academy all the way back to *Starlight* in the time they had.

"It was *maybe* four hours from us teleporting away from the Academy to them challenging *Starlight*. They made that connection too damned quickly."

Niska sighed.

"That's because that isn't the connection they made," he said quietly. "I had Augment Nichols trying to dig up some of our old contacts on Manchester. They didn't catch us. They caught her."

"And Nichols came back aboard with us," Damien concluded grimly. "And just what was Ms. Nichols looking for that was so secret, Niska? I thought we were trying to keep each other informed of things that would at least threaten the mission."

"And you had a *stealth ship* tailing us," Niska replied. "We each have our own damn secrets, Montgomery. In this case..." He sighed. "I had Nichols trying to get her hands on a Link. The ability to eavesdrop on even the general news updates that they're sending out for RIN and RID ears only would give us a valuable tool.

"But *I* wanted to control that tool, Montgomery. There's a limit to what I can give up just yet."

Damien sighed.

"And that desire for secrecy nearly killed us all," he pointed out. "Can you safely use your authentications and so forth in Bolivia now?"

"I think so," Niska said after a pause. "Hopefully, only Nichols's IDs and clearances were flagged. Even if they cast a broader net, I have clearances hidden in the system that they won't know about."

"That they shouldn't know about," Maata said quietly. "What if they do?"

"I don't know," he confessed. "But we don't have a lot of options, do we? Unless anyone here thinks we're going to walk away from the mysterious disappearance of over two hundred teenagers at the hands of my government?"

CHAPTER 22

TWO DAYS INTO the slow process of moving nearly eighty warships across over a hundred light-years of space, Roslyn *finally* began to start feeling like she had her feet under herself.

It was a small moment, in the middle of a videoconference between Admiral Alexander and four other Mage-Admirals with regards to anti-gunship tactics. Alexander made an unthinking gesture toward Roslyn and asked her a question they hadn't discussed in advance.

"Lieutenant, do we have any estimates on where the Republic is manufacturing gunships?" she asked.

"We're not entirely sure," Roslyn replied instantly. "Current estimates from MISS have sixty to seventy percent of the manufacturing going on in Legatus, with another twenty percent in Nueva Bolivia and the rest scattered across half a dozen other systems."

As she was answering the question off the cuff, she was digging through her file structure and grabbing the most recent relevant report and flipping its summary page onto Alexander's screen.

The Mage-Admiral gave her an approving nod and turned back to her peers.

"As Lieutenant Chambers's data suggests, we're not going to eliminate gunship production by besieging Legatus," she told the Admirals. "That's something we need to keep in mind."

"That raises the question of whether the RIN command is ruthless enough to keep building new gunships, loading them into carriers, and flinging them at our siege force," Medici said grimly. "That's probably the most effective thing they *can* do, at least in terms of wearing us down over time."

"It depends how many carriers they lose trying to dislodge us initially," Admiral Marangoz noted. He was checking something with his own staff as they spoke. "We still don't have solid numbers on how many of the damn things they have."

"Only how many they've lost," Medici said with a wicked grin. "Though that number isn't nearly as high as I'd like."

"And the price for them has been too damned high," Alexander replied. "Officers, we cannot underestimate our enemy. Our entire strategy in Legatus is to try and *avoid* engagement with the fixed defenses. As far as the gunships go, defeat in detail is the name of the game.

"We can engage the gunship forces from Legatus, *or* Centurion, *or* the entire mobile force in the system. We cannot allow them to concentrate those three forces. Our mobility advantage and control of the space between the two planets is the key to this."

"What happens if they start jumping ships out and arming them out-system?" another Admiral asked. Roslyn quickly checked the system to ID Admiral Arline Pender.

"The current assumption from MISS is that the jump drives are being installed at Centurion," Alexander replied. "That's why my intent is to lock down Centurion primarily. We will have some leakage from Legatus under the deployment plan. We can't avoid that.

"The priority is to make sure that no new jump ships are deployed, and that means we must keep jump-capable hulls from leaving the facilities at Centurion."

Roslyn hid a shiver. Their entire plan was hinging on assumptions and intelligence of mixed value. Even if it worked, the Republic was going to move everything in their power to dislodge Second Fleet.

She trusted Mage-Admiral Alexander and was starting to feel confident in her own tiny contribution to the machine Alexander had built—but she was *terrified* of what they were about to try and do.

The conference closed up several minutes later, and Roslyn already had Alexander's coffee ready the way the Admiral liked it. Alexander took a sip and gestured the Lieutenant to a chair.

"I didn't think we'd need that production data," she admitted. "Solid catch, Lieutenant. Well done."

"Thank you, sir."

"You're doing okay," Alexander said with a smile. "I haven't had many Flag Lieutenants over the years, Chambers. They have, to a one, been young Mages without the political connections to rise far in the Fleet. Young officers, all Mages by Right except you, that people I trust told me needed a leg up to get where the Protectorate needed them to be."

"So, we're all terrible political appointees?" Roslyn asked.

The Admiral laughed with coffee in her mouth, managing to spray steaming liquid across her immaculate dress uniform and desk.

"Ow," the commander of the Royal Martian Navy's Second Fleet declared in a pained voice, brushing hot liquid off of her wrist. "Could you have let me *swallow* before you said that, Lieutenant?"

Magic flurried around the Admiral as she spoke, instantly bleaching the stain out of her uniform sleeve and sweeping the liquid onto a tissue she tossed into the middle of the desk.

"You and your predecessors have been the opposite of political appointees," the Admiral replied. "You are probably the most-connected Flag Lieutenant I've ever had, though to be fair, you've been shepherded a good way by Hand Montgomery.

"And because you've worked for me, you are now known by face and name by about a fifth of the flag officers in the RMN. You've done well, and that means you're known *positively* by those officers.

"It'll help you in the future."

"And right now, sir?" Roslyn said quietly. "I just hope I'm doing well enough that I'm not hindering you."

"You're doing okay," Alexander repeated. "Which means, of course, I'm going to make you work harder. It's been two days since we received any updated reports on anything. By now, Captain Menendez should have *something* complete for an assessment of the shipbuilding at Legatus."

Captain Mirjam Menendez was the senior intelligence officer in Second Fleet. She and her analysts were tucked away in a secluded part of *Righteous Shield of Valor*'s copious corridors—not least because even Menendez's rank was a courtesy. She and her team were seconded from the Martian Interstellar Security Service, and she'd been commissioned to give her a leg to stand on with Navy officers.

"She's sent over some summaries," Roslyn said carefully.

"And they're crap and she knows it," Alexander said grimly. "I know we don't have perfect data, Chambers, but we've got information. We had enough for me to plan this damn operation, so I need you and Menendez to make sure that I have the most up-to-date assessment of the Legatus System's defenses, focusing on Centurion and Legatus, as possible."

"You want me to kick an RMN Captain and senior MISS agent into getting to work, sir?" Roslyn asked carefully.

"I want you to kick her in the ass until the job is done, Lieutenant," Alexander replied. "She knows who you report to—and I want your hands in the analysis as well. You've seen more battles against these people than anyone who *didn't* serve on *Stand in Righteousness*'s bridge from the beginning.

"You have a background Captain Menendez can't match. Let's see what you find that she couldn't."

It turned out that Roslyn had underestimated just how tucked away the MISS detachment was. She pulled the location from the ship's computer and started hunting for it. Eventually, after passing underneath a massive assembly that she *thought* was one of the primary missile magazines for the upper starboard broadside, she found the listed location.

Despite the sheer size of the battleship, these corridors were cramped. They'd lost at least twenty centimeters of the usual height to scrape in extra cubage for the magazine. Despite that, it looked like there were an entire block of quarters, several offices and a conference room tucked away down here.

Who exactly the designers had intended this section of the ship to serve—other than short people—was beyond Roslyn Chambers, but it was where they'd stuck the intelligence section.

She stepped up to the office that her wrist-comp told her held Captain Menendez and knocked sharply.

The admittance chime automatically sounded in response, and the door slid open.

"Come in. Who is it?" a tired voice shouted.

Roslyn stepped in and crisply saluted.

"Mage-Lieutenant Roslyn Chambers, from Mage-Admiral Alexander's staff, sir," she introduced herself. "I'm looking for Captain Menendez?"

The woman leaning on the desk didn't say anything initially, just examining Roslyn in silence. It was hard to tell with her sitting, but she looked to be of a similar petite build to Roslyn herself, though she was blonde to Roslyn's redder hair.

"I'm Menendez," she replied. "Drop the *Captain* bullshit, Chambers," she continued as Roslyn realized the other woman was wearing a suit, not a uniform. "It may make the Navy feel better about having me aboard, but I'm a data analyst, not a soldier."

"There are a lot of people in uniform aboard this ship who are data analysts, Agent Menendez," Roslyn told her. She took a seat without asking, studying the other woman in turn.

Menendez looked...exhausted. In fact, unless Roslyn missed her guess, Menendez looked like she was on the wrong end of a two-day bender.

Roslyn had shared that experience, *once*, and decided to limit her exposure to the Protectorate's legal and illegal pharmaceuticals afterward. She'd helped a few friends through them afterward, though, and she recognized the signs.

Signs it made no damn sense for the senior intelligence agent aboard Second Fleet's flagship to be showing.

"Sir, are you all right?" Roslyn asked when she realized Menendez hadn't said anything for several seconds.

"I'm fine," she snapped. "What does the Admiral want?"

Roslyn considered the various approaches available to her, and then decided on "tough love."

"The Admiral wants to know what the hell you're doing down here, since apparently it *isn't* assembling the updated report on Legatus's defenses she asked for," she said flatly. "And from your current state, I'd guess something closer to a two-day drug bender than your actual job."

Menendez finally showed a reaction to *that*, lunging to her feet as her face flashed red.

Unfortunately for her, she lost her balance and fell *over* her desk. Slamming her stomach into the cheap plastic surface, she promptly vomited everywhere.

A shield of magic kept the mess away from Roslyn—she'd expected something similar—and she rose to calmly look down on the intelligence officer.

"What the hell is going on, Agent?" she snapped.

Menendez groaned.

"I don't... I don't... What the *fuck*?" she managed to moan. "I've just had coffee... I haven't even left my offi..." She pulled herself sufficiently off her desk to look up at Roslyn.

"What time is it?" she asked.

"Nineteen hundred twenty-six hours OMT," Roslyn replied. "June thirtieth."

The intelligence officer stared at her.

"I haven't left my office in forty hours, Lieutenant," she said slowly, careful to enunciate each word clearly. "Something's not—"

Menendez passed out on her desk and Roslyn swallowed, wincing at the smell.

She stepped over to study the coffee cup. It was a third full and still warm. Someone had topped it up for the senior intel officer relatively recently, but...

Roslyn tapped a command into her wrist-comp.

"Chief Sinclair?" she said into it as the com channel. "I need somebody to run a drug test on a sample for me and keep it entirely under wraps.

"Know anyone in the MPs we can lean on with Her Highness's name?"

CHAPTER 23

CHIEF OLIVIA SINCLAIR arrived roughly ten minutes later with a dark-skinned middle-aged man in the uniform of shipboard Military Police, plus standard-issue turban.

"Sergeant Chetan Hersch," he introduced himself tersely as he studied the room.

Roslyn had managed to get Menendez off her desk, laying the woman on the ground in the recovery position. She'd checked to be sure the woman's airways were clear and that she was breathing, but then left her be.

Managing to not touch anything else in the room had been a struggle, but she couldn't be sure just what had happened yet.

"Sergeant," she greeted the MP. She gestured to the unconscious woman on the floor. "That is Captain Menendez, our senior MISS analyst. She looks to me like she's now sleeping off a multi-day bender...but she didn't seem to have a damn clue what was going on."

"That's not an uncommon effect of a bender," the MP said calmly.

"And if she were anyone *except* the person supposed to brief Admiral Alexander on the status of Legatus's defenses, I'd write it off as that," Roslyn agreed.

"Doesn't all new intelligence come through Captain Menendez's desk?" Chief Sinclair asked in a concerned tone. "If she's out of it..."

"Damn." Roslyn looked over at the unconscious woman again. "That would explain why the reports we were getting didn't look like they had new data at all. If she's out, then our entire intelligence team is running on old data."

Hersch grunted.

"And *I* know the Captain's reputation," he said gruffly. "Her staff don't bother her when she's working. She's notorious for ripping off heads and asking questions later."

"Depending on what drugs she was on, that would have been made even worse," Roslyn replied. "I need to know what she got hit with, Sergeant, and how it was delivered."

"I'm guessing you don't think she's an addict?" the MP asked dryly.

"It's possible," Roslyn conceded. "But given that the Admiral's *operations officer* was a Republic spy, I'm not going to rule out enemy action just yet.

"Check her coffee first," she ordered. "The rather abbreviated conversation I had with her suggested she'd been in here drinking coffee for at least twenty-four hours straight."

Which would, now that she thought about it, explain one of the smells wafting through the place.

"Her coffee was fresh when I checked, so she has a coffeemaker here somewhere...but I'm damned suspicious of it, no matter where it's hiding."

Hersch was already producing a portable chemistry kit and a set of thin blue gloves.

"You make a compelling case, sir," he conceded. "Even if you didn't, well, the Mage-Admiral is a powerful name to conjure with. I should be able to identify most drugs that could have been snuck into the coffee with the kit.

"Give me a few minutes." He glanced around the office. "And don't touch anything else. Everything in here could be a clue."

It took Hersch about fifteen minutes to complete the analysis, by which point Menendez was loudly snoring in the corner of the office.

The MP shook his head as he looked at the results.

"Kite," he told Roslyn. "Not sure which variety, the analyzer is confused. It's giving me sixty percent likelihood of Silver Kite, but also a sixty percent likelihood of Red Kite."

"That's because Red Kite is White Kite with caffeine added," Roslyn said with a sigh. Kite, in its several varieties, had been three of the top six best-selling illegal street drugs on Tau Ceti in her misspent youth. White Kite was the basic form, but Red and Silver were probably more popular.

"Most people wouldn't add Silver Kite to coffee," she continued. "By the time you've laced the Kite with cocaine to smooth some of its nastier effects, well, it's too damn expensive to mix with caffeine pills or pour into anything else."

"Why the hell would they put Silver Kite in coffee?" Hersch asked, the MP also clearly wanting to ask how the Admiral's Flag Lieutenant knew so much about illegal drugs.

"Because Kite screws with your sense of time normally and Silver Kite is *worse* for that," she said grimly. "Red Kite, on the other hand, augments the existing high from the base drug but leads to the worst crash. You can get the same high with two-thirds of the amount of White Kite, so dealers make Red Kite to stretch the supply and make more money."

"And the addicts keep coming back, regardless of the crash," Sinclair said grimly. "That's fucked up."

"Yes. And because it's a common street drug on half a dozen Protectorate worlds, it's hardly out of the question for Menendez to have been dosing herself on it," Roslyn said quietly. "But if there's some still in the coffee, she's been repeatedly dosed over multiple days."

She shook her head and turned to Sinclair.

"Chief Sinclair, we need to get her to the infirmary," she continued firmly. "Quiet is better, but the only person I know who ran this kind of bender with recurring doses of *any* kind of Kite died. And he died *ugly*."

"I'll handle it," Sinclair promised. "You good here?"

"Sergeant, I need you to do whatever you need with her computers ASAP," Roslyn ordered. "Then you're going to go over the rest of the room while I go through her data."

"You'll need the Admiral's codes for that," the Chief pointed out.

Roslyn paused carefully and then forced a nod.

"Of course; I'll touch base with her."

The thought that Alexander could open up the computer hadn't even occurred to her. *She'd* been planning on hacking in.

"Somebody wanted to be damn sure that the latest updates on Legatus got hung up at Menendez's desk. They were relying on the hard crash she's about to have to make people stop questioning why the reports had been delayed, and on her staff being distracted," Roslyn said grimly.

"I don't know about anybody else, but I guarantee that Mage-Admiral Alexander is going to want to know why...and who."

"I might be able to find out who, Lieutenant," Hersch told her. "Why...will take a while longer."

"I think the answer to why, Sergeant, is in Ms. Menendez's computers," Roslyn said. "Which means I need to make that call."

"What's going on, Chambers?" Alexander asked. Roslyn knew perfectly well she was interrupting the Admiral's supper, but she didn't have a choice—and Alexander sounded surprisingly calm about it.

"I need your authorization codes to break open Captain Menendez's data files," Roslyn said as quickly as she could. "She's headed to sick bay. Someone was dosing her with dangerous levels of a nasty street drug from Tau Ceti to keep her stoned out of her mind and unable to work.

"She's going to have an ugly crash, and the entire intelligence update we received before leaving Ardennes is locked up in her computer."

Alexander was silent for a few seconds.

"That is a *terrible* way to run a department," she noted. "Are you certain?"

"Our intel officer apparently has a reputation, sir."

"We'll deal with that later. You have the situation under control?" the Admiral asked.

"I think so," Roslyn admitted. "I have an MP searching Menendez's office for evidence, and Chief Sinclair is moving her to sick bay. Everyone is under orders to keep things quiet until we know more. I'm..." She sighed. "I'm guessing we still have a Republican Agent aboard."

"I'm sending you the codes you need," Alexander told her. "They're one-time keys, though they can be abused in a few ways. Don't abuse them."

"Wouldn't dream of it, sir."

"I'm also going to get a Secret Service detail down there ASAP," the Admiral continued, her voice still calm. "If someone put this much effort into keeping that intel buried, I suspect they're watching her office—and that means you and the MP are moving rapidly up their target list."

That thought hadn't occurred to Roslyn.

"Yes, sir." She swallowed. "Would appreciate the backup, sir."

"They'll be on their way in a moment. Be careful, Lieutenant Chambers. I don't want to have to train a new Flag Lieutenant; am I clear?"

"Perfectly, sir."

The channel cut to silence and Roslyn's wrist-comp chimed to tell her it had received the one-time override codes. She shivered, looking at the innocuous file that she suspected could open *any* computer aboard *Righteous Shield of Valor*.

"I probably should have asked this sooner, Sergeant," she said, her voice admirably calm to even her ears, "but you do have your sidearm on you, yes?"

Hersch coughed.

"Yes, sir?"

"Admiral Alexander just pointed out that we're currently undoing *somebody's* clever plan," Roslyn noted. "They might get cranky."

"Ah. Of course, sir."

The dark-skinned Tau Cetan officer seemed to take that in stride—but Roslyn also saw him pause his search to draw his sidearm, check its magazine...and take the safety off.

Both of them had work to do, and the young Mage-Lieutenant suddenly found herself wishing for eyes in the back of her head.

If that was possible with magic, though, it was outside *her* skill set!

The document that was live on Menendez's computer was potentially the single most garbled piece of text Roslyn had ever attempted to read—and she'd actually *managed* to read her gang-leader ex-boyfriend's attempt to write fiction while stoned.

It looked like the intelligence agent had been trying to put together a summary of the intelligence, but her drugged brain had been uncooperative at best and actively sabotaging her at worst.

With a sigh, Roslyn closed that file and pulled up the actual intelligence. *Rhapsody in Twilight* had made a pass through the Legatus System three days before Second Fleet had left Ardennes. The stealth ship had reached an RTA in time to transmit before they'd moved, but that meant that all Menendez had received was a transcript of an audio conversation transmitted across a hundred or so light-years by magic.

And it was horrendously confusing to Roslyn, a slew of acronyms and shorthand used to make sure that the information was communicated as quickly as possible. Fortunately, it looked like Menendez had kept a glossary on hand for translating the shorthand, which helped.

CBG-ID-A reloc Cent. New CBG, ID-B, arrv at Legt. CBG-ID-B BBs, 3, reloc Cent.

Carrier Battle Group A relocated...to Centurion? A new carrier group, designated B, had arrived at Legatus—but their battleships had been sent to Centurion. Three of them.

That was...potentially problematic. Second Fleet could certainly take those forces, but with the carrier group they expected still at Legatus, they might miss that another one was at Centurion—and a full carrier group reinforced with three battleships would be a nasty surprise as they tangled with Centurion's outer defenses.

There was more, but there was a *reason* that piece of intel was at the top of the transcript. It had taken Roslyn far too long to decode even that one line, but that one line could change every—

The door sliding open interrupted her thoughts and she looked up. She was expecting the Secret Service detail the Admiral had promised... and she should have known better.

There was only one person in the door, a tall man completely unknown to her holding a gun.

Training and years of practiced paranoia got Roslyn's personal shield up in time to stop the bullets.

The attacker kept moving, dodging sideways as Hersch turned, drew and fired in a single smooth motion. Unfortunately, Roslyn wasn't a good enough Mage to establish a one-way shield, and the MP's bullets slammed into the same defense that had saved them both.

The stranger slammed some device on the door control panel, which promptly flashed red and slammed the door shut. He studied her and Hersch for a few silent seconds, then grinned and charged.

He was too fast. Roslyn's shields were designed to stop small objects moving at a high velocity, not a *human* charging through them. The solidified air disintegrated under the impact, and the attacker collided with Hersch.

The two struggled for a moment and Roslyn tried to intervene. Bands of force slammed down across both men...and then a gun went off.

Several more gunshots followed and she saw Hersch jerk as the bullets struck home.

She tightened the bands of force. She was almost certainly making Hersch's injuries worse, but she *had* to keep the attacker pinned down.

She failed. The stranger moved with impossible speed and strength, slipping out of half of her bars of force and *breaking* several of them as he lunged back to his feet.

Most of the bullets had apparently been Hersch's. The MP was lying on the ground, dying if not already dead, but there were four clear bullet wounds in his attacker.

"Get back," Roslyn snapped, drawing her shield tightly to herself. She couldn't stop him charging, but she could keep bullets or blades from hitting her.

But this time, the attacker didn't aim at her. He aimed at the computer console—the console her tight defense around herself didn't cover. Bullets hammered into the system and he tossed another strange device after them.

She felt the magnetic pulse trigger. The computer was Navy equipment, hardened by default—but the bullets would have undermined most of that. The short-range EMP had almost certainly wiped the data.

Roslyn forced herself to focus and flung fire at the stranger. He sidestepped it and grinned at her again as he approached. He'd discarded the gun in favor of a blade of some kind...a narrow-pointed dagger she was quite certain an Augment could punch through her shields.

And there was no way her attacker wasn't an Augment. It seemed that their intelligence motherlode had missed an assassin or two in the data dump!

She glared at him and drew a deep breath. Roslyn Chambers was *not* going to die whimpering on her knees, begging for mercy. As the Augment lunged toward her, she flung her shield out. She wasn't trying to block his attack, just deflect it. The dagger plunged into the barrier— but that just gave her enough of a hold to throw it aside.

The cyborg's inhuman grip betrayed him and he was thrown aside with the dagger. That gave Roslyn a moment to reach for the Mage training the *Navy* had given her. Lightning flashed from her fingers, hammering into the Augment's back.

At a low level, the spell could disable a human without killing them... but Roslyn didn't know how much disabling an Augment could take, and she knew she wasn't going to get a second chance.

Cyborg or not, she roasted the man alive.

CHAPTER 24

MAGICAL HEALING was a surgeon's speciality, requiring years of education and libraries' worth of medical knowledge. To fix the human body with magic required you to *understand* the human body.

Magical combat first aid was a far more brute-force practice and one prone to causing almost as much damage as it fixed. Mages were trained to use regular first aid first and to call on their magic as a last resort to stop an injured person from dying.

By the time Roslyn reached Hersch, that was her *starting* point. Magic provided compression for her as she tried, desperately, to save the MP's life. He'd already lost a lot of blood and she wasn't sure that compression was going to work.

There had to be help on the way, but if she didn't stop the bleeding quickly, it wasn't going to matter.

The one thing that magic was *really good at* for medical treatment was also reserved for last-ditch options: cauterization. There was almost certainly internal damage, but there was nothing Roslyn could do about that.

She *could*, however, stop the bleeding.

Neat sparks of fire appeared inside the MP's wounds, searing the still-bleeding holes shut. It wouldn't hold—his injuries were too severe for that—but it would buy him time.

As she dared to hope, he stopped breathing.

Cursing, she placed her hands onto his chest and started pushing. Magic wove around Hersch's face as she began compressions, adding the air-transfer component of magically assisted CPR.

Ten seconds. Thirty. Between the cauterizing and the necessary strength of CPR, she knew she was causing as much damage as she might be fixing...but he was going to *live*, dammit.

Roslyn barely even recognized the sound of a vibroblade hitting the security door behind her. Her focus was so complete, whoever it was had been *sawing* through the door for ten seconds before she registered them.

Then the door fell from its frame. Roslyn kept her focus on Hersch as she heard footsteps...but she wove a defensive shield around them as she did.

"Fuck," a woman swore behind her. "Call it in, Hammond. We need medical *now*."

Roslyn kept compressing. Someone knelt beside her, studying the wounds over her shoulder as Hersch drew several ragged breaths beyond those the young Mage was forcing into him.

"Medtech should be under three minutes," a calm voice said in her ear. "Keep compressing."

She'd been about to stop, but she followed instructions...and Hersch stopped breathing again.

A noise started a few seconds later, causing Roslyn to start. Then she realized it was a metronome beat—exactly the rate she needed to be keeping up—and she adjusted her compressions to match.

She was weakening and a hand squeezed her shoulder.

"Keep up the air; I'll take over compressions," the stranger ordered.

Roslyn obeyed, also using magic to sustain the compressions for the seconds of the changeover. A narrow-set woman slid past her with an experienced motion and took over.

There was no concern in her movements for the fact that Hersch was covered in blood and that she was wearing an expensive suit.

It seemed the first to arrive had been Alexander's Secret Service team.

Roslyn would never, not even with access to the timestamps of everyone else's actions and arrival, be certain how long passed between Sergeant Hersch being shot and the medical techs' arrival.

All she knew was that she was being suddenly gently ushered away as an oxygen mask replaced her magical efforts and two white-uniformed young men took over from the Secret Service Agent.

"We've got him, sir," the lead medtech told her as they gently slid a stretcher underneath Hersch. "Everything says he's still with us. It's up to us now."

Roslyn stepped away and almost fell over Menendez's desk. One of the Secret Service agents had already produced a white sheet from *somewhere* and covered the crisped corpse that had been a Legatan agent.

"You need to head to medbay yourself, sir," the woman who'd been helping her deal with Hersch told her. "You're showing every sign of shock. You need to get checked out."

"Not yet," Roslyn told her in a distracted voice. She was going over the desk, trying to link to its systems with her wrist-comp.

She was unsurprised when she got nothing. The Augment had done a brilliant job of wrecking the hardware and Roslyn had been looking at the data on Menendez's local console.

"Agent...?"

"Aryana Escarcega, Mage-Lieutenant," the woman replied. "And I'm going to have to argue with you on the medbay. I was sent to guard you, and that includes taking care of you in my book, sir."

"Not. Yet." Roslyn bit off the words as she studied the wreck of the intelligence officer's desk. She plugged a command sequence into her wrist-comp.

"Communications, Lieutenant Peti Vida speaking," an officious voice responded.

"Lieutenant, I need to know what happened when we got the intelligence dump from the Ardennes RTA before we left the system," Roslyn said crisply. "I know Captain Menendez had a copy, but were there any others? Was a copy kept in the coms buffer?"

"Intelligence communications are confident—"

"This is Mage-Admiral Alexander's Flag Lieutenant," Roslyn said sharply. "Captain Menendez is in sick bay after a murder attempt made to keep that intelligence from getting to the Mage-Admiral.

"Answer my damn question, Lieutenant, or explain to the *Admiral* why you didn't."

Roslyn was well aware that the Lieutenant should have held her ground and insisted Roslyn get authorization from the Admiral directly. She'd have got that authorization, though, and Roslyn was out of patience.

There was a pause as the officer went through the same thought process, then sighed.

"Menendez insisted that all intelligence communications went through her for distribution," Vida told her. "No copies were distributed to anyone else or kept."

"And *why the fuck* did we let her do that?" Roslyn snapped.

"Because she was MISS and we were told she had that authority," the coms officer replied. "From the sounds of it, we should have pushed back harder, I take it?"

"Menendez is down and her console is destroyed. I don't suppose she would have been keeping the data elsewhere?"

"It's got to be backed up, no matter how controlling she was being," Vida replied. "I can pull the file metadata and give it to IT to track down, if that would help, Mage-Lieutenant?"

Roslyn swallowed.

"Check with Mage-Captain Kulkarni for authorization before we go that far," she suggested gently, "but yes, Lieutenant Vida, that would help greatly."

The channel closed and she could feel herself wavering.

"Sir." Escarcega was there, inserting a well-muscled arm under Roslyn's shoulder to keep her upright. Roslyn noticed, somewhat distractedly, that the woman had very thick black hair that had been carefully tied into short braids over her head.

"Not yet," she told the Agent. "I need to talk to the Admiral."

She tried to stand and fell over onto Escarcega.

"I'll let her know and she'll meet us at sick bay," the Secret Service Agent said firmly. "Because that's where you're going, sir. *Now.*"

Escarcega was as good as her word, at least, and Mage-Admiral Alexander was in the sick bay when Roslyn arrived.

"What in the black tombs is so important you can't see a damned medic before telling me, Chambers?" Alexander demanded, gesturing for a medic to start checking over the Flag Lieutenant.

Roslyn shivered at the medic's cold, gloved hands. Escarcega was probably right, a part of her mind noted in a calmly rational tone. She was crashing from an adrenaline overload *and* in shock, and the fact that she'd killed a man with her magic was probably going to catch up to her pretty quickly.

She'd killed in battle before, with missiles, lasers and amplified magic, but it was something else to kill in person. To see the man's flesh crisp under her magic as he screamed.

"Chambers?" the Admiral repeated, and Roslyn tried to shake herself.

The medic's iron grip stopped that.

"Lieutenant, you need to rest," the young man—the *very attractive* young man, a distant part of Roslyn's brain noted—told her firmly.

"Admiral," she forced out. "Intel came through Menendez. She kept it under her thumb, no other copies. Don't think she was hostile, just... controlling.

"Her console was wrecked but I saw the dispatch."

"And someone tried damn hard to make sure no one did," Alexander agreed. "Tell me, Chambers—then get some damned rest."

"They moved the battle group from Legatus to Centurion. Brought a new group in so Legatus looked right, but moved *their* battleships to Centurion. Wanted to...wanted to..."

Roslyn knew enough about the Operation Bluebell plan that she was sure she could see how this made them vulnerable. But it wasn't coming.

"They wanted us to think nothing had changed and let us move in around Centurion before hitting us with a massive gunship strike," Alexander finished for her. "Damn, they knew our ops plan in detail...but they didn't count on us getting the intel."

The Mage-Admiral gripped her shoulder firmly.

"Go with Dr. Rostami, Lieutenant," she ordered.

Apparently, the attractive young man wasn't a medic. He was a doctor. She should probably have recognized the insignia.

"Yes, si..."

CHAPTER 25

DAMIEN'S REACTION to Nueva Bolivia, he supposed, was a sign that he was getting far too calm about his life. He ran through a mental checklist as the scanners updated.

Eight planets. One habitable, in the liquid-water zone. Two gas giants, useful sources for hydrogen and helium for the fusion plants that powered an UnArcana World. Two massive ice balls too far out to be useful for anything. Three rocky uninhabitable worlds and an asteroid belt, providing multiple easily accessible sources of minerals.

Then he realized that he'd reduced an entire *star system*, one of the most fundamental building blocks of the universe, to a list of resources, and shook his head at himself. Nueva Bolivia the star was a golden furnace, brighter and more intense than Sol, that created a wide liquid water band.

Sucre was still the only world in that liquid-water zone, and it was right in the middle of it, creating a world with as many contrasts and different climates as Earth itself. Sucre had jungles and ice plateaus and immense world-straddling oceans.

Even for a habitable world, it was surprisingly Earth-like. And like most Protectorate and now Republic worlds, it was going to stay that way. Most of the heavy industry was kept in orbit, massive space stations that took in raw materials and spat out the refined goods that fueled an interstellar economy.

Nueva Bolivia had always built gunships. He doubted that their production of the sublight warships had *decreased* under the new management, though his expectation of shipyard complexes were unmet.

That was odd in itself. Nueva Bolivia was one of the most industrialized UnArcana Worlds. With the Republic of Faith and Reason at war, he'd have expected to see military shipyards sprouting up like mushrooms.

Instead...nothing. The military reservations scattered here and there across the system were gunship yards and component factories, not shipyards.

"Okay, so I see gunships and missiles, and I *think* that's a production facility for your ridiculous heavy lasers," he said aloud on *Starlight's* bridge. "Why the hell aren't they building warships here?"

Captain Maata and her crew were silent for several long seconds.

"I never thought about it," she admitted eventually. "I guess the Republic is still keeping their FTL drives secret enough that they're only building them in Legatus."

"But not even hulls being built here," Damien challenged her. "Just components. Doesn't that seem weird?"

"If Legatus can build enough hulls to match their jump drive production, why not?" she asked. "Build the components here and elsewhere, ship everything to the Legatus System for assembly."

"That's one hell of a strategic vulnerability," he countered. "Why would the Republic embrace that?"

"To control the secret of our jump technology," Niska told him, the spy clearly having entered the bridge in the middle of the conversation. "I was present in some discussions where those exact points were made, Montgomery. The jump drives are built into the hulls, and the jump drives are made at Centurion, inside the reservation we didn't let Mages inside."

"So, all of the hulls are made there?" He shook his head.

"Which is why Centurion is now the most fortified planet in existence," Niska replied. "But yes, it's a vulnerability. One your Navy is probably going to try and take advantage of—and one the RIN is expecting an attack on."

He shook his head grimly.

"That's not a battle we can influence, Montgomery. Our task is here." He gestured at the system's fourth planet. "The records to tell us where that liner ended up will be on Sucre, in the system traffic-control archives if nowhere else."

"You can get us in?" Damien asked.

"Yes."

"Good, because there's a *carrier* in orbit, Niska, and she's not alone," Maata told them both. "Looks like a *Bravado*-class with a pair of *Andreas*-class escorts." She snorted at Damien's confusion. "Forty-megaton carrier, fifteen-megaton cruisers. It's not a full carrier group and it's the smaller ships, but it's more than enough to handle us."

Damien snorted.

"As we saw before, a handful of gunships is enough to handle us," he pointed out. "Let's play nice little merchant ship this time, shall we?"

"I've already applied for an orbital slot," Maata confirmed. "We're about nine hours out. We'll know in plenty of time if there's going to be a probl..."

"Captain?"

Maata was staring at her screen as a response came in, then tapped a command to toss it up on her screen.

"Merchant freighter *Starlight*, this is Captain Edward Thatch of the Republic Starship *Ancestor*," a tall dark-haired man greeted them. "Your orbital slot is denied. You will surrender immediately and stand by for my vessel to match courses with yours. Any resistance will be met with overwhelming force.

"I know who you are, Captain Mere Maata," he said calmly. "You are a deserter and a traitor to the Republic. If you do not immediately stand down and surrender on receipt of this message, I *will* destroy your ship."

One of the cruisers, presumably *Ancestor*, was already leaving orbit at five gravities. Two dozen gunships were falling in around her, their accelerations more variable as they matched the cruiser's velocity.

"Anybody know this Captain Thatch?" Damien asked quietly.

"Yeah," Maata said flatly. "He's my bloody ex-husband. He divorced me when he found out I was an Augment who moonlighted as a spy."

Being an Augment was *probably* something that should have been discussed before the wedding, Damien figured, but it wasn't his place to judge other people's relationships.

If he was *very* lucky, Grace would be content with the unclassified version of this particular adventure, after all, and would forgive him for once again risking himself in the line of fire.

Maybe.

"I'm guessing that doesn't cover *quite* everything, since most people aren't quite so willing to blow their ex-spouses to pieces," he noted.

"*Willing* has nothing to do with it," she said. "If he thinks he has to, he will. End of story. Man has an iron rod jammed up his ass." Maata glanced over at him. "It's not a quality without value, as I'm sure you can attest to yourself."

Damien was pretty sure she meant him.

"So, can we outrun our lovelorn friend over there?" he finally asked.

"I'm not sure," *Starlight*'s captain responded. "We've already flipped and are burning for the outer system, but..."

The main screen had the unfortunate answer to Damien's question. They'd already built up a velocity heading toward Sucre, and it would be hours yet before Liara Foster could jump them. They could match the cruiser for acceleration, but the gunships could probably outmaneuver them, and the RIN ship had the velocity advantage.

"We run. They pursue," Damien agreed. "And it's all down to when Captain Thatch decides to shoot."

The range was long—almost thirty light-seconds—but they were definitely inside *Ancestor*'s missile range.

The first missile launched a couple of minutes later, but no one on *Starlight*'s bridge took the weapon overly seriously.

"I have it dialed in with our turrets," Maata told Niska and Damien, "but I'm pretty sure that's a warning shot."

With almost nine million kilometers of range, the missile charged after them for several minutes before desultorily detonating its antimatter warhead a hundred thousand kilometers clear of the freighter.

The next message played immediately on the screen.

"*Starlight*, that is your only warning shot," Thatch said grimly. "You know I can hit you. You know I can blow you to hell." He paused. "My math says you're eighty minutes from space clear enough to jump.

"You have thirty to surrender or I will vaporize your ship. My orders leave me no choice."

He paused, his face softening from the harsh lines of the mask of duty.

"Please, Mere. Stand the hell down," he said quietly. "Don't make me do this."

The recording ended.

"Do you want to reply?" Damien asked.

"What's the point?" Maata replied. "We aren't going to haul over and surrender, and he is going to blow us up if we don't. So, options, people?"

"Liara is at least four hours from being ready to jump," he told them. "I can't jump us, for obvious reasons."

He could barely hold a damn glass. He was a *long* way from being able to inlay new silver runes into his scarred palms.

"What about your stealth ship?" Niska asked.

"She's here," Damien agreed. The plan had called for *Rhapsody in Purple* to come in much farther out than *Starlight* and hide in the asteroid belt. "Even if she managed to sneak into point-blank range again, however, her laser and missiles aren't going to do much to a cruiser.

"And she'd be ripped to shreds by the gunships even if she could."

"So, we're fucked," Maata said harshly. "Great. Always wanted to get vaporized by the man I thought was the love of my life. Seems to fit with my judgment."

"No," Damien corrected, studying the screen. He tapped a command on his wrist-comp and a new green icon appeared on the screen. Unlike *Starlight*'s crew, he *did* know roughly where *Rhapsody in Purple* was—or at least where she'd been thirty minutes earlier, when he received the last encrypted update pulse.

"*Starlight* is fucked," he continued. "We are only in trouble if we remain aboard the ship." He looked at Maata. "How many shuttles do you have?"

"Enough for everybody but not all of the gear," she admitted. "And I have no way to hide them."

"So long as we keep them *really* close together, I can take care of that," he said firmly. "Your ex just gave us a deadline. Let's see how much crap we can fit around ourselves on your shuttles, Captain Maata."

"And *Starlight*?" she demanded.

"She's a damn fine ship, Captain, but I don't think she'd want you to die with her," Damien told her. "But I think her computers are enough to keep her running until Thatch vaporizes her."

Maata looked torn between fury and tears, but she slowly nodded.

"Then we'd better get started."

CHAPTER 26

MAATA HAD understated how little space the shuttles would have left after cramming the crew aboard. These weren't designed to be personnel transports, after all. The shuttlecrafts' primary purpose was to haul the standard ten-thousand-cubic-meter cargo containers around.

They could also carry people, but by the time all of *Starlight*'s passengers were crammed aboard, there wasn't enough space for such niceties as food, let alone exosuit power armor.

Niska and Maata had tried anyway, which had left the interior of the spacecraft quite cramped.

Damien could barely tell. He was wearing a helmet that completely covered his head, filling his entire view with a virtual reality projection of the space outside the shuttle. He could see the other six shuttles drifting nearby, ejected from *Starlight* as carefully and sneakily as possible.

"The others aren't close enough, Captain," he murmured.

"If we get them any closer, this goes from unsafe to insane," she pointed out.

"Slave their controls, match velocities with minimum thrust while we have *Starlight* to hide behind," he ordered. "I can shield a bubble *maybe* five hundred meters across, so everyone needs to be inside that."

He heard her swallow.

"We'll do what we can," she promised.

As he watched, the shuttles slowly condensed. "Safe distance" between two ships running fusion engines was generally set at around the ten-kilometer line unless you were docking the ships.

They'd already had less than a kilometer's space between each shuttle, but Maata did as he asked. The shuttles got closer, each of them slotting into a spot two hundred meters away from the shuttle Damien was riding and surrendering control of their engines.

"And now."

His voice was soft, but he could feel power ripple through him. The three Runes of Power that remained to him warmed with the energy as he projected an illusion around his new charges. Light hit one side of the illusion...and emerged on the other side, unchanged.

There was no sign that six shuttles were inside that bubble.

"You're clear, Captain Maata," he announced. "Let's try and keep this nice and gentle for the moment. I'm not sure how much engine heat I can hide, but one gravity should be safe."

"All right. Everyone hold on."

He was pressed back into his seat by the acceleration. Ignoring that, he checked the rest of his charges. Each was matching the vector and acceleration exactly, six ships moving in a staggered formation with Damien's shuttle at the heart.

It was the closest he was going to get to flying again anytime soon. Even as the Hand of the Mage-King, he'd flown himself as much as possible. It had been a refuge, a safe zone where he was fully in control.

Now, as First Hand, he was no longer physically able to fly. The controls of a ship would have to be heavily modified to allow him to use them, and the cost in reaction time and flexibility could easily be dangerous.

So, Damien lost another refuge and let others fly him. Right now, however, the VR helmet allowed him to pretend he *was* the shuttle he was hiding.

Six ships and sixty people fled under the cover of his magic, and he really had no way to tell if *Ancestor* was fooled. In theory, his spell was impenetrable to their scanners, but the Republic had surprised them before.

"Breathe, my lord," Denis Romanov said quietly in his ear. "Everything is good, but we need you to hold that spell. So, *breathe*."

Damien chuckled and felt some of his stress leave his shoulders.

"Which of us is in charge again?" he asked.

"You," Romanov agreed cheerfully. "Right up until I need to keep you safe. Isn't that how being a bodyguard works?"

The first few minutes were the scariest. For about ten minutes, they were still close enough to *Starlight* that they could be in trouble if Thatch opened fire.

Thankfully, they were almost a full light-second away from the freighter when the deadline ran out. Edward Thatch might not have *wanted* to shoot down his ex-wife, but he certainly didn't hesitate once his time limit was hit.

An *Andreas*-class cruiser carried one hundred missile launchers. Damien probably would only have fired a third of them at most, but he supposed they had an update on the fate of the gunships that had tangled with *Starlight* in Arsenault.

Thatch launched a full salvo. A hundred missiles blazed into space, closing the distance at ten thousand gravities.

Starlight was running on autopilot, but Maata had turned on the automated defense protocols. RFLAM turrets came to life under computer control as the missiles charged in. Lasers swept space, catching *some* missiles.

Three. Maybe four. Possibly even five—it was impossible to tell, given the scale of the swarm.

Even five would have been a miracle for the computers, but it wouldn't have changed anything. Over ninety one-gigaton antimatter warheads detonated as one, and *Starlight* ceased to exist.

"Stealth spell is holding," he murmured. "We're a hole in space and they don't see us."

"And the bastard didn't leave enough behind for it to be worth investigating," Maata said. "God damn it. I always knew duty came first for him, even more than for me, but still!"

"You don't expect to see your ex vaporize a ship you're presumably standing on," Niska agreed. "On the other hand, I find it interesting that he vaporized *Starlight* quite so thoroughly."

"What?" Maata demanded.

"Like you said, there isn't enough left for it to be worth investigating, and he's already slowing down to return to orbit," the spy told her. "By utterly vaporizing *Starlight* and turning back, he's making our sneaking away significantly easier."

"You think he saw us get out?" she snapped.

"I doubt it," Damien interjected. "But he *might* have seen something that was enough to make him suspicious...and not enough that he had to do anything about it."

"So, you're saying he overkilled on killing me in case I had escaped, so I could keep escaping?" Maata asked. She didn't sound convinced.

To be fair, neither was Damien.

"I'm saying it's possible," he conceded. "You know the man better than any of us, apparently. All I can say is that it looks like we're clear. Give *Ancestor* an hour or so to move further away, and I'll ping LaMonte for a rendezvous point.

"I hate to lose a good ship, Captain Maata, but *Starlight* served us well. She got us clear."

Damien wasn't really one to anthropomorphize ships, but if ships *did* have souls...well, *Starlight* had to be happy her crew were safe.

Damien certainly was.

"What happens now that we don't have Niska's accesses to get us on-planet?" Romanov asked.

"We'll have to take a look at what we've got in terms of fake shuttle beacons aboard *Rhapsody*," Damien said. "We can get her pretty close in, but her usual courier guise isn't going to cut it here. She has to stay invisible—but we should be able to insert a couple of shuttles into the regular traffic without drawing too much attention."

"Get me on the ground and I still have resources," Niska promised. "If we're burned, there's only so much I can do from orbit. I have some electronic accesses they might not have IDed, but at this point...well, at this point, we're better to go for an entirely different kind of authority and access."

Damien was pretty sure he followed, and he chuckled.

"We're at 'beg friends for help,' aren't we?"

After six hours of not being able to move, Damien wasn't sure he ever would be able to stretch his arms again. The strain of sustaining the stealth spell was starting to get to him as well. He'd been lowering the intensity of it as they got farther and farther away from the RIN, but his skin was now itching from the gentle heat of his Runes of Power.

"I've got something on the scanners," Maata reported. "We're at the rendezvous point and..."

The main thing that separated Damien from other Mages was that, as a Rune Wright, he could *feel* magic. He felt the amplified stealth spell being run by *Rhapsody in Purple*'s mages sweep over his own shield and finally dropped the illusion with a sigh.

"We are inside Captain LaMonte's protective envelope," he told the Captain. "You should be able to see her now."

"We've got her on the screens," Maata confirmed. "We've got six shuttles to dock; this could take a while."

"I know." Damien sighed. "The good news to all of this is that I at least get to see my cat."

"You have a cat, Montgomery?" Niska asked.

"My physiotherapist suggested it where the Princess of Mars could hear," he replied. "Never let a sixteen-year-old know there's an excuse to get a kitten; trust me. Persephone is the finest princess-approved rescue cat in the Protectorate, but she was rather foisted on me originally!"

The Augment laughed.

"That's...not the image I would expect of the terrifying First Hand of Mars," he pointed out.

"Major, when was the last time *you* argued with a friend's teenage daughter?" Damien asked. "Believe me, it's not a game you can win. *Especially* not when kittens are involved."

"I haven't had a home anywhere for long enough for anyone to pressure me to get a cat," the Augment spy replied. "The thought has been tempting, though. I like cats."

"I didn't understand why anyone would," Damien said. "Until the first time a furball jumped up on my lap and informed me that it was physical therapy time." He grinned. "By which, of course, she meant time to pet her."

The first shuttle was docking as they spoke. Damien hadn't taken the VR helmet off and wasn't planning to, either.

He was feeling crowded enough *without* being able to see how cramped the actual confines of the shuttle were.

Damien was honestly surprised to find himself wrapped in LaMonte's tight embrace moments after he exited the shuttle. Even he could tell it was platonic, but her fear was real.

"You need to stop doing this shit," she whispered in his ear.

"We were never in danger," he reassured her. He returned the hug and stepped back, surveying the crowded shuttle bay. "We were the last shuttle. Everything is aboard?"

"I don't have a damn clue where we're putting everyone or the crap, but everything's aboard," she confirmed. "If we weren't intended to carry more troops than we currently are, we'd be in serious trouble. As it is, everyone is going to be doubling up in staterooms and I think my armory is about to start resembling a trash heap."

"Better than losing the gear that the Augments need," Damien said grimly. "Do we even *have* extra gear for the BCR troops?"

"No." LaMonte shook her head as she guided him and Romanov out of the shuttle. She glanced at the Marine. "We've got a few exosuits for your Marines, but most of *our* battle suits are designed to interface with

BCR implants—and my commandos apparently use a different data interface standard than the Augments."

"Of course they do." Damien shook his head. Humanity had taken two centuries to standardize *power* connections. Data interface ports were still...idiosyncratic. Add different software protocols to go with the different hardware, and he wasn't surprised the Augments couldn't use BCR armor.

"You realize it's going to take Niska less than five minutes to realize I have an entire platoon of cyborgs aboard, right?" she asked. "I don't know how much the Republic knows about the Bionic Combat Regiment."

"I would honestly assume that the Republic is fully aware of anything we were doing prior to the Secession," Damien admitted.

They reached a door and LaMonte opened it, leading the way into a spartan stateroom. The room appeared to be unoccupied...until Persephone leapt from the couch to Damien's shoulder.

"You're the only one of our passengers getting a private room," LaMonte told him. "And you only get it because half of *Rhapsody*'s senior officers sleep in the same bed. We were keeping Persephone in our quarters, but I figured she'd want to see you."

Damien carefully supported the kitten—cat now, he supposed, at over a year old. His hands hurt a bit, but he was getting better.

"True." He shook his head. "I don't *like* bringing Niska and Maata aboard a *Rhapsody*," he conceded to LaMonte's earlier point. "But I prefer it to getting everyone killed."

"That's fair. If they know everything, though... Plowshare? Weyland?"

Damien winced.

"Part of the reason Plowshare exists is to help hide Weyland," he admitted.

Project Plowshare had been the black construction program, funded under the table by loyal Core Worlds, to build a new fleet for Mars. Unfortunately, the only ships Plowshare had been going to complete soon were destroyers...and Damien himself had signed off on the recommendation that no new *Lancer*-class destroyers be completed.

Weyland, though...

"We buried Weyland deep. Not even all of the Hands were cleared for Project Weyland," he told LaMonte. "Though, to be honest, I didn't think *you* were cleared for Weyland."

She grinned at him and he swallowed a curse.

"I'm not. But I am cleared for Plowshare and had heard the name bandied about in that context. So, when high muckety-muck people are talking about reinforcements, they're talking about Weyland, huh?"

"Captain LaMonte, you of all people should know better than to ask questions I cannot answer," Damien told her, letting his voice drop into the cold register of "Angry Hand."

The effect was probably somewhat undermined by the small black cat purring on his shoulder, but from the way LaMonte recoiled, it was still effective.

The room was silent for several long seconds before he sighed.

"I am privy to some of the greatest secrets of our Protectorate," he reminded her quietly. "Weyland may be our only hope of winning this damn war. I know Alexander has a plan to destabilize the Republic war effort, but it's a long shot at best.

"I can't tell you what Weyland is, beyond *hope*."

"Fair enough," she conceded, recovering from the shock of seeing Damien in full Hand mode with surprising aplomb.

"Leaving the war to Her Highness, what do we do now?" she asked.

"We answer the damn question we came here for," he replied. "Can you get a shuttle into Sucre orbit?"

"Not directly, but there's enough in-system traffic floating around, I think I can get you on a course to the planet that no one will question," she said after a moment's thought. "Still need some answers from the planet, huh?"

"A ship entered this system with two hundred teenaged Mages aboard," he confirmed. "Someone on Sucre knows where those kids went. We're going to find out."

"What happens when we find those kids, Damien?" LaMonte asked. "I'm not a Mage, but...more people died at Ardennes than that. Two hundred kids...is a drop in the grand scheme of things already."

"I know. And yet...if the Republic shot two hundred kids and left them in a mass grave, that's an atrocity that can't be forgotten in silence." He shook his head. "But worst of all, Kelly, I can't see Bryan Ricket having turned on the Republic for *merely* the mass murder of children.

"I think we're following the right thread, but I am *terrified* of what we're going to find at the end," he admitted. "I don't think we're going to find mass graves...and having stood on the slopes of Olympus Mons and looked out on the nameless graves of the children sacrificed to create the human Mage, I have to wonder—I have to *fear*—how far short of the reality my imagination has fallen."

CHAPTER 27

"STAND BY FOR JUMP."

The calm words from *Righteous Shield of Valor*'s bridge echoed across the battleship's flag deck.

Roslyn's seat was barely a meter from Alexander's, putting the Flag Lieutenant in a position to watch over the Admiral's shoulder as Alexander controlled the main display. Like everyone else on the battleship's bridge, Roslyn was strapped in—but she was ready to unstrap and leap into action to get anything Alexander needed.

Her role in battle was…limited. This was the part of the job where she shut up and learned, more than anything else.

"Remember, Chambers, if you see something strange, tell me," Alexander told her quietly, overriding her assumptions even as she thought them. "Everyone else in the fleet has spent years in the structure and training of the RMN. You have that training, but you're not trapped in it the way I know I can be."

The Admiral reached out and squeezed Roslyn's shoulder. She was barely able to reach, but the gesture sent a surge of confidence and determination through the young woman.

"You know this enemy, Mage-Lieutenant. Don't hesitate to tell me if you think they're playing games with us."

"They did that when they moved their ships and hoped we wouldn't notice," Roslyn replied.

"They tried damn hard and almost killed a few people to pull that off," Alexander agreed. "*You* made sure we knew about it."

Roslyn didn't challenge the Mage-Admiral out loud—one didn't argue with Admirals, let alone Princesses of Mars—but she was well aware that she'd only found the attempt to neutralize their intelligence because Alexander had sent her to check in on Menendez.

The intelligence officer was still unconscious, the aftereffects of a multi-day round of the drugs she'd been on still ravaging her body. The security she'd put on her console and her intelligence had prevented the Augment assassin—who'd apparently been working as a missile tech, requiring Engineering to go over every missile the man had touched—from simply deleting the intelligence.

That same security had almost caused them to *lose* that same intelligence. Roslyn suspected, though she hadn't asked, that most Admirals didn't have the override codes that Alexander had given her. Her suspicion was that those were a *Royal* prerogative.

"All ships report at battle stations and ready for jump."

"Chambers, get me a channel to the ship captains," the Admiral ordered.

Roslyn had the channel waiting to turn on at Alexander's command, and nodded swiftly to the Admiral.

"Everyone," Alexander greeted her COs. "You know the plan. You know the orders. Battleships, lead the way. Engage!"

Righteous Shield of Valor was only one of the six battleships in Second Fleet, and those six ships represented the greatest concentration of force at Admiral Alexander's command. She'd augmented them with her ten *Honorific*-class battlecruisers, the next-heaviest units of her fleet, and then that entire sixteen-ship-strong task force was the spearhead of the strike.

Taking a course that strained the Mages jumping the ships to their limits, that task force appeared forty light-seconds, twelve million kilometers, from the planet of Legatus itself.

They were launching missiles already. The Martian ships were *inside* their active missile range of the defenses—and orbital platforms couldn't dodge.

When a carrier battle group centered on two heavy carriers had been positioned in Legatus orbit, engaging the defenses would have been dangerous at best and suicide at worst for Second Fleet. But the RIN had shifted those ships to Centurion, and the replacement battle group was much lighter.

Two heavy carriers remained in orbit along with sixteen cruisers, but there were no battleships to support them now...and those carriers weren't moving right now either.

"RIN has picked us up. Missiles are on their radar," Kulkarni reported grimly. Forty light-seconds meant they'd had forty seconds to act before the Republican ships detected them. Now it was a test of how rapidly the RIN crews could get to their stations.

They still had six minutes, and Roslyn would have been shocked if the crews weren't at their positions by the time the missiles reached them.

There was a difference, though, between *at their stations* and *ready*, Roslyn suspected. *Righteous Shield* trembled underneath her as a third salvo of missiles blasted out.

"Third salvo away, fourth is loading," Kulkarni reported. "No gunships deployed, no return fire."

"Maintain the plan," Alexander said calmly. "No changes."

Protectorate warship design was predicated on pursuit. The vast majority of the battleships' and battlecruisers' weapons pointed forward, which meant that they couldn't engage and withdraw at the same time.

None of the RMN ships were accelerating. They hung in space as their launchers spoke again and again.

Seven salvos were in space by the time the RIN finally returned fire.

"Three minutes, thirty-two seconds," Kulkarni reported. "That's after they saw us." She shook her head. "That's not bad. Not at all."

The defenses might have been reduced to augment Centurion and attempt to surprise Second Fleet, but there were still twenty fortresses, sixteen cruisers and two carriers in orbit. Only the first handfuls of gunships were getting into space, but the capital ships and fortresses alone mustered almost five thousand missile launchers.

"Still almost seven minutes to impact," Alexander said calmly. "Adjust the plan, Mage-Captain Kulkarni. Let's give ourselves ninety seconds, just to be sure."

"Yes, sir."

More salvos lit up space as the defenders got more and more gunships into play. Thousands of missiles might be coming out at the battleship formation, but the RMN had already flung thousands of their own.

The first round of Martian missiles landed as Roslyn watched. The Republic crews were as ready as they could be to deal with the surprise attack, but there were almost three thousand missiles in the salvo, and they targeted only two of the defensive platforms.

More than enough missiles made it through to vaporize the two twenty-megaton fortresses. The next salvo went for a new pair, which shared the same fate. One of the stations targeted by the third salvo survived, but the scan codes suggested it was crippled.

More salvos crashed home as the Martian ships continued to fling fire into space and the defenders returned fire in overwhelming numbers.

"Enemy salvos at one hundred twenty seconds."

"Ship's Mages are ready?" Alexander asked.

"Yes, sir."

"Damage assessment?"

"We've destroyed six platforms and badly damaged two more," Kulkarni said. "The remaining salvos *will* be less effective."

"We shall see," Alexander replied. "We're done here, Mage-Captain. Pass the order. All ships to jump to Rendezvous Point Alpha."

Seconds later, sixteen Royal Martian Navy warships vanished. Tens of thousands of missiles would find only empty space and memories when they arrived.

Second Fleet had brutalized Legatus's defenses without taking a single loss of their own.

It was a solid beginning, but Roslyn was looking at the records of what had *survived* the strike too. Despite the damage they'd inflicted, there were *still* enough ships and fortification in Legatus orbit to stand off the entire fleet.

They wouldn't manage this kind of hit-and-run again...but the Siege of Legatus had begun.

CHAPTER 28

RENDEZVOUS POINT ALPHA was closer to Centurion than to Legatus—and it was where the rest of Second Fleet had jumped to when the strike force had gone for the homeworld. Their mission had been less dangerous, if no less important.

Roslyn started cataloging their successes and mission reports as soon as *Righteous Shield* emerged from jump. A dozen in-system freighters had already been corralled into place under the guns of the destroyers, their vectors converging on a zero point a long way from anything.

Shuttles flickered between the civilian ships as Marines took control of them and concentrated crews onto the vessels picked as prison ships. Most of the ships would be destroyed, but the Royal Martian Navy wasn't going to kill civilians.

The mission reports were brute-force at this point, computer-generated summaries of less than an hour of rapid movement and engagement. The cruisers had held down the fort at Alpha while the destroyers had dashed out at fifteen gravities.

Quite sensibly, the Republic had been guarding the transfer orbit between Centurion and Legatus. Unfortunately, they'd done so with squadrons of ten gunships apiece—enough to take down a single raiding destroyer, but not enough to deal with the entire fleet.

Two of those squadrons were gone. Five more were still within the fleet's operating radius, and the destroyers were heading their way. One destroyer against ten gunships was an even fight until the gunships ran out of missiles.

Four destroyers against ten gunships was a massacre.

"Reports show twenty gunships destroyed, fourteen vessels captured and six military freighters destroyed after refusing to surrender," Kulkarni reported, her numbers matching Roslyn's.

"There are fifty more gunships in escort position along the main traffic route between Centurion and Legatus," Roslyn added. "They will be engaged over the next three hours."

She continued to run through the data in front of her, then grinned coldly as she picked out the holy grail.

"I also have six twenty-megaton hulls heading toward Legatus, still seventy hours from their destination," she pointed out, highlighting them on the screen. "Intel says they're probably already fitted out with jump drives but that their guns will be installed at Legatus."

"Three days out, huh?" Alexander replied. "Kulkarni—pass that information to Mage-Admiral Medici. He's to take his cruisers and wreck those hulls. If he believes he can safely capture them, he is to do so, but the priority is that those hulls do *not* reach the fitting-out yards at Legatus."

"Yes, sir."

A minute or so later, eight cruisers disappeared as Admiral Medici set off to demonstrate just how this siege was going to work.

"What about Centurion?" Alexander finally asked. "We know they moved the battle group over there. How heavily reinforced are they?"

Kulkarni shrugged.

"Fixed defenses haven't changed. Four major nodes, each with ten fortresses. Eight high-orbit fortresses for missile defense. It looks like their mobile forces are primarily at the antimatter harvesting center.

"Two heavy carriers, nine battleships, twenty cruisers." She shook her head. "Almost a quarter-billion tons of warships. We could probably take them, but..."

"But they've another few hundred million tons of fortresses," Alexander agreed. "We'll clean up the traffic lanes and watch for new activity. For now, we hold position."

"They'll try to dislodge us, sir," the operations officer pointed out.

"That's the plan," Alexander agreed as Roslyn smiled coldly. "We can fight their forces in detail—and if they're willing to feed them to us like that, I will happily tear them to pieces.

"So, let's see just how clever our friends actually are."

Two hours later, it was clear that the RIN understood the problem. The mobile forces had moved out *toward* Second Fleet, but when they flipped to decelerate, it became clear they weren't trying to challenge the RMN fleet.

"Looks like they're settling in around the nearest of the cardinal forts," Kulkarni reported. "Not even going to try and save the ships Medici is jumping."

"They'll blow the hulls before we can take them," Roslyn said quietly. "That's what they've done every time. They *really* don't want us getting a look at the jump drive."

"Would you?" the ops officer asked. "Right now, we have a magical solution and they have a technological solution. They're not going to be able to acquire any Mages to jump their ships, but there's nothing stopping *us* from installing their jump drive on ours.

"We already have better strategic and tactical mobility than they do. Adding their drive on top of our Jump Mages would only make that worse."

"If they didn't have FTL coms, they'd be screwed," Alexander agreed. "No, you're right, Chambers. They'll destroy anything with a jump drive before we can take it. They've proven willing to kill their own people to make sure of that."

"Fanatics," Kulkarni said, half under her breath.

"Yes. We always knew Legatus had them. It seems the Republic is drawing them from all across its territory."

"We have gunship launches," Roslyn reported, not quite interrupting the Admiral as new icons speckled her screens. "Looks like the cardinal stations farthest from us are launching half of their parasite craft."

"Interesting," Mage-Admiral Alexander said softly. "Two thousand ships?"

"Yes, sir."

"The yard stations are doing a partial launch as well," Kulkarni noted. "Looks like another thousand ships from there. Vector has them all arriving at the station closest to us around the same time."

"Let me know if the other cardinals launch gunships," the Admiral ordered. "What do you think they're doing?"

"I see a few possibilities," the ops officer replied. "Most likely, they're reinforcing the forces closest to us. An extra three or four thousand gunships would stiffen their missile defenses a lot."

Roslyn shook her head as she studied the vectors. That made sense, yes, but it didn't feel right.

"Chambers?"

Admiral Alexander had clearly seen her gesture.

"They're keeping their velocities low and coming in at an angle where gunships from all of the fortresses will be able to converge," Roslyn said slowly. "That convergence point isn't a zero-velocity rendezvous with the nearest cardinal. The convergence point is about a million kilometers *past* the cardinal station at almost three hundred KPS.

"A million kilometers closer to us on an attack vector," she clarified. "They're far more willing to deploy their gunships independently and expendably than we keep expecting. My guess is that they'll hold the carrier gunships back and send half of the fortress gunships right at us.

"They're hoping to get most of them back, but they're testing to see how much damage they can do with a pure gunship strike." She shook her head. "They're also testing if we're actually willing to take a punch. We jumped away from the missiles at Legatus and they know that.

"They also know that this siege is meaningless if they can just chase us away anytime they want to send ships out."

Both of her superiors looked at the massive holographic display at the heart of *Righteous Shield of Valor*'s flag deck.

"She's not wrong, sir," Kulkarni said slowly. "They could still adjust their course for a zero-velocity rendezvous with the existing fleet, but I think Mage-Lieutenant Chambers is correct. In about ten hours, we're going to be looking down the launchers of about five thousand gun-ships."

Alexander studied the display and then nodded herself.

"Worst-case scenario, I look paranoid," she said aloud. "The fleet is to go to one-quarter watches for the next eight hours. Every ship is to stand down to status three for at least six hours and make sure their alpha watches get some rest.

"We'll prepare for heavy fire in ten hours." She smiled. "And that 'get some rest' applies to you lot, too. Send the orders, call your replacements and sack out.

"That is *also* an order."

CHAPTER 29

NINE HOURS LATER, Roslyn was back on the bridge with the rest of Mage-Admiral Alexander's core staff, watching as the scenario they'd predicted unfolded in front of them.

Space battle lent itself to that. Even the Republic gunships were limited to eight or so gravities at best, which meant courses were built up over hours or days. The gunships from the cardinal station closest to them had launched just over an hour before, accelerating at that full eight gravities for the entire time.

Now all of the various gunship forces had converged at the same point and the same velocity, a masterpiece of maneuvering that would have been far more impressive if it wasn't assembling almost *thirty thousand* missile launchers to come at Roslyn and her companions.

She wouldn't have turned down a few thousand gunships of her own. The *Aegis*-class destroyers would, in theory, make up some of that difference when they became available. The new destroyer class was primarily a defensive ship, trading half of the *Lancer* class's offensive armament for over three times as many anti-missile turrets.

The new cruiser and battleship designs being considered were planning to squeeze in more RFLAM turrets anywhere they could fit. The current round of construction was *Honorific-* and *Peace-* class ships, though. Those were the warships they'd fight this war with unless it lasted far longer than anyone hoped.

Right now, however, the entirety of Second Fleet mustered forty-nine hundred launchers and six thousand anti-missile turrets.

That was less than one missile launcher per gunship coming their way, and the gunships had over twice as many RFLAM turrets as the Martian ships.

Worst of all, the Excalibur V missiles in the Republic's magazines outranged the Martian fleet's missiles by a lot—almost two million kilometers at this closing geometry.

"They're never going to enter our range," Kulkarni said quietly. "They chose their velocity carefully. They'll launch their missiles and flip. Their zero-vee point will be almost four hundred thousand kilometers out of our range."

"So, we get to face ninety thousand missiles and just, what, smile and take it?" Roslyn asked. That was...terrifying.

"We *need* to deplete their gunship numbers," Alexander replied. "Amplifiers and missiles in defensive mode should get us through this attack, but they've got the ships to do this again even if we wipe this force out.

"We can't let them get away untouched."

"Then we have to pursue," the ops officer said quietly. "If we bring the fleet forward at fifteen gravities, they'll get into range faster, but they won't be able to evade our range."

"They've only got three missiles, Kulkarni," the Admiral said grimly. "So long as we stay out of range of the defensive platforms, I will chase them to the end of the stars. Pass the orders."

The timers on the main display shifted as Second Fleet's engines came to life. When Second Fleet had been staying basically in place, engaging only in defensive maneuvers, the RIN gunship strike would have reached their weapons range in just over thirty minutes.

Now that timer was starting at seventeen minutes and counting down. A second timer had joined it—this one counting down from over an hour. When that one ran out, Second Fleet would finally range on the gunships.

As Roslyn was studying the big holodisplay, more icons and circles drew themselves in. Weapons range for Second Fleet and the gunships were joined by a bright crimson threat sphere drawn around the cardinal station and the fleet gathered around it.

"We have weapons to spend," Alexander said quietly. "They don't. As soon as they open fire, the fleet will engage with extreme-range missiles."

"They'll be ballistic by the time they reach the gunships," Kulkarni objected. "We'll be throwing away missiles."

"We have them to spend," the Mage-Admiral repeated. "More importantly, there are *five thousand* targets out there. Relatively lightly armored targets, at that. We only need to get a warhead within a few hundred meters of a gunship to take it down.

"Proximity kills are the name of the game, Mage-Captain. We can't guarantee hits through their defenses, so let's swarm them with weapons they can't even *see.*"

"Yes, sir."

Kulkarni started to run numbers and feed them to the rest of the fleet. Roslyn mirrored the operations officer's screen, virtually watching over Kulkarni's shoulder as the attack patterns took shape.

She didn't have any more confidence in a swarm of ballistic missiles than Kulkarni did, but they could easily send twenty salvos of missiles at the gunships while closing and have half of their magazines left.

And if the Republic thought they could run Second Fleet out of ammunition, they'd have some ugly surprises waiting for them. Dozens of freighters packed full of munitions were hidden in the deep dark a lightyear from Legatus, waiting for a courier to summon them forward to rearm the Martian fleet.

A siege would take a long time. They were going to run through their magazines a *lot,* and Alexander had made sure they had the supplies to do it.

Right now, however, they needed to prove that the Republic couldn't break the siege with their current resources.

"We need better damned missiles," Alexander muttered, her voice quiet enough that only Roslyn could hear her. "They've been promising us an improved Phoenix since the penny dropped, but I needed a million of them two weeks ago."

Roslyn could only nod. Second Fleet's need to stay in position to prevent traffic leaving Centurion meant that the enemy would always get to choose the velocity of the engagement. That meant they had the chance to set up fights where the Protectorate fleet wouldn't range on them without taking risks.

Even if the Navy's suppliers had finally come up with a schematic for a Phoenix IX, they definitely hadn't produced enough of them to fill Second Fleet's supply train.

"Enemy range in sixty seconds; standing by for defensive fire," Kulkarni reported. "We'll launch ten salvos to counter theirs, then twenty ballistic salvos." She paused. "We're only going to get two fully powered salvos when we reach range. We're going to have to flip immediately after launching the second and go to full power away from the enemy."

"They *will* be able to bring warships out after us," the operations officer warned, "but we'll avoid missile range of the station."

"We'll deal with that then," the Admiral said grimly. "For now..." She studied the holodisplay and grimaced.

"For what we are about to receive, may the Lord make us truly thankful."

At some point, Roslyn was going to have to research that silly prayer.

Five thousand gunships launched thirty thousand missiles in a salvo. They only carried three missiles per launcher, leaving their impact on a battle immense but short-term. Once all three salvos were launched, the Republican ships flipped in space and began accelerating toward the cardinal fortress.

They were accelerating at five gravities, though. Second Fleet was accelerating at fifteen, and the velocity was with Mage-Admiral Alexander's force.

Moments after the light showing the launch of the first missiles reached the fleet, Roslyn felt *Righteous Shield of Valor* shiver underneath her as the big warship's missile launchers spoke. Again and again the battleship fired, until ten full salvos of missiles were in space.

The RMN's answer to having ninety thousand missiles coming toward them was to put fifty thousand missiles in their path. The orgy of mutual destruction started disturbingly quickly, with massive explosions of antimatter lighting up the stars. The Republic's heavier warheads only added to the usual gunsmoke effect of the radiation and debris of the explosions, making it harder and harder for the gunships to guide their own weapons.

The Protectorate forces were the target of the incoming fire, which meant that the missile swarm left the radiation fields of the cataclysmic intercept behind as they continued toward the Martian ships.

RIN missiles were smart enough for this environment, better designed for true war than the RMN weapons were. The Republic, Roslyn was grimly aware, had been expecting to fight a war with the Protectorate for longer than it had existed and had studied every RMN action to date.

The Protectorate had specialized its lighter ships for piracy pursuit and then unconsciously scaled many of the same concepts up when they built bigger ships. Neither side, though, had dedicated counter-missiles, something that Roslyn forced herself to think about intellectually as the waves of missiles crashed toward her.

Using full-size missiles with regular warheads meant they could get proximity kills and create the radioactive gunsmoke effect, but the weapons weren't really designed for this purpose. A dedicated weapon with a smaller warhead, less flight time and potentially even less acceleration but more maneuverability...she could see the value.

Right now, they had what they had. Their missiles suicided against the Republic's and the entire first gunship salvo vanished before it reached the inner defensive perimeter.

The second was *almost* obliterated. Only a few thousand missiles reached the defensive perimeters, and twice as many RFLAM turrets came to life to engage them.

A handful of missiles made it through, vanishing as the battleship *Thunderer*'s Mage-Captain reached out with her amplifier to defend her ship.

"Drop the escorts back," Mage-Admiral Alexander said quietly. "Let's get the battleships in front. If we're going to take a hit, let's take it where we can."

The formation adjustment took mere seconds, the battleships continuing to accelerate at fifteen gravities while the rest of the fleet dropped to thirteen for a moment.

A lot more of the third salvo was going to make it through. The last of their defensive salvos was gone and there was no time to launch any more. Over ten thousand missiles hit the laser and amplifier perimeter at over an eighth of lightspeed.

At the tactical console, Roslyn would have focused on the missiles heading directly toward her own ship. On the flag deck of the entire fleet, she had no easy basis to filter down the conflict and found herself almost losing track in the chaos.

Thousands of missiles died. Second Fleet had over seventy amplifiers and almost six thousand RFLAM turrets, and their Mages and gunners alike had been trained to a razor edge over the last few months.

Hundreds of missiles made it through, flinging themselves at the battleships in the front line. Last-ditch sweeps by the individual ships' lasers claimed dozens, but missiles began to strike home.

A two-gigaton warhead didn't need to make contact, but it needed to get close. Those last few seconds allowed for desperate maneuvers and magical illusions that could fool even the computers aboard RIN missiles.

Hammerblows hit *Righteous Shield,* and Roslyn inhaled sharply, half-expecting a bright flash of light and nothing.

When the impacts faded, they were still there.

"Report," Alexander said flatly.

"Every battleship took at least two hits," Kulkarni said swiftly. "*Shield* took four, but none were direct. *Pax Marcianus* took two direct hits, but..."

"But?" the Admiral demanded.

Roslyn was pulling up the status on the *Peace*-class battleship and swallowed a silent curse.

"Her armor held, sir," Kulkarni reported. "She's down three launchers. That's...it."

"Apparently, we did something right with these battleships," Alexander said brightly. "The gunships are done?"

"They've shot their bolt and are running for home. We're in pursuit." Kulkarni shook her head. "We're still almost forty minutes to our weapons range."

"Engage with ballistic phase as previously indicated," the Admiral ordered.

"We're going to waste a *lot* of missiles," Kulkarni warned.

"We have them to spend, and they're more easily replaced than those gunships. Use them."

The problem with every plan was that the lighter warships only carried fifteen missiles for each of their launchers. This time, however, the RMN had a solution. Several munitions ships had jumped into Point Alpha with Second Fleet, and they'd left behind hundreds of containers of missiles.

Dozens of those containers had been towed to the current fight by the cruisers. As the first wave of ballistic salvos began to spew forward, those containers were released from their tows and destroyers swept in to scoop them up.

Five ballistic salvos emptied the escorts' magazines and then the Fleet paused, waiting for five minutes as the destroyers and cruisers rearmed.

Then the fire resumed, more and more missiles flashing into space in a cascade that Roslyn knew was going to be almost useless.

"It's a mind game, Mage-Lieutenant," Alexander told her, the Admiral's voice quiet enough that no one else could hear them. "We won't score many hits with these, but we'll score some. And we'll remind the Republic that while Legatus may be the most industrialized Core World, we have *twelve* Core Worlds to their one.

"They can't out-produce us. We can afford to spend missiles like this for limited kills."

Roslyn considered the number of missiles aboard Second Fleet and their logistics train.

"Not...really, sir," she pointed out. "We'll have shot off fifteen percent of our total munitions load by the time we pull back from the cardinal station. We can't keep doing that."

"Agreed," Alexander conceded. "I know that. You know that. The Republic? They *don't* know that."

The gunships were out of missiles, and there was no way they would bring the fleet to laser range without a miracle. If the warships came out, Second Fleet would pull back, but Roslyn didn't expect the Republic to risk warships to save the parasite fighters.

Republican doctrine ranked the jump ships far above any number of gunships. They'd stand by and watch Second Fleet shatter their fleeing brethren.

It was really only a question of how many gunships would die before Second Fleet had to let them go.

CHAPTER 30

THE ABSENCE of ten people, multiple exosuits and several dozen crates of supplies left *Starlight's* former shuttle feeling almost spacious to Damien as their pilot inserted them into the regular traffic.

"Bringing the beacon online now," Kelzin reported, looking back over his shoulder at Damien. *Rhapsody's* First Pilot had insisted that no one else was flying the Hand into this stunt.

"We're flagging as a personnel courier for one of the companies that does high-speed transits from the outer system to Sucre," he continued. "According to MISS's files, the company intentionally rotates their own beacons to cover the fact that they're smuggling on the side."

"What are they smuggling between planets in the same system?" Niska asked.

"Depends on who's paying, I imagine," O'Malley said grimly before Kelzin could respond. "But most likely people."

"People?" Damien said.

"Most of the metal extraction in the system is either on Camibol or based there, since that rock is closest to the belt," the Augment explained. "Camibol is a frozen hellscape with a hyperactive tectonic system. Your options on the planet are freeze on the surface or burn in the mines."

She shook her head.

"It's not a popular place to work, so Camibol uses a lot of long-term indentures to keep people there. They're not *quite* slaves, but they can't leave until their ten- or twenty-year terms are up."

"That's illegal," Niska said coldly. "...Isn't it?"

"In Legatus," O'Malley replied sadly. "Republic law was carefully written to allow the loophole, so Nueva Bolivia can continue their century-old practice of transforming debt and prison sentences into indentured-service terms."

"So, people run," Damien concluded with a glance over at Romanov. His bodyguard and the two Augments were the only people accompanying him to the surface. Mike Kelzin was flying them down, but would stay with the shuttle as their emergency backup. There wasn't much he'd be able to do on a relatively advanced MidWorld like Sucre, but a shuttle with concealed weapons was nothing to sneer at.

"They run and pay people to smuggle them to Sucre, where they try and grab a ship to anywhere else," O'Malley confirmed. She grimaced. "I was too young to understand what was happening to my family when my dad got sent out to pay off his debts.

"Wasn't much more understanding when he suddenly came home and we all shuffled onto a ship for Legatus." The Augment shook her head. "A lot of star systems have their dark sides that they try not to think about. Nueva Bolivia's is just darker and uglier than most."

"And helps fuel the industry that's supporting the Republic war machine," Damien agreed. "What a mess. Is that cover at least going to get us onto the planet?"

"I don't know much about that background," Kelzin admitted. "Our files do note that they smuggle people and gemstones, but nothing about the reasons for the people. The debt-slavery thing is probably *in* our files somewhere, but I was focusing on Sucre and getting us there."

He shook his head.

"That said, yes, it'll get us to the planet and down. Getting everyone *off* the planet is going to take some more chicanery, but that's why I'm coming with you." Kelzin cracked his knuckles. "I haven't worked for MISS this long without learning a *few* tricks I can play to get us into the air without questions."

"Good. Based off last time, we might need to run fast," Damien said. "We might not even know in advance!"

"Everyone's sticking together," Niska promised, his voice tired. "We're in hostile territory here, Montgomery. Once we're down, I'll book a meeting with an old friend, but...I don't know how far friendship will go."

"We find out the hard way, then," Damien said calmly. "But one way or another, we find out where that damn liner stopped."

"Worst-case scenario, we have to break into the archives for traffic control."

The Hand snorted, remembering a time when he'd broken into a set of corporate archives in Tau Ceti. Roslyn Chambers had served Mars long before she'd put on a uniform, after all.

"And me without a convenient juvenile delinquent," he murmured.

Spacer hotels were much the same the galaxy over, in Damien's experience, though the one they booked into after landing was an unusually run-down example of the breed. This one was a concrete block barely five minutes' walk from the landing pad they'd come in through, with an automated check-in that asked for only the most perfunctory of IDs.

"I'm guessing this is a hub for those people-smugglers we were talking about?" Damien asked under his breath as they selected a block of four rooms and paid without the system even asking for a level of ID complex enough to require any significant faking.

"At the very least, the people running it are perfectly happy to take money without asking questions," O'Malley agreed. "Want to take bets on the number of lumps in the beds?"

"I'll settle for no bugs," he told her. "I can deal with the rest."

He could deal with bugs, too, if he had to. Of course, dealing with lumps on the bed meant ignoring them, and dealing with bugs meant magically fumigating the room. One was a tad more active.

"Check out the rooms, make your calls," he instructed the two LMID Augments. "Meet up in the bar across the way in an hour?"

"*Bar* might be overvaluing that institution," Niska replied. "I imagine it's as likely to be asking questions as this place is, though, and that has value all its own." He nodded. "An hour, then. Should be enough to at least make contact."

Leaving the rest of his companions behind, Damien stepped into his room and studied the setup. He was glad he hadn't taken O'Malley's bet—he'd have bet high and it looked like the bed was perfectly serviceable.

Nothing in the room was new but it was all solid. Threadbare and worn but still clean and comfortable—more than he'd expected for the level of hotel they'd found.

He sighed and dropped carefully onto the bed, letting his suitcase roll across the room untouched. The process of pretending to be using his hands while actually moving his bag with magic was frustrating if not particularly draining.

It was risky, too. Thaumic detectors were notoriously unreliable, using scans for thermal bloom as much as any ability to actually detect magic, but they kept being used because they *did* work.

Any time Damien used magic to do something someone else could do with their hands, he created a small heat bloom around the area he was manipulating. The illusion he had woven around himself to appear as a different person was less obvious in many ways. It was a more powerful and extended spell, but any given point was less energetic than his telekinesis.

And that energy was easily lost in the background heat of a human. An unexpected bloom around his suitcase handle might draw unwanted attention from a smart Augment—and raise questions about Mages with crippled hands.

Damien was sure there were other Mages in the galaxy without the full use of their hands, but there was no question that the First Hand of Mars was the most famous.

He needed to be careful. His presence there was necessary—he didn't think anyone else could ride herd on Niska—but it was also a risk.

He might look like a blond man five centimeters taller than Damien Montgomery right now, but Damien Montgomery was the Republic's Enemy Number One. Even the slightest hint of his presence could bring down hell.

But somewhere in this mess was the secret of what had happened to the Mage children of the Republic. A secret that Bryan Ricket had died for.

And if Damien needed to bring down hell himself to find that secret, well...he could.

And he would.

The hotel had failed to live down to its appearances, managing to provide exactly the kind of cheap and private lodgings needed near spaceports without sacrificing on the fundamental quality. It might have appeared run-down, but Damien had been impressed by its actual quality.

The bar across the street had apparently tried to live up to its run-down drunk spacer bar appearance and failed to rise to even that low standard. Something had spilled on the floor next to the table they'd taken, and been allowed to dry to stickiness. The table itself had clearly had more interactions with violence than with cleaning cloths, with a head-sized dent on one side connected to a crack that ran the whole length of the table.

There was no wait staff visible at all, and Damien suspected that the reason the bartender seemed anchored to a specific part of the bar was because that was where the shotgun was hidden. The other end of the bar contained what had probably been electronic gambling machines at one point, but one of the man-high devices had been knocked over and the other two had clearly been introduced to the stool in front of them.

When O'Malley joined them at the table with four beers, they were in bottles and still sealed.

"I'm not sure I trust the lines to the tap here," she confessed as she popped all four lids with a rapid, practiced gesture.

"The tag on the door says it was inspected two months ago," Damien pointed out, surveying the space. "I'm *presuming* that means they passed, but..."

Shouting at the other end of the bar covered him trailing off. There were half a dozen spacers there watching some kind of sport, but the holographic display had just shorted out.

The bartender shouted back, one of the women in the group struck the projector with the side of her bottle, and the game flickered back to life.

"I glanced at those guys' food as I walked by," O'Malley said. "It's *possible* the kitchen is clean, though I'm not taking bets that what was poured over those nachos is actually cheese."

"Find somewhere else to eat," Niska said, the Augment looking tired as he dropped a covert white-noise generator on the table. "We're here to talk in private, not judge the damn décor."

"Fair enough, boss. What have we got?" the redheaded Nueva Bolivian native asked.

"I reached out to three people I know are on this planet via the old codes and dead drops," Niska told them. "All three *were* LMID and were people I trusted."

"And the but?" Damien asked.

"They're RID now," Niska said flatly. "I don't think I gave enough information in the drops to get myself picked up, but the only friends who can help us work for Republic counterintelligence."

Damien sighed.

"And this is why nobody told me who we were reaching out to beyond 'friends,' isn't it?" he asked. Sooner or later, he was pretty sure Niska was going to get them all killed.

"I trust these people," the Augment replied. "There are two more ex-LMID agents on the planet I *don't*, and we're not talking to them at all."

Further conversation was interrupted by a ping on Niska's wrist-comp. Damien took a swallow of his beer as the Legatan went over the message.

It wasn't bad. He suspected O'Malley knew the beer there relatively well, though, and had picked something safe. He'd rather have a good coffee, really, but he wasn't trusting the coffee in *this* bar.

"I have a bite," Niska said slowly. "*Not* one of the people I intentionally contacted, but he'd have access to the same codes and dead drops."

"That's not a great sign, Niska," Damien pointed out.

"No. Except that unlike the people I was aiming to get in touch with, Connor's area of responsibility is orbital," the Augment replied. "He'd be the man responsible for countering any attempt to steal STC's information."

"And if he's responsible for orbit and in-system space here, he's almost certainly been tasked with trying to catch runaway indentures," O'Malley pointed out. "So, either he has no soul...or he might be broken enough to be looking for a way out."

"If he wants a way out, we can give him that," Damien said. "Presuming he has the information we need."

"There's a meet location and time," Niska replied. "About an hour from now...and at a *much* nicer restaurant than this!"

CHAPTER 31

THE TAXI DROPPED Damien and Niska off a block or so from the meeting ground, and the Hand carefully did not notice the second taxi traveling farther with Romanov and O'Malley.

"Keep your eyes open," the Augment spy told him. "I don't trust this."

"Who is this 'Connor'?" Damien asked.

The sidewalk was quiet and there were enough vehicles on the street to cover up their conversation. There was nowhere safer to talk about this available.

"Connor De Santis," Niska said. "An LMID counterintelligence analyst before the Secession, primarily working with law enforcement. He took a transfer to RID for a big promotion and ended up assigned out here."

Niska shook his head.

"He's an ass," he concluded. "I don't think he ever met a woman he didn't at least *try* to make a pass at, and his taste in men was equally enthusiastic, if generally more directed. I never worked with him, but he had a reputation around the Directorate.

"I got analysis from him a few times and it was good work, but I could avoid working with him. So I did."

"Wonderful," Damien said grimly. "So, you have no idea how he feels about the Secession or the War?"

"Not a damn clue," Niska replied. "I'm not even sure why he responded to the breadcrumbs I left out. I wouldn't have thought he knew *me* well enough to put the pieces together—and even if he did, we weren't friends. We weren't even *acquaintances*."

"You just said he was an intelligence analyst," Damien pointed out. "Are you really surprised he put together the pieces?"

"In the long run? No," the older man admitted. "This quickly? Yes."

The restaurant De Santis had sent them to was a rooftop patio on the top of a three-story mall. The open sightlines made Damien nervous as he glanced around. He'd had bad experiences with meetings at rooftop restaurants in the past.

A ping on his wrist-comp told him that Romanov had the patio under observation from a nearby building. The Combat Mage couldn't leap onto the patio from the ground, but he *could* quite handily smuggle in the components of a disassembled sniper rifle.

O'Malley, on the other hand, *could* leap onto the patio from the ground floor. If De Santis was planning trouble, it was going to be a messy day for a lot of people.

"Party of two," Niska told the neatly dressed older man at the front desk of the restaurant. "We're part of a reservation, should be under De Santis."

The man flipped through a digital screen for a few seconds.

"Ah yes, of course. Follow me, please?"

He led them out onto the patio and then, to Damien's surprise and discomfort, to a door into an additional two-story extension of the main mall structure. He could see the glint of glass above them, suggesting that there were more rooms at the top of the building.

"Señor De Santis booked one of our private rooms, just up the stairs here," the host told them. The door slid open at a touch. "Follow me."

This wasn't great to Damien's mind, but he tapped a command on his wrist-comp telling Romanov not to *immediately* leap into action. The lack of live overwatch wasn't great, but it wasn't going to change the end result.

Not when they had an Augment and a Marine Combat Mage for backup...and the people in the room were an Augment and the First Hand of the Mage-King of Mars!

The room the host escorted them to held a single man, currently facing away from them and looking out over the city with his hands clasped behind his back.

De Santis—presuming this *was* Connor De Santis—was a tall man with pitch-black hair and heavily tanned skin. His reflection suggested that he was heavily bearded but that his eyes were definitely on Niska and Damien.

"We'll have three of the chef's special," the RID agent told the host. "A bottle of the house red, three glasses, and waters. Knock before entering, please."

"Of course."

The host withdrew and De Santis chuckled as the distinctive buzz of a white noise generator filled the room.

"If you're wondering, James, I own the restaurant," he told them. "Sean and I have a number of investment properties here in Nueva Bolivia, though we've been moving funds toward Legatus as well.

"This system doesn't sit well with either of our tastes, we discovered," the agent said with a sigh. "Sean says hello, by the way. There was no way he could get free to meet you—it's *his* department that's investigating just what a certain rogue ex-LMID ship was doing here."

"That answers part of my first question, I suppose, if you're working with Sean Jezek," Niska said as he took a seat. "I was wondering why you answered my drop instead of him. He was the one I was expecting to hear from!"

"'Working with' is one way of phrasing it," De Santis said with a chuckle. "I *married* Sean six months ago."

He sighed and turned to face them. The beard was even more impressive from the front than it was in the reflection, covering almost all of De Santis's face in thick black hair. It was well taken-care-of and evenly cut, but there was enough of it to be shocking all on its own.

"I'm guessing you were aboard *Starlight*," he said bluntly. "Which means you were involved in the attempt to steal a Link in Arsenault, which leaves me with one pressing question of my own, Niska:

"Who the *hell* are you working for now?"

"No one," Niska said quietly. "Maata is working for me. I'm operating alone."

"Bullshit." De Santis pointed at Damien. "I'm not a combat Augment, Niska, but my eyes are no more organic than yours. I can recognize the heat bloom of a full-body illusion spell when I see it.

"You arrived in the system aboard a former LMID covert ops ship gone rogue—a ship that has now been destroyed, so how you're standing in my restaurant arguing with me is a matter of some question to begin with—accompanied by a Mage and in the wake of trying to steal a Link.

"You're working for Mars."

Niska sighed.

"I'm working *with* Mars," he conceded. "But I'm operating under LMID authority. Black protocols activated on Ricket's death."

"I'll accept that, for now, but you'd better talk quickly if you expect me to let you leave," De Santis told him. "Sean trusts you more than *me*, so you get this meet. I'll even allow that I'll probably let you leave for that. I don't really want to piss off my husband, after all.

"But if you want the help your message asked for, you're going to have to sell me hard. Because smuggling an illegal Mage onto Sucre is a crime at best—and if he's an MISS agent, easily treason."

"Oh, we're well past treason," Niska murmured. There was a knock on the door. "How about we get our food and then I tell you why I'm here...and who I brought with me."

After the waiter delivered the food and drinks and slipped back out, the room was silent for several long seconds. Damien took a moment to study the plates out of sheer awkwardness.

The "chef's special" was some kind of fried chicken on top of what might have been pancakes of some kind, along with strips of lettuce and other vegetables. It looked like someone had heard of the concept of chicken and waffles and tried to create something healthier...and then someone else had turned it into pub food.

"You have my attention, Niska," De Santis finally said. He picked up a glass of wine the waiter had poured and shook his head. "Just from the fact I'm *here*, you can guess I think something's rotten—but I'm a long way from contemplating *treason*."

"Damien, drop the illusion, please," Niska asked.

With a chuckle, Damien obeyed, and then grabbed his own glass of wine with magic as De Santis tried not to choke.

His face had been all over the Protectorate even before the Secession. Any intelligence officer in the Republic who *didn't* recognize him was terrible at their job—though he'd found his height confused people.

"That is Damien fucking Montgomery," De Santis finally said.

"Yes," Niska confirmed.

"The Sword of Mars. The First Hand of the goddamn Mage-King." The RID agent was staring at Damien, who silently toasted the other man with his free-floating wineglass.

"You're right. This is way past treason. I don't know if there's a *word* for what bringing *Darth Montgomery* onto a Republic world is!"

"Desperation," Damien suggested. "And I hate that nickname. Right now, however, Agent De Santis, I think we share an objective—or at the very least, a moral and ethical duty and calling."

"I really can't see that," De Santis snapped. He put the wine glass down and glared at Niska. "This is too much. I can't not turn in the *Sword of Mars*."

"Agent, do you really think I'm going to let you leave before Niska says his piece?" Damien asked gently. "I'm not going to hurt you unless you make me, but you *are* going to hear us out."

Unspoken was that if De Santis pushed too hard, Damien would have to kill him. He wouldn't *like* doing so, but one more face in his nightmares was much less likely to wreck their mission.

De Santis met his gaze and seemed to consider for a moment. He hadn't tried to rise yet, though, so he was taking the warning seriously.

"Talk," he ordered.

"You were with LMID long enough to see Case Prodigal Son written," Niska said. "That's the authority I'm operating under."

"*Bullshit*. Only Ricket could activate that—and Ricket would never contemplate treason."

"Ricket is dead, Connor," the older spy said very quietly. "You knew that. But you're RID...did *you* know the RID killed him?"

The room was silent again.

"No," the heavily bearded man said quietly. After a moment, he picked up his wineglass again and drained it. "I believe you," he admitted. "I've heard enough strangeness around Ricket's death that it fits, but no. I didn't know that."

"He was investigating something," Niska said levelly. "I don't know what. All I originally knew was that he triggered Prodigal Son. An old friend left more information in the datanets for me and others to find.

"It hadn't made it to Arsenault yet, but I scanned it as we were coming in. All encrypted and concealed, of course. New LMID protocols nobody else knew."

Damien sighed. Eventually, Niska was going to tell him everything as it came up.

"We're still not sure of what he was investigating, but it caught the Lord Protector's attention," the Augment continued. "Solace invited him to a meeting to discuss his concerns. Instead, Ricket was kidnapped by three RID agents.

"They didn't even interrogate him, Connor," Niska half-whispered. "They drove him out into the middle of nowhere, shot him in the back of the head and dumped his body in a river."

"How the hell do you know that?"

"Because the last LMID agent on Legatus stayed because she was too damn angry to let things slide," the Augment snapped. "Brecker captured one of the agents who carried out the hit—and she *did* interrogate the bastard.

"From the codes she sent, Brecker's dead now. There are no agents of the Legatus Military Intelligence Directorate left on Legatus. Any who survived have at least fled our homeworld...or defected."

"You defected."

"It's complicated, but basically, yes," Niska admitted. "The Republic Intelligence Directorate murdered Bryan Ricket, Connor. They murdered one of our *founding fathers*. What the hell did he find that was worth that?"

De Santis grimaced and rose, turning away from them to look out the window again.

"There shouldn't have been anything for him to find," he admitted. "If there was..."

"Then our country might not be what we swore to serve," Niska agreed.

"I was Ricket's right-hand man, one of the last senior agents left after the RID transfers," he continued. "Even I didn't know he was carrying on the investigation until the end, and all *I* knew was where he started: the Mage Academies."

"Fuck me." De Santis's curse hung in the air. "I never even thought to ask the damn question."

"Neither did I. So, Hand Montgomery and I went poking around Arsenault—and every one of those kids is missing, Connor. Two hundred–plus teenagers got loaded up onto a transport."

"And sent here, I'm guessing," the RID agent concluded. "Because this system is the Republic's secondary hub at this point, with all of the *bullshit* that entails."

He was still staring out the window.

"I was vaguely aware of Nueva Bolivia indentured workers on Legatus," he said quietly. "I assumed it was, well, what they claimed it was. Long-term work contracts with attached statutory deductions to pay off debts or whatever.

"Then I got here, and supporting the people making sure no one escaped become part of my job."

No one interrupted him as he paused, marshaling his thoughts.

"Twenty-six percent, Niska," he finally said. "That's the fatality rate of a ten-year indenture contract. There's no life insurance, no payout to your family. No payment at all unless the contract's complete.

"So, the people who die...their families get nothing. And a quarter of the men and women who get caught up in the contracts died.

Twenty-year indentures are worse...and guess what there have been *more* of since the Secession.

"Those mines fuel the factories that are building weapons for the Republic Navy," De Santis concluded. "The factories, too, are now primarily operated by indentures. There weren't *enough* indentures before the Secession, but the Republic rules for who they can sell into *fucking slavery* are looser than the old Nueva Bolivian government's rules."

"Any sacrifice for the war," Niska said quietly.

"If our war machine—our *nation*—is fueled by slaves and lies, who do we serve?" De Santis asked. He turned around and looked at Montgomery.

"Answer me one question, 'Lord' Montgomery," he snapped. "It was you who laid the case for the Inquest before the Council of the Protectorate. Here, they say it was lies. Was it?"

"No." Damien let the word stand alone. He didn't need to say more. The Protectorate had made sure that the Inquest files were made public, even in the Republic, as they pulled the Mages out.

"The Lord Protector claims we didn't want a war, that our first strike was a functionally defensive countermeasure against the attack you were preparing," De Santis told him. "I'm guessing that *is* a lie?"

"From the moment Councilor McClintlock declared the Secession, we planned to let the Republic go," Damien told him. "We were concerned about Republican aggression, yes, and moved some ships to the border and began building more, but...we weren't planning a war."

He snorted.

"And believe me, Agent De Santis, if we *had* been planning a war, I'd have been involved."

The room was silent again.

"I want out," Connor De Santis finally said. "Two tickets to Mars, *safe* tickets, for my husband and me. I don't want to defect, I don't want to betray the Republic...I just want out."

"We can make that happen," Niska told him. "But we need you to help us first. That transport with two hundred teens aboard came here. I can give you its registration, name and expected arrival time.

"I need you to tell me where they went."

"We'll have to pull you out with us," Damien noted carefully. "And believe me, I'm not any happier about you on my covert ops ship than you are, but I can't guarantee that we can get you out another way."

De Santis stared out the window for a full minute.

"I'll talk to Sean," he finally said. "We can only liquidate and move so much money. Fleeing the Republic could cost us everything, but...I don't know if I can serve this nation anymore.

"Regardless, Niska, Montgomery, I'll find out where that ship went to. I don't know what answer you're going to find at the end of your search, and I'm not sure I *want* to know.

"But if Bryan Ricket died for it, then the least I can do is help dig it up."

CHAPTER 32

THE NEXT EVENING saw them in a different restaurant, much closer to the spaceport. This time, Connor De Santis had brought Sean Jezek. The RID agent's swarthy, hook-nosed husband wasn't what Damien would have called attractive, but from the way the two men treated each other, De Santis clearly doted on him.

"Do you own this one, too?" Damien asked as they were ushered to a table on a raised section overlooking the main dining area. Looking around the small restaurant with its old-fashioned wood panels and flooring, he saw that there were two other similar areas, though those both held more tables.

Theirs only had the one four-person table right now, though he suspected it normally held more.

"No, I just paid for their chef's special dinner table," Jezek replied, his voice just as gravely as Damien would have expected from his appearance. "On no notice, but they had an opening tonight so it was only five thousand pounds."

Damien was only vaguely aware of what his salary was and operated with a budget that was functionally "yes, sir." The concept of a five-thousand-pound table hurt his head, even if that was "only" thirty-five hundred Martian dollars. He'd paid that for meals, but not for just four people!

"It's a polite way of buying private space, I suppose," he conceded.

"Agreed." Niska dropped his white-noise generator on the table and covered it with a napkin. Their waiter would notice it, but at a five-thousand-pound entry price, Damien suspected it would go un-remarked.

"Connor and I talked last night," Sean told them. "Just by meeting you, we're putting ourselves in danger. I'm back-office for counterintelligence here, and I've already heard a lot that makes me uncomfortable."

He sighed.

"And CI's people are bad enough. The Internal Security team, well..." He shrugged. "They're unabashed secret police and going downhill by the day. As I believe Connor told you, we want out."

"You're rich," Damien pointed out bluntly. "You'll lose that."

"*I* was always rich," Jezek said with a chuckle. "Connor is still getting used to the idea. We have assets in the Protectorate as well. We'll be fine so long as we get across the border safely."

"We're not heading straight home," the Hand warned. "We need specific intel from you and we'll be actioning that. You'll be riding shotgun for a while before we can drop you off in Protectorate space."

"We'll survive," De Santis said bluntly. "Better than I'll survive running down any more runaway slaves."

"Exactly," Jezek agreed. "Connor is probably going to be all stuffy and honorable and refuse to help you lot beyond what we've already promised, but I've seen too much." His eyes were suddenly distant and haunted.

"I've seen too much," he repeated after a moment of silence. "The Republic is not what it was meant to be. I don't know where we went astray, but I fear it was long ago. Certainly long before the Secession. We were just blind."

"Did you *miss* Antonius?" Damien asked sharply. "LMID killed a hundred thousand people there."

There was a new edge to the silence for a moment as the three ex-LMID officers half-glared at him.

"Yes," De Santis conceded. "And that was too much, even for us, but remember: so far as we were concerned, we were at war. Perhaps those of us with shreds of a conscience should have thought that through, but we were deep in the heart of the echo chamber."

Damien let that hang.

"Do you have the intelligence we wanted?" Niska demanded.

"I do," the intelligence officer replied. "Tracking space traffic control for stuff people are trying to hide is my job, after all." He snorted. "Found your shuttle's insertion, by the way. It was well done. If I hadn't been looking for it, I never would have seen it."

"And?" Damien asked.

"Well, the records now show that it was flagged as a problem, investigated, and IDed as a systems problem on the shuttle that has been resolved," De Santis told him. "It may not hold forever, but it will hold until we're all long gone.

"As for your freighter, she was *New Orleans Delight*, chartered to Amber." He shook his head. "From the files I saw, she's an RID ship and has been for a decade. Used for covert and overt personnel and cargo transfer.

"The trip you're looking for was in cold storage. Requesting it had a risk of drawing attention we didn't want, so I tried something else first: I looked to see when *Delight* had visited that *wasn't* in cold storage."

"And?" Damien asked.

"She hasn't been to Nueva Bolivia in about six months," De Santis told them. "Before that, she swung through about every six to ten weeks. Came into orbit, dropped off her official cargo, left."

De Santis unrolled a smart-paper flimsy onto the table and dropped an image onto it. It was a two-dimensional representation of the Nueva Bolivia System, with green lines drawn on it.

"These are the six courses that are in live storage," he told them. "They all come in from different systems. They all end in Sucre orbit. And they are all coming in from *odd* emergence points."

"I guess you work traffic control," Niska said. "You'd see that. What are you saying?"

"They're all passing through the same orbital slot," Damien told the old Augment. He had been a pilot and a Jump Mage first, after all. He could pick up that pattern.

"Exactly." A curving thick orange line appeared on the flimsy. "There isn't supposed to be anything *in* that orbital slot, it's pretty far out...but an unassisted orbit at that distance would be moving at exactly that speed. *Delight* kept rendezvousing with somebody out there."

"We can project forward, see where it should be," Damien concluded. "That's more of a lead than I expected."

"Unfortunately, we may need to move faster than any of us would like," Jezek said quietly. "After talking to Connor last night, I poked at our records on the Mage Academies on Sucre today. I hit a bunch of data roadblocks and ended up called into my boss's office."

The dark-skinned man shook his head.

"I think I may have attracted the exact attention Connor was trying to avoid by not digging into cold storage, but...there's *nothing* in our data files on the Academies. Five hundred teenage Mages? We should have them under constant surveillance—and we don't."

"If you've drawn attention, then we need to move sooner," Niska said sharply. "You said our shuttle is covered?"

"For now," De Santis confirmed.

"I don't think I've drawn enough attention to get followed or anything of the sort," Jezek pointed out. "But I've flagged enough that when I disappear, questions are going to get asked."

"Either way, the faster we move, the better, I think," Damien told them. "If there are no Mages in the Academies here, either, then we need to check out this space station ASAP. We should move."

And it certainly didn't *reduce* his urgency that the known number of missing teenage Mages had just quadrupled on him.

CHAPTER 33

"THIS IS A NICE SHUTTLE, but I'll admit I'm wondering just how you plan to leave the system," De Santis said dryly several hours later.

Damien ignored the man, his focus over Kelzin's shoulder as the pilot weaved them through the orderly chaos of the traffic routes leaving Sucre orbit.

"Not on this ship," Niska said bluntly. "Right now, however, it looks like this shuttle might be our best plan to check out the station."

"I've got a course filed and everything," Mike Kelzin confirmed cheerfully. "I'm a little surprised that it didn't flag as a no-fly zone or anything like that."

"They might not want to draw that much attention to it," Damien told them. "Or we could be missing something."

"I'm just a jarhead," Romanov said dryly, "but I looked at the same numbers as all of you. Unless I'm misreading it, we're not exactly on an intercept course, are we?"

"We should pass by five light-seconds away," Kelzin agreed. "That's more than close enough for us to detect a space station. You can't hide anything in space at that range without magic."

"And even with magic, it's hard," Damien noted. "At that range, I'd trust a Hand to do it. Probably no one else."

The spells that could conceal a ship's heat signature were only so good, after all, and the energy still had to go somewhere.

"So, they can't hide from us, and that course looks like it's heading toward one of the larger refining facilities in the asteroid belt," Kelzin continued. "Unless our personnel transport company ID has been flagged by someone, that shouldn't raise questions."

"Even if it was, we search the ships we think are trying to smuggle people on the way back," De Santis pointed out. "We need to find the indentures who are violating their contracts for there to be a crime, after all."

"So, we fly out being nice and non-suspicious and scout out the station from a distance," Damien concluded. "There's no point in bringing in the big guns until we *know* we have a target."

"And...what kind of big guns do we have, again?" Jezek asked. "There are seven of us on this shuttle. Two Augments and two Mages, yes, but that seems...insufficient to assault a space station engaged in some kind of mass kidnapping."

"We have other assets," Damien assured him. He could tell the two new recruits, he supposed, since they were going to end up on *Rhapsody* regardless, but he was feeling paranoid.

The two seemed aboveboard, but this whole affair could easily be a trap. They'd find out in about sixteen hours, one way or another.

The shuttle was equipped for long-distance trips, but not overly well. By the time they were approaching the target point, everyone had retreated into their own individual corners of the spacecraft.

"We're coming up on where we should be finding our ghost," Mike Kelzin reported from the cockpit. "Our closest approach should be in about twenty minutes unless I bring the engines online, but...I'm hoping one of you lot sees something I don't."

With a tiny bit of magic, Damien took off the helmet he was wearing, leaving the system to automatically turn off the VR sleep program he'd been using. He'd set it to let Kelzin communicate with him but ignore everyone else.

He was getting tired of sharing cramped quarters with a bunch of LMID agents. Niska and O'Malley, at least, seemed completely dedicated to finding out just what was going on behind the scenes of the Republic, but they'd still helped fight the shadow war that had led them all here.

Regardless of their anger *now*, they'd helped build the very state that had kidnapped the children they were chasing. Over seven hundred kids gone. Most of the Republic's systems had smaller Academies than Arsenault, but Legatus had five to Nueva Bolivia's three.

If every Academy was empty, then there were *three thousand* teenagers missing. If no one knew where they were and Damien wasn't turning up mass graves, he wasn't sure just what their fate had been.

Pushing aside that thought, he stepped past the Legatans and joined Kelzin. The scanner displays didn't look much different than they had at any point in the last sixteen hours, which wasn't right.

"Mike, can you show me where we thought the station would be?" he asked. It was easier to have the other man manipulate the scanners than try to change it by magic or voice command on a ship that wasn't really designed for either.

"Here." A chunk of space highlighted in orange. "And there's nothing there. I don't think I'm missing anything; I don't think it's hidden behind magic. There's just nothing there."

"That's impossible," De Santis said from the doorway. "Or at least damned unlikely. The courses *New Orleans Delight* took lined up with something in a stable, unpowered orbit. If it was in the same orbit for two years that we know of...why would it change?"

"Maybe they were done?" Damien asked. "Finished whatever scheme they were running?"

"Maybe they thought they were compromised," Niska suggested. "If we trace back along the orbital path, would we be able to find any trace of debris? Or maybe a rocket burn?"

"You think they would have destroyed the station?" Damien demanded.

"Or moved it," the old LMID agent told him. "It doesn't take much to move a station, after all. What takes a great deal is moving it *quickly*."

"They couldn't have destroyed a space station without it attracting everyone's attention," De Santis noted. "Space traffic control can be easily convinced to ignore a platform with the right authority, but no one would have ignored an explosion of any kind."

"So, we need to trace back and find out where they moved the platform," Niska suggested. He met Damien's gaze. "You'd know better than I would, Montgomery. Can this shuttle do that?"

"No," Damien admitted. "We'll make contact with LaMonte, bring in her ship. There's no way we can do this with the shuttle."

"If it helps, they probably would have tried to drop it into one of the gas giants if they wanted to wreck it," De Santis suggested. "We're far enough out that they could have adjusted the vector to fling it toward Santa Maria relatively easily—and if they wanted to do that with any kind of efficiency, there was only one two-week window in the last six months."

"And we know they got a shipment six months ago," Damien conceded. "Let's reconvene with real scanners and a real ship, people," he decided aloud. "Whatever we're close to finding, the Republic wanted to bury it pretty hard.

"So, let's close the gap, people. There's a space station out here somewhere, and I *want* its databanks. Let's make it happen."

Rhapsody swam up on them out of the dark without warning.

Well, without warning for De Santis and Jezek, anyway. Damien had known the stealth ship was coming for a while. LaMonte had brought her ship near to where they expected to find the space station, so when they started taking the shuttle back along the orbital path, it was easier for her to find them.

Nueva Bolivia was active enough that even this far out, they were running a lot of the stealth systems. Directed venting and radar baffling were enough to keep the ship concealed for now...and enough that the shuttle's limited sensor suite didn't even see her coming until she was on top of them.

"Initiating docking protocols," Kelzin said aloud.

"With wha— The fuck!" De Santis looked up at the ship diving toward them "Where did that come from?"

"Around," Damien said gently. "She's not being as sneaky as she could be, but this shuttle's sensors suck. Meet *Rhapsody in Purple*, Mr. De Santis. She's your ride out of here."

The agent snorted, looking up at the stealth ship.

"So I see. I've never seen anything like her."

"So far as I know, she's a first in the galaxy," the Hand replied. She wasn't *unique*, but he wasn't going to tell the RID agent that the Protectorate had six of the stealth ships. De Santis didn't need to know that.

"And if anyone can find where they buried that space station, it's Captain LaMonte and her crew."

The shuttle bay swept over them like a consuming maw, sending a chill down Damien's spine. They slowly dropped to the deck and he exhaled. Home.

"You're not going to get private quarters," he admitted. "We've got a lot more people crammed onto the ship than she's supposed to carry. We were doing okay, but then the Republic blew up *Starlight*."

"Give me a *shoebox* heading away from the Republic, and we'll fit ourselves in," Jezek told him, taking his husband's hand. "Any course that lets us keep what's left of our souls."

Damien grimaced.

"You know, I really did hope your Republic was going to be a positive thing," he admitted. "At the least, I figured it would end the damn shadow war. Looks like I was wrong on all counts."

"Yes," Niska agreed bluntly. "Now. Let's go see what Captain LaMonte has discovered, shall we? If there are answers to what kind of cancer my country had birthed hidden here, I need to know them."

The Augment stalked out of the shuttle, and Damien looked at the other Legatans.

"Remember, Lord Montgomery, that this is harder for us than you in many ways," O'Malley said quietly. "You fought LMID and fought the

Republic. Finding out that there is evil at the heart of the nation Legatus birthed can't be unexpected for you.

"We fought *to create* that nation. And its leaders may have betrayed everything we trusted them to build. We'll find the truth with you and we'll trumpet it to the heavens for you, but don't expect us to find this *easy.*"

Damien sighed and nodded his understanding. As she said, this was bad enough for him.

"As Niska said, let's go find out what this system is hiding."

CHAPTER 34

"**COLONEL CHIANG** reports that Decurion's orbital defenses are now under our control," Kulkarni told everyone.

Decurion was the uninhabitable world closest to Centurion, used to supply much of the raw metals and minerals fueling the shipyards attached to the accelerator ring.

No remotely habitable planet would have been subjected to what had been done to Decurion; that was for sure. The images of the planet on Roslyn's display showed literal chunks carved out of it that were visible from orbit, thousands of square kilometers of rock blasted into space with nukes.

Those massive gouges marked the source of the raw materials for the immense accelerator ring, but the continued smaller-scale mining operations were fueling the Republic war machine. There was no way they could leave Decurion operating.

Of course, Decurion was heavily defended. Unlike Legatus or Centurion, however, those defenses were older. No gunships or RIN warships, just massive batteries of missile launchers on artificial asteroids in orbit.

Those launchers had been updated...but they were mostly automated and linked to a single command center. One that Colonel Chiang Wen's Second Battalion, Bionic Combat Regiment, now controlled.

"I assume Admiral Medici has already started to move in, but confirm his orders," Alexander said with a chuckle. Medici's cruiser detachment would have received the report from Colonel Chiang two minutes earlier.

"Yes, sir," Kulkarni confirmed. "And General Tone?"

"Her Marines are to move in as soon as Medici confirms the orbital space is clear," the Admiral replied. "Taking the defenses intact means we don't have to worry as much about our rear, but I want Medici to make sure we can get the transports through."

General Alexis Tone had fifteen thousand Marines, the only complete division of the Royal Martian Marine Corps that Roslyn was aware of. They had exactly *one* specially-designed combat transport. The rest of the Marines were being delivered on regular civilian freighters carrying specialized transport containers.

The RMMC had trained for assaulting a planet from orbit, but they'd never expected to actually do it. Interstellar assault ships were expensive, so they'd only ever built the prototype.

Like the rest of the Martian military, they were making do.

"Any reaction from Centurion or Legatus?" Alexander asked.

"Nothing from Legatus yet," Roslyn confirmed. "It'll be over an hour before we see the moment they would have known Chiang arrived. It's not like there's much at Legatus they can send at Decurion, either."

Their initial attack had wrecked Legatus's orbital defenses. The RIN starships in orbit were chained to the Republic's capital now—Second Fleet could obliterate the carrier group in an open engagement, and—worse from the Republic's perspective—the remaining fortresses couldn't defend the planet against the Protectorate fleet.

Legatus was quite handily contained, so long as Second Fleet was in position to jump over and take out any attempt to run.

Centurion remained a concern. They were a lot shorter on gunships than they had been, but the mobile forces there were the only force in the system that could actually challenge Second Fleet. The fixed defenses were sufficiently spread out that it was *possible* that Second Fleet could evade the mobile forces and attack the accelerator.

"The Centurion forces are continuing to hover around the closest cardinal station," Kulkarni reported. "They're going to hang out between us and the accelerator ring forever, from the looks of it."

"Whoever is in command over there realizes that we only need one missile to end the damn war," Alexander said. "I'd prefer they sent ships out to attack us. The more we can grind them down, the closer we get to actually being able to engage one world or the other."

"With Decurion under our control...there isn't much else in the system we can take away from them," the operations officer admitted.

"Nothing obvious, anyway," the Admiral confirmed. "That's why I have you and Chambers, Mage-Captain. Find me the *non*-obvious weaknesses.

"Besieging this system cuts off the reinforcements for their entire Navy, but it isn't going to end this war. All we've forced is a stalemate... unless we can find a way to actually *take* Centurion or Legatus."

As the Flag Lieutenant, Roslyn had her own office. It wasn't much of an office, but it at least recognized that her job wasn't *quite* just being Alexander's secretary.

While the battle for Decurion wrapped up, over two light-minutes away, she was studying a strategic map of the system on one screen.

Another was showing the latest updates from Decurion. There *had* been some gunships amongst the defenses, and several platforms had enough crew aboard to wrest control of their launchers away from the command center.

Six cruisers had made short work of all of that, and uninhabitable worlds didn't have many places to hide when the Marines came dropping from orbit. A planet of ten million souls was falling in front of Roslyn's eyes, and all she could think was that it wasn't enough.

Mars didn't have the troops to assault Legatus. The Marine Corps was recruiting, but they didn't have the gear or ships to equip and move the hundreds of thousands of troops necessary to take a world of five billion people.

They'd have to make Legatus surrender, and she wasn't sure how they could do that without engaging in atrocities that she didn't even need to *ask* to know weren't on the table.

If they could separate the starships guarding Legatus from the planet and its defenses, they could take the orbitals of the Republic capital. That was check...but Roslyn wasn't convinced it was checkmate.

Not against a society that had forged itself for decades on opposing Mars—and not against the dictator who'd used that fear to make himself ruler of eleven worlds.

Taking control of Legatus was a fool's game, Roslyn concluded. They'd lose ships and people taking the orbitals, and then the Lord Protector would call their bluff. Somehow, she didn't see Alexander finding the ruthlessness to order cities nuked from orbit.

Perhaps that was weakness. Roslyn was somehow sure that Solace would call it weakness...but she couldn't.

If Legatus wasn't the key, then it had to be Centurion. She refocused her map, then looked up at a chime at her door.

"Come in."

She was somehow unsurprised when Kulkarni stepped in.

"Poking at the impossible task our Princess assigned us?" the older woman asked, pulling up a chair with a flicker of magic.

"Yeah." Roslyn shook her head. "Legatus is a trap," she concluded. "Even if we somehow took the orbitals, we couldn't *do* anything. Not without a million or so Marines we don't have."

The operations officer was silent.

"I'll admit, I was thinking that Legatus was the most vulnerable point," she admitted. "We *could* smash through the defenses and starships left. It would hurt, we'd lose good people, but we'd be in control of the orbitals. Checkmate, right?"

"Checkmate means the king can't *escape*," Roslyn noted. "Solace won't surrender just because we control the orbitals. We don't have the troops to dig him out, and we won't blow up cities."

Kulkarni was silent as she studied the strategic map, then nodded.

"You're right," she conceded. "I hadn't even got that far. I was thinking maybe drop Marines to grab him in person, but he'd be ready for that."

"So, Centurion is the key," Roslyn replied, studying the map. "And the key to Centurion is the cardinal forts."

"We've smashed a bunch of their gunships, but they're all still heavily armed battle stations with hundreds of parasite warships," Kulkarni pointed out. "Sensor networks, antimissile defenses, the works. They'd pick up a stealth ship before we could pull the trick we pulled at Decurion. Hell, they'd pick up a ballistic *rock* before it could hit them. They planned for that."

"And no approach to the planet doesn't pass within laser range of two of them," Roslyn concluded. "We could take any one of those forts. Maybe two of them—but while we were doing so, the entire mobile fleet would arrive and kick the crap out of us."

Her superior nodded and sighed.

"I don't see an answer to Centurion, Lieutenant," she admitted. "Except for more ships, and we're not getting those anytime soon."

"The Admiral keeps talking about reinforcements we'll get before the rest," Roslyn said. "Do you know what she's talking about?"

"You caught that too, huh?" Kulkarni shook her head. "I asked. I got told the answer was classified and I didn't need to know yet."

"So, what, we just besiege Legatus until the answer falls into our lap?" Roslyn asked.

"I wish I saw something else, Chambers," the Mage-Captain admitted. "But right now...that's all I see. I'll keep poking at it, though. There's got to be an answer somewhere."

Roslyn snorted.

"I see *an* answer," she admitted. "It's 'Give me twenty more battleships.'"

Kulkarni laughed.

"I'll check behind my couch, Lieutenant, I'm sure they must have just slipped out of sight!"

CHAPTER 35

FOUR DAYS.

That was how long *Rhapsody in Purple* sneaked through the outer void of the Nueva Bolivia System, creeping ever closer to Santa Maria.

The largest gas giant in the system was the farthest out. Edging close to brown-dwarf territory, it was highly energetic and its orbital spaces were generally not considered safe to colonize. Most of the inevitable industrial work that needed to be done at *a* gas giant took place at the closer-in and calmer Cochabamba.

That meant that Santa Maria made a useful place for the people they were chasing to dump an entire space station. Unfortunately, it also turned out that the system security force was carrying out an exercise with their monitors far beyond their normal operating ranges.

None of the dozen sub-million-ton sublight warships would have been a threat to any real starship on their own. Together, though, they could probably stop a cruiser—and any of them could have taken down *Rhapsody* without breaking a sweat.

"It is just coincidence they're out here, right?" Damien asked. "I'm starting to get twitchy."

"They run these exercises three times a year," Jezek told him. "Nueva Bolivia Security had two squadrons like this, and they want them ready to deploy anywhere in the star system.

"I didn't check when this one was scheduled for, but I don't think they're looking for us."

"Well, they're behind us now and they didn't see shit," LaMonte replied.

"And I've got something," Xi Wu reported. "Check out seventeen by sixty-five."

That part of the screen on the simulacrum chamber bridge flickered at the Mage's command and zoomed in.

"We're not getting much of a heat signature, but..." The screen zoomed in further and an odd dot resolved into a slowly spinning circle.

"That's a centripetal-gravity ring station," Damien said. "Legatan-style. Do we have dimensions?"

"One kilometer. It isn't powered, but it's still spinning. Full rotation about every ninety seconds. Half a gravity or so, I'd guess."

"No power," LaMonte said quietly. "Fusion plant offline. Evacuated and abandoned. Damn, that's creepy."

"Do you think you can get anything out of her computers?" Damien asked.

"Can't tell you until we're aboard," the covert ops captain replied. "I'm coming with you this time, Damien. You need me."

"Agreed." He glanced over at their Republican partners, then back at LaMonte. He wasn't going to trust Niska to break into the station's computers, let alone any of their other Republican allies.

"We go over in force," he continued. "Niska, O'Malley, Romanov and at least three of our people. Everyone in exosuits. Treat it like we're assaulting a fortified enemy position."

He shook his head and studied the abandoned but still-spinning ring.

"I don't trust that place to be as dead as it looks."

Eight people in exosuits would have crowded the shuttle they'd taken from *Starlight* to the breaking point. Fortunately for Damien's calm, they no longer needed to pretend to be a Republican spacecraft, which meant they were back to his old standby RMMC assault shuttle.

His hands itched to take the controls over from Kelzin, but it wasn't like he currently *could*. Regardless of his desires, he was still a year away from being able to reliably use his hands.

So, he and LaMonte waited in the main passenger compartment. Unlike their hulking companions, they wore simple vac-suits. Neither was trained in the heavier gear, and Damien, at least, didn't need it.

"You stay behind the Marines," he ordered LaMonte. "I can shield myself against most threats, but that vac-suit's armor is all you have."

"I've played combat hacker before, Damien," she told him with a chuckle. "This isn't my first rodeo any more than it's yours."

He nodded his understanding and swallowed. It was easy, sometimes, to forget that LaMonte had spent the years since they'd both left *Blue Jay* behind just as actively and interestingly as he had.

Damien had become the First Hand of Mars, but LaMonte had earned command of a covert ops insertion ship and had then *commanded* that covert ops ship through the shadow war against Legatus—and the early days of the open war against the Republic.

"Contact in sixty seconds," Kelzin reported. "I don't suppose these people could have left the centerpoint access behind?"

"The Legatan design doesn't have one," Damien told him. "They've got some *very* good computers to manage the latch-on."

"Yeah, well, those are currently turned off, so I'm doing this on my own," the pilot replied. "So, everyone hold on, because this is going to be one hell of a bump."

Damien brought up the shuttle's display on his suit HUD, then concealed a chuckle.

Kelzin was preparing everyone for a problem, but from what Damien could see, he was coming in for a perfect landing. There was barely even a noticeable impact as the shuttlecraft latched on to one of the docking ports, Kelzin having exactly matched the rotational velocity.

"Well, welcome to the latest in the Republic's line of mysterious, creepy, abandoned space stations," the pilot told them all. "Thanks for flying aboard an MISS spacecraft and make sure you take your guns with you.

"That place looks *real* creepy."

Damien snorted and unbelted himself. He rose, adjusting for the angular acceleration that acted as gravity on a spinning station. Less than half a gravity, he confirmed. Enough to stick them to floors as designed, at least.

"Let's go, people."

Damien had lost count of the number of space stations he'd been on in his life, but he'd never been on one with no power. The complete lack of lights, moving air, or any kind of feeling of life was strange at best.

"Air is present," Romanov noted. "It's safe, even, though it reads like it would stink. I guess the life-support plant was running up to the end."

"If they left the place with breathable air and no one is breathing it, well." Damien could hear the shrug in Niska's voice, though the Augment's body language was invisible inside the hulking exosuit.

"Also tells us there are no leaks," LaMonte noted. "They abandoned a perfectly functional station. That's...weird."

Their lights weren't picking out much of anything. The access corridor they'd ended up in was larger than most, but it was still a short connector between a docking port and the actual entrance.

"Get that door open," Damien ordered, gesturing toward the door at the end of the corridor.

O'Malley stepped up to it and prodded the metal a couple of times.

"How much damage do we want to do?" she asked. "We can cut it out of the way or power it up."

"Power it up," Damien said after a moment. "We want this place's secrets. Let's not get in the habit of just punching our way through everything."

"Your call, Montgomery."

The Augment removed the access panel next to the door and poked around in its guts. After a few seconds, she pulled a cord from the arm of her suit and hooked it into a port inside the door's systems.

The door promptly and smoothly slid open.

"Systems are working just fine," she reported. "There's no power, but nothing is damaged and it responded immediately."

That added up. The Republic hadn't abandoned this station because it was damaged or useless. They'd abandoned it because they believed destroying it quietly was the easiest way to keep it secret.

"What the..."

Romanov's shocked words brought Damien forward into the main loading bay. The access tube they'd connected to had been intended for larger ships, but the bay they'd now entered was where shuttles would have landed and where passengers from those larger ships would have been met.

The lights picked up bits of bright, cheerful banners. None of their flashlights were really wide enough to read a full sign, but they quickly picked out that there were a lot of them.

"Let me make some light," Damien ordered. He had air to work with, after all, and air was the key component to a lot of a Mage's spells.

He conjured a tiny ball of light and let it float up into the air to illuminate the entire space. The bright banners were mostly declaring WELCOME in large blocky letters. A mural of semi-anthropomorphized animals covered one wall, culminating in a single fox twice the height of man holding another WELCOME sign.

"What the fuck," Niska finished Romanov's prior sentence. "What is this place?"

Damien's vacations tended to include such "low-pressure" tasks as speaking to schools and other collections of teenagers. Motivational speaking wasn't really his forte, but the First Hand of Mars carried some weight, even with kids.

He had enough experience to recognize the space he was standing in.

"It's a school," he said softly. "Or, at the very least, it's *pretending* to be one."

CHAPTER 36

DIGGING AROUND the loading bay some more, Damien at least knew the name of the place they were standing in. Supposedly, this was the University of Tau Ceti Special Satellite Campus.

He would have been very surprised if the University of Tau Ceti knew it had apparently branched out into specialty Mage schools in the UnArcana Worlds.

"Whoever came up with this has never actually *been* to UTC," one of Romanov's Marines observed over the radio. "Logo is wrong; they changed it from that one twelve years ago. Text is wrong; the University has a brand standard and it isn't that.

"Plus, well, UTC's high school outreach is on a much lower scale," the trooper concluded. "I *went* to UTC, sirs."

"That's about what I figured, but the confirmation is good," Damien replied. "Stick in pairs, people, but let's move out and explore this place. If it *isn't* a school, what *is* it?"

There was no question who was coming with Damien. Romanov hadn't left his side since they'd come in, and he switched to a private channel.

"Make sure the Marine with LaMonte is one of your best," he ordered quietly. "We need her to rip open this place's brains once we find them."

"I'll see to it," Romanov confirmed.

A few moments later, everyone had shaken out into their pairs and the Marines were opening up several cases they'd brought with them.

"Let's hold here while we get the drones up," Romanov told Damien. "I'll be linking them to everyone, and they should give us a better idea of what we're heading into."

"All right."

Damien left the Marines to their work and studied the room. There wasn't much to see, really. Half of the space had been designated for shuttles, but there hadn't been that much shuttle traffic. As far out in the system as the station had been, larger ships had delivered the cargos and passengers for this place.

There was a map, he realized, and he waved LaMonte over.

"Can you grab a picture of this and upload it to the tacnet?" he asked her. "My wrist-comp only works so well with my hands and a vac-suit's gloves."

She chuckled humorlessly and obeyed. "That's funny," she said aloud.

"What?"

"This map isn't complete by a long shot. It only covers forty percent or so of the station." LaMonte leaned in to study it more closely. "Kind of looks like that's all they wanted the students to know existed."

"Pass that on to everyone," Damien ordered. "If the 'school' is less than half the station, then the odds are that what we're looking for is in the other half."

"Gives us a starting point," Romanov rumbled, the Marine interjecting himself into the private channel with the ease of long practice. As Damien's bodyguard, Damien had to specifically exclude the Special Agent Mage-Captain from a channel for him *not* to hear what the Hand was saying.

"And a starting point gives us somewhere to send the drones," Damien agreed. "Get to it, Romanov. This place makes my teeth itch."

The drones the Marines had brought were designed for this environment. In true gravity, the head-sized ion-thruster-equipped orbs would never have stayed in the air. In the pseudogravity of a rotating space station, they simply needed to make sure they never touched the "ground."

Twenty-two of them were launched and sent off into the station, their networked artificial sequential intelligence—an ASI or "artificial stupid"—making sure they moved sufficiently far apart to build up their own map of the space station.

Thanks to LaMonte, that map was now overlaid on the HUD of Damien's helmet on top of the map of the school.

"So far, everything's lining up with the map and the drones haven't encountered any difficulties," Romanov reported after a moment. "Doors are mostly open so far, too. We're flagging closed ones for follow-up."

"That's a good starting point," Damien agreed. "Move our teams out; check on the closed doors. Most are going to be nothing, but who knows what this place is going to hide."

Romanov set to organizing the teams, then he and Damien set off.

"I've flagged this door for us," he told the Hand. "It's next to what the map says is the boys' dormitories. None of the doors to the dorms are open."

"Do we have any other areas closed off like that?" Damien asked.

"No. Not yet. The drones are still drawing their own map." Romanov sighed. "Even with the map we have only covering forty percent of the station, that's a *lot* of real estate. The station is a kilometer across, after all."

Damien's nod was visible through his lighter vac-suit as he considered the math. A ring a kilometer across, so three and a seventh kilometers or so of circumference. The ring was fifty meters "high" and four stories "thick"—plus a triple-height inner level that was entirely rotation and power systems, per the original design.

That forty percent they'd found the map of was most of a square kilometer—and the unmapped segments were a full square kilometer.

Searching that was going to take time, though the drones were going to take on most of that work.

They reached the door they were after, and Romanov immediately set to opening it up. The exosuit had a collection of tools for that purpose, though in this case he simply powered the door up rather than cutting it open.

Stepping through was surreal. There were still no lights in there except for Damien's floating ball of sunshine, but that was enough to pick out the calmly organized nature of the rooms. They'd entered a common area with a dozen tables, clearly used for gathering and snacks.

There were gaming consoles along one wall, disabled from the lack of power. Even books. The place had been neatly cleared away and shut down, then abandoned.

Wordlessly, Damien crossed the room and pushed open the unpowered door to the actual dorm rooms with a burst of magic.

Fifteen beds, all neatly made up. Stepping back into the corridor, he counted eight doors.

"Hundred and twenty kids here," he noted. "How many dorm sections are on the map?"

"Four." Romanov replied.

"We know they brought more than four hundred and eighty kids here." Damien shook his head. "It's supposed to *look* like this was their long-term home, but it clearly wasn't...so who were they trying to fool? And where did the kids go?"

"So far, the drones are finding that we're running up against walls where the map says the station ends," Romanov reported over the channel an hour later. "Is anyone finding anything behind the closed doors?"

Damien already knew the answer. Their people had been flagging areas on the shared map as they'd been exploring them, and the answer was much the same.

All they'd found so far was a "school" that happened to be in space that exactly matched the map they'd pulled from the landing bay. It was definitely a school for *Mages*, with several classrooms set up for the rather destructive process of teaching young Mages self-control, but it was otherwise relatively, well, normal.

"Kelzin," he addressed the pilot once everyone else was aboard. "Were there other access points?"

"A couple, but they weren't primary connectors," the shuttle pilot confirmed. "I targeted the one that looked like where they'd be bringing in ships." He paused. "I didn't expect half of the station to be cut off like you're saying it is."

"I doubt they took shuttles from the school area to the rest of the station," Damien replied. He and Romanov were now in the girls' dormitory, which was basically identical to the boys' dormitory, barring the additional storage cabinets in the bathroom for sanitary supplies.

He studied the map.

"The dormitories are all up against the edge of the map on this side, and the main administration area and teachers' apartments are up against the edge on the far side," he noted. "LaMonte, I suggest you get some of the computers booted up and see if there's a control program for opening a secret door."

Rhapsody's captain had ended up on the far end of the "school" from Damien and Romanov.

"We could just go through the walls," Niska suggested.

Damien studied the outer wall of the dormitory. Half of the actual dorm rooms with their neatly arranged beds backed against that wall. He had a grim suspicion that it could be opened, but...

"Yeah," he confirmed. "We're recording everything, right?"

"Everything is being recorded in the tactical network and relayed to the shuttle," Romanov confirmed. "And *that* is being backed up on *Rhapsody*. Even if this station blew up right now, everything we've seen would make it back."

And most importantly, no one there could edit or censor the footage, Damien realized. Whatever they saw, the Protectorate would eventually see.

"I don't know what kind of time limit we're facing, beyond that it's only two weeks before this thing hits Santa Maria," he noted. "The faster we know what we're going to find out, the better."

He grimaced.

"Cut 'em open, people. Let's gut this place and see what falls out."

Suiting actions to words, Damien took a second to inhale and study the innocent-looking wall barring his way. Force flashed from his hands and the metal came apart in tatters, the rotation of the station flinging the debris away from him into the space on the other side of the wall.

The piping and tanks in that space sent a chill down his spine.

He charged forward, studying the wreckage of the wall with a terrified eye.

"Romanov? You seeing this?" he asked.

"Concealed vents hooked up to a piping system and a set of tanks holding compressed gas," the Marine confirmed, his voice very flat. "More piping on the roof and to the other rooms. All eight rooms were hooked up to this setup."

Damien checked the tanks and swallowed hard. The source tanks were a standard size provided by the manufacturer, still labeled with their contents.

"Nix-Seven," he said softly. Neutralization Solution Seven, a low-lethality knockout gas. "They gassed the kids."

"Dosage controls over here," Romanov told him. "They're set by... room." He coughed, his voice breaking from the deadly calm flatness. "All of them are off now, but the last setting shows. They were keeping them at low dosages, to keep the ones sleeping asleep."

A row of stripped beds, identical to the ones in the room behind him, were lined up against the wall on the other side of the room. Without the bedding, it was more obvious that they all had wheels.

"Wait till the kids are asleep, pump in Nix-Seven to keep them asleep, unlock the wheels and roll them out," Damien said slowly. "Room by room. Clean out an entire dorm in a night. Want to bet the classes were segregated by dorms?"

"So no one would notice when an entire dorm of kids was suddenly missing?" Romanov asked. "Yeah. Where the hell did they take them?"

"We'll find out," Damien promised grimly. "What are the rest of you seeing?" he demanded.

"Dorms have...a fucked-up setup with gas and rolling beds," O'Malley replied instantly.

"This one, too," he confirmed.

"Then they all do, I'm guessing," Niska told them, the Augment's voice deathly cold. "What about the other side?"

"We're just seeing more administration capacity here," LaMonte said quietly. "I recognize the layout, though, so I'm going to try and find this shithole's real computer center."

"You follow that," Damien ordered. He turned to study the beds and swallowed down a wave of nausea.

"We're going to follow the path of these damn roller beds and see where they took their victims," he told them, the word slipping out unconsciously.

The channel was deathly silent for several seconds.

"Damien, I swear to you, by all that is holy, by all that I believe in, *we did not know*," Niska told him. "No one here with you knew any of this."

"I know." Damien stared blankly at a wall. "I know," he conceded again.

If he hadn't been certain of that, Niska would already be dead.

CHAPTER 37

THE LAST TRANSFER of beds, presumably with students in them, had never been cleaned up after. The people running the station had swapped the beds out with freshly made ones, probably by sheer habit and routine, but they hadn't cleaned up the inevitable scuff marks left by rolling beds on unmaintained wheels.

With Damien's mage-light hovering in the air and Romanov's flashlight trained on the scuffs, following the trail was easy. The corridors around them were blander than the ones in the school area of the station, more institutional.

"Are the drones sweeping into the new areas?" he asked the Marine.

"Yes, my lord. Two are sweeping ahead of us, but they're hitting a lot more closed doors here," Romanov told him.

"Looks like a hospital," Damien muttered.

"I prefer my hospitals less abandoned," his bodyguard replied. "This is...creepy."

Damien didn't answer, but he did increase the energy he was feeding his light. As the light starkly lit up the corridors and doors, he shivered.

No, that was not helping.

"Here," Romanov said as he suddenly stopped. "Looks like a bunch of them kept going, but this was where the first ones stopped."

Damien brought his light around to examine the door more closely. There were more scuff marks in front of it, rolling beds slowing and turned against the rotational pseudogravity of the station.

The door itself looked like a hospital door. Metal with a frosted glass pane, a panel where a wrist-comp could rapidly download data on the patient.

And a sign.

CRYOGENIC INTAKE ONE.

The door probably wasn't even locked, but Damien vaporized it anyway. Flame and metal hung in the air, frozen in his magic as he regarded them flatly. The fragments cooled under his power and he tossed them aside, leaving the doorway empty.

The sterile room beyond it wasn't familiar to him, but he knew it would be familiar to Romanov. The Marine's stony silence told him that.

The reason *Damien* wasn't familiar with it was that he'd been dying when his thaumic burnout coma had been stabilized and he'd been placed in partial cryo-stasis. Romanov had been the one to stand over the doctor while the risky process was completed.

Six operating suites hung open, their built-in IVs and oxygen lines hanging limply against the wall. Empty tanks were neatly stacked against the wall, and Damien didn't even need to look at them to know what they contained.

Cryogenic freezing required specific chemicals to be added to the blood to even make it possible, let alone safe. It was a complete violation of medical ethics to apply it to any person who wasn't already dying, because a notable percentage of the population had a fatal allergic reaction to the chemicals.

"They rolled them in here and hooked them up to oxygen and a more measured anesthetic gas while they pumped the cryo chemicals into them," Damien said onto the open channel as he walked into the room.

"The kids would never have known anything was wrong," he continued. There was only one actual cryo-stasis pod left in the room, an empty two-meter-long container still waiting to receive its precious cargo. "They wouldn't have woken up. They went to sleep, probably after a day or two of regular-seeming classes to lower their stress levels, and then they were frozen before they woke."

"*Why?*" Niska demanded. "I've never seen this kind of mass cryof-reezing outside of a fucking *war zone.*"

"Captain Rice had," Damien said in a very cold, very flat tone. He knew he was burying his emotions and he'd pay for it later, but he need-ed to focus now. "It was one of the advantages the Blue Star Syndicate had over their rivals. They had the gear to move into a system, sweep the cities for the vulnerable and weak, kidnap or convince them to sign up for sex work, then cryo-freeze them and move them to other systems where the demand was higher."

Modern slavery, after all, was almost never about labor. It was about power and sex—and the Blue Star Syndicate had been eager to provide whatever their clients would pay for.

Damien had never regretted killing the Syndicate's leader. Right now, part of him was wishing he could have made it more painful.

"There is no way that the Republic was selling these kids into slav-ery, Montgomery," Niska replied. "I can't assume we were *above* that any-more, but there'd be no point—and these were *Mages.*"

"No," Damien agreed. "They were frozen for transport. For ease of movement. But...they got them here easily enough. Why move them further?"

"Because then they moved them to Legatus," O'Malley said, her voice very quiet. "They needed an extra separation. People would wonder why Mages were going to Legatus. It would raise questions—the Republic wouldn't want more Mages at their capital.

"Nueva Bolivia, though?" She hissed. "No one would pay that much attention. Nueva Bolivia did well over the years by being worse than Legatus but never drawing as much attention as the biggest UnArcana World.

"So, they brought the kids from all over the Republic to here...and here, they froze them and moved them to Legatus."

"We're running out of answers, O'Malley," Damien snapped. "So, what, every Mage in the Republic was brought here for *processing?*"

"That's what it looks like," the Augment replied. "Thousands of kids. This wasn't murder... It was something else."

"We need to know what."

"I might have some answers," LaMonte's voice interjected, sounding very, very tired. "They did a good job of wiping the computers, but I got a few useful tidbits...including what looks like the Director's final report.

"I'm transferring it to all of your systems. I suggest you find a place to sit down before you play it. I'm digging for more, but..."

There was pain in LaMonte's voice and it wasn't physical.

"You need to see this, Damien," she said in a half-whisper.

Somehow, Damien knew he didn't want to be sitting in the cryo-prep suite when he saw the file LaMonte had found. He and Romanov retreated to the main lounge of the dorm, and he took a seat in one of the couches.

His vac-suit could interface with his wrist-comp to put a hologram in front of him. Activating that, he loaded in LaMonte's file with a verbal command and started it.

The man who appeared in front of him looked like he wasn't much taller than Damien himself. He was a squat, heavily muscled man with a shaven head and a white lab uniform. There were no insignia or name labels or anything on the uniform.

The stranger had been standing behind a desk when he recorded the hologram, and he leaned against it and smiled.

"This is Director James Paulson," he said calmly. "This will be the final progress report for Project Prometheus's Nueva Bolivian facility.

"The last phase of subjects has completed cryo-prep. I have con-firmed with the sourcing teams that there are no further waves of sub-jects en route, so I will be commencing the cleanup protocols. This will be the final message sent by the Link aboard Prometheus Station Nueva Bolivia."

Paulson paused, seeming to marshal his thoughts.

"As the head of Prometheus Station Nueva Bolivia, I'm not sure I agree with the decision to concentrate production at the Centurion facility, but I understand the logic. We will no longer have the supply of juvenile subjects we've been working through, and removing the cryo-stasis from the process removes that wastage factor.

"Our average ratio has been one point two percent," Paulson said calmly, as if he was talking about damaged microwaves, not dead teenagers. "I understand that Dr. Finley has brought the final wastage down under three percent, so even with transport, we are ahead of where we were when Finley was operating here.

"The final shipment will be one hundred and sixty subjects. While I presume Project Prometheus has plans for future supplies of subjects, that is the end of our internal sourcing."

The Director paused again.

"I will be exercising my termination authority under the cleanup protocols for a number of the staff; information to be attached to this message. Several of the teachers, especially, seem to have suffered significant erosion to their commitment to the project's goals.

"This has been a difficult project for us all, but the individuals listed represent a potential threat to Prometheus's security. The remaining two hundred and eighteen members of the Nueva Bolivian Station's staff will relocate to the Centurion Facility."

Paulson smiled.

"I hope you have room for us," he concluded. "We are eager to continue our work in helping protect the Republic.

"Director Paulson, out."

The recording froze and Damien sighed.

"Kelly?" he asked.

"Our data access was limited to what was in active memory when Paulson wiped the computers," she told him. "The message he'd just sent. A recent map."

"And his termination list?"

"We got it. I sent Niska to check out the quarters of the couple I could locate."

"And I'm there," the Augment told them.

The cyborg spy sounded very, very old.

"That doesn't sound like good news," Damien pointed out.

"I don't know if Paulson did it himself or sent someone else to take care of it, but the quarters were hermetically sealed," Niska said. "We cut the doors open, but the seal had mummified the body."

"That's what I expected," Damien admitted.

"Shot in the head, short range." Niska sighed. "All the hallmarks of an Augment assassin, as if my cohorts needed *more* blood on their hands."

"Fuck." Damien swallowed. "What about this Finley?" he asked. "Do we have any idea where they were working on the station?"

"There's a sealed area on the map I found, marked as blocked under a Colonel Samuel Finley's authority," LaMonte told him. "It's near you."

"Flash me and Romanov a waypoint," he ordered. "If they wanted to hide it even here, I want to see it."

CHAPTER 38

THE LAST THING Damien was expecting to find on a Republican station—a *pre*-Republican station, really—dedicated to some horrifying project involving thousands of teenage Mages was a runic defense.

Years of practice, however, meant that he scanned a wall for the energy signatures only a Rune Wright could see before slicing into the space Finley had sealed.

"Wait, what the hell?" he demanded aloud.

"My lord?" Romanov asked.

"There's a runic shield on the interior of the wall," Damien said slowly. He stepped carefully along the wall, running his fingers along the metal and studying the magic. "If I cut the wall open with magic—or with vibroblades, for that matter—it'll explode.

"There's got to be a door that's been flagged to check for a token."

"It's also possible that it was just sealed to explode no matter what," Romanov pointed out. "Wait...could you teleport through it?"

Damien studied the magic as best as he could through the wall.

"Yes, it couldn't check for a token when teleporting into the space, so that has to be safe." A chill of familiarity ran down his spine. "How did you know that, Denis?"

"Asimov, my lord," the Marine replied. "The defense on Kay's apartment."

Kay had been an ex-Keeper, an agent of some kind of conspiracy inside the government of the Protectorate. He'd been involved in wiping out the *rest* of the surviving membership of the Royal Order of the Keepers of Secrets and Oaths, using a squad of borrowed Legatan Augments to do it.

The magic on Kay's apartment had been near-unique in Damien's experience, a complex spell designed to counteract the capabilities of Hands and other powerful Mages.

But the shield here was identical; and that suggested...

"It's the same shield," Damien breathed. "What the hell was a *Keeper Mage* doing here?"

"I don't know," Romanov said grimly. "But I think the answer is on the other side of that runic shield, my lord."

"Stay here," Damien ordered. This station was getting creepier by the second. He studied the wall for a few key seconds, then *stepped.*

Damien appeared inside the lab. Teleporting inside a rotating station, however, had thrown off his mental calculation for the short jump, and he appeared about twenty centimeters in the air and ended up face first on the metal floor.

Groaning, he rose to his knees and studied the walls. Like the rune matrix in Kay's apartment on Mars, it was designed to explode if severed—but there were *always* weaknesses a Rune Wright could find that someone writing code in Martian Runic wouldn't see.

He cut the matrix, exhaling as its energy drained off. Once that was done, he slashed open a door for Romanov and struggled to his feet to look around.

Other than the runes, there was nothing to make him think this was a Mage's facility. The room he'd stepped into looked like any general practitioner's office on any world he'd visited. There was a mock skeleton, pictures of the brain, cupboards, a screen to link to the doctor's wrist-comp.

Dismissing all of that, Damien pushed through a door and into the rest of the space. Even more than the rest of the facility, this space gave off a massive sense of *research institute*. The runes continued along the wall as he studied the space.

There were operating tables with dozens of cameras pointed at them. Holographic projectors that would once have held models of whatever the researchers were working on. A large-scale 3-D printer in the corner.

No answers. Just a sterile, neatly cleaned-up and put-away lab that someone had sealed behind a spell that could have destroyed the entire station.

"There's another sealed unit back there," Romanov noted. "Given the security, why would they have sealed a second layer?"

Damien crossed the lab and checked his map. The closed-off room that Romanov had indicated was next to a set of double doors close to where the cryo-prep suites had been. At some point, a subject could have been rolled down here and into that section of the closed lab.

He blew the double doors open almost absently as he turned to the remaining sealed unit.

"Enough space for half a dozen operating rooms in there," Romanov said quietly. "Is it sealed magically?"

"No," Damien replied after checking. "Though..." He paused and stepped up to the door, running his finger along what should have been the seam.

"They welded it shut. Paranoid much?"

"Not paranoid enough?" Romanov asked.

"Not paranoid enough," Damien agreed. He stepped back and obliterated the doors. Stepping into the debris, he found six...somethings. They weren't operating rooms, though they definitely had the equipment for them.

There were operating table–like structures. Cryo-chemical IVs. Oxygen. Everything that had been in the cryo-prep chambers...except...

There were two sets of IVs at each section. One positioned for the usual wrist insertion and the other...around the neck?

"Those are preset saws," Romanov said in a sick voice, and pointed. "What the hell?"

Damien followed the Marine's pointing gauntlet and approached the table. The Marine was right. There was a set of saw blades attached to the table, in a set that would neatly close around the top of someone's skull.

A second piece of equipment was clearly intended to hold some kind of canister.

The full realization of just what he was looking at finally struck Damien, and he struggled away to throw up.

"Damien?" LaMonte asked in a desperate tone. "Damien, what the hell are you looking at?"

"It's a brain extraction facility," he said quietly, trying to activate the systems to clean the inside of his helmet before he threw up again. "They murdered the kids and pulled their brains out. There are life support canisters here; presumably, they had some kind of brain implant to interface with the canister systems and keep the brains alive."

"Dr. Finley's mysterious process," Niska said, the Augment's voice slow and careful. "My god. But why? What the *hell* would they be doing with Mage brains?"

"I don't know," Damien said, letting his cold anger suffuse his voice as he gave up and used magic to clean the inside of his vac-suit. "But there was a facility at Centurion, Niska. At the fucking heart of your fucking Republic. The kids were taken there, murdered and frozen alike.

"*Why?*"

"I don't know," Niska replied in a choking sob, and Damien realized he was hearing something he'd never heard before. The Augment was fighting against the same tears and rage as he was.

"I don't know, Damien Montgomery," he finally said, his voice still trembling. "But there are only a handful of facilities at Centurion covert enough that they could have hidden this.

"LaMonte and I will go over the data as we're on our way. I will work out which one. We will find the answers, Damien. I know what Bryan Ricket died for now...and I swear to you, we will *end it.*"

"On our way where?" O'Malley asked into the silence.

"Legatus," Damien and Niska replied simultaneously.

CHAPTER 39

"THAT'S A LOT OF GUNSHIPS. I'm not sure they're bluffing this time, sir."

Mage-Captain Kulkarni's words echoed on the flag deck. On the main display, the Republic fleet orbiting Centurion had formed up behind a shield of gunships.

The defenders had once again combined gunships from multiple cardinal forts, though their losses had reduced how many the fortresses could spare. They'd also launched the gunships from the two heavy carriers in the battle group, allowing them to assemble a shield of roughly four thousand gunships.

That shield made it hard to see just what the capital ships were doing, but it was still clear that they were moving out.

"Their course isn't toward us," Roslyn reported as she studied the vector. "They're vectoring for Decurion." She shook her head. "Those gunships alone could overwhelm the defenses General Tone has taken control of."

"And they quite possibly have some way to shut down Decurion's orbital platforms," Kulkarni agreed. "It looks like all of the cardinals are holding on to a thousand gunships and they've stripped the inner forts this time. We might be able to press through, but not easily."

"We could disable the accelerator ring, but we'd lose half the fleet and they'd retake Decurion," Admiral Alexander said calmly. "And then we'd be trapped against the gas giant by the RIN."

Roslyn shivered. She could see how that would wrap up in her head. A battered and depleted Second Fleet, short on munitions and trapped by an enraged enemy. There'd be no retreat for them.

The destruction of the Centurion Accelerator Ring would wreck the Republic's logistics for years, but if the Protectorate lost Second Fleet...it was possible, even likely, that the Republic would still have enough fuel to finish the war.

"They're leaving the Ring vulnerable, but they know we can't take the risk of launching an attack," Kulkarni concluded. "Still seems rather... blasé about their most critical strategic asset."

"They're counting on their psych profile of me," Alexander replied. "I haven't even seen that profile, and I can tell you it says I won't leave General Tone and her people to die when I can protect them." She smiled wryly. "That would be because I won't.

"Take the Fleet to battle stations and set an intercept course. If they want to give us a chance to reduce their mobile forces, let's take it."

Roslyn could think of a dozen reasons why that was a bad idea—not least among them the fact that the starships in Centurion orbit were very nearly a match for Second Fleet.

If they were concerned about not having a combat-capable fleet after attacking Centurion, the same concern had to apply to engaging the enemy fleet.

But the Admiral was right. There were thousands of Marines and Navy spacers at Decurion. The fixed defenses could stand off a few ships, but the Republic battle group would retake the planet in hours and kill or capture them all.

"Chambers," the Admiral said quietly, gesturing Roslyn over to her.

"Yes, sir?"

"Everyone else is going to be watching the RIN battle group," Alexander told her. "That's their jobs. I want you watching everything else."

"Sir?" Roslyn was confused. That was also part of the sensor crews' job—but her job was to support the Admiral.

"They know as well as we do that the margin on this fight is razor-thin," her boss replied. "If they're courting it, something has changed—and I don't know what. So, I want you to keep an eye open for their game."

"I can do that, sir," Roslyn promised.

"I know," Alexander confirmed, then sighed. "Two more bloody days. All I needed was two more bloody days."

"Until what, sir?"

"I trust you, Chambers," the Admiral told her. "But I'm going to hold that card close to my chest a while longer. We've been too badly penetrated for me to completely trust anyone yet."

"They chose their course well," Kulkarni noted. "Just far enough off and pushing just fast enough that we're going to need to jump to intercept them." The black Mage-Captain shook her head.

"It's not going to *help* them, since we can jump out to meet them," she continued. "It's like they're courting a full fleet engagement."

"That's exactly what they're doing," Alexander agreed. "But why?" The Admiral shook her head. "I guess it doesn't matter. Even if it's a feint, we have to honor it.

"Move us out from Centurion, heading for here." The Admiral flagged a point on the display. "Let's call that Point Alpha."

Point Alpha was almost sixty minutes' flight away at fifteen gravities, well into safe territory for the Fleet to jump. It was also, Roslyn noted, in the opposite direction of the Republic fleet—but along the same line.

"From Point Alpha, we'll jump to Point Bravo, *here*." Another icon dropped onto the screen. "That will move our velocity to being directly toward them, and we will emerge inside missile range. Let's avoid their range advantage if we can, shall we?"

Righteous Shield shivered beneath them as the battleship's engines came to life.

"Fleet is moving as ordered," Kulkarni confirmed. "Fifteen gravities to Point Alpha."

"And send..."—Alexander considered—"TK-5331 back to the current RV point with the logistics fleet. Make sure the captains there are fully updated on everything we're seeing."

"Yes, sir."

It was an odd order in Roslyn's mind, though it wasn't like a courier ship like TK-5331 was going to change anything. But the freighters at the RV weren't really going to change anything either.

"Keep the rest of the couriers receiving full telemetry updates and cycling at ten-minute intervals," Alexander continued. "If this battle doesn't go our way, I want the Protectorate to know why."

Roslyn glanced over at the Admiral in surprise. If they could dodge the problem of being in the Republic's range before they were in their own range, then it didn't seem likely they'd lose this battle.

The Admiral met her gaze levelly...and then winked.

Something was going on—something related to the two more days Alexander had wanted.

Right now, however, Roslyn's responsibility was keeping an eye on Centurion. Fighting the battle was everyone else's job.

Her task was to find out why the Republic had decided to fight at all.

Fifty-five minutes at fifteen gravities left the Protectorate fleet with a significant velocity away from Centurion and a rapidly growing distance.

The Republic battle group wasn't accelerating as quickly, though they'd started sooner and had known their destination all along. If they'd been a Protectorate force, Roslyn would have been half-expecting them to jump toward Decurion in the near future.

Certainly, the jump that Admiral Alexander was planning was a tricky calculation, if safe enough. It was *hard* to teleport a ship less than a light-hour. Part of the reason for the hour-long delay accelerating away from the Republic ships was to give the Mages time to make those calculations.

It was also giving Roslyn time to go over the sensor data available from Centurion. There had to be a reason the Republic had chosen this moment to launch their breakout.

It might be as simple as they knew what the Admiral was expecting in two days, but it was more likely that they had something else in the works. Some plan that required getting Second Fleet's attention.

And pulling them out of position. Roslyn swallowed a curse as the realization hit her. A few moments later, her attempt to check into her suspicion ran into a roadblock.

There were drones on the far side of Centurion, keeping an eye on what was going on. Right now, however, the telemetry from those drones wasn't being processed. It was going straight into cold storage as the sensor teams focused their computer cycles on the enemy fleet.

"Tactical, I need the sensor feed from the far side of Centurion updated and fed to my console," she said into her headset, linking herself to the tactical team.

"We're a bit busy, *Lieutenant*," the Commander running *Righteous Shield's* tactical department replied sharply. "We need our processing cycles for the battle, not your curiosity."

"Myopia kills, Commander," Roslyn said, equally sharply. "If we don't know what our enemy is doing, we get surprised—and in war, surprise means death. I need that feed, Commander—or you can explain to the Admiral why we don't have it."

The channel was silent.

"I'll have a Chief run it for you," the Commander replied. "I don't know what you expect to see, though."

The channel dropped and Roslyn set up her console, waiting for the data to get properly processed. She had *minutes* before Second Fleet jumped, and if she was right...

There.

The drones weren't smart enough to be able to flag any given set of data as more important. They encrypted everything they saw and transmitted it to a relay drone that packaged all of the data from its subordinates, encrypted it again and fired it off to Second Fleet.

Decrypting that data and turning it into something humans could process took computer cycles, a precious resource on the edge of battle, and that was what the Republic had been counting on.

"Admiral! We have a convoy breaking free on the far side of Centurion," Roslyn reported. "Looks like four battleships escorting multiple antimatter tankers."

Unless she missed her numbers, that was enough fuel to operate the entire RIN for months. It was probably every scrap of antimatter that had been produced since Second Fleet had arrived two weeks earlier.

The flag deck was silent as Alexander zoomed the main display in on the convoy.

"If there are four battleships there, the deployed battle group is weaker than we expected," she said aloud. She sighed. "But still powerful enough that we can't spare the ships to deal with four battleships. Damn it."

Catch-22. To take down a hundred and sixty million tons of RIN battleships, they'd need to send two-thirds of either their battleships or cruisers. That would leave the remainder facing *five* battleships and twenty cruisers, plus four thousand gunships.

"Two days," Alexander repeated. "I swear these people get the same updates I do."

"Sir?" Kulkarni asked. "Jump is in sixty seconds."

"Get a courier updated and send them to the logistics train," Alexander ordered. "We might get lucky. For now...proceed as planned.

"We can't stop that convoy, so we'll take the advantage they gave us to get it out. We may pay for it later, but they'll pay for it today.

"Second Fleet will engage the enemy."

CHAPTER 40

THERE WAS the usual moment of chill from a jump...and then everything was pain. Roslyn doubled over as her gut rebelled. Her lungs rebelled. It felt like every muscle was spasming as pain wracked through her body.

She'd been involved in short jumps in training, down to three light-hours. Those had been uncomfortable but tolerable. This jump was less than three light-*minutes*, the shortest jump she'd ever been on by an order of magnitude.

Everything hurt. She lost precious seconds to stifling the pain and trying to focus, and as she took a gasping breath and looked around, she realized she was doing better than most of the flag deck crew.

Missiles sparkled across the display as she looked, though, as the fleetwide targeting plan activated automatically.

They'd emerged close enough to fire on the enemy and far enough away that the enemy wouldn't see them until well after they'd arrived. The unexpected consequences of the short jump had cost them that "free" time, even with the computers reacting faster than the humans.

It would be another thirty seconds before they saw the Republic force's reaction to their movement, but the Republic force would have been aware of their presence before they fired.

There were Mages who could carry out shorter jumps than this—the *Picard Maneuver* had been covered in her classes, for example—but most of the records she'd seen on microjumping suggested that it was a task best left to Hands and the insane.

Alexander took longer to recover than Roslyn did, and the Flag Lieutenant was about to undo her restraints to check on the Admiral when she finally raised her head and smiled grimly.

"How bad, Lieutenant?" she asked.

"We launched at jump-plus-thirty-five seconds," Roslyn reported crisply. The display was now showing where the Republican forces had been at roughly that time, and the gunships were shifting to new formations.

"Enemy initial reaction appears to be their new standard anti-missile doctrine," she continued. "And...there we go. Incoming missiles."

It was an insane number of missiles. The Republic's gunships had almost no ammunition capacity, but for the three salvos they launched, they increased the firepower of RIN forces almost tenfold.

"Twenty-seven thousand–plus incoming."

"Leave it to Kulkarni and the others," Alexander ordered. "We have a doctrine for this now."

Mostly, from what Roslyn could tell, the RMN's doctrine for gunship strikes was to expend a *lot* of missiles in defensive mode. Their first two salvos had been launched offensively, but she could see the icons shifting as their next salvos went out looking for missiles.

"Look for the trick, Chambers," the Admiral continued. Alexander's gaze was focused on the display. "I need to run this battle, but you don't. The itch on the back of my neck says they're still playing games."

"Watching like a hawk, sir," Roslyn promised.

"That's funny."

The third Republican salvo was in space now, but missile flight times were long. Over two minutes had passed since the first salvos had launched. It would be five more before the first RMN salvo hit and six minutes before the first Republican missiles arrived.

Hopefully, the defensive salvos would reduce how many of the Republican weapons made it through. There were over seventy-five *thousand* hostile missiles on the display.

But Roslyn had been told to ignore all of that, and distracting as it was, she was trying. Her focus was on the enemy formation, and there was an odd energy signature.

"Tactical, can I borrow a sensor cluster?" she asked. "I need active sensors pointed at a very specific spot."

"Fine." The Commander didn't say anything beyond the one word, and Roslyn wasn't even offended. They were in the middle of a battle, after all.

Roslyn trained that one sensor cluster—*Righteous Shield of Valor* had some three hundred of the things—on her strange energy signature and pulsed active sensors as hard as she could.

Almost a minute round trip. Missiles were going to start blowing up and wrecking her ability to see what the RIN was doing, but she needed her answer.

And there it was. Speaking of things blowing up...

Where she'd seen the spike of mysterious energy, there was now an expanding debris cloud that, from the scans, had been a twenty-megaton Republican cruiser with a crew of a thousand people.

"Why did one of their ships just blow up?" Roslyn muttered aloud, then silenced herself. Everyone else was fighting the battle. Her curiosity wasn't *that* important.

She pulled up the energy pulse she'd IDed. It was familiar...really familiar. Where had she seen it before?

Santiago.

The realization hit Roslyn like a ton of bricks. Santiago. She'd seen that energy signature before at Santiago, when the Republican transports had jumped to avoid the RMN capturing their jump drives.

It was the signature of a ship coming apart when they jumped—and there was no reason a single RIN cruiser would have jumped on her own. She pulled the historical data...and there it was.

"Admiral Alexander, sir," she exclaimed, finally turning to the fleet commander. "The RIN starships are *gone.*"

"What?" Alexander demanded.

"They jumped just after the last gunship salvo, sir," Roslyn explained. "They lost a couple of ships, but most of the battle group is gone. I don't know where they went, but they left the gunships as sacrificial lambs."

"But they're still launching missiles," Kulkarni said. "That makes no..."

"If the gunships are running on autopilot, they could dump their entire life support system and use the extra engine power to strap additional missiles to the hull," Roslyn pointed out. "They don't need to duplicate the full firepower of the gunship formation, just of the two dozen starships that are missing."

Both of Roslyn's seniors were now staring at the display.

"She's right," Kulkarni said grimly. "Where could they have gone?"

"It doesn't matter where they fled to," Admiral Alexander replied. "What matters is where they could *hurt us most.*

"Orders to the Fleet: Admiral Medici's squadron is to jump to Decurion and reinforce the defenses there.

"The rest of Second Fleet is to *immediately* jump to the location of the logistics convoy!"

They'd fired off over half of the missiles Second Fleet was carrying. If the RIN had somehow located the munitions ships hiding a light-year from Legatus, they could end the siege in one strike.

Despite their fears, the supply fleet was alone and intact. Three dozen freighters of various sizes hung in deep space with no reference points. They'd been cycling in and out over the course of the siege, ships joining Second Fleet to drop off their supplies and then heading back into Protectorate space.

Without the thirty-six ships currently present and the twenty more somewhere between Legatus and Ardennes, the Siege of Legatus would have been impossible.

"Everyone's still here," Kulkarni reported. "Courier TK-626 is reporting in as well." She paused, looking at the display suspiciously. "I didn't think TK-626 was attached to Second Fleet."

Roslyn was watching the Admiral and could *see* the tension leaving her shoulders.

"She isn't. I know who she's attached to, though, and that's the best news I've had all day," Alexander told the operations officer. "Someone get me a link to Commodore Iceni."

It only took a couple of moments to link the Admiral to the man commanding the two Armed Auxiliary Fast Heavy Freighters providing security for the supply ships.

The AAFHFs weren't warships, but the pair under Commodore Warren Iceni's command were brand-new, built after a decommissioned AAFHF had served with distinction in covert operations.

Anyone who decided to tangle with the supply fleet was going to get an ugly surprise.

"Admiral Alexander!" Iceni greeted her. "I'll admit, I wasn't expecting to see all of Second Fleet suddenly arrive out here. What happened?"

"A significant Republican battle group escaped the siege," Alexander said bluntly. "Here was where they could have done the most damage, and given the degree of RID penetration we seem to suffer on a regular basis, I had to be sure the convoy was safe.

"I see TK-626 here. Where is Admiral Hovo Tarpinian?"

That wasn't a name Roslyn recognized. At all. *Who* was Tarpinian?

"Tarpinian jumped less than ten minutes ago to see if he could cut off the runaway convoy," Iceni told her. "His ships are—"

"Still classified, Commodore," Alexander cut him off. She shook her head. "Damn. I need to know where the Republic went."

"At the least, sir, I'll move the supply fleet to rendezvous sequence, mmm, Kappa," Iceni replied. "We should be safe, but I'll have courier ships on standby in case we aren't."

"Thank you, Commodore."

The channel cut and Alexander was silent in thought for a moment.

"Mage-Captain Kulkarni, can the fleet jump again?" she asked.

"All of our ships have four Mages, sir," Kulkarni replied. "We haven't made any jumps before today, so even with the medical casualties from the microjump, every ship has at least one Mage ready for action."

"Then take us back to Centurion," Alexander ordered. "Let's intercept that convoy if we can."

She shook her head.

"We're probably too late, but it will at least let us rendezvous with Admiral Tarpinian."

Kulkarni's gaze was questioning, but she set to work. That left it to Roslyn to ask the question she knew the operations officer wanted to.

"Who is Admiral Tarpinian, sir?" she asked quietly.

"An old friend of my family," Alexander told her. "None of you would know him; he's been retired for twenty years. We dragged the old warhorse away from a Mediterranean beach house because we needed someone we could trust beyond all reason.

"As for why he's here, well." The Admiral smiled. "Project Plowshare was the covert, *semi*-official attempt to expand the Martian Navy for this war.

"But we had a black project before that. Depending on who you talked to, it was Project Weyland or Project Mjolnir...and I was told its first fruits would be mine *very* shortly.

"And it seems that Admiral Tarpinian has been as reliable as ever."

CHAPTER 41

"WHAT THE *HELL* ARE THOSE?" Kulkarni demanded.

The tanker convoy was gone, but a cloud of radiation and debris suggested that the tankers hadn't escaped. Admiral Tarpinian had clearly cut them off and destroyed them and their escorts before they could escape.

Instead of the convoy, twelve ships orbited Centurion at a distance. Only three of the twelve ships were recognizable, and all of them were *huge* to Roslyn's eyes.

"Officers, those would be the reinforcements I've repeatedly promised," Alexander told the operations officer. "Twelve ships under Admiral Hovo Tarpinian, including some of the largest warships we've ever built.

"Okay, so these are *Peace*-class battleships," Roslyn noted, highlighting the three sixty-megaton ships. "These are cruisers and look like ours, but I'm reading them as *fifteen* megatons."

The *Honorific*-class ships were the newest cruisers in the RMN's inventory that Roslyn knew of—and were twelve-million-ton ships.

"And then...I have no idea what these three are," the Flag Lieutenant admitted, highlighting the heavy warships at the heart of the new battle group. Each was a full kilometer long. The core hull was a pyramidical spike, four hundred meters across at the base and a hundred meters across at the top, topped by a half-kilometer wide, two-hundred-meter-thick, cylindrical hammerhead.

"I don't know what they are either," Kulkarni agreed. "But they're a hundred million freaking tons."

"Before there was Project Plowshare, there was Project Weyland," Mage Admiral Alexander said quietly. "Inside Project Weyland was Project Mjolnir, the program to design and build an entirely new type of warship.

"Your three mystery ships are *Mjolnir*, *Masamune* and *Durendal*," she continued. "They are *Mjolnir*-class dreadnoughts of the Royal Martian Navy, our closest-kept secret for the last four years.

"*Mjolnir* has been ready for a while, but we didn't want to commit a single dreadnought to action alone. So, we rushed two of her sisters to completion—which gave us the chance to finish the only fully covert set of *Peace*-class ships and to construct the testbed vessels for the *Salamander*-class cruisers.

"They're the only reinforcements we're getting for another year, but they're the doorknocker I plan on kicking in Centurion's teeth with," Alexander concluded. "And it seems like Admiral Tarpinian has made an appropriate opening impression.

"Mage-Captain Kulkarni, please get the Fleet and Task Force Mjolnir on a rendezvous course that will keep us out of range of the cardinal fortresses. We'll need to coordinate with Admiral Tarpinian and complete a plan as the rest of Second Fleet rearms."

Alexander smiled broadly.

"Because the *other* thing Admiral Tarpinian brought with him should be the first production runs of the Phoenix IX. Enough for at least one full load for every ship we have."

Assuming the IX outranged the Republic's long-range missiles, then the tide of the battle had just turned, and Roslyn joined the rest of the flag deck in a drawn-out noise that was somewhere between a chuckle and a growl.

They'd held Legatus under siege for weeks. Now, with Phoenix IXs and the dreadnoughts, well...

It might be time to finally end the damn war.

"How the hell did they manage that?"

Roslyn and Kulkarni were locked in the operations officer's office, going over the specifications for their latest arrivals.

The exact toy earning the older woman's surprised comment was an entirely new weapon system aboard the *Salamander*-class cruisers and the *Mjolnir*-class dreadnoughts: a heavy bombardment missile with thirty thousand gravities of acceleration.

"It's six times the size of the Phoenix IX with a warhead only twenty percent larger," Roslyn pointed out. "Most of that extra mass goes to engines and fuel. They managed it by giving her twice the power-to-weight ratio."

"The IX already involves an entirely new generation of thrust modulators and engine tech." Kulkarni shook her head. "The VIII only had a five-hundred-gravity increase over the VII. A full twenty-percent increase in acceleration for only a thirty-second decrease in flight time?"

"That's what we had with the VII, wasn't it?" Roslyn asked. "And for all that, I'm not entirely sure it's enough."

Numbers and vector diagrams splashed across Kulkarni's office wall.

"We have less of a range advantage now than the Republic had yesterday," she pointed out. "The IX accelerates faster but it only has half a million kilometers more range than the VIII. The Samurai has eight hundred thousand, but we only have nine ships with Samurai launchers and they're damned expensive."

If the newly reinforced Second Fleet fired off a full volley of the new heavy missiles, it would cost as much as a new destroyer. There were definitely times it would be *worth* it, but Roslyn could see the Samurai remaining a special-circumstances weapon.

"How long until we're fully reloaded?" Roslyn asked her boss.

"Longer than I'd like. Shockingly, our ships aren't really designed to *remove* missiles from our magazines except by firing them," Kulkarni replied. "The Admiral gave me a few more hours to build a plan, but I think the easiest way is to actually cycle ships back through the supply fleet by squadron.

"Plus, I'm nervous about the fact that those starships ran away," she noted.

Roslyn nodded. *Nervous* understated her own feelings. Two full carrier groups had decided to pull out of Legatus, leaving Centurion to Second Fleet's gentle care.

The only thing that was stopping them from launching an attack against the accelerator ring *right now* was that they'd take fewer losses if they attacked with the new missiles.

"They have FTL coms," Roslyn reminded her boss. "We don't. The moment we're stuck in against the defenses, they're going to jump in behind us."

"That's my reading as well," Kulkarni agreed. "But...what worries me, Chambers, is that they had the force to go toe-to-toe with Second Fleet. They would probably have *lost* in the end, but it wouldn't have been a sure thing."

"They went for reinforcements, you think?" Roslyn asked.

"I think they went to meet reinforcements that were already on their way," Kulkarni replied. "There are at least half a dozen more carrier groups' worth of ships floating around, guarding the Republic's systems. Even without pulling back their offensive forces, they could assemble a fleet that could kick us out of Legatus with an overwhelming advantage."

"*Mjolnir* will help with that." Roslyn was hoping aloud more than she was stating an opinion.

"To a point. To a point," Kulkarni repeated with a sigh. "I don't think they're going to be able to field a force that can really beat us head to head without pulling back most of their fleet."

That was, after all, basically what the Protectorate had done to assemble Second Fleet.

"That was the minimum mission objective for this plan," she continued. "By attacking Legatus, we'd force them to pull ships back from the front. Buy ourselves time.

"I'm worried we've concentrated enough force to make ourselves overconfident," Kulkarni admitted.

"And not enough force to actually get ourselves out if they come at us with everything," Roslyn finished the thought for her old boss with a shiver. "They're good; we have to give them that. The question is whether they have the fuel to push a major attack in on us."

"My only hope is that they'll be short on gunships," her superior replied. "They'll have the missiles, but if we can cripple their gunship forces' fuel supply..."

Roslyn shook her head.

"They were flying fusion engines in Nia Kriti," she reminded Kulkarni. "That was to fool us into thinking they weren't a threat, but I doubt those were specially built ships. What do you want to bet that they can change the gunships' engines over to run as fusion drives? They'll lose in operating range and acceleration, but they won't need antimatter for them."

"I forgot that," the older woman admitted. "Damn. I won't take that bet, Lieutenant Chambers—because the only thing I have to bet with is the entirety of Second Fleet."

CHAPTER 42

THE TEAM GATHERING aboard *Rhapsody in Purple* was a quiet group. The ship itself was crowded to the nth degree, but there were only so many people aboard that Damien trusted completely.

And regardless of anything else, Damien had no intention of surrendering command of the mission. That meant that the planning meeting was with the people *he* trusted, which meant that only Niska and Maata were present from the Legatans aboard the ship.

He also trusted O'Malley, but that was why she was one of the people guarding the door to the room.

The MISS contingent was represented by Captain LaMonte and her wife, Xi Wu. Damien and Agent Romanov represented the Protectorate government.

The six people in the room represented a surprisingly wide cross-section of humanity from both the Protectorate and the Republic. They also represented the only people outside of whatever horror show the Republic was running who understood the true failing of the Republic.

"I've put the pieces together," Niska told them all. "It was the name that was the final puzzle piece, and it all adds up now."

"Can you lay it out for the rest of us?" Damien asked. "I'm guessing you'd heard of Project Prometheus?"

The old cyborg bowed his head.

"Yes," he said softly. "Only in passing, never directly. *I* heard about it so rarely that I can only assume that it was and remains the most classified of projects in what is now the Republic of Faith and Reason. For obvious reasons."

"Hell, I'd never heard of it, and I dealt with a lot of strange shit for LMID," Maata noted.

"It was tied to Project Hephaestus, and that's our biggest lead here," Niska told them all. "Hephaestus was the overarching project for the covert creation of what became the Republic Interstellar Navy. Greek names for the components: Athena was the new sensors, Ares was the warship hulls, Apollo was the missile upgrades...et cetera, et cetera."

"So, Prometheus fit right in," Damien said.

"Except I knew the full org chart for Hephaestus, and Prometheus wasn't on it," the old Augment admitted. "It was a secret project, one operating under the cover of another...and I think I know which one."

"And?" LaMonte asked bluntly. "You're dancing around the point, Niska. What do you know?"

James Niska buried his face in his hands for several long seconds.

"I'm sorry," he whispered. "It should have been obvious to us all. Prometheus was buried in Project Daedalus. Everything about Daedalus was classified beyond the highest levels; it's the only organization that would have had the authority and the power to carry out something like Prometheus." He shook his head. "And even then, only with the cooperation of the people in charge of everything."

"Daedalus?" Damien asked.

"The jump drives, Damien," Niska told him. "In legends, Prometheus stole fire from the gods. We didn't steal fire from the gods; we stole it from our brothers.

"The Republic doesn't have a technological jump drive. They have an apparatus that uses the brains and magic of murdered Mages to jump their ships."

The silence in the meeting room was now sharp enough to cut with.

"It makes sense, doesn't it?" Damien finally asked, swallowing down his rage. Niska wasn't his enemy. The Legatan might have helped this come to pass—but he was also the only reason they knew any of this.

"We should have known," Niska snarled. "Two hundred years of research and not even a *hint* of an answer, and then suddenly we have one? We should have suspected. *I* should have suspected, should have looked deeper."

"And now thousands of children are dead," Damien told him. It was harsh but true. "You can't change that, so what are you going to do to try and fix it?"

"It's worse than you think," the old cyborg replied. "It was only rumor on the Republic worlds I visited, so I ignored it, but now it makes sense."

"*What* makes sense?" Damien demanded.

"The civilian Mages on the occupied worlds were being rounded up and shipped somewhere," Maata said quietly. "That's the rumor you're talking about, isn't it?"

The chill in Damien's spine turned to ice.

"They're going to murder prisoners to fuel their fleet?"

"It's the only thing that makes sense," Niska whispered. "My god, what did I make possible? What did I help create?"

"We'll stop them, Niska," Damien promised.

"That won't be enough," the old cyborg said flatly. "I asked you to help me restore my nation's honor, but this had to have been going on all along. These programs would have started while I was working for LMID, possibly before.

"My nation, my leaders...they never *had* any honor," Niska spat. "I can't make this right. I can't find honor in what my people, what my *planet* has done. All I can do is help destroy it."

The room was silent again.

"We need to know where the actual facility is, then," LaMonte said. "We can get *Rhapsody* in. If we're careful on cycling Xi's Mages, we can get anywhere. But getting *out* is a different story."

"We can't get it wrong," Damien concluded. "We need to hit the right facility the first time, free the prisoners, find *proof* of what's fueling the Republic fleet."

"They've got to know," Romanov snapped. "They can't have warships that they don't understand."

"With how black they kept the jump drives, they can," Niska pointed out. "I don't think most of the RIN's *engineers*, let alone the rest of the Navy, know what's inside their jump drives. They're black boxes, maintained at heavily secured facilities."

"Facilities that would have to have Mages," Damien growled. "This couldn't have been done without Mage help. Every type of humanity has their monsters, so let's not pretend Magekind is innocent in this horror."

"So, we want one of those repair facilities?" Romanov asked.

"No," Niska replied. "We want the origin point. The production facility, where they'll have shipped frozen children and prisoners of war alike. And I know where it is."

"Where?" LaMonte demanded.

"Centurion," the Augment replied. "All of the hulls pass through a specific secondary yard to get fitted with their jump drive. All of this is done under a shroud of secrecy and apparently lies, but at the heart of it is the space station Minerva, hidden under Centurion's moon Trajan.

"It's supposed to be a specialized zero-gee production facility where the jump drives are constructed," Niska explained. "Now I suspect Minerva is the heart of this horror. It's where we'll find your prisoners and your proof, Lord Montgomery.

"I have some access still, I think. Back doors Ricket installed that no one would know about." The old spy smirked. "I'm not sure Ricket even knew I had them.

"If you can get us *to* Minerva Station, Captain LaMonte, I can get us aboard. After that..."

"After that, the Republic will learn the truth of their worst fear," Damien said levelly. "Get me to Minerva Station, people, and the Republic will learn what it means for a Hand to go to war."

"You're not actually planning on going in alone, I assume?" Romanov asked later, the Marine looking...twitchy.

Damien actually laughed. After the last few weeks, it was almost as much of a surprise to him as it was to his bodyguard.

"With as many Marines, commandos, Augments and former LMID fighters as we have aboard? I don't think any of you would let me," he noted. "Even if I was dumb enough to try."

He shook his head.

"No. We don't know nearly enough about this Minerva Station for me to try anything that stupid. All we really know is where it is."

"Yeah." Romanov looked at the image still on the wall of the conference room. "In the middle of a fortified side facility hidden from the Republic, surrounded by more purely automated defenses than I've seen just about anywhere.

"If the Mages' stealth spells fail, we're going to be staring down a *lot* of missiles and lasers with only a computer deciding if we live or die."

According to Niska, there were four major complexes attached to the Centurion Accelerator Ring, big shipyards that would be visible from well into deep space. The Daedalus Complex, however, was concealed in the shadow of Centurion's largest moon.

Like the station they'd left behind in Nueva Bolivia, Minerva Station was a Legatan prefab. Unlike Prometheus Station, it was made of five of the ring stations and it *did* have a central zero-gravity section the rings rotated around.

That section was connected to a number of shipyard slips, designed to take anything up to the Republic's new fifty-million-ton carriers. There, those ships would have their "jump drives" installed.

Now Damien and his people knew that process involved installing a concealed jump matrix, a simulacrum...and a collection of Mage brains hooked up to life support and control systems.

All of this was surrounded by defensive platforms, clusters of the triple-shot missile launchers built for the gunships, mounted around twenty-gigawatt lasers.

Niska didn't know how many platforms, beyond "a lot."

Rhapsody had to sneak past those platforms, board Minerva Station, and find proof. Something they could throw at the feet of the Republic's government—and more importantly, the Republic's *people.*

Damien had to believe that the citizens of the Republic wouldn't stand for the horror their government had committed in their name. If they didn't, the proof they were after would bring the Republic of Faith and Reason to its knees.

If the people of the Republic didn't care, at least they'd destroy the production facility for the horrific engines and free the Mage prisoners.

"One way or another, this horror show ends, Denis," Damien said quietly, studying the stations on the screen. "We'll free the Mages. Wreck the Daedalus production facilities. *End* this."

"And if the Republic tries to start again?"

Damien shook his head, swallowing down the spike of rage that answered his bodyguard's question.

"Then we burn them to fucking ash."

CHAPTER 43

"JUMP...NOW."

Liara Foster's soft voice carried across the silence of *Rhapsody in Purple*'s simulacrum chamber bridge. The void of deep space vanished in a moment of nothingness, and then the Legatus System appeared around them.

"Taking over the simulacrum," Xi Wu announced calmly. She and Liara swapped positions in the carefully practiced dance of military Mages. "Casting our veil of shadow."

Rhapsody's dozens of technological stealth systems were already online. None of them would cover the jump, any more than the stealth spell would. Anyone watching would have seen them arrive.

Of course, they were hoping that there weren't very many people watching out beyond Triarii, the next gas giant out from Centurion. The two gas giants were close to each other right now, which made the smaller planet a useful hiding spot.

"Drives online; we are heading in for a slingshot around Triarii," LaMonte said. "I'm definitely seeing some sensor platforms and what looks like a gunship squadron guarding the extraction facilities."

"Did they see us?" Damien asked.

"Oh, almost certainly," the spy captain said cheerfully. "But we'll run the stealth spell for six hours as we get the hell out of dodge and they won't find us."

He nodded and studied the screens. *Wait...*

"Those gunships are sticking pretty close to the planet," he noted. "They almost look like *they're* hiding. From what?"

"We don't have a clear shot of the rest of the system," LaMonte admitted. "Not without deploying drones, and we can't hide those nearly as well."

Rhapsody's stealth requirement defined everything from her power source to her hull shape. Her drones were harder to see just because of their size, but they simply *couldn't* have every aspect of the bigger ship's stealthy design.

And they couldn't carry a Mage.

"How long until we can see?" he asked.

"Maybe three hours," LaMonte replied. "At that point, we'll be coming around Triarii on a course for Centurion.

"Once we're clear of Triarii, we'll bring the drives online at full power under our stealth spell for several hours. We'll be pushing pretty hard, but we should be able to keep our presence concealed and still make it to Centurion in roughly twenty-two hours."

"So, we'll have about nineteen hours' warning of what's going on in this system," Damien concluded. "I can work with that."

"I can't see there being anything going on that can change our plan," she said.

"Alexander might be here," he replied softly. "That was the plan, anyway. We've been out of touch for a while, but she was considering a long-range strike on Legatus. Potentially even an attempt to besiege the system."

"Well, a distraction would certainly make this easier," LaMonte replied. "But I didn't think we had the ships to take Legatus."

"We don't," Damien admitted. "But she *might* have had the ships to make sure no one left Centurion or Legatus. A stalemate, not a victory. A siege."

"We'll see in a few hours," LaMonte said. "In the meantime, I suggest you go get some rest. Even if this goes wrong, we can deal with the enemy here at Triarii without you."

"And at that point, the whole plan is screwed anyway."

Unable to sleep and unwilling to break into his stash of sleeping drugs, Damien ended up "resting" by playing with Persephone. The black cat was always happy to see him, alternating between purring on his lap and chasing a tiny ball of magical light across the room.

His wrist-comp eventually chimed and he answered it instantly.

"I hate to wake you up, Damien," LaMonte apologized.

"I wasn't sleeping," he admitted. "Persephone isn't enthused with the interruption, but since *everyone* on this ship spoils her, I think she'll be fine."

His ex chuckled.

"Fair enough. We need you on the bridge. We've got scanners on the rest of the system, and it looks like you were right."

"Alexander is here?" he asked.

"With friends," LaMonte confirmed. "We're still resolving Legatus, but it looks like the orbital defenses there have had the shit kicked out of them. Centurion's defenses look intact, but there is a *huge* fleet flying Martian IFFs...including ships I've never seen before."

"How big?" Damien asked, his attention entirely focused.

"Sorry?"

"How big? I may know what they are, but I didn't expect them to be ready yet."

"We're not sure," she admitted. "But there are three ships out there at least half again the size of anything else in Alexander's fleet."

"Damn. They did it."

"Damien?" LaMonte asked.

"Three of them, right?" he checked.

"Yes."

"Those are dreadnoughts," he told LaMonte. "One was done. The yards promised me they could strip parts from some of the incomplete ships to finish two more in time to actually join the fight, but I didn't expect them to succeed."

"Dreadnoughts." Her response wasn't really a question. More an exclamation.

"And if we have those and Alexander has her fleet gathered, this siege might be changing into a real fight sooner than I expected," he told her. "Which means I need to talk to her. We may need a distraction to get out—but we absolutely need to get *in* before Alexander introduces the Daedalus facility to antimatter warheads!"

He shook his head.

"I'll be up on the bridge shortly, but I'll need to record a message for Alexander in private. Can we get it to her without being detected?"

"We'll drop a relay buoy that will fire an encrypted pulse after we're clear," LaMonte promised. "Hell, I'll drop three to make sure the message gets through. Can I make a suggestion, Damien?"

"Of course."

"Send her everything," *Rhapsody's* captain suggested. "Everything we've learned, every scrap of data we have. My ship was designed for this kind of mission and my crew are the best, but I can't guarantee we'll get in, let alone escape alive.

"We can't afford—*humanity* can't afford—for all we've learned to be lost."

Voice commands and touch screens with overlarge icons were Damien's life these days. His hands were recovering, but he was still barely able to hold a cup or a glass. He certainly wasn't up to *drinking* without magic—or using a computer that wasn't specifically set up for him.

LaMonte's crew had copied the setup from *Duke of Magnificence*, his usual cruiser flagship slash transport, which made things a lot easier. He got everything set up and faced the camera.

"Mage-Admiral Jane Alexander, this is First Hand Damien Montgomery," he greeted her. "There will be a large data dump attached to this message. It needs to be transferred to a courier and relayed to Mars and the rest of the Protectorate ASAP."

He paused and considered.

"For now, you will want to keep its contents classified. I fear the potential consequences if our crews here in Legatus learn what we have learned.

"That said, I am aboard a stealth vessel heading to a concealed facility around Centurion. I need you to delay your final attack until I have completed my mission. If we fail..." He shook his head.

"If *I* fail," he echoed, "you now have everything we have learned, extrapolated and guessed. It will fall to you to decide what happens after that, Jane. Desmond has to know what we've learned, and my own feeling is that *everyone* in both Protectorate and Republic needs to know what has been done."

Damien swallowed, considering how best to summarize what they'd learned.

"You have everything," he repeated. "But the core discovery is this: the Republic *does not* have a technological jump drive. What they have done instead is murder Mages and extract their brains.

"Those brains and souls are trapped in an apparatus that makes them able to jump. They have concealed this from their crews and their main population, but this is why they could not permit peace.

"They started with children, Jane," he admitted quietly. "They kidnapped the populations of their Mage Academies and murdered their own children. Every ship you see, every starship that flies Republic colors, represents half a dozen murdered Mages.

"We believe this process is taking place at Minerva Station in the Daedalus Complex. There is evidence in the files attached of every part of this horror up to the use of the brains of their victims."

Anger stabbed Damien again and he exhaled carefully. He would do no one any good by setting his quarters on fire.

"We may need a distraction to escape, but I will be in touch as needed," he told Jane. "I can't give you orders, but we both know we share a goal. I need to find the proof at Minerva. Their crimes may break the Republic...and I don't even care anymore."

He looked at the camera levelly.

"The Mages taken prisoner on the occupied worlds are believed to be held prisoner aboard Minerva Station, awaiting...processing," he said quietly. "I will save them. I will destroy the bastards responsible for this.

"Then—and *only* then—will you turn this entire hellhole to ashes."

CHAPTER 44

RHAPSODY IN PURPLE **WAS INVISIBLE.** Not just hiding be-hind a low radar profile and heat sinks, but entirely invisible. Xi Wu's hands glowed to Damien's Sight, magic pulsing out from the Mage as she concealed all evidence of the starship's existence.

Their engines were burning at full power, decelerating the stealth ship to a rendezvous with Minerva Station, and the weapons platforms around them saw nothing.

Damien had more power than Xi Wu and could have managed the same concealment if he could use the amplifier. Captain LaMonte's wife didn't have that power. She had no Runes of Power. No Rune Wright gift.

She was simply an above-average Mage who had studied this particu-lar spell, this specific trick, very, *very* well.

Every scrap of heat and light was being spread across half the star system, a spell that mixed the teleport and stealth spells to create an utterly impenetrable invisibility.

Damien was watching her carefully. In Xi Wu's hands, it made for an amazing cloak of invisibility. In *his* hands, once he could use an amplifier matrix again, the same spell could easily render a starship invulnerable.

For a few moments, anyway, depending on what weapon attacked them.

"Contact in one hundred ninety-five seconds," LaMonte said from the Captain's seat. "We would match velocities exactly in one hundred ninety-seven seconds without the impact. It's going to be one hell of a bump, people."

"This is so freaking weird," O'Malley breathed softly. "This is insane. We won't even know if the stealth failed; we'll just be dead."

"We'll see the platforms maneuvering to fire before they shoot," Damien replied. "We'd know."

He looked past O'Malley to Niska.

"If we're ninety seconds out, it's time for us to go," he told the two Augments. "Let's load up.

"I'll be right behind you," LaMonte promised. "The rest of this is on autopilot. Human involvement in this kind of high-speed docking is a bad idea."

"I'll hand off once we're in contact," Xi Wu assured them. "Will you need us aboard the station?"

"Romanov and I will have it," Damien told her. "Keep your Mages aboard. Making sure *Rhapsody* goes unseen is damn important. We've got the station."

"Good luck, my lord."

He traded a nod with the Ship's Mage.

"Thanks. We're probably going to need it."

Impact.

A momentary crushing sensation hammered Damien even through his magic, and he wavered against it. That was one *hell* of a hit. *Rhapsody* was designed for this, but that was going to leave a dent in Minerva Station.

"Go! Go! Go!" Captain Jalil Charmchi's voice echoed through the boarding tube Damien was waiting in.

The Bionic Commandos led the way, punching through the station's hull moments after the cutting lasers finished their work.

Damien and Romanov were with the Commandos, but Charmchi's command was only one of four forces boarding the space station. This was what *Rhapsody* was designed for, after all.

Each tube was delivering a force of twenty boarders. Damien and Romanov followed twenty Commandos aboard. A second tube held Romanov's Marines, and the last two were a mix of Maata's people and the Bionics and Augments.

Damien didn't know what was waiting for them, but *his* team was going for where Legatus design said the computer core would be. They needed data. Proof of the Republic's crimes.

And that was why LaMonte was with him. The other teams were looking for prisoners to rescue, but Damien and LaMonte were going for the heart of Minerva Station.

"No contact, repeat, no contact," Charmchi reported. "Alpha Team, sweep left, Bravo, sweep right. Charlie, you're with me. Delta, watch the package."

Damien snorted. It was far from the first time he'd been called "the package" in his life. It probably wouldn't be the last.

Five Commandos fell in around his three-person party.

"Let's go," he told them. "Believe me, people, I'm safer unarmored than you are in those walking tanks. Let's move."

Like the Augments, the Bionics had specially designed exosuit armor. Damien and LaMonte were once again the only people *not* wearing the immense armor in this team.

"Let me get into the computers here," LaMonte said. "That'll give our friends time to check out the immediate area while I work out where the hell we're going."

She didn't wait for him to approve it or not, and Damien smirked behind his vac-suit helmet as one of the Bionics ripped a wall panel off for her.

Some things never changed.

A few seconds of plugging in wires and LaMonte was in. Damien didn't even bother trying to watch over her shoulder—he knew his skill set, and cyberwarfare wasn't in it.

"Force Three has contact," Niska reported. "Regular security troopers. No Augments or exosuits. We're continuing moving toward the cargo bays."

Minerva Station was built around multiple versions of the standard Legatan ring station. They'd picked the middle ring as the most likely to hold the prison and command centers, but the stations had a relatively fixed layout. The computer center might be somewhere odd, but there were only so many big cargo bays.

Those bays were the most likely location of the imprisoned Mages.

"Got it!" LaMonte snapped. "Dumped a bunch of viruses into the system to keep them confused, but they've still locked me out. I got a full map, though, unredacted."

"Send it to everyone," Damien ordered. It appeared on his heads-up-display before he even finished giving the order.

"Teach your grandmother to suck eggs, Damien," LaMonte told him with a chuckle. "Looks like everyone is close to their intended target except Force Four."

Force Four, under Captain Maata, had been one of the teams hunting prisoners.

"They're close to the support system control," Damien noted. "Captain Maata, do you see what I see?"

"We're a long way from the prisons and pretty darn close to life support. I'm going to go play with the lights."

"Good luck, Captain."

"Same to you."

Damien turned to his people.

"All right, we've flagged the computer center. Kelly—how long until they start wiping data?"

"They can try whenever they want, but you know those viruses I mentioned?" she replied.

"Yes?"

"They aren't wiping *shit* until they clean those out of the computers, and that should take them at least twenty minutes."

"Okay." Damien grimaced. "We have twenty minutes to secure and physically isolate the computer center. Let's *move*."

"Contact!"

The shout over the radio was redundant. Damien could hear the gunfire coming from up ahead. Worse, he recognized the distinctive *SNAP-CRACK* of the discarding-sabot tungsten penetrators used against exosuit battle armor. Whoever was in charge of Minerva Station's defenses had held back until they could properly equip their people.

His HUD was rapidly updating with new information as he ushered Kelly to cover. The access to the computer center was behind an intentionally designed choke point. Three corridors converged and a single accessway led to the hardware cores.

Additional defenses had been physically built into the station. They couldn't have truly expected that this place would come under attack, but the Republic had prepared for it anyway. At least two dozen troops, seemingly half Augments, were holding the line in exosuit combat armor.

They clearly *hadn't* been expecting to face Protectorate Bionic Commandos. In general, Legatan Augments were still the *better* cyborg by any standard—but they hadn't expected *any* cyborgs.

By the time Damien had ducked his way around half of Captain Charmchi's troops to be able to see the fight, the defenders had lost over a third of their number—but several of the BCR troops were down and they didn't look like they were getting back up.

"Drop to the ground and shield your sensors on my mark," he ordered calmly.

"What?" Charmchi replied.

"Just do it," he barked. "Three. Two. One. *Mark.*"

They obeyed. The seven armored Commandos in front of him hit the ground like a small earthquake.

The defenders didn't even have time to respond before Damien struck. He wasn't able to point particularly well, but the one advantage his injuries had provided was that he'd become much less dependent on gestures to conjure his magic.

Lightning risked the very computers they were there to retrieve, so he reached for one of the simplest spells a Mage learned for self-defense. Except where a Mage in training was taught to heat a small ball of air to create the classic fireball, he heated every scrap of matter in the corridor the Legatans were guarding.

The defenders weren't even cooked alive. They simply turned to ash in a moment of extreme heat. It took almost as much power to contain the heat in his target area as it did to spike it.

Exhaling slowly, he released his power and slowly lowered the temperature ahead of his people.

"Go," he ordered softly.

"*Fuck me*," someone murmured on the local channel.

Damien ignored it, walking slowly ahead as the Commandos swarmed forward around him.

"There's a sealed door he—"

He obliterated the door before the Commando finished her report, shattering three tons of iron to rusty sand in a moment.

"Carry on."

"Why do we need an army, again?" LaMonte murmured. She'd apparently caught up with him.

"Because I only have one set of eyes and can only be in one place," he replied. "Get into those computers, Kelly. I need proof of what they were doing here and everything you can get on the station itself—in that order."

"On it."

She was past him and drawing her working computer again as they spoke.

Everyone was stepping very judiciously as they moved down the corridors. Damien had cooled the temperature to one safe for people in vac-suits, but it was still easily fifty degrees Celsius in the corridor.

A corridor that was covered in a layer of ash that *had* been over twenty people.

Damien took the time to check in on the rest of the teams as LaMonte started to hook in. Force Four had run headlong into heavy fire, at least a full platoon of exosuited troops and Augments dug in around the life support section.

Force Three and Force Two were running into resistance, but not nearly as tough as they'd expected. There were hundreds of Mages in the prison sections—possibly *thousands* across all of the rings of Minerva Station.

Just their presence there left Damien cold and furious. Occupying planets was one thing, but rounding up people and shipping them there to murder them? That brought back old memories for any Mage.

He'd stood on the slopes of Olympus Mons and looked at the fields of unmarked graves where the tens of thousands of children who had failed Project Olympus's tests had been buried—along with the older teenagers who had been forced to bear multiple children and then been executed when they became too troublesome.

The Mages wouldn't have struggled, not without knowing what was coming. Once the knowledge of what the Republic was doing made it back to the occupied worlds and the rest of the Protectorate, none of them would go easily.

The great families of any Protectorate world were not to be underestimated. Once they knew what was coming...Damien shivered.

The Republic didn't know what they were unleashing. To spare their neighbors and friends, the Mages they'd captured already would have kept their resistance to the reasonable. Faced with mass murder?

The Mages would burn their worlds to the ground before they would yield. The UnArcana Worlds had struggled with the fact that Mages had been held to separate laws and judged by separate courts under the Compact.

But this...this was *why* the Compact existed.

"Damien, we have a problem," LaMonte snapped. "Running both of your searches, and I just found something really, really ugly."

"Tell me."

"The prison bays are set up to be dumped into space from a completely separate control center," she told him. "They're trying to lure our people into a trap—exosuits or not, if they expel the prison bays into vacuum, our people will go with the Mages."

And the very people Damien was there to rescue would die.

He crossed the room to LaMonte, looking over her shoulder.

"Who can activate it and where are the controls?"

"Looks like just Dr. Finley and from here." She highlighted a space. "It's a general control center for those prison bays."

"I'll stop him," Damien told her.

"Damien, the prison bays are runically sealed," she warned. "You might be able to get in—but I'm not sure even you can get out."

"Then you're all going to have to come get me, aren't you?"

He fixed the coordinates in his mind, adjusting for the continuing rotation of the station, and then gave his companions a firm smile.

"I am the Sword of Mars," he told them gently. "This is my job."

He *stepped.*

CHAPTER 45

ROSLYN AND KULKARNI were holding down the fort on the flag deck, neck-deep in the logistics headaches of replacing every missile in over seventy warships, when Mage-Admiral Alexander calmly walked into the mostly abandoned space.

"Sir!" Roslyn exclaimed, scrambling to her feet. The last she'd heard from the Admiral was that she'd been going to sleep, barely an hour earlier. As the Flag Lieutenant, that meant that Roslyn should be heading to rest herself, but the logistics situation was a mess.

"Sit down, Chambers," Alexander ordered. "I didn't get to sleep before I was interrupted by an old friend of ours."

"Sir?" Roslyn asked.

"Apparently, Damien Montgomery is in-system. He's polite enough not to give me orders, but he probably should have," the Admiral said. "Bring up the map of Centurion space."

Roslyn obeyed and Alexander walked up to the hologram and poked one of the moons.

"This one is Trajan, right?" she asked. "What does our intel say about it?"

"Largest moon of Centurion," Kulkarni replied instantly. "Flagged for potential long-term colonization during the initial expeditions. That project fell by the wayside, as most major artificial habitation projects do."

Why live in a dome when you could live somewhere with a sky, after all?

"Is it inhabited, then?" Alexander asked.

"We don't believe so." Kulkarni said. "No colonies, no stations. Might be some mining operations, but it's mostly ignored."

"If there was a major shipyard complex hidden underneath it, would we be able to see it?"

Alexander's question silenced both of her subordinates.

"No," Roslyn finally said, glancing at Kulkarni for confirmation. "They'd have to have placed it very carefully, and I'm not sure why..."

"Because apparently they're hiding it from most of their own people," Alexander said. "Not just us. That complex is where the Republic's ships are fitted with 'FTL drives.'"

There was something in the way Alexander said *FTL drives* that sent a chill down Roslyn's spine. Just what had the Admiral learned from Montgomery?

"Is that where Montgomery is going?" Roslyn asked.

"Yes. And we're to hold off our assault until he calls us," Alexander told them. "I can't share all of the intelligence he sent me, not yet, but I *can* tell you that he's looking to rescue thousands of prisoners from that complex."

"Has he found another ship?" Kulkarni said. "He left us aboard *Rhapsody in Purple*. That ship would be hard-pressed to carry even *a* thousand people from Trajan to us. They'd be packed like sardines, but I think the air would last that long."

"He hasn't, which means he hasn't thought that far ahead," the Admiral said grimly. "Given what he's told me, I'm not surprised.

"So, what I need from you two is a detailed attack plan that will take out the cardinal forts on this side of Centurion and any of the inner forts that threaten us...and gets Second Fleet to the Daedalus Complex in the shortest time possible."

"Sir, we're fifteen point four million kilometers from the cardinal forts. Those forts are six hundred thousand kilometers further out from Trajan—that's a sixteen-million-kilometer trip."

"At maximum acceleration for a zero-velocity-zero-distance rendezvous, six hours," Alexander agreed.

"What about the RIN?" Roslyn asked. "As soon as we commit to an attack, they're going to jump in behind us and try to pin us against Centurion."

"We're going to let them," the Mage-Admiral told her. "I can't tell anyone, even you two, what Damien found yet. What I *can* tell you is that the Republic can bloody well come.

"We're going to kill them all."

Alexander left the flag deck and Roslyn shared a long look with Kulkarni.

"We need to get Medici's cruisers back ASAP," the younger woman said calmly. "Six *Honorific*-class cruisers could change all of this, even if they're only carrying Phoenix VIIIs."

Medici's ships—and the six destroyers who'd gone with them—were the last ships that had been sent back to the logistics fleet for rearming. Every other ship was now fully armed with the new Phoenix IXs.

"We'll get a courier moving," Kulkarni agreed. "But to get to Trajan? What are you thinking?"

"Minimum-time course doesn't leave us a lot of options," Roslyn admitted. "We were thinking about trying to keep our new range advantage hidden, but I don't think that's an option. Bull in a china shop, sir?"

The Mage-Captain laughed.

"That's a good description. Lock in the course as soon as Montgomery contacts us, blow the cardinal forts away with the Samurais and then hit everything they throw at us with Phoenix IXs. No subtlety, just hammer our way through."

"We have the firepower and the range, but if the First Hand is *inside* a Republic shipyard, we don't have time for anything more complicated," Roslyn agreed. "We send that courier right now, muster the entire fleet and then kick the door in when Montgomery calls."

"TK-5331 is next up on the docket; I'll get them moving," Kulkarni said. "I want you to see if our tactical group can get a drone into position to look under Trajan's skirts. If they were concealing this yard from their own people, it's almost certainly defended, and I want to know what we're sending people into."

"On it," Roslyn promised.

The flagship was currently part of the one-third of the fleet on full stand-down, but Roslyn didn't need to go through the tactical team, anyway. After the last fight, she'd been linked into the tactical network directly.

She'd *been* a tactical officer until relatively recently, so it only took her a few seconds to put together the retasking request. There weren't any drones in position to *subtly* take a peek at the complex, but she could send one of their closer-in drones much closer in.

A tight orbit of Centurion, underneath most of the facilities, risked running into the systems defending the accelerator ring itself. It was the only option she saw for getting a look at the mysterious hidden shipyard.

One probe would probably get shot down. She retasked six and passed the orders for the active ships to launch new ones to replace them.

The drones left their positions, diving toward the gas giant at maximum acceleration.

"The hell?" someone snapped on the com channel attached to the network. "Who ordered those drones to suicide?!"

"This is Admiral Alexander's staff," Roslyn interjected. "We have intelligence on a facility we may have missed. Those drones are going to tell us if that intel is correct."

"All those drones are going to get is shot down!" the voice objected. A quick check showed that Roslyn was arguing with the Lieutenant Commander acting as tactical officer aboard *Mjolnir*.

As they were arguing, one of the drones *was* shot down. Antimissile defenses weren't perfect at shooting down recon drones, but they could certainly handle the task.

"That's why I sent six, Lieutenant Commander," Roslyn said calmly. "Because we *need* to know what Trajan is hiding, and if that requires us to lay a trail of wrecked drones thick enough to walk on, that's exactly what we're going to do."

There was silence on the channel, and then the stranger laughed.

"If it's the Admiral's orders, it's the Admiral's order," he concluded. "But those drones aren't cheap. It better be wo..."

Four of the drones had died. Two made it far enough to get a look at the underside of Trajan.

The fifth died even as the survivor twisted toward the Daedalus Complex to get better data. The sixth lasted long enough to get them a solid image of the entire miniature shipyard and its defenses.

"Never mind, Lieutenant," *Mjolnir's* officer concluded. "Do you want assistance setting up the next pattern? We're going to need a better number on those defensive platforms, if nothing else."

Medici's ships returned thirty minutes later. Their ammunition status updated on Roslyn's displays almost immediately.

Only half of the Mage-Admiral's cruisers and destroyers were armed with Phoenix IXs, with the other half still carrying the older missiles. It would hopefully be enough, combined with the heavy Samurai missiles and the full rearmament of the rest of the fleet.

With the entire fleet reassembled, Second Fleet was an utterly overwhelming wall of steel in space. Eighty-six warships, massing over a billion tons and carrying the most advanced technology available to the Protectorate of the Mage-King of Mars.

There was a reason that the bull-in-a-china-shop approach was going to work to get them to the mysterious shipyard complex. Roslyn's second sweep of drones gave her the details she needed to help Kulkarni plan the attack.

There were a hundred and ten weapons platforms guarding the shipyard, primarily laser platforms that would utterly devastate anyone who came around the moon without expecting them.

Unfortunately for the defenders, Second Fleet now had enough data to target missiles on those platforms from the other side of Trajan. They probably had the sensor relays to return fire, but the platforms had only a few hundred missile launchers.

There was nothing in Centurion orbit now that could stop Second Fleet. The RIN presumably had a significant force in place to try and pin them in place, but doing so was going to risk the accelerator ring.

Right now, the only thing stopping Second Fleet from destroying the structure underpinning the entire logistics structure of the Republic's military was that Damien Montgomery had told them to wait.

So, they were waiting. Still waiting. There was no way that Roslyn could tell whether *Rhapsody in Purple* had penetrated the Daedalus Complex. They were waiting for the First Hand's call.

But he'd told the Admiral he was attacking the complex hours before. Roslyn would have expected him to call. How long, she wondered, would Admiral Alexander wait to hear from Montgomery?

How long until they had to conclude that something had gone wrong?

CHAPTER 46

SOMETHING HAD GONE WRONG.

What should have been a momentary blink out of reality, a short-distance teleport like Damien had done a thousand times before, stretched out into seconds of darkness.

There was no pain, no discomfort—none of the issues of a blocked jump or teleporting a starship too close to a planet. Just...nothingness.

He emerged from the jump and fell to the floor. Even that floor was wrong—and he realized that, somehow, his jump had been redirected.

"Well, *that's* a surprise," a calm male voice declared.

Damien dragged himself to his feet and realized he was inside a glass cell of some kind. The outside of the cell was covered in silver runes and hung in the middle of what looked like a mix of a control room and an office.

A single man had clearly been in the process of crossing between the two halves of the room when Damien appeared, and was now studying him.

"Rune Wright, but only three Runes of Power," the stranger said calmly, studying Damien through the glass. "Crippled hands. Platinum icon, hidden under the vac-suit. That leaves only one potential guest.

"Welcome, Damien Montgomery, to my space station. I am Dr. Samuel Finley."

The stranger was a tall older man. He looked like he normally shaved what was left of his hair, but enough had grown in to reveal that he was also naturally mostly bald. Something about him poked at Damien's Sight.

This wasn't a conversation Damien wanted to have while locked inside a cage. He tried to teleport out...and failed.

"Did you really expect that to work, Lord Montgomery?" Finley asked. "This entire facility was built to hold captive Jump Mages. The main bays are simply blocked against jumping, but a soft block over the rest of the facility always seemed handy."

The Mage smiled.

"Of course, it's not like it works on me," he concluded. "You might even be able to power through it. It will be fascinating to watch you try. I've never had the privilege of meeting someone else with the Sight.

"Rune Wrights, that's what you call us, right?"

Us.

That was what Damien was feeling and seeing. The runes that wrapped around him weren't the precise lines of the Martian Runic script, standardized and shaped to control the flow of magic. They were the flowing lines and twists of *true* runes, silver that shaped magic as it *was*, not as it was expected to be.

"I didn't expect to meet a Keeper here," Damien said quietly. "At the heart of this horror show."

Finley snorted.

"I've *met* a Keeper," he conceded. "He called himself Partisan. Obviously not his real name, but I didn't care. He had such *fascinating* concepts and information to share. I was halfway to the Promethean Drive before he helped out, but between us we perfected the system."

"A system of murder and torture?" Damien asked.

"Some things are necessary to achieve grander designs," Finley told him. "I continue to refine the system. In the long run, the Promethean Drive will jump further and more reliably than any mere trained human. If sacrifices must be made, then that has always been the price of progress.

"Besides, what are those who are only half a true Mage really worth?"

Power flared through Damien, fueled by his anger...and was drained away by the magic that surrounded him.

"Surely, you've realized that much, Damien," Finley continued. "You and I represent the *true* nature of a Mage, able to wield power and *understand* what we do. The rest? The mundanes? The half-bloods who can only do what they are taught by their betters?

"They are expendable."

"I'm going to kill you," Damien said conversationally, forcing himself to calm the homicidal rage that ran through him. "I am going to tear whatever excuse for a Rune of Power you've carved into yourself from your flesh and use it to cut your head off. You will join the children you murdered."

"Those Mages are very much alive," Finley replied. "Crippled, perhaps, but you should be the last to say that the loss of the usual limbs is equivalent to death. The Republic doesn't fully utilize all of the capabilities inherent in the Promethean Interface. Using them as shipboard AI enhancers would be far too risky for them."

This time, the rage was enough. Damien couldn't teleport out of the cell, but he *could* channel enough power to sever part of the runes. The glass shattered around him and he dove forward.

Power channeled around him as he charged Finley—and then he and his power alike were thrown across the room.

"I don't have a Rune of Power," Finley told him. "Partisan refused to provide me a sample of the design, and it's a hard one to come up with from scratch."

He smiled coldly as Damien struggled to his feet.

"I managed the reverse, though," he said calmly. "Any Mage except me in this room is badly weakened—and your Runes of Power won't function. I'll examine them once you're dead; then I should be able to augment myself."

The door to the room slid open, and Damien looked up to see Connor De Santis walk in. The ex-RID agent had abandoned his exosuit somewhere.

"Well, Agent?" Finley asked without even looking at the RID agent.

"The assault on the life support section is still going to be a problem," De Santis said calmly. "My husband is among them, so I'd rather talk them down. Once the rest are dead, that should be easier."

"And the assault on the prison bays?"

"Almost inside your target zone."

"You betrayed us," Damien snapped. He tried to channel magic against De Santis this time, but it failed to come.

Without his Runes, Damien was actually a *weaker*-than-average Mage, and the runes on the room were robbing him of much of even that power.

"He can't harm you, Agent," Finley told the Republican, keeping his gaze on Damien with a disturbingly warm smile. "Everything that has been set into motion has led here. We would *rather* have stopped you in Nueva Bolivia, but there was no opportunity for De Santis to make contact there."

"There is one thing you set into motion that you forgot about," De Santis said quietly.

"What?" Finley demanded, turning to face the Agent.

He never completed the turn before De Santis shot him. It was the classic perfect headshot of a combat Augment, designed to take down a Mage before they could act. Most likely, that wound would have killed him, but De Santis apparently wasn't taking any chances.

He shot Finley in the head again, leaving little but a stump. He then shot Finley three times in the chest, then crossed to Damien to offer his hand.

"I'm sorry," he murmured. "I made contact before I saw the nightmare at that school station, and they told me to play along.

"I don't think they realized that my loyalty had a limit—and it was somewhere short of cutting brains out of teenagers!"

"Why didn't you say something?" Damien demanded as De Santis helped him up.

"I wasn't sure there wasn't anyone else who was leaking to the RID," De Santis admitted. "Their defense of the life support has failed, and this is the control center that could dump the prison bays into space.

"I couldn't let him do that, Montgomery. I needed Finley to trust me enough to get me in here."

Damien leaned on the Augment and sighed.

"Fair enough. Now, this room utterly sucks for me," he admitted. "Can we wreck those controls and meet up with everybody else?

"It's time to call for our ride out of here."

CHAPTER 47

"BOARDING FORCES, report in," Damien ordered. The advantage of voice communication was that none of his subordinates could see him leaning against the wall in exhaustion. Whatever Finley had done to his office had left the Hand exhausted.

"This is Force Four; we are now in control of the life support systems," Maata reported. "We've taken multiple casualties and we can't find De Santis, but we're now in control of the air systems for this ring."

"De Santis is with me," Damien replied. "Situation under control. What about the systems for the other rings?"

"It looks like there *is* a central control, but cutting the individual sections of the station into local control is stupid easy from the actual systems," Maata told him. "Even if we found the central system, the people in charge of each ring could take local control without any trouble."

"Damn. Everyone else?"

"This is Niska. Forces Two and Three are in the prison bays, and we have full control," the Augment told him. "We have a lot of *very* angry Mages who don't have a clue what's going on." He paused. "Do I brief them, Montgomery?"

"As much as necessary," Damien ordered. "Those Mages are probably our best chance to take the rest of this damn station."

"This explanation is the least punishment for what I helped happen," the old spy said softly. "I'll talk to them."

"Force One?" Damien asked a moment. "LaMonte, what's your status? I don't suppose you have the evidence we need?"

"Would the briefing slides Finley used to explain this mess to the Lord Protector count?" LaMonte replied. "Because apparently, the director was a data packrat. Everything is in here...and surprisingly well organized, once I convinced the encryption and security protocols to fuck off and die."

"You have proof?" he demanded. "Like...sourced, easily transmittable proof?"

"Well, I don't have a recording of Finley giving the damn lecture to George Solace, no," she said. "All I've got are his slides, but those have pictures and attached video, and the bit I watched made me very sick."

"It'll have to do," Damien replied. "Pull everything. See what you can get packaged up into a neat box we can hand the Republic and watch explode. First, however, I need to know how to take full control of this station and the defense network."

"Minerva Control is in the central zero-gravity hub," LaMonte told him. "I'll pull the exact coordinates." She paused. "Damien, it's the control center for a hundred defensive satellites. It's going to be defended. Do we have the numbers to hold this ring *and* assault the command center?"

"Even if I were to call Alexander right now, it'll be six hours before they get here. We'll secure the command center and *then* call for backup. Get me the exact coordinates."

"What are you going to do with them?" LaMonte demanded.

"Everybody, I need five exosuited troopers from each team headed to my location right now," Damien ordered. "I'm going to take those coordinates, Captain LaMonte, and teleport a strike team right into the command center.

"Their defenses won't matter much if we're inside them."

First, though, he needed to go back into Finley's hellhole and make sure that the cell that had trapped his *last* teleport was completely disabled. It was more than big enough for one person.

It wouldn't hold twenty.

Minerva Station Control was well aware that their station was under attack. Every security measure was engaged. Armored bulkheads had sealed every entrance to the command center. Augments and Republic Space Assault Troopers had dug in around every approach.

Unlike many places in the Republic, the command center even had shields against teleportation. Unfortunately for them, Damien was the First Hand of Mars. He tested the defenses from where his troops had gathered, judging how much power he was going to need.

He was tired, but he was far from tapped out.

"Most of the defenses are outside the actual command center," he said aloud, "but most of the crew are armed and there are Augment security troops in there."

"We'll deal with them," O'Malley promised, the ex-LMID Augment joining Romanov to lead Damien's newly assembled strike force. "Captain Romanov?"

Romanov's suit turned to study the Augment.

"Agent."

"We've got this, right?" she asked.

"We do," he confirmed.

"Then it's down to you, Lord Montgomery."

Damien smiled thinly.

"Then gather closer. They tried to seal it, but that only means I need you within touching distance."

"Don't you need to actually touch us?" Romanov asked.

"I've been practicing," Damien said. "Sadly, I don't think this is going to be any pleasanter for you lot."

He *stepped*.

Minerva Station Control was thankfully large enough for twenty exosuited soldiers to fit in it with room to spare. It consisted of several concentric rings; each one half a meter lower than the one outside it. Even the smallest ring was wide enough for a dozen men, and the entire room was over twenty meters across.

Jump-sickness disabled Damien's assault force for a few moments—but it didn't disable *him*. Low-energy lightning sent a dozen crew sprawling back from their consoles, sparking like they'd been shot with taser darts.

A shield protected his people from the gunfire that opened before they could react, but none of the defenders had expected an assault force *inside* the control center. Damien's people were throwing up in their suits, but they didn't react that much later than the guards who hadn't been expecting them.

"Throw down your weapons and surrender!" Damien shouted; magic augmented his voice over the gunfire. "Anyone who surrenders will not be hurt!"

The station control crew clearly weren't prepared to die for the Republic today. Most of them hit the ground, sidearms skittering away on the floor.

The Augment security was more determined, but after about ten seconds of fierce gunfire, the handful of survivors threw down their weapons as well.

"Romanov, see to the injured," Damien ordered. "O'Malley, can you get me control?"

"On it," she replied. "Sylens, get the Hand coms. I believe you have a call to place?"

One of the crew tried to grab a penetrator rifle the Augment security had dropped. Damien's magic caught her in mid-slide across the floor and yanked her over to him, holding her in the air with a firm-but-not-dangerous grip around her throat.

"Miss, this station has murdered several thousand Mages and installed their brains in spaceships," he said in as calm a voice as he could manage. "My usual rules of engagement call for me to take prisoners wherever possible, but I am *very* angry right now. Don't push me, all right?"

Calm or not, his tone seemed to get the message across. He could *see* the difference in the body language of his prisoners as they went from looking for ways to turn the situation around to looking for ways to stay alive.

He wasn't going to kill them, not outside of open combat. He would have hated himself for it later, and he liked being able to shave with a mirror.

"Coms console is over here," the tech O'Malley had ordered to find the coms told him. The man's exosuit gauntlets had retracted, allowing him to work on the computer with free hands.

"It was already logged in; I've broken what security was left. We now control this station's coms."

He stood back and made an inviting gesture.

"It's waiting for you, Montgomery."

With a small smile, Damien let the woman he was holding in the air slide to the ground.

He had work to do.

"You're going to need to help me," he muttered to Sylens as he joined the tech. "I doubt this is set up for someone with no usable hands."

"I can set up the call," the tech agreed instantly. "We're using a group of relays in a polar orbit of Trajan. They're not always in the same place, but there's always one on the edge of the planet, so we can tag it."

"Who are we transmitting to?"

"Second Fleet," Damien replied. "Doesn't really need to be more specific than that."

Sylens poked at the console, then gestured toward a camera as it rotated to face Damien.

"You're live whenever you want. They're almost a light-minute away, though, so it's not going to be a live conversation."

Damien nodded and eyed the camera.

"Admiral Alexander, we have now secured control of the core facility of the Daedalus Complex and, most importantly, of its defensive network.

"I have an unknown but large number of Mage prisoners in the station that we are in the process of liberating. While we *should* be able to break them all free before you can get here, I wouldn't object to a few Marines—or a few thousand, if you've got them.

"Please refrain from firing on the Daedalus Complex, as its existence alone is proof of the Republic's crimes. Beyond that..." He shook his head. "I leave the fate of the rest of Centurion's infrastructure to you, Admiral Alexander. That's your area of expertise.

"My math says I won't see you for at least six hours, but my admittedly uneducated assessment of the situation is that you won't have many problems getting here.

"I look forward to speaking in person again. Montgomery out."

CHAPTER 48

THE NEW SAMURAI heavy-bombardment missiles were unlike any-thing Roslyn had ever seen before. The cardinal forts had barely even begun launching their gunships, secure in the knowledge that even Second Fleet's maximum-acceleration charge would take them almost two hours to reach missile range, when the handful of ships in the fleet with the new missiles opened fire.

Second Fleet had been accelerating for over an hour and a half before they launched, but the Samurai missiles still launched well before the Republic was expecting them to fire. When *Mjolnir* and her friends had ambushed the task force, they'd intentionally stepped down their missile accelerations to match the older missiles' ability.

The new range was a shock—they launched just over five minutes before the Republic would be in range...and the Samurai I only had a five-minute flight time.

There were only two hundred and seventy of the heavy-missile launchers in the fleet, but the Republic had no data on their perform-ance—and few of their defenses could really handle missiles coming in at ninety thousand kilometers a second.

The fortress closest to Second Fleet only had five hundred gunships left, and only two-thirds of them survived long enough to launch their missiles. As the rest of the salvos of Samurais and the new Phoenix IXs swarmed in afterward, they didn't manage to launch twice—and the fort-ress didn't survive her gunships by long.

A single salvo of a "mere" two thousand–plus missiles flung themselves at Second Fleet, only to die to the RFLAM fire.

They weren't even applying missiles to their own defense, Roslyn realized. As soon as the first fortress was gone, Samurais and Phoenix IXs were being flung at the other fortresses. Short ballistic periods of a few seconds were more than enough to make certain every fortress that wasn't protected by the planet itself was badly outranged.

Fortresses couldn't dodge.

Even the gunships were scrambling. There were still over six thousand of the small ships aboard the defenses of Centurion, but their deployments rapidly showed that Roslyn's guess had been right: they *could* be easily refitted to run on fusion drives, and the Republic was reserving their antimatter for their missiles.

Second Fleet ignored them all. The fortresses were reduced one by one, overwhelmed by missiles from just beyond their range. Then, once the bases were gone, the missiles focused on the gunship formations.

None of them tried to surrender. To the last, they were desperately trying to coordinate the one massed salvo that would have been a real threat to Second Fleet.

They failed.

"The good news, everyone, is that Centurion is now functionally defenseless," Mage-Admiral Jane Alexander announced to her flag officers a few minutes later. "We took minor damage across the fleet from the gunship salvos, but they weren't expecting the range advantage to be flipped on them.

"But remember that the Republic was prepared to risk the Accelerator Ring to lure us in here. They'll expect our range advantage when the trap closes," she concluded. "If nothing else, we're out of Samurai bombardment missiles. They're too big for us to carry many of them."

"We still have the range advantage with the IXs," Medici pointed out. "They'll be expecting it, but there's only so much they can do about it."

"Agreed. We'll turn over in fifteen minutes," Alexander continued. "In just over three hours, we'll rendezvous with the Daedalus Complex. Unfortunately, General Tone and the majority of her Marines are at Decurion. We don't even have our complete regular shipboard detachments."

She smiled grimly, and Roslyn felt a moment of pity for anyone who thought that shortage was going to help them.

"That still leaves us with roughly three thousand Marines, all of them with combat exosuits," she noted. "That should be more than sufficient to finish the task of securing the Daedalus Complex.

"Without that complex, the Republic does not have FTL warships. We now control it...and we are *not* letting it go."

"What about the Accelerator Ring?" Medici asked. "We could take it out now, easily."

The Ring was far from defenseless, but even a *million* RFLAM turrets would have paled against the immense scale of humanity's only true megastructure. It had, according to their intel, twelve thousand such turrets.

That was less than one for every kilometer of its circumference. Less than one for every *ten* kilometers of its circumference—and given the inherent vulnerabilities of a giant particle accelerator, it would only take one missile to take it out.

"No," Alexander said slowly. "Right now, unless the Republic's trap is *far* more powerful than I expect, we are going to end up in control of at least Centurion, if not the entire Legatus System.

"I see no reason to destroy one of humanity's greatest technological and engineering achievements in that case."

"And if you're wrong, sir?" Mage-Admiral Marangoz asked. "We won't have another opportunity like this."

"We will have plenty of opportunity to destroy the Centurion Accelerator Ring before the Republic can bring us to battle, Admiral." Alexander shook her head. "That was the bait for this trap, and I am still stunned that they were prepared to take the risk."

"It can't be the only one," Roslyn said aloud before her mortification caught up with her. Her job in these meetings was to shut up and take notes, not interject.

"I'm so—"

"No, you're right," Marangoz cut off her apology. "Out of the mouths of Flag Lieutenants, people—we've been bloody blind. We've assumed all along that Centurion was the only accelerator ring they had, but they wouldn't have taken this kind of risk if they didn't have a backup ready or close to ready."

"Then taking Legatus won't end this war," Alexander said. "But it's a damn good start, regardless. We'll destroy the accelerator ring if we have to, but we'll preserve it if we can.

"For now, let's go fetch ourselves a Hand. As usual for my brother's chosen representatives, the good Lord Montgomery seems to have dug himself into a *very* deep hole he needs the Navy to collect him from."

CHAPTER 49

"ALL RIGHT, EVERYONE, we have a winner," Kulkarni said in a forced bright tone. "The pool is closed; whoever bet 'two hours after turnover' for the Republic closing the trap wins."

"I don't think I bet on that," Roslyn replied. "There was a pool?"

"I don't think we're supposed to let the kids gamble; I'll have to check with the Admiral," the ops officer replied.

Roslyn managed a moment of mock huffiness, but then her gaze was inexorably drawn back to the main holodisplay. They were still an hour from reaching the target complex, which meant they were easily seven or eight hours from being able to escape—and that was if they abandoned everyone they'd come this deep to collect.

Escape was suddenly looking like the best option. The Republic had clearly been preparing for this moment for a while.

"Let's run the numbers, people," Alexander said calmly. "What am I looking at? Ten carrier groups?"

"Looks like," Kulkarni confirmed. "Roslyn, do we have a split?"

"Yes, sir," she confirmed. "Tactical makes it six fifty-megaton *Courageous*-class ships and four forty-megaton *Bravado*-class ships. Twenty-one hundred gunships aboard."

"Twenty battleships; evenly split between their thirty- and forty-megaton models," Kulkarni continued, the operations officer running through the data herself.

"And seventy cruisers," Roslyn finished. "Forty twenty-megaton ships, thirty fifteen-megaton. This has to be their entire damn fleet!"

"Quite possibly," Alexander agreed. "They've probably still got a couple of carrier groups floating around, but you'll note..." The Admiral flagged one of the carriers. "*This* group is slightly off from the rest. They jumped from Legatus while we were distracted.

"They've concentrated everything they have. That's over two *billion* tons of warships." Kulkarni said in a soft voice. "They've got us out-massed, outnumbered and outgunned."

She snorted.

"I guess we should have expected that. Except for *Mjolnir* and her escorts, we've all been here for quite a while. They know exactly what they were facing."

"And now they have us pinned against the planet. I wonder what their plan is," Alexander said calmly.

"For now, we will continue as planned. If they want to enter the gravity well and give us a chance to run on our terms, I'll take it.

"If not, well, we'll find a way out. But we're going to do it with those rescued prisoners aboard and leaving their shipbuilding and antimatter production facilities in ashes behind us," she concluded.

"The good news is that they're not coming in after us," Kulkarni pointed out. "The bad news is that they have the metaphorical high ground. I don't know if they can microjump, but if they can, we're screwed."

"They can do anything a Mage can do," Alexander said with a sigh. "Because that's what they're using."

"Sir?" Roslyn looked over at her boss. There was something in the Admiral's tone... "They've made a big deal about their technological solution to FTL. You know something?"

"That's what Montgomery found," Alexander told them. "It doesn't leave this room yet, all right?"

Roslyn glanced around the flag deck. There were easily thirty people in there, and yet...she was pretty sure no one was going to tell tales outside of school about anything Alexander told them to keep quiet.

"Their 'technological solution' was to murder Mages, extract their brains and hook them up to an interface that can force them to cast the jump spell into a specially designed amplifier," Alexander told them, her voice tired. "Every starship in the Republic Navy represents at least three or four murdered Mages...most of them teenage Mages by Right from the UnArcana Worlds."

Roslyn's gaze snapped over to the fleet waiting for them to try and run. There were a hundred ships out there. All told, she'd probably seen at least twice that in Republic starships over the last year.

Those ships represented hundreds of dead Mages, murdered so that their powers could be stolen to fuel the Republic's rise to power.

"My god," she whispered.

"I was fourteen years old the first time I stood at the black tombs and truly *understood*," Alexander said, her tone still drained. "We buried a Hand that day, but it was the mountainside above the black tombs that really hit home. We always thought that Project Olympus would be the worst crime committed against us.

"We were wrong. At least Olympus only killed us when we were no longer useful." The Admiral's face twisted into a snarl. "The Republic had found ways to make us useful even *after* they murder us."

"This has to stop," Kulkarni said. "We have to stop them."

"Montgomery already has," Alexander pointed out. "There are almost certainly other places where they carry out this horror, but the vast majority of their ship construction and FTL drive installation was here—at the Daedalus Complex."

That complex was already growing on their sensor screens. They were only a few minutes from swinging around Trajan now, and Roslyn hoped that the Hand had been correct when he said he'd taken control of the complex's defenses.

A hundred twenty-gigawatt lasers would make a mess of even Second Fleet.

The flag deck was silent as the terminator line approached, then Alexander sighed.

"Orders to the Fleet," she said crisply. "All ships are to launch their assault shuttles as soon as we have clear line of sight. I trust the Marines to divvy up their own targets, but they *will* make contact with Montgomery's people in that task."

"And us, sir?" Kulkarni asked.

"We'll be making contact with Montgomery directly," she replied. "He's done his job. Now I need him aboard *Righteous Shield* while we do ours."

Alexander smiled coldly.

"If the Republic thinks they can deal with this fleet, they have underestimated me...and they have underestimated the Sword of Mars."

CHAPTER 50

NISKA INTERCEPTED DAMIEN outside the shuttle intended to take him to *Righteous Shield of Valor*. Despite everything they'd found, Damien was prepared to give the old cyborg *some* credit.

It was pretty clear that a large portion of LMID hadn't known what they'd been fighting for. The ideal James Niska had fought for had been for an equal world, one without special rights for Mages. The kind of horror included in Project Prometheus was far beyond whatever lines the covert ops soldier had drawn.

"We need to talk," Niska said.

"We are talking," Damien pointed out.

"I need time," the cyborg replied. "I know what's waiting for you out there. I need to come with you."

Damien sighed.

"I trust you, James," he said gently. "But there is no way in hell I can bring you aboard the flagship of Second Fleet as we face the massed fleets of the Republic. We can't afford a single false step, a single error... or a single betrayal."

Niska gestured around them.

"Do you think we would have made it this far if I was going to betray you, Damien?" he replied. "Please. We've come this far together. Hear me out. I'll stay on the shuttle when we get to Alexander's flagship, but you and I need to talk about what happens next."

Damien sighed, then gestured for the cyborg to come with him.

"You stay on the shuttle," he told the older man. "Romanov, you make sure of it."

"Yes, sir."

It was probably telling that Damien's bodyguard wasn't even blinking at Niska's request. If Romanov, whose job was to be paranoid on Damien's behalf, figured this was fine, they were probably okay.

Aboard the shuttle, he led the old cyborg into the space usually set aside for a Marine unit commander. It had full coms and tactical networking capacity, and Damien eyed them with a moment of paranoia.

Then Denis Romanov *closed the door behind them* and Damien swallowed. His bodyguard had just left him alone with a professional mage-killer, a cyborg trained from his teen years to take down Mages like Damien.

If Romanov left them alone, then the bodyguard was trusting beyond all reason...and Damien realized that James Niska had *earned* that trust.

"That is a reminder that I owe you more than this," Damien said quietly, gesturing at the closed door. "Talk."

The shuttle's engines flared around them, but Damien calmly conjured gravity around him as he held Niska's gaze.

"You need to give the RIN a chance," Niska said quietly.

"They outgun us two to one," Damien pointed out. "I'm not sure you're talking to the right people."

"Damien, I have seen the records of you in action—*and* the records of other Hands," Niska told him. "I know the Mage-King is something more than a regular Mage. I know his *sister* is the same—and I'd bet the survival of Second Fleet that you are too.

"I don't know what that level of raw magical power means to a fleet battle, but I doubt it's going to end well for my people," Niska told him. "So, yes, I think I'm talking to the right person."

"Fine. Keep talking," Damien instructed.

"They don't know any better than I did what's been done," Niska said. "A few of the engineers and captains may have guessed, and I'd presume most of the flag officers have been briefed, but the crews? The gunners? They don't know. They've been lied to from the beginning.

"Just like I was."

Niska inhaled, looking at the display behind them.

"We have the proof to show them. Let me show it to them," he asked.

"It's the RIN that shipped Mages back here in job lots," Damien noted. "It's that Navy that has broken world after world, that provided covering fire for the invasions, that carried out those kidnappings.

"Why the hell should I give them a chance?"

"Some of them are rotten, yes," Niska conceded. "But most aren't. Gods, Damien, if there was one group I'd have called rotten to the core, it would have been LMID and RID, and De Santis saved your life!"

"I can't give you access to fleet coms in the hours before a battle, James," Damien said. "It can't happen. It *won't* happen."

"Damien, please," the old cyborg said. "We've come this far together, and we both know that the honor of the nation I swore to serve is garbage and lies.

"But the honor of her *people* is not. The RIN has been led into atrocity and horror, but *they don't know that*. Let me tell them," he begged. "Give me this chance, to test the honor of the nation I swore to serve.

"Give me the chance to redeem the *soul* of the people I swore to protect."

Protect.

That was one hell of a word to conjure with to the sworn servants of the Mage-King. The Protectorate of the Mage-King of Mars was a nation, yes, ninety-plus star systems swearing fealty to the throne at Olympus Mons.

But it was also something else. A concept. A duty. The Mage-King's Protectorate, it was called among those who knew Desmond Alexander... the duty of the Mage-King to guard and protect *all* humanity.

Even those who didn't owe him allegiance.

Even those who had betrayed him.

And if not, perhaps, those who had committed grand atrocities, perhaps those who had been led astray by others.

"The soul of the Republic is broken," Damien said quietly. "George Solace smeared it with shit and blood before it was ever born. Anything else must build from that truth."

"I know."

Niska faced him levelly, but the man's eyes were something else. Something old and dark, that even electronic pupils couldn't conceal.

"You don't owe them anything," he admitted. "But *I* do...and you owe me. You never would have made it this far on your own."

That was true enough, and Damien sighed.

"What purpose is his protectorate if we don't protect people?" he asked. A deadly question, he supposed.

"I can't let you talk to them," Damien admitted. "But *I* can. Despite the Republic's propaganda, I suspect your people know me well enough to believe what I have to say. Especially since we can send them proof."

"I can give you codes and backdoors to make sure they can't shut you down," Niska promised. "They won't let you do more than talk to them, but they can make sure that every screen and speaker carries your message—and that your proof gets through."

"We will do what we can," Damien conceded. "What comes after that...that I leave to the honor of your people, James Niska."

"For the sake of all of our souls, I hope that honor is more intact than I fear."

CHAPTER 51

PUTTING TOGETHER the appropriate setting for the transmission took time. Unlike *Duke of Magnificence*, Alexander's flagship didn't have Damien's normal working space.

The thought of having Damien actually go to *his* ship didn't occur to anyone until it was too late.

Despite everything, as Second Fleet set its course to meet the Republic fleet, Damien had a properly set-up office. The wall behind him was the flag of Mars: a stylized mountain in front of a red planet on a black background.

He sat behind a standard RMN-issue desk, facing a camera. The suit and black gloves he wore were almost aggressively the look he'd adopted as his uniform over the last few years.

The platinum hand of his office hung visibly on his chest, and the gold medallion at his throat caught the light. He laid his hands on the desk, wincing as he slowly straightened them, and faced the camera.

"How long?" he asked quietly.

"Just over forty minutes to weapons range," Romanov told him. "Enough time to let the message sink in."

"I've put together a supporting package that should convince people quickly," Niska said. "I have a pretty good idea of what's going to hit the buttons of loyal Republicans."

He shook his head.

"I can't believe it's come to this."

"Blame George Solace," Damien suggested. "Whatever has come to pass, the Lord Protector has had his fingers in it since the beginning."

"I know. I just can't believe I fell for this." The old cyborg shook his head. "I can't believe *Ricket* fell for this."

"You were told what you wanted to hear. Now we need to convince a few hundred thousand of your fellow citizens of something they *don't* want to hear."

"If anyone can, it's you." Niska stepped backward, making sure he was out of the line of the camera. "My package will go with the transmission. It's your show now."

Damien nodded and inhaled.

It was show time.

"Start recording," he ordered.

"My name is Damien Montgomery," he told the camera. "You know who I am. I am the First Hand of Mars. I am the man who brought food to Kormar when they were starving. I am the man who saved Ardennes from a dictator.

"I am also the man who gathered the fleet that stopped you at Ardennes. I am the man who cleaned up after LMID's massacres in the Antonius System. I am one of the people who have fought the shadow war against your Republic since before it was born."

Damien smiled thinly.

"I am the Hand who laid the charges of treason against Legatus and triggered your secession."

He paused, letting that sink in.

"You know me," he said again. "I am your enemy, but you know my word can be trusted. I speak for Mars and you know that I will not lie to you...so I beg you to trust me now when I tell you that you *have* been lied to.

"You have been made accomplices in an atrocity beyond your worst nightmares, servants to a horror that you would not have supported.

You have been betrayed by the men who led you into first secession and then war.

"There is no technological jump drive at the heart of your ships," he told them. "Your ships are carried through the stars by something your leaders call the Promethean Interface. It is a technological wonder, yes, but not a jump drive.

"It is a tool of torture and control, designed to force a Mage to jump... except that they realized they didn't need the whole Mage. Or even a Mage *trained* to jump.

"At the heart of your supposed technological wonders are the tortured brains of murdered Mages, forced by this interface to provide the interstellar travel you would not accept from the Guild.

"Thousands of Mages have been taken prisoner by your fleets and delivered here, to Legatus, to be sacrificed on that altar...but I beg you to think. To question.

"Your ships were built before the war, before you could murder prisoners of war to fuel these devices. Where did the Mages whose brains power your ships come from?"

He paused again.

"They came from the UnArcana Worlds," he said quietly. "From the only place in the UnArcana Worlds where there were Mages: the schools for the Mages by Right. Your leaders kidnapped and murdered *children*, by the hundreds—the *thousands*—to fuel the war machines you ride. The proof of *all* I have said is attached to this message, organized by one of your own."

Damien winced as his hands clenched into fists.

"There can be no mercy for the people who authorized or executed this plan," he said harshly. "Only justice. Your Republic is built on lies and death. We were never your enemy until you brought this war to us—but if we had learned what lies hid behind the Lord Protector's smile, *we would have been.*"

His speech was supposed to be urging them to surrender, but his anger was taking over, and he rose to his feet as he faced the camera.

"*I am the Sword of Mars,*" he snarled. "I am charged to bring justice to the weak, freedom to the oppressed.

"I will bring justice to Lord Protector George Solace and anyone else I find who supported this horror. The horror that lurks in the heart of *your* ships.

"You are in my way. Leave, surrender or die."

Anger swirled through Damien as he glared at the camera.

"I am past caring which."

The office was silent after Damien had finished speaking and collapsed back into the chair. He looked over at Niska, meeting the ex-LMID spy's gaze.

"Well?" he asked.

"Recording attached to the package and sent," Niska told him. "It's up to them to decide what they want to do now."

Damien had been expecting the Legatan to object to the tone he'd ended up taking, and arched an eyebrow at him.

"It's more powerful, my friend, for you to say what you truly feel than for you to soften the blow," Niska told him. He offered Damien his hand to help him rise. "We've been through this together. We'll finish it together. Our next step is Legatus itself, regardless of what the fleet does."

Damien raised his arm, letting the cyborg grab his upper arm. Even knowing Niska was augmented, he was still surprised by how easily the other lifted him to his feet.

"Solace is the key," he agreed. "But we do have to deal with that fleet first."

"You should get to the flag bridge," Niska told him. "And shut all the computers in here down before you leave me. There's trust and there's being irresponsible."

"Romanov?"

"My lord?"

"Stay with Niska," Damien ordered. "Set the systems to passive and put the tactical display up. He deserves to see how this ends."

"Yes, my lord." Romanov smiled. "So long as you take the team outside with you to the flag deck."

"Of course." Even here, even now, Damien couldn't be sure there were no hidden RID agents. The Republic had done a *damn* good job of infiltrating the Protectorate—but then, their enemy had known the war was coming long before they had.

CHAPTER 52

THERE WAS a stunned silence on the flag deck as Damien entered, three suited Secret Service Agents in tow. Every gaze turned to him as he crossed the room, an uncomfortable situation at the best of times.

"Admiral Alexander," he greeted the Princess of Mars with a bow.

"I ordered your message played for our people as well," Alexander told him without preamble. "They needed to know what happened, too, and it seemed like the most efficient way."

"Ah." Damien concealed a sigh. It made sense, but it explained why everyone was watching him.

"My flag deck crew knew the key parts, but you did lay it out rather... succinctly." Alexander nodded toward the consoles nearest her. "I know you've met Lieutenant Chambers. This is Mage-Captain Kulkarni, my operations officer.

"Kulkarni is watching to see what impact your speech had," she continued. "Captain?"

"We're still at over forty seconds of lightspeed delay on transmission and sensors," Kulkarni pointed out. "They got your message two minutes ago. What we're seeing is roughly a minute and twenty seconds after that."

"So, what we're seeing is nothing, I presume?" Damien asked. "It's not like they're going to change their minds dramatically in a few seconds, after all."

"But a few minutes is possible?" Alexander replied.

"Possible, yes." He shrugged. "If not, well, when are you getting to the simulacrum?"

She snorted.

"Weapons range in thirty minutes," she told him. "I'll be on the bridge and taking over the amplifier in twenty-five."

"Sir?" Kulkarni said in surprise.

"I am the sister of the Mage-King of Mars," Alexander said calmly. "I am my brother's equal, his match, in every way. That's something we go to great lengths to conceal, but today...today it is time for our enemies to realize what it means to face the rulers of Mars in battle."

Damien was probably the only other person in the room who realized what that meant. Romanov would have had an idea—he'd seen Damien stretch to the full limits of his power before—but the number of people who'd seen a Rune Wright with five Runes of Power go all-out was very small.

"It's still going to be a hell of a fight," Damien murmured to the Admiral. "Every trick in the book."

"It's been a long time since I could fully unleash," she admitted. "I should still be able to shield the fleet, if nothing else."

The geometry of the battle was...brutally simple. They were too deep in Centurion's gravity well to jump away, *and* they weren't prepared to surrender the Accelerator Ring or the Daedalus Complex.

In Alexander's place, Damien would probably have destroyed both. He was not in command of Second Fleet, though. He might be using his face and reputation to sell the truth of what they'd discovered to the Republic, but Alexander commanded the military operation.

His role was purely political.

"Wait...I have an aspect change," Kulkarni barked. "Multiple aspect changes, throughout the RIN fleet."

Damien checked the time. Receipt plus about seven minutes. Enough time for a determined engineer to removed the sealed casing around their "jump drives" and find the truth.

He knew starship crews. You never trusted your ship to anyone else. You verified the problem yourself—and the engineering crews of those warships *had* to have suspected something.

Given the extra pressure of his call, he suspected that at *least* half of the jump drives in the Republic fleet had been torn open.

"*Holy shi*—" The curse was cut off, but everyone else had seen what the exclaiming sensor tech had seen.

One of the forty-megaton battleships had just blown up. The gunships closest to her were reeling, even as other battleships and cruisers fell out of the line. Suddenly, at least a quarter of the Republic fleet wasn't accelerating toward the Protectorate force...and some were outright running, flipping in space to accelerate away.

A second ship, one of the cruisers, exploded.

"What the hell is going on?" Alexander demanded. "I'm not seeing weapons fire."

"What you're seeing are the ships whose engineers weren't good enough to disable the failsafes," Damien said quietly. "At a guess, fusion warheads inside the jump drives to make sure no one examined them."

"Not even their own crew."

"My god."

More ships were dropping out of formation now. The self-destruct sequences seemed to be changing minds that Damien's message hadn't.

"I'm picking up the edges of a lot of chatter," a com tech reported. "It's encrypted, but we've got the codes for some of it... Oh."

The tech sounded ill.

"Pictures of the interface?" Damien asked. "I've seen them."

"Yes, my lord," the tech half-gasped.

For the first time, a *carrier* stopped accelerating. One of the big fifty-megaton ships turned back.

The Republic formation was a mess. Ships were attempting to retreat. Others were holding their vector as they tried to work out what was going on, Captains buying themselves time to make a decision.

It was only a matter of time, and Damien closed his eyes as laser fire lit up the screen.

"Two battleships just fired on the withdrawing carrier," Kulkarni reported. "Three *other* battleships just opened fire on *them*. My god..."

The last vestiges of a formation disintegrated. Whatever flag officer had ordered the carrier destroyed had made a critical mistake. Up to that moment, the confusion would have resolved itself before the battle was joined.

Regardless of the bombshell Damien had dropped on them, less than a tenth of the RIN fleet had actually gone so far as to run. There was, after all, a Martian battle fleet in their star system. They would fight.

The self-destructing ships had tested that resolve, but the order to kill their fellow officers and crew broke it.

Ships scattered in every direction and laser fire cut through the void. Explosions marked the display, and from this distance, Damien couldn't see if they were self-destructing or being fired on.

"I have jump flares," Chambers said quietly. "They're not all making it...I don't know if that's voluntary on the ships' part."

"It's not," Damien replied. "We've seen it enough: their fleet commanders can force other ships to jump. The poor bastards at the heart of the Promethean Interfaces have no ability to refuse the order, no matter who's sending it."

Or how dangerous it was.

"Looks like there's a solid core resolving around three of the carriers, but the rest of the fleet is running," Kulkarni finally reported. "A lot of the runners have converged around the retreating carrier, one of their big ones."

She shook her head.

"That group isn't shooting back, but they are defending themselves."

"And the rest?" Damien asked.

"Running in every direction. It looks like whoever's left has disabled any failsafe bombs or remote-jump functions," the operations officer concluded. "Between wrecked ships and fleeing ships, they're down over half their numbers."

"That solid core is running, sir," Chambers noted softly. "I make it forty-one capital ships around three carriers."

"Are they heading for Legatus?" Damien asked.

"No. They're vectoring sideways to reduce our engagement time now, but they're moving in formation." The young woman shook her head. "Those are the only ships out there actually keeping formation; the other grouping is just a cluster."

The numbers weren't clear, but it looked like at least twenty ships were dead. Battleships, carriers, cruisers, the full gamut of the Republic's order of battle.

Forty-one remained in an intact formation, retreating in an organized fashion.

Twelve had clustered around the rogue carrier, running with no clear destination beyond away from the intact formation.

The other twenty-five ships were...lost. There was no other description for it. Some were running solo, desperate to escape *everyone*. Six were on their original vector, their drives shut down—quite likely with fighting throughout their hulls.

"Orders to the Marines," Alexander said softly. "They're to prepare for boarding actions. Search-and-rescue teams are to stand by to deploy as well.

"Navigation departments are to adjust our course: I want to be *damn* certain we can retrieve any survivors of that mess."

"What about the intact formations?" Kulkarni asked.

The Admiral swallowed something and looked to Damien.

"I think that's a political question, First Hand?"

"They're both running," he pointed out. "We're *guessing* this group are loyalists and this group are mutineers, but we don't know.

"We don't want to shoot down potential allies, whatever horror show is running on their ships right now. Let them go."

If they *were* potential allies, he suspected that they wouldn't have jump drives for much longer. In their place, he'd run to somewhere safe and then destroy the Promethean Interface.

There wasn't much they could do for the poor people inside the Interfaces other than give them mercy.

"I think this battle is over," he noted quietly. "May I make a suggestion, Admiral?"

"Of course."

"We need to secure Legatus's orbitals," he told her. "Send *Mjolnir's* group under Admiral Tarpinian and myself. We'll bring my Legatan contacts with us, see if we can convince the planet to surrender, but we *need* to secure Legatus."

"We don't have the forces to take the planet," Alexander pointed out.

"So, we secure the orbitals and the Siege of Legatus becomes of the planet rather than the system," he agreed. "The battle is over. Let's make sure we grab every lever we can to try and end the war."

CHAPTER 53

LEGATUS DIDN'T LOOK any different from orbit than it had five years earlier, when Damien had visited aboard the merchant freighter *Blue Jay*.

The orbital space around the planet certainly looked different, though. Dozens of what the younger Damien had thought were storage or industrial stations had turned out to be secondary nodes in the defensive network.

They were gone now. So were the new-build fortresses installed after the Secession.

It hadn't even been a fair fight.

"The Republic Legislature is still refusing to surrender," Mage-Commodore Kole Jakab told Damien. "They've evacuated the main Assembly Hall, too. It's like they expect us to bomb them from orbit."

"Should we?" Damien asked.

"I never wanted to," Jakab said calmly. "Certainly, I don't want to bombard civilian targets from orbit. We could still do a number on legitimate military targets, though. Clear the way for the Marines."

For the first time in weeks, Damien stood in his observation deck office aboard *Duke of Magnificence* and surveyed a world beneath him. The computer screens overlaid on the window marked the military bases of the Legatan and Republic Armies. All of them were legitimate military targets...but they also represented somewhere around two million people wearing those uniforms.

"I'm not ordering the deaths of two million people just yet," Damien replied. "I don't think it's necessary. Time will give us what we need, Kole. Any further resistance in orbit?"

"No. None of the orbital stations that are left have any significant weapons, and they're all terrified of what will happen if they cause the Marines too many problems. Based off my coms with the rest of Second Fleet, we now control the Legatus System."

"Everything except the planet," Damien agreed. "Has Niska reported yet?"

"Solace is gone," the cyborg replied. Damien looked up to realize that the spy had just slipped into the office, one of Romanov's Secret Service Agents hanging right behind his shoulder.

Aboard *Duke of Magnificence*, Niska wasn't going anywhere without a guard.

"How gone are we talking?" Damien asked.

"A cruiser remained behind when the rest of the defensive task force jumped out to Centurion," Niska explained. "When your message turned that into a nightmare for him, Solace and key members of the Legislature boarded that cruiser and got the hell of the system."

"Damn. Where did he go?"

"I don't know." Niska joined the Hand and the Martian officer in looking out over Legatus below them. "I don't have the depth of access on the planet that I hoped," he admitted. "LMID no longer exists. The entire organization was proscribed for treason after those of us who got the Prodigal Son order fled.

"Most of my friends and contacts are dead," he said heavily. "My name is known to enough people to open some doors, but not enough doors to make it safe for me to go down there."

"I have no intention of assembling an army of millions and taking Legatus by force," Damien said quietly. "Hopefully, Solace's flight will change some minds. In any case, nobody lands or leaves without permission from me or Admiral Alexander."

"Figure he's fled where, Nueva Bolivia?" Jakab asked. "That's their second-biggest industrial center."

"It's not the Republic's fallback position, though," Niska said. "There was always a base—a star system, I presume—outside Legatus for the leadership to retreat to. As an LMID operative, it wasn't in my need to know."

"And if they have a second source of antimatter, it's there," Damien concluded. "No ideas, Niska?"

"There are only ten systems left in the Republic," the spy pointed out. "Surely, we've sent stealth ships to them all by now?"

"Our focus was on the ones closest to the front," Jakab admitted. "There are at least three or four that we've only done the most cursory scouting of...and it's not like we were looking for an accelerator ring. Big as the things are, on the scale of a star system they're easy to miss."

"I don't know where it is," Niska told them. "I don't know where Solace ran to. Hopefully, they don't have another facility to stick bits of Mages into Promethean Interfaces, but I can't even hope for that much."

"They aren't getting the Daedalus Complex back," Damien said grimly. "We're going to tear that place apart piece by piece to make sure we know *everything* Finley and his people did—but Alexander's people are already placing the antimatter charges to make sure it doesn't fall back into the wrong hands."

"So, what do we do now?" Jakab asked.

"We've sent a courier with a reinforced crew back to Sol," the Hand told them. "The Mage-King will know what's happened here in a few days...and that courier is carrying a Link."

They'd captured seventeen Republic warships intact in the aftermath of the fighting at Centurion. They now had the samples of the Promethean Interface and the quantum-entanglement Link communicators the Republic had tried so hard to keep out of their hands.

"Once the Link arrives, we'll be able to have a live conversation." Damien shook his head. "Well, at least once Mars' electronics techs have gone over it with a fine-toothed comb. I'm pretty sure that Solace will be listening in if we just boot the damn thing up."

"I'm shaking down my contacts to see if I can get details on what ships they had in commission," Niska noted. "I think we'll know pretty quickly how much of the RIN is left."

"Enough to be a hell of a pain," Jakab noted. "We're going to need to keep a lot of Second Fleet here. Hunting down the remaining active formations of the RIN is going to suck—and some of those guys who ran are going to choose darker paths."

"Because what we need is a generation of pirates with capital ships." Damien sighed. "We'll deal," he promised. "It'll take months, maybe a year or two, for us to clean up the mess Solace has left us with, but we'll neutralize the RIN and take control of the Republic's systems."

There was a long pause.

"What happens then?" Niska asked. "The Secession was under false pretenses, but..."

"We didn't want this war and we don't want to be conquerors," the Hand told him. "The Republic is doomed. With all that they did, we can't permit it to re-form. The individual systems can make their own choices about rejoining the Protectorate or not."

"Best I can hope for, isn't it?" the old spy asked. He shook his head. "All that we did, fueled by lies and hate. It wasn't what we were after. I doubt that helps."

"Not really," Damien said. "But we are where we are. The Republic as it currently stands must be destroyed. The RIN and their ships will be destroyed or captured."

"And then maybe we'll know some actual peace," Jakab replied. "After the last few years of LMID trying to stab us in the back, that will be strange."

"The Republic will be enough of a threat to keep the shipbuilding program going for a while," the Hand pointed out. "The Navy will expand before we plateau it again. Without a new enemy, though, yes. I think we'll finally have some peace."

"Welcome, Lieutenant Chambers."

Roslyn stepped into Admiral Alexander's office slowly. The battle might be over, but there were still a thousand calls on both the Admiral's time and hers.

"You called for me, sir?" she asked.

"It's a moment to breathe, as much as anything," the older woman told her. "Have a seat. Grab a coffee."

Roslyn obeyed.

"You've done well, Lieutenant," Alexander told her. "We're going to be here in Legatus for a while now. We're going to be digging into the Link manufacturing facilities. Once we're certain we have clean units, we'll start installing them in our ships.

"Actual command-and-control across interstellar distances is going to be weird. I'm going to need a damn fine Flag Lieutenant to keep all of that straight."

Roslyn swallowed and nodded.

"If you feel you need to repl—"

Alexander cut her off with a laugh.

"Stars, no," she told her. "You're doing a damn fine job and I expect to continue getting the best work possible from you. But it's always a question: right now, you're the most junior staff officer in the fleet. If you wanted a more traditional career, we could transfer you to a tactical department somewhere."

"You just said you needed me, sir," Roslyn pointed out.

"I do. I could find a replacement, but training her would be a pain in the ass." Alexander shook her head. "This kind of role is considered a solid foundation for later command and flag rank, Roslyn, but it also usually comes later in your career. Flag Lieutenant to the Admiral of a fleet is usually one of the *last* things you do before your promotion to Lieutenant Commander.

"Eventually, for the sake of your career and the good of the Navy, I'm going to have to give you up," the Admiral pointed out. "If you wanted to be back at a tactical console somewhere, I wouldn't begrudge it. The *Mjolnirs* are short enough on staff, I could probably fast-talk you into an assistant tactical officer slot on one of them. You could do a lot worse."

"Or I could be where you need me, sir," Roslyn replied. "Which is likely to do more good for the Navy...and the people we protect?"

"Right where you are," Alexander told her. "If you stick with me, you might end up promoted early again, just to make my life easier—but the hint of favoritism and patronage will haunt the rest of your career, Roslyn Chambers.

"I'm selfish enough to want you here, but I want you to know the risk for you."

"I swore an oath, Admiral Alexander," Roslyn said. "Choosing my assignments for my own benefit wasn't mentioned anywhere. Doing my best to serve the Protectorate and the people Mars protects was."

"All right." Alexander smiled. "Good. In that case, Lieutenant Chambers, can you grab me Colonel Sang's report on the orbital production facilities at Decurion?

"It seems we have work to do."

CHAPTER 54

THE OLD MAN with the cane had gone by many names in his life. He'd been Winton when he'd met Damien Montgomery. Partisan when he'd worked as a mercenary for the conspirators who eventually became the Republic.

The secret warriors in the organization he'd built over his lifetime called him *sir*. In his own head, he'd started regarding them as his children, and himself as their Father.

The cane was new. Despite the best in medical technology, Father's body was failing him. Fortunately, the events that had led to the Secession had identified the best candidate to succeed him at the head of Nemesis.

He stood in the magical gravity of his ship, leaning on the cane as he studied the reports out of Legatus. *He* wasn't restricted to the speed of a Mage-jumped courier. He'd long since cultivated sources on the Republic capital, many of which thought they were reporting to a legitimate Republic official.

Who else, after all, would have access to one of their Links?

Father's purposes had never truly aligned with the Republic. He had enabled Finley, but it was in pursuit of a higher goal.

Still. He'd worked more closely with Finley than he had with any other person alive except Kent Riley, his new protégé. He'd once thought the Rune Wright could succeed him. Even if the other man's megalomania had made that too dangerous to allow, he'd been close to Finley. The man the First Hand had killed had been a personal friend.

But personal was not the same as important.

"They transferred an extra half-dozen Mages onto TK-421," Riley said behind him. "She'll reach Mars within a few days."

"They think the war is over," Father said quietly. "The Republic will soon disillusion them of that."

"We need the buildup to continue," Riley replied. "Should we deploy assets to make sure the Republic remains in the fight?"

"That won't be necessary. Our prior assistance with their project at Chrysanthemum should be enough," the old man said. "They have a second accelerator ring, a shipyard and a stockpile of extracted minds."

He wasn't looking at Riley but he could sense his protégé's reaction.

"You *should* be angry, Riley," he pointed out. "We enabled a horror unlike anything humanity has seen—your anger at the Republic and at me is entirely justified."

"The alternative was to see the same horror unleashed on a far greater scale," Riley admitted. "I understand."

"But you are still angry." It wasn't a question. Father turned away from the screens. He'd seen all he needed to. A gesture sent the Link system retracting back into the ceiling, and he slowly hobbled over to the wallscreen showing the space outside the ship.

There was nothing visibly special about the luxury yacht. It was one of dozens orbiting Earth, serving as home bases for wealthy visitors from across human space. Father's yacht was more able to defend itself than most, concealing several powerful lasers and a full amplifier, but if he ever had to use those weapons, his grand quest would have failed.

"That is what we fight for," he told Riley, gesturing at the world outside the window. "Ten billion souls on Earth. Another two billion on Mars. A hundred billion humans, all told. Almost a hundred million Mages.

"If our true enemy came upon us without warning, every one of those Mages would face the fate of the few thousand sacrificed to allow the Republic to fight this war." He shook his head.

"I know all of their names, Kay," he admitted to his protégé. "There will be memorials built to honor their memory, and I will make sure the lists of names are complete and correct. They will not be forgotten."

Riley stepped up next to him, casting a worried glance at the cane.

"You push yourself too hard," the ex-Marine Mage pointed out. Kent Riley was *ex* many things. He'd been a Combat Mage of the Royal Martian Marine Corps. While he'd worn that uniform, he'd been recruited to the Royal Order of the Keepers of Secrets and Oaths.

In *that* service, he'd killed a Hand for Father. There were no higher proofs of loyalty to the old man.

"I know," Father conceded. "But I have some years left in me, years to bring you fully up to speed."

It was the first time he'd admitted his plans to Riley.

"Me, Father?" Riley asked.

"You killed a Hand for me," Father pointed out. "You've stood at my right hand since. Hell, boy, you evaded a Voice under your own power *without* having to kill her.

"No, it is and must be you who takes over. It will take time to fill you in on everything, but you know the core of it already."

They studied the planet together for several minutes.

"Montgomery has all of the pieces now, doesn't he?" Riley finally asked.

"I think so. And he's a smart man, if too honest to join us directly. We must make certain he has the power to act when he puts all the pieces together."

They were silent again.

"I thought you'd offered him the throne once," the younger man pointed out.

"Oh, yes." Father rubbed his throat gently in memory. He'd found himself suspended in the air with the life being choked out of him at the end of that meeting. Montgomery wasn't the type to settle for a simple no.

"This time, we won't give him a choice. You know what Desmond's will says about Montgomery, if the Mountain falls to Kiera."

"That won't be easy to arrange."

"We own the Councilor for Centauri," Father pointed out. "So long as he doesn't know *why* we want them both somewhere, he'll cooperate. He's a dead man if we reveal his crimes."

Riley was silent for a moment.

"You hesitate." Again, it wasn't a question.

"Desmond is a good man."

"He is. But he doesn't have the strength for what is to come. The man he made his Sword will. It must be done, or all humanity will perish."

Riley bowed his head.

"It must be done," he echoed.

ABOUT THE AUTHOR

GLYNN STEWART is the author of Starship's Mage, a bestselling science fiction and fantasy series where faster-than-light travel is possible–but only because of magic. His other works include science fiction series Duchy of Terra, Castle Federation and Vigilante, as well as the urban fantasy series ONSET and Changeling Blood. Writing managed to liberate Glynn from a bleak future as an accountant. With his personality and hope for a high-tech future intact, he lives in Kitchener, Ontario with his partner, their cats, and an unstoppable writing habit.

OTHER BOOKS
BY GLYNN STEWART

For release announcements join the
mailing list or visit **GlynnStewart.com**

STARSHIP'S MAGE
Starship's Mage
Hand of Mars
Voice of Mars
Alien Arcana
Judgment of Mars
UnArcana Stars
Sword of Mars
Mountain of Mars
The Service of Mars
A Darker Magic
Mage-Commander
Beyond the Eyes of Mars (upcoming)

Starship's Mage: Red Falcon
Interstellar Mage
Mage-Provocateur
Agents of Mars

Pulsar Race: A Starship's Mage Universe Novella

DUCHY OF TERRA
The Terran Privateer
Duchess of Terra
Terra and Imperium
Darkness Beyond
Shield of Terra
Imperium Defiant
Relics of Eternity
Shadows of the Fall
Eyes of Tomorrow

SCATTERED STARS

Scattered Stars: Conviction
Conviction
Deception
Equilibrium
Fortitude
Huntress (upcoming)
Scattered Stars: Evasion
Evasion (upcoming)

PEACEKEEPERS OF SOL

Raven's Peace
The Peacekeeper Initiative
Raven's Course
Drifter's Folly
Remnant Faction (upcoming)

EXILE

Exile
Refuge
Crusade
Ashen Stars: An Exile Novella

CASTLE FEDERATION

Space Carrier Avalon
Stellar Fox
Battle Group Avalon
Q-Ship Chameleon
Rimward Stars
Operation Medusa
A Question of Faith: A Castle Federation Novella

SCIENCE FICTION STAND ALONE NOVELLA

Excalibur Lost

VIGILANTE
(WITH TERRY MIXON)
Heart of Vengeance
Oath of Vengeance

**Bound By Stars: A Vigilante Series
(With Terry Mixon)**
Bound By Law
Bound by Honor
Bound by Blood

TEER AND KARD
Wardtown
Blood Ward

CHANGELING BLOOD
Changeling's Fealty
Hunter's Oath
Noble's Honor
Fae, Flames & Fedoras: A Changeling Blood Novella

ONSET
ONSET: To Serve and Protect
ONSET: My Enemy's Enemy
ONSET: Blood of the Innocent
ONSET: Stay of Execution
Murder by Magic: An ONSET Novella

FANTASY STAND ALONE NOVELS
Children of Prophecy
City in the Sky

Made in the USA
Las Vegas, NV
30 July 2024

93103739R00208